The Sol

MW01223119

Sam Crescent and Jenika Snow

Books Included

Book 1: Owned by the Bastard
Book 2: Bent, Not Broken
Book 3: Hard As Steel

The Soldiers of Wrath MC: Volume 1

Sam Crescent and Jenika Snow

CrescentSnowPublishing.com

Published by Crescent Snow Publishing

Copyright © March 2016 by Sam Crescent and Jenika Snow

Digital Edition

First E-book Publication: March 2016

Edited by Editing by Rebecca

OWNED BY THE BASTARD

The Soldiers of Wrath MC, 1

OWNED BY THE BASTARD (The Soldiers of Wrath MC, 1)

Sam Crescent and Jenika Snow

http://www.CrescentSnowPublishing.com

http://www.SamCrescent.wordpress.com

sam_crescent_fanmail@yahoo.co.uk

www.JenikaSnow.com

Jenika_Snow@Yahoo.com

Published by Sam Crescent and Jenika Snow

Copyright © January 2015 by Sam Crescent and Jenika Snow

Digital Edition

First E-book Publication: January 2015

Edited by Kasi Alexander

Demon, the President of The Soldiers of Wrath MC, is a vicious bastard, a heartless killer, and has no regrets about any of the violent things he does in life. It is how he survives, and how he keeps his club and his men safe.

Deanna Monte has stayed in the life of her drug addicted, low-life father since her mother passed away. She may hate her dad, but after her mother's dying wish for Deanna to not give up on him, she knows she can't walk away.

When Deanna is given to Demon as payment for her father's debt, she fights with everything inside of her and refuses to submit. But she's never met a man like Demon, a cruel man that is big and powerful and can take her life as easily as he breathes. She shouldn't want him the way she does, not after he takes her away from her life, refusing to let her go, and tells her that she is his now.

But she does, and that frightens her most of all.

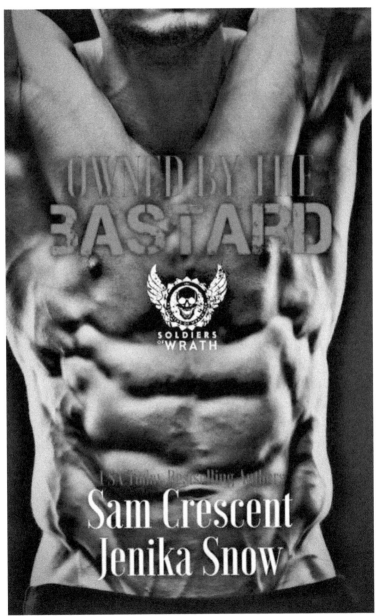

OWNED BY THE BASTARD (The Soldiers of Wrath MC, 1)

Sam Crescent and Jenika Snow
http://www.CrescentSnowPublishing.com
http://www.SamCrescent.wordpress.com
sam_crescent_fanmail@yahoo.co.uk
www.JenikaSnow.com
Jenika_Snow@Yahoo.com
Published by Sam Crescent and Jenika Snow
Copyright © January 2015 by Sam Crescent and Jenika Snow
Digital Edition
First E-book Publication: January 2015
Edited by Kasi Alexander

Chapter One

"What the fuck, man?" Shakes said and took a hit off the joint he was smoking. "He actually wants to trade his daughter for the fucking debt he owes us?" He shook his head, disgust on his face.

"He's a desperate motherfucker, that's for damn sure," Joker said, and grabbed the joint that Shakes handed him. He took a hit off the roach, stared at all of them, and exhaled. The backroom they were in was in the Soldiers of Wrath clubhouse, and currently filled with marijuana smoke, smelling of the green, and holding club members that were pissed that a father would trade his only daughter for a clean slate with the MC. "You want a hit, prez?" Joker asked.

Demon leaned forward, the leather chair he was in creaking from his weight. He took the joint, puffed off the end, and took in as much of the sweet smoke as he could. To calm down he usually liked a little something stronger. Although cocaine was a stimulant, it seemed to have the opposite effect on Demon. He calmed the fuck down with it, let the flow of pleasure hum through his body, and it was what he was itchin' for right now after he had gotten word about the trade. He finished off the smoke, snubbed it out in the already overflowing ashtray, and leaned back in his seat. He looked around the table at his men, the members that would lay down their lives for him and this club. He'd do the same for them in a heartbeat, because that was what a brotherhood was all about.

"What do you want me to tell him?" Joker, his VP, said from beside him.

Demon looked at his other men. Joker sat to his left and his Sergeant-at-Arms, Dark, sat to his right. There were Striker, Weasel, and Nerd that stared at him, waiting for the answer on how to proceed. Shakes and Steel wore hard looks of concentration on their faces. These men had been with him from the very beginning, had death in their eyes, hatred and loyalty in their blood, and right now they were wanting to go and kick that father's ass for even wanting to sell his daughter to them. Although Demon wasn't a good man, not by any stretch of the imagination, he also didn't give a fuck on how someone paid off their debt.

Maybe he should have given two fucks that the lowlife piece of shit junkie wanted to give an outlaw biker gang his twenty-something-year-old little girl. But he didn't. In fact, he was a sick bastard because he wanted her. He had seen the pictures of the busty little redhead. She had a pair of big fucking tits, ones that would be overflowing in his hands when he grabbed them. Her ass was nice and round, big and just the right amount of meat on it that the thing would shake like a warm bowl of Jell-O when he was fucking her good and raw. And her hips, *fuck*, her hips were wide as hell, and perfect for when he held her as she bounced on his dick. He shifted in his seat, his cock getting hard at the thoughts and images moving through his head.

He looked down at the table, at where the picture of the daughter was. Her face was one that could make a sane and practical man go on a killing spree just to get her attention. But Demon was already a dangerous man, had killed plenty already, and would just have to get her attention in other ways. He thought about the things he could do to her, could show her.

He'd pull out his big dick, let her see what he'd be plowing into her sooner rather than later.

"Yo, Demon, you with us here?" Steel asked, clearly trying to get his attention because he was sitting here thinking about fucking a woman that would be in their compound against her will.

He looked at his club members again, cleared his throat, and pushed the picture of the woman away. "Do it. Make the deal, and bring her here."

Deanna pulled her piece of shit Toyota into her father's driveway. The underside of her car scraped on the pavement, and she grimaced. Her father's place was a small two-person home in a cracked-out part of town. She was afraid to come here, even when it was broad daylight—like it was now— because there were usually hookers on the street corner, and drug dealers patrolling the streets in their cars. She reached into her bag, felt the small .38 Special her mother had given her before she died, and sighed.

Yes, her mom had handed her a gun on her deathbed, told her to keep it close, and to knock a fucker down if he even came sniffing around her. Deanna chuckled at the memory, but on the heels of that happiness the sorrow had come crashing in. It had only been a couple of years since her mother died of leukemia, and although she had fought hard to survive, in the end she had lost her battle.

Deanna stared at the front door of her father's place. God, she really didn't want to go in there, but she hadn't been able to get ahold of him for three days. Yes, her dad was a junkie, a drug addict, and a crack head. Whatever someone wanted to call another person hooked on drugs, that was her father to the nth degree. He disgusted her, infuriated her, and she shouldn't even care what he did with his life. He hadn't been there for her mother when she was sick for all those years, hadn't given two shits about them or sent money to help with medical bills, and he hadn't even gone to the funeral. Deanna had hated him for so long. But when her mother had told her that being angry wasn't the answer, that her father was sick and needed family, Deanna put away all of her hatred. She had tried to get her father into rehab, only to see him relapse over and over again. But she hadn't given up, not because she loved her father, but because her mother had asked her to be there for him.

The truth was she hated him, despised everything that he was, but being there for him had been her mom's dying wish, and so she was seeing it through to the very bitter end.

She climbed out of the car, glanced around the street, and saw a woman standing on the corner in fishnets, a black pleather mini skirt, and a cropped shirt. Deanna moved quickly toward the door, knocked on it once when she reached it, and looked behind her again. The sound of what had to be a gunshot echoed, and she grabbed the door handle and turned it. Fuck this and waiting for him to get his druggie ass up.

Once inside, she shut the door and wrinkled her nose. It stunk like a warm, humid armpit, and didn't look any better. Trash littered the ground, graffiti marred the walls, and the sound of someone coughing in the next room had her turning and walking toward the noise. The living room was a mess of ratty, holed-up couches, stained covered drapes, garbage and hypodermic needles on the ground. And there was her dad, passed out on the couch with a middle-aged naked woman on his lap. They were both sleeping with their mouths hanging open, and the stench of piss and body odor lingered in the air.

"Dad?" she called out to him. The woman stirred slightly, but her father only gave a loud snore in response. He shifted on the couch, slowly cracked open an eye, and pushed himself up, groaning.

"Hey there. Didn't hear you." He pushed the naked woman off of him. She fell to the ground with a *thump*, but didn't make so much as a sound.

"I've been calling you."

He stood, grabbed his cell off the coffee table, and looked at it. "Oh, yeah. You've called me a few times."

"Try for the last three days. I know you don't care about your life, and I shouldn't really either, but I made a promise to Mom. The least you can do is pick up the phone."

He was busy typing something out on his phone, glancing up at her every few seconds. He closed the phone shut, and set it back on the coffee table, very slowly, too slowly for her liking. She looked around the hovel again, knew that he was still high or he'd be tweaking more than usual, and lifted her hand to rub her eyes. She was so tired of this shit. Deanna needed to wash her hands of him, because all he was doing was bringing her down.

He picked up his glass pipe, put some white crystals in the bowl, and lifted it to his mouth. She turned away disgusted after he heated the end of the pipe with a lighter. Here he was, smoking meth right in front of her like it wasn't anything, like she wasn't his daughter and standing here watching.

"You're doing good?" he asked in a tight voice as he held in the toxic smoke.

"What's wrong with you? Aside from the obvious," Deanna said, knowing he was acting stranger than usual.

"Nothing now." He exhaled the smoke, set his pipe down, and sat back on the couch. "You want something to eat or drink?"

Deanna didn't even bother responding because there wasn't any food or anything sanitary to consume in this shithole.

The sound of motorcycles in the distance, coming closer, becoming louder, had her moving toward the dirty, cloudy window. She saw three massive Harleys pull into her dad's driveway, blocking in her crappy car. The engines cut, and the silence descended. "You expecting three big ass bikers?" she asked without turning around. The men climbed off their bikes, removed their sunglasses in unison, and she swore the one in front stared right at her. They moved forward in sure, arrogant, and deadly steps, and something inside of her went on alert. She moved away from the window, turned and faced her father, and saw him pacing.

"I'm sorry, Deanna. I had to tell them you were here, had to do this to get myself out of this mess. It was the only way, and they said they'd take a trade."

A trade?

Deanna didn't know what he was rambling on about, but when there was a loud banging on the front door, everything inside of her stilled. She knew she needed to run, and she needed to do it now.

Chapter Two

Demon banged on the door, waiting for it to be answered. He didn't like the response he felt at seeing the bastard father's text. The name of the man was unnecessary to him. Once they took the daughter, this bastard would cease to matter, as they would no longer be doing business with the fucker. This one and only debt would be paid out in flesh, his daughter's flesh. The very thought made him sick to his stomach. He was going to stay back at the clubhouse instead of coming on this long journey to claim a woman that wasn't his. Then he thought of the other brothers getting hard for her. He wasn't risking her being passed between the brothers. They were a horny lot of men without a woman for a few hours. Deanna wouldn't survive two minutes without one of the bastards trying to get between her creamy thighs.

You want first pick.

There was also the fact he wanted her before anyone else did. Demon liked to test out all the new women in the club. He rarely let anyone get past him, least of all fresh meat. That's what Deanna would be to the Soldiers of Wrath, fresh meat. From the way she looked he doubted she'd be a virgin. She'd probably already had plenty of dick in that sweet pussy of hers.

"I wonder what's taking him so long," Shakes said, smiling.

"Bitch is probably loading up on our shit." This came from Joker.

Shakes and Joker had joined him for the ride to collect their payment. Admittedly, taking a woman as payment wasn't something he was used to. The women he took were always willing.

One look from Deanna and she'd be begging for all of them. Demon was confident in getting a woman into his bed. He had a big dick and knew how to use it. No woman left him unsatisfied. All of the club whores went out of their way to please him. Demon loved being able to snap his fingers and to have pussy on tap. Being the president of one of the biggest MCs gave him free access to it all.

Reaching out, he banged on the door, only to come up short when the redhead in question opened up.

"What can I do for you?" she asked.

Her voice was small and he heard the wobble in it. Demon instantly didn't like the nerves he was seeing inside her.

Cut that shit out.

It wouldn't do him good to care about her. She was payment for services, nothing else.

Pushing past, he made sure to brush his body against hers. Her tits were large, fleshy, and he wanted to touch them, suck on them. His dick went into overdrive at the thought of getting her naked and fucking her.

Soon.

"Boys," her father said, smiling at them.

There was a half-naked woman on the floor by the sofa. Demon turned his nose up at the state of the apartment and the smell. The scent of decay, sex, desperation, and fear clung in the air.

Glancing back at Deanna who still stood by the open door, he knew the fear came from her. She kept her gaze outside on her car. They'd trapped her vehicle in on purpose. There was no way she was getting out unless they allowed her out of their sight.

"Demon, take a seat. It's good doing business with you."

The father moved a little closer. Putting his hand in the man's face, he pushed him off. "I'm not here to do business. I'm here to take what is mine." He'd not gotten to be president of the Soldiers of Wrath by being nice. Demon was hard, cold, and lethal. No one saw any other side of him.

He didn't look away from Deanna, who still hadn't looked at him. She was going to be his no matter what.

Could she get to her car, run the motorcycles out of the way, and be home before the three angry-looking bikers even noticed she was gone? Deanna kept looking at her old car, wishing she could see any sign of escape. There wasn't any escape from this. The three men were scary, large, and could tear them all apart if they chose to.

Her mouth ran dry as she turned to face the room. Standing from the outside staring in, her father looked like a small bug that needed to be squashed. If she could, she'd take him out. Her mother was wrong all along. She shouldn't be here trying to protect and care for her father. The only thing the man cared about was himself. The way he looked at all the men with this greedy look in his eye let her know shit was going down. It was things she didn't want to know about.

Deanna stayed by the door, refusing to get involved in anything relating to her father.

He's not your father. He's a fucking monster.

Crossing her arms underneath her chest, she surveyed the room. The woman sleeping with her father was still passed out, which was starting to concern her. No woman should be able to sleep through all the crap going on around her. The man with the leather jacket marking him as president of the Soldiers of Wrath kept staring at her. His gaze scared her the most. He wouldn't look away even as he spoke to her father. The show of disrespect wasn't lost on her.

"You're not getting any more shit. You can't even pay like a real man."

"But we've got a deal. You'll take her, and I'll be debt free?"

She tuned into what her father was saying, and frowned. Take who? The woman on the floor?

Something turned in the pit of her stomach. Whatever was going on wasn't going to end well for her. Staring at all three men, she knew, part of her knew, they were here for her.

"I think it's time I should go," Deanna said, walking back into the room to pick up her purse. Stupidly she'd left it on the floor next to *his* chair. She walked into the room, leaning down to grab it.

"You can't go," her father said, raising his voice.

Grabbing her purse, she whirled around to glare at the man who wasn't really her father. Donating sperm didn't make any man a father. It only made him a man capable of fucking.

"What the hell is wrong with you?" she asked. "You've got to be kidding me. You don't answer your phone and now you're raising your voice at me?" She was losing her temper, overreacting, and it was all because of the three men who were in the room watching them.

The men scared her. She did everything in her power to avoid being around men who looked like they'd laugh while killing someone.

"You're not going anywhere."

She turned toward the man she knew only as President. His dark hair was short, and his eyes were hard and cold, the color of molten silver. What had her father called him? Demon? Surely that wasn't his real name. There was no way anyone would have the name Demon; it was wrong on so many levels.

"What? You can't stop me from going anywhere," she said, putting her purse over her shoulder and starting to make her way out of the room.

Deanna didn't get far.

Demon reached out, snagging her hand. Before she knew what was happening she was sitting on his lap. She fought to be released but within quick moments, he had her hands trapped to her sides. He held her tightly, firmly, with no chance of escape.

"Get off me. Let me go!" She shouted, screamed, cursed, and wriggled. Boy, did she wriggle, but not once did he loosen his hold. Deanna felt the evidence of what her shifting on him was doing. The man beneath her was getting hard. His cock was pressed against her ass, showing her exactly how much he was enjoying it.

She stopped instantly.

Licking her lips, she stared across the room at the horrid walls. The whole place was in need of some tender loving care.

Don't think about it. Don't think about his arms wrapped around you, trapping you.

"You're a little wildcat, aren't you? Is she a natural redhead?" Demon asked. His breath was across her neck.

"Don't ask him, ask me," Deanna said through gritted teeth. She hated how her body responded to being captured by him.

"Well, little red, are you all natural?" Demon's lips brushed against her cheek. He was so large compared to her. His presence alone had her tensing, waiting for him to strike.

"Go fuck yourself," she said.

Bad, Deanna, bad. This is a fucking biker, not some twerp in high school.

He didn't respond how she expected. Demon burst out laughing.

"She's got fire inside her," Demon said.

"You'll tame her." One of the other men spoke up. She didn't even bother to look to see who had spoken. This was a nightmare.

She shouldn't have come over.

"Well, do we have a deal?" her father asked.

He looked nervous.

Demon grabbed her chin and forced her to look at her father. "Your father owes me a shit load of money, Deanna." How did he know her name? "Do you know what he offered me?" he asked.

She shook her head, more afraid of what he was about to say than what he could have already said.

"He offered me you as payment."

Deanna stared into her father's eyes, the eyes of an addict. Hatred filled her to the core at what he'd done. There was no mistake now. When he'd been on his phone, he'd made sure these three men knew to come for her.

"I'm not going with you," Deanna said.

"You don't have a choice. If it's not our club it'll be another club. Before long, you'll have so many men taking payment out of your pussy. Your father is scum, Deanna. The lowest of the low."

Her heart pounded at what he was saying. This was not news to her. Her father had always been a problem. The only reason she tried to help him before was because of her mother.

"I've got a life. I'm not going with you." She fisted her hands, preparing to break free.

"You don't understand, Deanna." Why did he keep saying her name? "If you don't come with me now we're going to kill your father, and then we're going to kill you."

She froze. "That makes no sense. How could he even earn you back the money if he's dead?"

"Because we wouldn't have to deal with him anymore. Your father owes too much. How much do you value him? Or better yet, how much do you value your own life? Do you want to die?"

Tears filled her eyes as she stared at the bug she called a father.

Look, Mom. Look what caring for him has done.

"I don't want to die."

"You're coming with me back to my club. It's for your own good."

Deanna started to struggle. She didn't want to go back with him. She didn't want to have anything to do with the man who was holding her captive. The only thing she wanted to do was escape.

Demon stood quickly, holding her against him. He wrapped his fingers around her neck and tightened until he cut off her air supply. She stopped fighting him to claw at his arms to be released.

Only when he was ready to release her did he do it.

He turned her around until she faced him, taking a gun out of the back of his pocket. Fright gripped her as she looked at the deadly looking piece. That could do a lot of damage. It could kill someone and if she wasn't careful, it would kill her.

"I *will* shoot you. Now, you're going to be quiet and get on the back of my bike. We're going to take a long trip back to the clubhouse."

"I've got a life here," she said.

"No, your life was over the moment you came to check on that useless piece of scum."

The tears that had filled her eyes finally fell. There was no time for arguing. Demon grabbed her arm, leading her toward the door. They stopped long enough for Demon to give instruction.

"Hurt him."

Glancing behind her, she saw the other two men surround her father. Before she even climbed on the back of the bike she heard his screams. For once, Deanna couldn't bring herself to care. Her own father had ruined her life.

Chapter Three

Demon had to all but toss her ass into the clubhouse. She had struggled to get on the back of his bike, but he had growled out his frustration, stared at her with this look that said "shut the fuck up and do what you're told," and the fear had been evident in her face. To say she had shut right the hell up was an understatement.

His men entered the clubhouse and went straight for the bar. The night was winding down, and he knew it would be a long while before this sweet piece of ass was comfortable being here. The sweet butts made their way toward the guys, their tits and assess all on display. His cock got hard, but it wasn't because of the easy access cunt that was around him. It was because of this one woman that was staring daggers at him.

"You can't keep me here. It's illegal, immoral, and kidnapping." She all but spat out the words, and he grinned.

"Honey, I can and will do whatever the fuck I please with you." He snarled out, feeling his patience wear thin, even though he was aroused. She straightened her shoulders, pursed her lips and looked like she was about to go toe-to-toe with him. He felt a rise of pride in him that she wasn't putting up with his shit, but then again he was also getting pissed because no one fucked with him. They did what he said when he said it, and if they fucked with him he made sure they never did it again.

"This is insane," she stuttered out, and he could tell she was trying to be strong despite the fact she wanted to break down. "How can you even be okay with some junkie piece of shit trading off his daughter to pay off a debt?" The tension was flowing now, and he was surprised she had lasted this long without calling him a derogatory name. He was a bastard plain and simple, and he didn't try to pretend otherwise.

"Taking you as payment is pretty fucking easy, honey. You see, your old man owed us big-time, and anyway he saw fit in paying us back is good with the club." He moved over to the bar, slammed his palm down on the counter for a drink, and glanced over his shoulder at Deanna. Yeah, he had said her name over and over again in his head. He had seen the text from her lowlife father, saw that he wanted to trade her up right then and there, and he had gotten excited at the prospect that she'd finally be here.

She was leaning against one of the tables, her gaze jumping to the door. Joker was standing by it, his focus on Deanna, and this smug fucking smile on his face. Demon laughed, took the shot from the prospect named Chucks, and faced Deanna again. "You want something to take the edge off, baby?" He grinned wide when she glowered at him.

"Like alcohol is really going to make this situation any better for me."

He shrugged, tossed the shot back, and loved that the burn was fucking wicked. He slammed the shot glass down, and Chucks refilled it. Demon tapped on the counter and Chucks filled a new glass with bourbon. Demon turned and walked over to Deanna. He held out the glass, and she eyed it for a second before taking it. He lifted a brow, tossed the second shot back, and watched her over the rim. She looked down at the alcohol, and then up at him. Before he knew what she planned on doing she tossed the liquor in his face and threw the glass across the room. The sound of the glass shattering, and of Joker cursing, had Demon turning and staring at the MC member.

"What the fuck?" Joker cursed out. "She fucking missed me by like an inch." He turned and looked at where the glass had obviously slammed into the wall since there were pieces of glass and liquid sliding down the brick.

"Fuck all of your crazy, kidnapping biker asses," Deanna pushed Demon out of the way, catching him off guard, and running toward the exit. For a second all any of the guys did was stare at her as she hauled ass toward the front door, but then Demon growled and went after her. He had her in his arms and thrown over his shoulder seconds later.

"Let me go, you fucking barbarian." She slammed her hands on his back, cursed out over and over again, and before Demon lost it he brought his palm down right on her full, plump ass. She stilled for a second, just long enough for him to take her to the back room, slam the door shut behind him, and toss her stubborn, trouble-making ass on the bed. She bounced on the mattress twice, stared at him with wide frightened eyes, and Demon had to make himself calm down and not lose his shit because of how she was acting. Yeah, she was here against her will, but she'd have to come to terms with that sooner rather than later.

"How can you not think any of this is wrong?" she all but shouted out.

Demon stared at her, feeling like a beast trapped in a human body, and smirked. "Because I'm a heartless motherfucker, Deanna, and the sooner you realize that the better off you'll be." He turned and left her alone, locked the door behind him, and went to get good and trashed.

He had spanked her, actually spanked her ass like she was this petulant child instead of being held here against her will. Deanna got off the bed and moved over to the door, knowing it was locked before she even reached it. She had heard it click when he had shut the door, and her anger and fear had mounted. This man could, and would not see reason. He was narrow-minded, set in whatever fucked-up ways he had adapted for himself, and she was stuck right in the middle of it all.

Deanna curled her hands at her sides, and using all of her strength she booted the bottom of the door. But all that accomplished was having her foot hurt and her anger rise. She turned and faced the room. A small bed sat in the center, a few posters of Harleys and engines lined the wall, and of course there were a few nude chicks hanging on the bikes, as if they couldn't help but rub their tits all over the metal.

She huffed out, felt her anger start to fade as the hardcore realization of this situation slammed into her. She had been stupid enough to think that these men could be talked to, seen that what they were doing, and whatever they wanted to do to her was wrong on every level. They were in this roughened biker gang, not caring that illegal activity and kidnapping someone were immoral. In fact, she was pretty sure they reveled in it all. She moved over to the bed, sat on the edge, and breathed out. The tears came before she even felt them on her cheeks. They burned, scorched, and pissed her off even more. Why should she cry over these assholes? Why should she cry over the fact her own father had sold her out?

Deanna wiped her tears away angrily, stared at the closed door, and promised herself she'd get out of here, and get even. She'd make her father pay for being the shittiest fucking dad in the world, and make these bastards realize that she wasn't this weak and timid wallflower. She'd give as good as she got, and they'd regret ever taking her in the first place.

Chapter Four

Demon slammed his fist on the counter, needing another hit of something strong. He didn't give a shit what it was so long as he got this desire under control. Her fighting him wasn't going to help her any. He relished the fire, and it only made him want to tame her more. She was a wildcat. Demon liked that.

The fire burning inside of her would help keep her alive in the club. The whores and the men would eat her up and spit her back out if she showed one sign of weakness. He didn't need to worry about that, though. No, he needed to worry more about his dick staying intact than anything else.

Running a hand down his face, he glanced out of the corner of his eye to see Joker join him.

"She's going to be a handful. Are you sure this is worth having her around?"

Demon slammed the shot back, demanding another one from Chucks. The sound of moaning drew his attention across the room. Nerd had one of the club whores bent over the table. He was fucking her good and hard. Three men were already waiting to take Nerd's position when he was finished. His club liked to share the club whores. The ones who had old ladies didn't allow them at the club. What would Deanna be in the club? He'd taken her as payment, yet didn't have the first clue as to what to do with her.

Nerd finished, and another man put a condom on, bent down, and slid into the whore's waiting cunt. They all had women waiting on them to fuck. He liked his sex easy. But Deanna was going to be anything but easy.

Had he made a mistake bringing her to the club? Fuck, it was tough shit now. If he reneged now, the brothers would have his hide. He'd be the one dead. The only way he became president was by showing his strength. Some of the brothers were loyal to him as they believed in his leadership, while others weren't strong enough to take the club from him.

"We can't do anything about it now. She'll learn her place."

"Which is?"

Chucks put another shot in front of him, then left them alone.

"Look, Demon, she's different. I don't see her bending over a table while the brothers take turns to fuck her."

Demon tightened his grip on the glass, already not liking the idea of any of the other brothers being near her. What the fuck was happening to him? He was never possessive over the women. Demon didn't claim just one. He liked variety in his pussy. Deanna was too uptight. It would take a lot of cock before she loosened up in any way to take his dick.

"She's not different. She'll fuck like the rest of the whores." He got up from his chair, heading outside to have a smoke. It was still too hot and he was looking forward to the colder nights coming in. His jacket clung to him with sweat trickling down his back.

If he didn't get his thoughts into focus, he was going to be screwed.

Lighting up, he stared up at the night sky. If he was poetic or some shit, he'd say it was a beautiful, starry night. Maybe it was fate that had brought her to him. Chuckling, he took another deep inhale on the cigarette.

"Hey, baby, I thought I'd find you here." Sarah was a whore through and through. She loved the club but she loved cock more. Like the woman lying down on the table, she'd taken all of the men, loving every second of it. She'd screamed, howled, and begged for more, like the woman was now doing.

"What do you want?"

"Your cock." She was also blunt, exactly what he liked.

Putting his smoke between his lips, he opened the buckle on his jeans. "Get to your knees."

She sank to her knees before him. He left her to get his cock out. In no time he was smoking and getting his dick sucked. This was the life.

Sitting on the bed feeling sorry for herself wasn't going to get her out of the club. Demon hadn't told her what to do. He'd trapped her in the bedroom. Whose room was she in? Getting to her feet, she made her way toward the window. Looking outside, she saw the man in question getting his dick sucked by one of the women. She didn't recognize the woman, but why would she? The sight of them together twisted something in her gut. For several seconds she watched him getting his nuts sucked off. The pleasure was clear on his face as he sunk one of his hands into her hair.

Sickened by the sight, she turned away, hating it. Deanna didn't want to be here in this club. She'd never smoked or drank in her life, let alone took drugs. There was no way she was going to sit quietly while they took her as payment because of her father.

She paced up and down the room. There was no way she was having sex with these men. They were probably infected with all manner of things. She imagined their dicks were close to rotting off. Glancing out of the window again, she hoped his dick was rotting the woman's face off.

Not nice, Deanna. Not nice at all.

Being nice wasn't all it was cracked up to be. Look what was happening to her. She'd been nice to her father and all he'd done was find a way to sell her off as if she was nothing but a thing to be used. God, she was going to cry again if she didn't get her emotions back under control.

She took several deep breaths, trying to calm herself once again.

There was no way she was about to give up on her life because this fucking biker club thought they could take her as payment. Walking around the room, she began tearing down the posters on the wall. She didn't care whom they belonged to. All she wanted to do was set about the destruction of the room.

The moment they saw she'd be a pain in their ass, they'd let her go. Her plan was stupid, not thought out, yet she was prepared to use everything at her disposal. Moving around the room, she grabbed everything, upending all the crap she could find. When there was nothing left on the walls, she smashed the mirror. Going to the wardrobe, which was a walk-in one, she started to trash it, tearing down everything she could find. Throwing sneakers across the room, hitting the walls gave her little to no pleasure. She'd never been a destructive woman in her life. This was an act of desperation.

When they'd taken her, they'd pushed her too far. She refused to be just another woman to them.

The door opened and she launched a sneaker toward the person invading the room.

"What the hell, woman?"

"I want fucking out!" Another sneaker flew at the man. He stepped out of the room again, and closed the door, barely missing him.

"I'm not some fucking payment. I want out of this club, you sick fucks."

She saw the shelf in the wardrobe wasn't fixed in. Pushing it forward, she dislodged it from the position and threw it at the closed door. Going for the rest of the shelves, she threw one out of the window, which smashed.

Going to the open mess, she saw Demon was no longer getting his dick sucked. The woman was glaring up at the room.

"Fuck you!" Picking up the clothes, she began to throw them out of the window. No way was anyone going to say she didn't fight this. Everyone was going to know she wasn't here willingly.

Out the window all the sneakers went, along with parts of the shelves. Several men stood outside, far enough away so her wrath wouldn't touch them.

She whirled around as the door to the room opened again.

Demon stood, glaring at her. There was nothing for her to throw at him, which only pissed her off more. She didn't have anything but herself. Charging at him, she threw herself in his direction, trying to hit him. He was far stronger than her. She had no chance of winning against him. The door was closed, leaving them alone.

"Let me go!" She screamed each of the words, hoping he'd get the hint.

He picked her up, overpowering her and slamming her down to the bed. Deanna cursed, going in for the kill. She bit his now exposed shoulder. Between being outside to upstairs, he'd lost his jacket. She sank her fingers into his skin.

"You fucking wildcat."

In quick moves he had her arms locked above her head in one of his hands, and gripped her jaw tightly with her other one.

Demon covered her mouth with his hand. "Do you think you're that fucking smart?"

She glared at him, begging for him to slip up so she could knee him in the nuts.

"No you don't," he said, spreading her legs open as she tried to knee him.

He held her open with no chance of escaping. His hand left her mouth, landing at her pussy. Through the material that covered her, she felt the heat of his palm. Pausing, she stared up at him.

"Ah, do you need some attention?"

"Get your filthy hands off me."

"I like this fire you're showing. However, you're going to be the one to clean up this mess, no one else."

"I'm nothing to you. Leave me the fuck alone. I've got a job, a life."

"I bet all are shit. I wonder how many men have got you on your back, panting for them."

"I'm not panting for you, asshole. I want to leave."

"You're not leaving."

"You don't need me. You've got more than enough women to suck your dick."

He glanced behind him at the window. Before she could react, his hand went inside her jeans, sliding her pants to one side. His finger moved through her slit. She wasn't even wet for him.

"You're not even turned on?"

"I don't deal with women's sloppy seconds." She struggled against his hold, wondering when he'd let her go.

Demon pulled away from her. She sat up on the bed, glaring at him. Her heart was racing as she stared back at him. What was he going to do to her?

"Clean this shit up," he said.

"No."

"This is my room and you'll be sleeping here as well. I suggest you clean it up, otherwise the brother who cleans this shit up will be fucking you first."

Deanna wanted to argue, curse, and throw shit at him. The look in his eyes told her he wasn't joking around. He'd do exactly what he said he would. Going to her knees, she started to pick up what she could.

"When this is done, you'll pick up the trash outside."

Once she was outside, she might be able to escape. Hope flared inside her once more.

Chapter Five

Demon left her alone to pick up all of the shit. She had destroyed his room, trashed the hell out of it, and although he was pissed as fuck at the fact she had done it, he also couldn't blame her. She was here against her will, and anyone with half a brain wouldn't lie down and accept it without putting up a fight. The women that were here, the pussy that spread for him and his brothers, did so because they wanted to. They didn't force them to suck their cocks, or to beg to be fucked by them. But Deanna was a different breed of woman altogether. She was feisty, didn't hold anything back, and he knew, after only having her here for this short fucking time, that she'd give as good as any of the brothers in this club.

"Joker, make sure she doesn't try climbing out the window and cutting herself in the process of trying to escape." Demon would have laughed at that fact, seeing her so desperate to escape him that she'd go to any lengths, but he couldn't laugh at the thought of her hurt. She was angry, hated him and this club, but she'd have to come to terms with it all sooner than later. He wasn't going to let her go, wasn't going to allow her to run all over him either. Having her fits in the beginning was fine, for now, but soon she'd have to see that he didn't put up with that kind of shit.

He was growing angrier by the second, and went to the bar and grabbed a shot. He tossed it back, asked for a beer, and did the same with that. Once he was feeling good, the alcohol moving through his body, he turned and glanced at the doorway. She needed to be taught a lesson. He should have done it when he had her under him, and his hand down her pants. He'd never rape a woman, no matter how much of a criminal he was. This was about putting the little wildcat in her fucking place.

He turned and stalked back into the bedroom. Joker stood by the wall, his arms crossed, the scar under his left eye more pronounced because of the scowl on his face as he watched Deanna. She was on her knees, picking up the broken pieces of furniture she had destroyed, and cursing every step of the way. She stopped, looked up at him, and glowered.

"What? Come to harass me more, or maybe touch me without my consent?" she all but snarled out, like she was some kind of cornered feral animal ready to claw his eyes out. When he didn't respond she smirked, actually fucking smirked like she thought it was funny or some shit. He grew so damn angry his blood felt like it was on fire. "That's what I thought." She chuckled in a sarcastic way now, went back to picking up the trash, and he looked at Joker. The biker shook his head as he stared at Deanna.

"Joker, leave, and shut the door behind you," he said in a low voice. The other member pushed off the wall, nodded toward Demon, and left them alone.

Deanna stopped cleaning and stared up at him. She didn't show any fear, but Demon saw the way her hands shook slightly, and the fact she was grinding her teeth, as if she wanted to curse him out some more.

"Whatever you're going to do, just fucking do it already," she spat out, and he saw her reach for a piece of the end table she had broken. She hurled the leg at him, and he dodged it.

The fucking thing missed him by an inch. He growled out low, watched as her face turned red and her eyes widened, and then he strode toward her. Without thinking, just taking action, he hauled her off the floor, moved toward the bed, and sat down. He turned her over so her belly was flat on his thighs, her legs hanging over the other side, and her ass in full display.

His palm itched, and before he thought about it he brought it down on the big, fleshy mound of her right ass cheek. She squealed in outrage, kicked her legs out, and tried to get away. He placed a forearm on her lower back, kept her stationed, and spanked her over and over again. She was screaming at him, swearing all these impressive names at him, and then stated gasping out. He was relentless in his actions, spanking her like she had needed it done her entire life. And when she was breathing heavily, moving on his lap, his fucking cock jerked in response. He was getting hard watching his hand come down on her ass, and seeing the mounds shake from the force.

"You asshole," she breathed out, and for a second he wondered if this was arousing her. She had to be able to feel his dick hard beneath her belly, but she didn't say anything.

"You needed this, Deanna. You need to know who is in charge, and that continuing to act like a child in my damn clubhouse isn't going to go over very well with me." He spanked her once more, felt her dig her nails into his thighs, and then flipped her over. Demon stared at her face, saw her cheeks red, her lips parted and glossy, and her chest heaving. And her damn nipples were hard, poking through her shirt, teasing him with the idea that she was aroused by the punishment. Demon didn't make it a secret he liked a little pain with his pleasure. And maybe Deanna was the perfect woman to give him that combination, and take a little agony and ecstasy for herself while with him?

"You bastard," Deanna said in a low voice, and the way she dipped her eyes to his mouth told him that she was fighting what this did to her. Well, she could fight all she wanted, because Demon wasn't going to let this go.

Deanna stared at the ceiling, feeling her anger, her self-disgust, and her hatred for the man named Demon and this fucking clubhouse grow to a breaking point. It had been hours since she had trashed this room. But she was alone, had picked up the mess just so she didn't have to hear any more from that behemoth Demon. They had boarded up the window, but they had refused to let her to go outside, so her chance at leaving was squashed.

It was already night and she was exhausted, but all she could think about was when the asshole had spanked her like she was a kid and needed to be punished for acting out. What the hell had he expected? Should she just roll over and accept it all? Deanna was not some shrinking violet, and she wasn't a submissive that would just suck his dick whenever he snapped his fingers. But she hated herself for getting aroused when he spanked her. That wasn't like her, and she wanted to curse herself out until she didn't have a voice for how disgusted she was with her reaction.

No, Deanna wasn't about to let this bastard or his club take control of her. Even if she had to take them all out to make her escape possible she would. Because Deanna wasn't going to let her father get away with this, or be the whore to a bunch of fucking bikers.

Chapter Six

"Have you tamed the beast?" Joker asked, smirking as Demon came downstairs. He'd been standing outside his bedroom waiting to see if she'd try anything funny. She clearly didn't have a death wish, otherwise he'd be dealing with a dead body now rather than a drink. Although truth be told he didn't want to harm her, and would never hurt her unless she compromised the club. The club didn't willingly hurt women and children, but she was a liability, especially with her resistance, and her fierceness could put the club into shit they didn't need to deal with. If he continued to let her get away with shit, he'd start to lose respect in the club. Joker had supervised her cleaning up the mess after he spanked her ass. He'd gone back up when it was all over to listen to see what she'd do. Deanna was the first woman to intrigue him like this. He didn't like nor did he trust these feelings she kept inspiring.

"Shut the fuck up."

He slung back a shot, waiting for Chucks to fill him another. All the time he stared at the ugly-assed prospect he couldn't get the feel of Deanna's body across his knees out of his mind. Slinging back the shot, he wiped his mouth, turning around to find Sarah making her way toward him. She was slender and he saw the outline of her hipbones above where her skirt fell. The skirt was too small, and the bikini top left nothing to the imagination. She looked dressed to fuck whereas Deanna looked dressed for business.

If he didn't get her out of his mind, he was going to lose it.

"Hey, Demon. Do you want to finish off what we started?" She traced a finger along his stomach.

When she'd been sucking his cock earlier he'd been so close to coming. Deanna stopped him with her shouts then the smashing of the window. He liked her spunk. Sarah did nothing for him. She had a nice, tight cunt, and was fucking easy. Demon didn't need to fight with her to get what he wanted.

"Not now," he said.

"Come on, Demon. I know you need some release."

He grabbed her hand when she went to grab his dick. "I said no. Step back before I hand you to one of the fucking prospects for the night."

Demon grabbed his refilled shot glass and made his way out of the clubhouse. He stopped at the same place where he'd gotten his dick sucked.

Staring at the pile of crap the members had piled off to the side, Demon smirked. He didn't think she had the guts to completely trash his room. His closet was useless. Some of his clothes had also been ruined in the process of her temper.

"I know what that smile means," Joker said, coming to stand beside him.

"What does it mean?"

"Deanna's not going to know what's coming to her. I almost feel sorry for her but then I look at that shit, and I know I can't wait to see how this is going to go."

Demon took another inhale on his smoke. "I can tell you there's only one way for it to end, with her beneath me, her cunt open and taking my cock." In the recess of his mind, Demon wondered if he'd locked the bedroom door.

Deanna stared up at the ceiling, surprised by how white it actually was. She expected the room to be in an awful state, as bikers never really gave a shit about being clean, or so the stereotype played through her mind. Titling her head to the side, she looked at the ceiling from all angles. She wondered what the other rooms were like.

Don't do it, Deanna. Don't give in.

She reached underneath her to touch her ass. The sting was no longer there, yet the memory of his hands on her body was. She'd never responded to any man like that. Biting her lip, she tried to contain the groan that was threatening to spill out. There was no way she should have been turned on by being spanked. Deanna knew deep down it wasn't just about the spanking; it was the way Demon held her down, masterfully. She was losing her mind. Turning over on the bed, she stared at the bedroom door. He wouldn't have left the door unlocked.

With her reaction to him she needed to get away from him, far away. In fact, the further away she was, the better it would be for her. She didn't want to respond to him in any way.

Getting to her feet, she walked toward the window that was boarded up. She couldn't see anything. Next, she walked across the bedroom to the bathroom. Deanna opened the door to gaze inside. This room had a smaller window. Even if she was a slender woman she wouldn't make it through that tiny little hole.

She walked toward the mirror to stare at her reflection. Her cheeks were flushed and she quickly splashed some water onto her skin. When that didn't help to cool her down, she walked back into the bedroom.

"What the hell," she said, going to the bedroom door. She doubted it would work but she wasn't going to not try it.

Gripping the handle, she turned it.

Her heart pounded inside her chest as the door clicked open.

What?

No, Demon wouldn't have left the bedroom door unlocked. That would be giving her the chance to escape. This had to be some kind of trick to lure her into a false sense of security. It didn't make any sense.

She closed the door, taking a step back.

What are you doing? Get your ass out of here.

Licking her lips, she opened the door wider and glanced up and down the hall. The music coming from the main room could be heard throughout the whole house. No one was around. Leaving the bedroom, she closed the door behind her, being quiet.

Deanna made her way down the long corridor, taking her time with each step. Each room she passed there were erotic sounds coming from inside. The biker club did nothing but have sex, or so it seemed. She hated it and would never give herself to the biker willingly, no matter what club Demon belonged to.

On the way downstairs, she panicked. She didn't know if she was going to get out of here alive.

She thought about her father and her anger renewed. When she got her hands on him she was going to kill him.

Running down the small flight of stairs, she turned left and then right, then froze. On her right was the front door. This wasn't the door Demon had brought her through. Surely this wasn't going to be her escape.

Deanna jumped as she heard a couple walking downstairs. Without waiting to assess her situation, she dived for the door, opened it, and closed it behind her. When she opened her eyes, she gasped and laughed. Freedom was hers.

The club had a long driveway, and it took her a moment to get to the road, but when she did she took off down the street, running as fast as she could go. She knew where she was going. Deanna had always been good at remembering directions, and she had watched where he had been going on the ride to his clubhouse. All she ever needed to do was look at a map once to remember the route.

She didn't stop, running like mad to get free.

When she got stitch in her side, she started to walk. She wondered if they'd found the bedroom empty of her presence. Deanna didn't care. They were all crazy if they thought she was going to accept them using her as payment for her father's sins.

Sorry, Mom, there's only so much crap I'll take.

Feeling in the pocket of her jeans, she found some money she'd stuffed in there earlier in the day.

Fate was on her side. She found a bus stop and within minutes she was driving away from Demon, away from his crazy-assed club. In about an hour, maybe a little more, she'd be at her father's place. She was going to give him hell, hurt him as well.

Fisting her hands on her lap, she gritted her teeth at the events of the day. She was so angry. Never in all of her life had she been this angry or even this vindictive. Trashing Demon's room was completely out of character. She'd gone through life being tame, calm, relaxed, and focused. Demon brought out a side of her she really didn't understand.

Staring out of the window, she rested her head against the glass. She remembered the dark look of desire in Demon's eyes right before he spanked her. He'd only ever looked at her as if she was something to eat, to savor. No man had ever looked at her like that.

She licked her lips, knowing she'd left all of that behind. Men like Demon were wrong to want. They were the bad boys who couldn't be changed. She closed her eyes, forcing herself to remember the other woman sucking his cock. That's what she needed to remember when she thought about him. The last thing she wanted was a cheating biker. With that in mind, nothing was going to stop her from kicking her father's ass.

Chapter Seven

Demon moved back into the clubhouse. The main floor was empty, and the sound of fucking from the back rooms came through. Beer bottles and joints covered the floor; even coke lines were on the table. He walked over a couple of club whores that were passed out on the floor by the couch, and shook his head and the fucked-up state everything was in. A prospect was slung over the piece of furniture, out cold as well, and Demon continued to make his way toward the back rooms. He had this feeling, this tingling in the pit of his gut that said some shit had gone down with Deanna. He relied on his instincts to lead him in the right direction, and right now it was telling him that Deanna was going to be even more of a handful.

He moved quickly down the hallway, past the rooms where moaning and grunting were coming from, and finally stopped in front of his room. He pushed the door open, saw that the bed was mussed from where she had been laying, but that the room was empty. He moved into the room and checked the bathroom, but already knew the little wildcat had fucking taken off.

"Motherfucking hell," he ground out, turned on his heel, and stormed back into the main room. "Put your dicks in your pants and get your fucking asses out here. Now." He roared out the last word, feeling his blood boil at the fact she had slipped right out from under their god dammed noses. "Get. The. Fuck. Out. Here. Now," he yelled out even louder, walked over to the stereo, and turned the music off. The club whores on the floor came to, looking around with their drunk and sloppy expressions.

"What's going on?" one of them slurred.

"You two," Demon pointed at them, "get the fuck out of here and take the rest of your girls with you." He was pissed, not mincing his words or trying to be sweet about it. The club girls crawled off the floor, gathered their things, and when the rest of the members stumbled out of the room all of the whores left the clubhouse.

"What's up, prez?" Shakes said, running a hand over his head and looking a little annoyed.

"Yeah, this better be important because I was balls fucking deep in Pinkie before we heard your call." Steel didn't know how to keep his mouth shut, glowered at him, reached down, and adjusted his dick behind his jeans. "I was minutes away from nutting inside of her cunt before you hollered at us—"

"All of you shut the fuck up." The room grew silent after Demon spoke. He glanced at his men, the brothers of his club that were more like family than anything else. "The redhead is gone," he ground out, glanced at them, and felt like fucking something up. No one spoke for several seconds, and their clueless expressions pissed Demon off even more.

"Redhead? Pinkie left already," Steel said through his teeth, adjusted his cock once more, and then leaned against the wall.

Pinkie was an artificially colored redhead, but the one Demon was talking about was all natural, and his crew clearly didn't understand who in the hell he was speaking about. "I'm talking about our payment." He growled out, went over to the bar, and grabbed the Jamison. He took a long swig, knowing that he should be out there hauling her ass back in, but needing something to ease his rage. He turned and set the bottle down, seeing the realization on all of their faces.

"Well, let's go bring her ass back home." Joker rolled his head around on his neck, and then cracked his knuckles.

Yeah, this was her home now, and her stubborn, troublemaking ass better get used to that.

Deanna got off the bus, her body sore, tired, and her mind screaming at her that she needed to keep going. But she wanted to rest, needed to in fact. The events of today had drained everything out of her, and now that she was away from Demon and his devil club she was so, so tired. But even though it was the middle of the night, and resting sounded good, she was amped up, adrenaline still pumping through her body at the thought of what her father had done to her.

Stepping off of the bus and heading toward the station, she walked inside and went straight to the bathroom. Her feet hurt, and the feeling of blisters along her toes made every step feel as if she were walking on broken glass. Pushing the bathroom door open, she squinted her eyes against the bright fluorescent lighting and moved over to the mirror. Deanna stared at herself, winced at her reflection, and started the tap. The warm water flowed seconds later, and after splashing her face a few times and resting her hands on the counter to catch her breath, she finally let the tears flow. She couldn't help it, had kept them in as long as she could, and she was just so fucking tired of it all. It wasn't just about her father selling her out like he had to save his own ass, it was also about the life she had led. She had stayed by him because of her mother, tried to do right by the asshole for her mom. But then he had just given her away as if she was a piece of property that meant nothing to him. He didn't love her, and she knew he never had. He had been a sperm donor, not a father, and she wished that her mother was still around so she could explain that she had tried. God, had Deanna tried so hard to keep him in her life and make things right. But nothing would be right with them, certainly not now.

But he had fucked her over, and she wasn't going to just forget about that. She wasn't going to let him get away with it, either. She planned on going over there, telling him exactly what a low-life piece of shit he really was, and then calling the cops on his junkie ass. Maybe some good old-fashioned prison time with drug withdrawal would slap his ass into shape. Probably not, but it sure as hell would make Deanna feel better.

She grabbed a few paper towels and wiped off her face, and then stared at herself. Her hair was an auburn mess around her too-pale face, and the dark circles around her eyes made her look as though she were half dead. Had they realized she had left yet? Would they take the time to come find her? It seemed smart that they would just cut ties with her since she clearly hadn't made her stay easy for them. But then again, when she had seen the look in Demon's eyes she had realized that he was a man that didn't give up easily, and because of that she knew he'd come for her.

Chapter Eight

"There's only one place she'd go," Joker said.

Demon already knew where Deanna was going to go. Her father was the only person she was angry at but he was also the only person she had in the world. He couldn't believe no other man had claimed her ass yet. Her fiery temper would put off any man who didn't have the guts to tame her. Demon was not only going to tame her, he was going to have her begging him.

He smiled, thinking about Deanna on her knees before him, begging to take his cock. Demon would own every inch of her skin. He'd have her on her knees, back, against the wall, on the back of his bike, whatever way he could have her, he'd do it.

The very thought of claiming her mouth, cunt, and ass had him hard as rock.

"We're going back to her father's."

"Why can't you leave the bitch?" Steel said, looking even angrier. "She clearly doesn't want to be here. What's the point in forcing her to stay?"

Demon smiled. "You don't come with me to go and get her, I'll make sure the only cock Pinkie will be sucking is six feet under." He'd not gotten to be president by making idle threats. Pinkie meant nothing to him. The only job she did at the club was making all the men happy. Everyone had been inside

Pinkie apart from him. He'd not wanted her. She didn't appeal to him in any way.

Deanna, on the other hand, appealed to him a hell of a lot. If she thought for one moment that her being difficult was a problem to him, she was mistaken. He loved a challenge, relished it even. Her fighting him only cemented in his own mind that she was going to be all his.

"We ride," Joker said, heading out.

Demon picked five more men to go with them. He wouldn't usually take so many but since they no longer supplied her father, he didn't want to risk it. Knowing the bastard the way they did, he probably already had another supplier set up and waiting for him.

He walked out of the clubhouse, scenting the warm air. When he got her back he was going to put her in her place. He'd put her back over his knee if he needed.

The thought of her squirming over his lap turned him on. He straddled his bike and started the motor. The vibrations of the bike turned him on even more. He'd take her on this bike as well. Her sweet little pussy was going to be spilling with his cum by the time he was through with her.

"Soldiers of Wrath, let's ride."

He led the men out of the compound. The blood pounded in his veins, anticipation and excitement clawing away at him.

Deanna was exhausted but her determination wasn't going to end. She had enough money left over to rent a room for the night, which she did. After she took a long shower and dried herself on the very short towel supplied by the motel, she changed back into her clothes. They stunk but she wasn't going to pay out more money for new ones.

She ran fingers through her red hair to get the worst of the knots out. Letting out a breath, she thought about her apartment. If Demon and the others searched for her then all it would take was for her father to spill where she actually lived. She'd need to pack her crap up and get out of town after she'd confronted her father. There was no way she was going to let that asshole go without her getting the chance to speak her mind for once. All of her life she'd held her tongue in respect of her mother's wishes. After what had happened to her, her father could go and fuck himself. She hated him, despised him even. He was no father to her. The very thought about him in a remotely nice way pissed her off. He'd sold her to pay off a debt for drugs. Bastard! Demon was just as big a bastard as well. What kind of man took a woman as payment? An unwilling woman at that?

The thought of his hand on her ass annoyed her. No, it didn't annoy her. It turned her on and she'd loved it.

Don't do it, Deanna. It's dangerous. Just forget about it. You're never going to be the kind of woman he'll need.

She glanced toward the small cabinet beside the bed. There was a clock with an alarm beside it and she set it to go off in the next four hours. If she slept through the night, there was a risk Demon would find her. She didn't know how long she had before he caught up with her, but she needed to rest before she moved on. She didn't doubt he could find someone if he really wanted to.

Those four hours passed so damn fast, she didn't even feel like she'd been in bed long enough for it to count before the alarm was blaring back at her. She made her way toward the bathroom, washed her face and refreshed herself.

Within minutes she was outside at the reception.

"I don't suppose I can organize a cab?"

The man behind the counter pushed the phone toward her. She glanced at the advertisement on the wall for a car company. Tapping her fingers on the counter, she waited twenty minutes for the vehicle to arrive. She thanked the man and left.

Once in the back of the car she watched the scenery go by. She'd already told the driver the address she wanted to go to. Deanna wasn't going to leave until she got what she wanted.

What did she want?

"You okay there, sweetheart?" the driver asked.

"I'm fine."

"You're looking a little troubled. You're not running from anything, are you?"

She gritted her teeth. The last thing she needed or wanted was a conversation about her troubles with a stranger. "Nothing. I'm good. I've just had a really bad night."

"Okay."

He didn't pry any more. She rubbed her sweaty palms down her jean-covered thighs. The journey didn't last long and she paid the cab driver, waving him off. She turned around and faced the house she'd come to hate. Her father was an asshole and her mother shouldn't have asked her to take care of him. She loved her mother, always would, but loving this man was her biggest mistake. Tonight would be her last night of taking care of him.

She walked up to the door and raised her hand. Deanna heard the pleasured moans coming from inside, which set off her anger. He'd sold her off to a biker group and he was here having fucking fun. She didn't think so.

Opening the door, she charged into the house. What she saw would be forever burned on her retinas but she didn't turn away. She reached out, grabbing the woman's hair and yanking her off her dad.

"Bitch, get the fuck off me."

She threw the woman away from her.

"I've got to talk to my fucking father." Deanna made sure she could see the woman in case she tried to attack.

"Deanna, what are you doing here?"

"You're surprised to see me."

"Demon and the boys wouldn't have let you go." Her father stood up from the sofa, tucking his cock back into his pants. She was sick to her stomach of this man. He was a vile person.

"They didn't let me go. I got out, but not because of you."

"You've got to go back. You've got to."

"What's going on?" the woman asked.

Deanna wasn't interested in her. "Get the fuck out of here before I make sure you can't suck cock with my fist in your fucking face." She turned back to her father. "No, I don't have to do shit. You used me to pay off your fucking debt."

She couldn't stop herself. Deanna threw herself at him, attacking her father. "You piece of shit."

He must have been high, as she got a couple of hits in before he grabbed hold of her, stopping her from hurting him.

"You need to do this for me, Deanna. They'll kill me."

"Fuck you. You're the one who can't keep fucking clean. I've never touched drugs. I've not even gone out to party. After everything that happened with Mom, I've not had a life. I've been too busy trying to take care of your pathetic ass." She was full-out shouting now. "You didn't deserve her."

She pulled away from him. Deanna saw the other woman was standing, opening and closing her fists. She didn't care. There was no way she was going until she'd said everything that needed to be said.

"You're going back to Demon." Her father snatched his phone from the table.

Deanna grabbed the device out of his hand, launching it across the room. The cell phone shattered on the floor. She had no doubt Demon was already on his way looking for her, assuming she might be here.

"What the fuck have you done?" he asked, turning back to glare at her.

"I'm not helping you. You can find someone else to use but I'm not going to be payment for your actions. You're a piece of shit and we're done."

She moved away from him, heading toward the door. This was the last chapter of this life.

"No, I don't fucking think so."

Her father grabbed her by her hair, pulling her back. Deanna screamed. Before she could stop him, he threw her on the floor. "I didn't put up with years of shit to go down. You're a fucking cunt and you're going to do this for me."

"Fuck you."

Deanna didn't know what happened, but in the next second his hands were wrapped around her neck, squeezing tight. She started to claw at his hands. She didn't want to die but the crazed look in his eye let her know she was going to.

Chapter Nine

Demon pulled his Harley into the parking lot of the rundown piece of shit hovel that the junkie lived in. His boys were right behind him, and once they all shut off their engines the sound of breaking glass coming from in the house had him getting off his bike and moving toward the front door. He knew Deanna was in there, could feel it in his gut, and he always went with his instincts. His crew was close behind, their anger tangible, fierce, and so potent that it matched his. He didn't knock, didn't wait to see if someone would come to the door. Demon booted the fucking thing with his foot, cracked the door right off the hinges, and stormed inside. The place reeked of stale smoke, spilled booze, sweat, and raunchy fucking sex. He scanned the inside, didn't see anything at first, and then heard a distinct sound of someone being choked.

Hell no.

This possessive side reared up inside of him, calling out the beasts that he reserved for killing men that crossed him or his club, or protecting what was his. Deanna might have been given to him as trade for payment owed, but she was his now, and he protected what he owned.

He rounded the corner, saw the junkie have his woman, *yes,* his fucking woman, in a chokehold, and he charged forward.

The motherfucker glanced up, stared wide-eyed as Demon came forward, and let go of Deanna.

"I'm sorry, Demon. She came to me. I was about to call you to come pick her ass up—"

Demon didn't let the fucker finish. He grabbed him by the neck, hauled the prick up and off the ground, and slammed his willowy, sickly body to the wall. "You thought you could hurt what is mine?" Demon roared out, and tightened his hold on the junkie's neck. "You think you could put your fucking hands on her?" He was growing more enraged, more insane by the second.

The man's face was starting to turn blue, but he didn't loosen his hold, and in fact squeezed tighter. He started to gurgle out, and clawed at Demon's hands. But Demon didn't let up in strangling the bastard that thought to hurt Deanna. He saw red, thinking about her father's hands on her neck, squeezing the life out of her, hurting her. No, Demon was going to be the one to take a life tonight, and that life was going to be this piece of shit.

"Demon..." Deanna said in a low, strained voice behind him.

He pushed everything else aside except for this one moment in time. He saw the way the junkie's eyes rolled back in his head, how his body sagged forward and his arms dropped to his sides. Demon was going to kill this man, take his life, because it meant nothing to him. He had dared go after one of his own, and Demon was about to show him exactly why they were called The Soldiers of Wrath.

Deanna stared at Demon as he held her father to the wall by his neck. Her father's face was now this ghastly blue, and even though she called out for Demon to let him go, the biker ignored her. But Deanna didn't even know why she was trying to stop this. Her father had ruined her life, brought her down, and this was what he deserved. But maybe she was trying to save his life because she was human.

There were a few other MC members that had followed Demon inside, but they were forming an almost barricade between her and Demon.

"Please, you'll kill him. He deserves to live his life in the gutter, remembering the shitty things he has done." But she didn't truly believe that either.

Demon looked over at her, and his expression had her taking a step back. "You want this motherfucker to live, Deanna?" he growled out. "You want me to show him mercy when you weren't shown any? He fucking turned you over to my crew, sold you off so he was free and clear." Demon pulled her father off of the wall, still holding his neck, and then threw him across the room with so much force that Deanna gasped out. There was a sickening crunch as her father slammed into the wall, and then his lifeless body slumped to the floor.

The silence stretched out, and she looked at the bikers. Demon was by the wall, this dark, hard look on his face. The other bikers had smirks on their faces as they stared at her now dead father. Deanna looked at her dad again, but the sorrow and regret didn't come. She took in the odd angle of his neck, at the way he stared at her with a lifeless gaze, and the only thing she felt was this hard hatred. It filled her, consumed every part of her, and then she broke down and started crying. It wasn't from sadness, but from this relief that filled her. She should hate herself, loathe the way she was happy that she was free of the man that had dragged her down to the bowels of his hellish life.

But she was crying and happy, and when the tears dried she started laughing uncontrollably.

"She's snapped, just fuckin' snapped, prez," one of the bikers said.

She threw her head back and laughed hard, not able to stop herself, and then she fell to the floor, landing on her hands and knees, and cried harder than she had ever cried in her life. She couldn't stop, couldn't control herself, and she knew that this was truly the beginning of the end.

"She's in shock," Demon said from right behind her now, and she looked over her shoulder at him. Her vision was blurry, her tears coming steadily. He got down on his haunches in front of her, lifted his hand, and she flinched away. He had just killed a man, and although she feared him because he was this hardened, dangerous biker, she also felt something else. He had protected her, went after the man—her father—that had been hurting her. She should hate him, loathe this fucking man and all he represented. But when he reached out and brushed her tears away, she found herself launching herself into his arms.

Yeah, Deanna was lost, fucking lost and insane, because she was finding solace and comfort in the arms of a murderer.

Chapter Ten

"Clean this shit up," Demon said. He didn't wait to see who stayed behind and who came with him. The only focus he had was on his woman, sobbing in his arms. He carried her out of the house toward his bike. Putting her on her feet, he gripped her face, forcing her to look back at him. "Deanna, look at me." He gave her a little shake, not enough to shock her but just enough to get her attention. Tears spilled down her cheeks and seeing them filled his heart with grief. "You do not get to cry for him. That man was a bastard. Those tears are not allowed." He wiped the tears away, wishing there was something he could do. Whatever happened there was no way he'd ever be able to let her go. She'd seen too much. Witnessing him murdering her father had cemented her future in his club. He couldn't let her leave. The club wouldn't allow him to.

"You killed him."

Demon nodded. "Yeah, and you don't speak another word of it."

"He's dead. My dad's dead."

Gripping the back of her head, he placed his palm over her mouth.

"Your asshole of a father is dead but you're alive. You talk about it and you're going to die along with him. Is that what you want?"

If he didn't get her to be silent now then his club would demand her death. He wouldn't go to jail for the slime ball.

"I don't want to die."

"Good. Now, you're going to get on the back of my fucking bike and we're going back to the clubhouse. Don't fuck with me, Deanna."

She jerked her head in a nod. Satisfied, Demon straddled his machine, waiting for her to climb on behind him. He didn't bother with a helmet. The quicker they got to the clubhouse the better it was for the both of them.

"Hold on tight."

Deanna wrapped her arms around his waist but she didn't put any effort in.

"Tighter," he growled.

She tightened her hold on him.

He headed in the direction of the clubhouse. Demon didn't make a stop on the way. The sooner he got home the better it was for him. He needed to keep her safe. The image of her father's hand wrapped around Deanna's neck entered his mind. He wanted to kill the fucker again. No one put a hand on his woman. He gritted his teeth, hoping by the time he got home, the anger would have simmered down; otherwise he was going on a rampage.

Climbing off the back of Demon's bike a couple of hours later, Deanna couldn't stop shaking. The man before her had killed her father, and yet she was indebted to him. Children should hate the men responsible for killing their parents. She was grateful to him. If he'd not arrived when he did she would be dead.

He took her hand, leading her into the clubhouse. Several men were waiting for them but he didn't stop to greet any of them. Demon didn't stop moving until they were inside his bedroom. She watched him slam and lock the door. No one was coming between them this time and there was no chance of escape.

Demon didn't talk as he led her through to his bathroom. He turned on the shower. She didn't know what to do or say. He began working the shirt from her body and her jeans.

His touch was a little rough as he got her naked. Deanna stayed still, letting him take the lead. He could have killed her but he hadn't. Demon saved her.

Taking a breath, she stepped under the warm water, shocked as he climbed into the shower behind her. He'd stripped his clothes off in seconds. She didn't dare look down at his cock. Deanna refused to think about what was going on.

You owe him your life.

Tilting her head back, she let the water spray her face, relishing the feel of it on her skin. She closed her eyes, gasping as she saw her father's angry face staring right back at her. He'd been so angry with her. Biting her lip, she couldn't help but tense up.

"He's not coming back, Deanna."

Demon stroked her arms, offering her comfort. She took it. Ever since her mother had passed she'd not gotten any comfort from anyone. She was all alone in the world.

"I know."

He washed her body, paying careful attention to cleaning her long length of hair. The patience he showed with her surprised her. Deanna really thought he'd find some way to punish or hurt her. His gentle touch didn't help her nerves.

When the shower was over, she crossed her hands over her breasts to hide herself from his gaze. She was too open, too exposed to his gaze. He looked past her naked body.

Licking her dry lips, she chanced a glance at his dark eyes. They gave nothing away. Demon was closed off. He didn't tell her anything.

Nodding her head, she stepped into the towel he offered her. He dried her body, carrying her through to the bedroom. Demon laid her on the bed and joined her.

"I'm sorry," she said.

She turned onto her side so that she was facing him. The towel gave her a little dignity as she stared at him.

"Why are you apologizing?"

"You didn't have to come and find me. He'd have killed me."

Demon stayed silent as she spoke but the moment tears filled her eyes, he started. "Why did you go back to him? He was a dangerous man."

"Mom told me to. Your parent isn't supposed to hurt you."

"What did your mom ask you?" He reached out, pushing some of her damp hair off her cheek.

"She asked me to keep an eye on him. Begged me to never turn my back on him. What kind of a father sells his daughter to pay for a debt?"

"It's not that unheard of, baby."

"I've never heard anything like it." Her throat felt tight, like something was clogging it. Staring at Demon, she shook her head. "I didn't want to be sold. I didn't want to lose my future."

"You're not going to."

"I won't run again. I promise. I'm so sorry."

"Shh, baby. You don't need to worry."

"I can't believe he tried to kill me." She buried her head against his chest, needing his warmth. There was nowhere else for her to go.

"You can't leave."

"I know," she said. For some strange reason, she didn't know why that comforted her.

"No more leaving. You'll do as you're told."

"Yes." She didn't have anyone. Her father was dead, good riddance. Her mother was gone but thank God she didn't have to see him at his lowest point. Closing her eyes, she listened to Demon's heartbeat. The sound soothed her, comforted her, and made her feel safe. She'd not felt safe in so long.

"I'm going to take care of you."

She murmured her agreement. He was so warm. Within minutes sleep claimed her.

Chapter Eleven

The feeling of hands skimming along her bare flesh had Deanna moaning slightly. The hands were big, warm, and there was a distinct pressure of ownership in the way she was being touched. She could have said she was dreaming, but even after she opened her eyes and stared at the still boarded up window, she knew she wasn't. Demon was touching her like he owned her, like there wasn't any part of her that wasn't his. Maybe Deanna should have stopped him, should have said this was wrong, that she didn't want it. But the truth was she did want it, desperately. She wanted to feel numbing pleasure that took away everything else, that made her life not matter at the moment. She wanted to feel him fucking her until she couldn't think, couldn't breathe, hell, couldn't even move.

"You're awake," Demon said huskily, softly, and continued to touch her. He moved his lips along the same path as his hands: over her shoulder, down her arm, and along her waist. It felt good not to think and just feel.

She rolled over, lay on her back, but turned her head so she could see him. It was still dark outside, and she knew she hadn't slept very long. "Be with me, Demon. Make me forget about everything except right here and now."

He groaned deeply, and didn't waste any time in grabbing her chin in a bruising grip, tilting her head to the side, and latching his mouth on her throat. He sucked and licked at her while he continued to move his hand over her stomach, along her hip, and finally touched her pussy. She wore no clothing because she had only worn a towel after the shower. God, she was already wet, and if that wasn't the sickest thing of it all, because of what she had been through, then she didn't know what was. But it felt good, and right now that was all that mattered.

He jerked her head back toward him and claimed her mouth. For several long seconds he didn't do anything but kiss her, stroked her tongue with his, and rub his fingers through her pussy lips.

"I couldn't help but touch you, smell you, memorize every part of you, but I wouldn't have taken it any farther, Deanna," Demon groaned against her lips. "I would have never taken something from you that wasn't freely offered, but I wanted to be able to feel your soft skin, especially after tonight." He slammed his mouth down on hers harder, and shoved a thick finger into her pussy. She arched her back and cried out. She wasn't a virgin, but she also hadn't been with a man in a while, and Demon had thick, long fingers. It was surprising the feel of herself being stretched by his fingers alone, but God, did it feel good.

Everything seemed to go fast and quick, but she was more than ready to put everything else behind her, and just feel Demon. He started kissing her neck, her collarbones, moved along her breasts, and sucked at the stiff peaks. For several long moments that was all he did, pump his finger into her and suck and bite at her nipple. And then before she knew what was happening he was removing his finger from her body. There she was, lying on this hardcore biker's bed, stark naked, dripping wet with her arousal, and unable to hold in her moan.

"You want my hands on you, my tongue along your flesh, and my cock deep in your hot little cunt, Deanna?" Demon groaned out, and she couldn't answer. She just nodded, panted for breath, and gripped the sheets beneath her.

He moved between her thighs, wedged his broad shoulders between her legs, placed both his hands under her ass, and lifted her to his waiting mouth. Their eyes locked for a heartbeat. The feel of his warm breath skating across her pussy could have made her come right then. He smirked, a hard slash across his mouth that was not one of amusement. He knew the effect he had on her and he was relishing in it.

And then he started licking her, lapping at her pussy like he was starving and her cream was the only thing that could sate him.

The feel of his tongue on her exposed flesh had her eyes involuntarily closing. He used that muscle to run up her center, sucking her wetness off and causing more to come. Demon was so incredibly slow with his ministrations that she found herself pressing closer to him, trying to tempt him to give her more. On any other occasion she might have been mortified by her actions, but pressing her pussy harder against his face, trying to have him lick and suck at her harder seemed so logical at the moment. And when she felt her orgasm start to climb, he pulled back, leaving her bereft. She opened her eyes and blinked several times. The arousal still pounded through her bloodstream, crying out for more.

"Put your arms above your head and keep them there." His tone brooked no argument, and she knew she had no intentions of denying him. Deanna needed this, needed him to control the situation because right now she felt like her life was out of control.

She did as he asked because she knew she needed his mouth back on her now. He moved back between her legs and resumed licking her. He moved his tongue up and down her slit, teasing her clit on the upstroke, and pressing minutely into her hole on the down stroke. She was so close to getting off. He was torturously slow, bringing her close to climax but not exerting enough pressure to actually bring her over the edge. Perspiration started to coat Deanna's flesh.

"Your cunt tastes so good, and you're so fucking wet for me, sloppy even, baby."

Her fingers hurt from the strain of keeping them together. All she wanted to do was grip his head and shove it more deeply into her pussy. And the erotic, filthy words he said to her had her crying out for more, unashamedly begging him.

"Please, Demon. Please let me come, give me this, and I'll be yours." God, those words came out of her, and she couldn't have stopped them if she tried. Would he think what she said was her declaration that she really wanted this life? Could she want this life with a biker and his illegal, dangerous and violent club?

"That's right, Deanna, you are mine. I'm not letting you go, and I'm not letting anyone have you. This pussy is mine," he licked her slit from pussy hole to clit. "These tits are mine," he reached up and grabbed the mounds, massaging them. "You are mine."

She opened her mouth on a soundless cry. He had to know she was perilously close.

"Say it, Deanna. Say you're mine. Only mine."

At this point she would have done anything to feel that crest of pleasure wash over her.

"Please. Please let me come, Demon."

"Say it." He roared out the words and sucked her clit into his mouth, bringing her right there over the edge and backing away before she went over.

"I'm yours," she breathed out. The words left her on a whoosh of air and she locked gazes with him. The look he gave her had her entire body tightening. As if he wanted to prolong her torture, she watched in rapt shock as he held her pussy lips apart with his thumbs and ran his tongue up her center.

"That's right. You're mine." A dark look crossed his face when she looked at him. He slowly moved his tongue back to her cleft. When he reached her clit he brought the tiny bud into his mouth and sucked hard. Rhythmic motions had her grinding herself against his mouth. He sucked on her clit, bringing the tiny bundle of nerves over his tongue and ever so gently running his teeth along it. The orgasm that moved through her was intense and heady.

When the tremors started to dissipate, she breathed out. He stayed between her legs, staring at her, the shadows moving across his face.

"I want you so fucking badly, so if you're not ready, baby, you need to tell me now. Once I start I don't know if I can stop, Deanna." He groaned out the last part, but a controlled expression stayed on his face. She didn't need him to warn her. She knew what she was getting into, and whether it was a bad idea or not, she would not tell him no.

Demon leaned back enough to see her slightly spread legs. He moved closer to her again, inhaled deeply, and growled low at the scent of her. Using his hands on her inner thighs, he pushed her legs open even wider until he saw what he ached for. She was swollen and wet for him. Demon went back to eating her out even though she had already come. He had to keep licking her, had to suck the cream from her pussy until he was drunk on it. He pressed his hips into the mattress, hoping to stem off his impending orgasm. Her slit, so ready for him, made his whole body tighten with need. He lifted his gaze to her breasts, those twin mounds that had his cock jerking with need. Her nipples were pink, tight and ready for him. A moan left him as he watched her bite the flesh of her bottom lip.

Again he pressed his hips into the mattress, feeling the sheets scrape along his throbbing cock, heightening his arousal instead of dimming it. Leaning forward, he let his tongue travel along the inside of her thigh and all the way to her core. A gasp left her and then she was pushing her cunt in his face. Using his thumbs, he spread her labia apart, flattened his tongue, and ran it up her center.

He sucked and licked her. He wanted her cream coating his mouth, wanted it running down the back of his throat. Sucking her clit into his mouth, he ran his tongue around the bundle of nerves. He started thrusting his hips faster against the mattress, dry humping the fuck out of the sheets. He needed his cock in her cunt, needed the friction and her wetness covering his cock.

"Fuck, baby. You taste so damn good." He groaned against her. He renewed his efforts and was rewarded when her back arched. Yeah, he was going to fuck her good and hard until she couldn't even walk straight.

Deanna couldn't breathe, couldn't even concentrate as she tried to get her bearings together after the second orgasm Demon gave her faded. Although Demon was rough in every way, she knew he would stop if she said no. But she had no intentions of stopping.

He settled his body on top of hers and placed his hand on the back of her neck, bringing her head closer with a fierce move.

"Everything about you drives me fucking crazy," he groaned out and looked at her mouth. "I am going to claim you so hard you won't be able to sit down without thinking of my cock in your body." Demon kissed her, and she tasted herself on him. He ran his fingers up her arms, and grabbed them around her wrists until a spark of pain filled her. "And your pussy is the sweetest thing I've ever tasted."

Her pussy became wetter and her arousal slid down her inner thighs. The sheet beneath her had become moist from her arousal, and she knew it would get more pronounced the more she was with Demon.

He moved his fingers back to her pussy, stroked her like an expert, and said in a low, heated voice, "If not for my self-control I'd be fucking you right now, but I want to savor this." He moved his mouth to the pulse point at her throat while he continued to run his finger over the opening of her pussy. "You're so fucking wet for me, Deanna." He dipped his fingers deeper into her body. "I bet this slick little pussy will be the tightest I've ever felt."

And more wetness spilled from her at his filthy words.

"Damn, my whole hand is drenched."

She gasped as he twisted his fingers inside of her.

"Soon my cock is going to replace these." He emphasized his point by scissoring his fingers deep within her. "And then you'll truly be owned by me. You'll be my woman, my fucking property, and no one will dare touch you without answering to me." He moved the digits faster, harder, and the sound of her flesh sucking at him seemed to fill the room. "I'd kill anyone that touched you, Deanna," he said in a deadly voice. Demon brought his thumb to her clit and started rubbing it back and forth. All other thoughts or actions ceased. In the next second she came. She cried out and pumped her pussy faster and harder on his fingers, lifting her hips up and down, trying to get him to go deeper. And when her orgasm faded in the background, and a pleasurable hum filled her, Deanna opened her eyes.

He still had one hand around her wrists, and she wondered if he was the type of man that enjoyed pain and inflicting it on others with his pleasure. The man before her was hard in more ways than one. He pulled back slightly and she stared at his body. His eyes were this cold, hard grey color, or maybe liquid silver would be more correct. His shoulders were wide, his chest defined and rippling with muscle. He had tattoos covering his arms and upper chest, and she could make out a frightening skull tattoo inked on his shoulder.

His erection strained forward, huge, long and thick, and the fleeting thought came to her that having that cock in her would be painful. But she grew bold, sat up slightly now that he had let go of her wrists, and reached out. She grabbed the root of his dick. Demon hissed when she wrapped her fingers around his length, but he was too thick that she couldn't fully grasp all of him. Looking up at him, she saw him watching her with half-lidded eyes.

"Suck my cock good, Deanna. Make me almost fill your mouth with my cum."

Even in the darkness she could see how deadly he was, how dominating and demanding Demon was.

Leaning down, she brought her mouth to the tip of him. She could feel his heat and opened her mouth wider to flick her tongue over the ridge of the tip. No noise came from him but she felt his body tighten. Deanna wanted him to ache for her like she did for him. She ran her tongue over the flared edge and engulfed him. The taste of him exploded in her mouth.

Salty, sweet, all male.

Her pussy was drenched and her clit throbbed, even though she had already gotten off twice for him. She sucked him hard and deep, and he gripped the back of her head and started thrusting into her mouth.

"I'm going to mouth fuck you until the crown of my cock hits the back of your throat." His whole body was strung taut and she knew he was going to come very soon. He tightened his fingers in her hair, but before she could taste him he pushed her back. She fell against the mattress hard, her breasts shaking, and her legs falling open. His breathing was haggard and the look he gave her heated and frightened her.

His gaze dipped between her spread thighs and he let out a gruff sound. "Jesus, Deanna." He ran a hand over his mouth, and flicked his gaze to her. "Tell me you want my cock in you. Beg me to fuck you."

Oh, God.

His words were like gasoline on a fire. She had never been with someone so incredibly compelling and forceful with their words, with their body, and just with one look. There was no doubt that Demon killed people, reveled in it, too, and here she was giving herself to him.

She started hollowing out her mouth, taking as much as she could, and when she was gagging from the hard, thick length of him, he pulled her head back with his hand in her hair. He stared at her for a second, and then in the next instant his hard body was blanketing hers, and he kissed her forcefully. "If we do this, we do it my way." His words brooked no argument.

Yes, she so wanted to do it his way. A nod was all she could accomplish, but it satisfied him nonetheless. He clasped her wrists in one of his hands and brought them above her head once again. Seemed he liked her restrained. She needed to feel his callused hands scrape over her flesh. He cupped one of her breasts, tweaked her nipples painfully until she gasped out, and then smoothed his palms over her skin. His hands were rough, worn, and all she could think about was how powerful he was when using them.

The feel of his dick pressing against her pussy had the desire to rub against him rising to the surface. For some reason, she knew that if she was patient and obedient, he would bring her to a place she had never dreamed of.

"Are you ready for me?" He squeezed her breast hard. "Are you ready for my cock?"

She parted her mouth and nodded.

"Does the idea of what I do, of how I live my life with my club, frighten you?"

"Yes."

"Good. It should, because I am a very dangerous man, Deanna. Very dangerous."

"Please—" Her words were cut off when he reached between their bodies, placed the big head of his dick at her entrance, and slammed into her. She threw her head back, groaning out her pleasure. He was like a wild man, thrusting, pumping, bringing her so close to the edge and then stopping right before she went over. Her pussy was so wet for him, and the sound of his skin slapping against hers reverberated in the room.

"So mine." He growled against her neck and picked up speed.

Soon she was falling over the edge into mindless, blissful completion. He let go of her wrists as he growled out and pumped in and out of her. She grabbed onto his short dark hair, pulled at the strands, and moaned out.

She screamed out, literally screamed when another smaller orgasm wreaked havoc on her body. Just as the high started to slowly dwindle, she found herself flipped on her belly. He lifted her ass, spanked her several times until the skin heated and her knees shook. Palms flat on the mattress and legs spread wide, she waited for him to dominate her further. Deanna closed her eyes when she felt his fingers skate over her slit to gather her cream. There was no tensing, no worries about what was going to happen next as he spread her juices over her anus. And then when he probed her hole, gently dipped his finger inside of her, she thought he'd fuck her then and there. But then he moved away from her only long enough to grab a bottle of lube from the dresser. He was back behind her in second, had the slick lube coating her ass, and then placed the crown of his dick at her back hole, but didn't penetrate her.

The fear of pain was present, but her desire was stronger.

"You're so responsive to my touch. Will you be this responsive when I have my cock buried deep in your ass?"

She didn't answer, couldn't. The sting of his hand coming into contact with her ass had her gasping once more. He spanked her harder this time. The pain was a sharp contrast to the pleasure he had just delivered.

"Answer me." His voice was dark, demanding.

"God, I want to feel you in my ass." She felt herself blush, not because she had said the words, but because she had meant them.

"I am so hard for you. Do you feel what you do to me?" He lifted off her back and she felt his erection slide across her ass.

"Yes," she breathed out.

In the next second he was slowly pushing all of his hard inches into her. Tears stung her eyes, and she started to feel the burn and stretch of being filled completely. It was like nothing she had ever felt. The sting of the tip of his cock popping through the tight ring of muscle had her squeezing her eyes shut.

"That's it, baby. Take all of my cock. Take it all, Deanna."

When he was completely inside of her he didn't move. Demon gripped the cheeks of her ass, intermittently as if it was agony being still. She pushed back against him, telling him without words she was ready. He hissed under his breath and gripped her hips hard.

"You're tempting a fucking beast, Deanna," Demon said low.

"Fuck me, Demon." She looked over her shoulder at him. "Make me feel something else tonight."

He started moving in and out of her and soon the burn of pain was replaced by something far more pleasing. Each time he pushed into her that desire heightened. When he reached in front of her and started rubbing her clit she didn't care that she was letting a bad man fuck her. Right now he was what was keeping her sane, and for that she wanted him like she wanted to breathe.

One thrust, two thrusts, and on the third one he buried himself balls deep in her ass and cursed loudly. His language was crass and vile, but it reflected the strong emotion they both felt. After his big body was no longer tense, he loosened his hands on her hips, and cursed out as he gently pulled out of her. Instantly she felt his cum start to slip from her ass, but she didn't care about the warmth of it, or the fact he had filled her completely.

He lay beside her, but he didn't push her away or leave her in the aftereffects of what they had done. He pulled her close and wrapped his arms around her. She let herself slip into an endorphin-filled coma. It was then, in the darkness surrounding them, that the idea of fighting him seemed abhorrent. Deanna let herself slip into the darkness, because being with Demon didn't seem so frightening anymore. In fact, it felt like the safest place to be.

Chapter Twelve

Demon held onto the fiery-tempered woman in his arms. He'd fucked her pussy and had taken her ass without really preparing her. Guilt hit him hard and square in the chest at the way he'd used her. Most women needed to take time to accept him. He wasn't a small man. Staring down into Deanna's sleeping face, he knew she was different. She wasn't like a lot of women. Deanna had given herself to him, trusted him when a lot of women would have gone running at what he did tonight.

He murdered her father right in front of her and he wouldn't hesitate to do it again if he could do it over. She was so breathtakingly beautiful that she made him want to be something he'd never been. He wanted to care for her. Demon didn't care about anything but the club. His one true loyalty held within the four walls of the MC to all the men who served him. They served him, and they served the club.

Pushing some hair off her face, Demon watched her sleep.

"You're going to cause me a shit load of problems. I can sense it."

Untangling himself from her body, he stopped when he saw his seed leaking out of her ass. He gripped the back of his head at the sight. Using a condom had been at the back of his mind while he fucked her. He didn't want anything to be between them when he was inside her body.

He wanted to possess this woman and make it so the only thoughts she had were filled with him. Moving into the bathroom, he ran the tap, splashing some water onto his face. Demon wiped the droplets out of his eyes before staring back at his reflection. This is what his life had come to. There was a woman in his bed that meant more to him than any other woman. He didn't want her servicing the other men in the club. The thought of Joker, Steel, or even Shakes touching her had him madder than hell.

Grabbing a towel, he headed into the bedroom where Deanna was still asleep. She didn't want to be part of the club life and yet that was all she'd get with him. He wouldn't give the club up for anyone, not even Deanna.

He wiped away his cum and made sure his touch was gentle so that she wasn't in pain or woken up. It had been a long couple of days for her. When he cleaned away his cum, he grabbed his jeans, heading out of the room. This time he left his door unlocked. Something in his gut told him she wasn't going to try to make a run for it again. She'd be in more danger out there alone than inside the clubhouse.

Sexual moans filled the long corridor as he made his way past doors. A few doors were still open showing off the couples fucking inside. Deanna had drained all need from him. Moving past the rooms, he headed down to the bar where he found Joker, sipping at a glass of scotch.

"Are you in a sharing mood?" Demon asked, pointing at the scotch.

"Sure thing, brother." Joker leaned over the counter, grabbing another glass and filling it to the brim with the alcohol. "To crazy-ass bitches and shit fucking luck," Joker said, clinking their glasses together.

Demon emptied his glass in several large gulps. Something had to be bothering Joker for him not to be using the shot glasses for scotch, but the full-sized ones.

"Do you want to talk about it?" Demon asked.

"Let's start with the shit that went down tonight. Nothing will come back on the club. He had a shit load of debt with a lot of people. We won't be touched."

"Good to know." Demon didn't expect anything else.

"I've got to head out for a couple of days," Joker said.

Out of all of the men, Demon trusted Joker the most. The man had taken a bullet for him years ago when he didn't need to. Joker had become one of his most trusted men, which was why he was the VP. He knew Joker would always have his back in a fight.

"Why?"

"Got shit to take care of. Proper shit."

"You're not going anywhere until I know what's going on. If it's to do with the club then we're going to have your back." Demon pointed for him to pour more alcohol. He wanted to be good and drunk before he went back up to his room. The thought of sliding inside Deanna's supple, pliant body was enough to make him ache. He needed to create some distance between them. Never in his life had he allowed a woman to have a hold on him. Deanna wouldn't be the last woman he fucked. Demon paused as he thought about fucking another woman. The very idea made him feel sick. His cock, which had been hard at the thought of Deanna, went limp at the prospect of another woman.

"It has nothing to do with the club. It's personal shit." Joker poured himself another shot, swallowing it back with one gulp before taking another. "The reason I'm letting you know is that I'm heading out tomorrow. I don't know if I'll be back for a couple of weeks."

"Personal shit?" Demon ran a finger over his lip. There was only one person he knew that would have Joker dropping all of his crap. "Amy?"

"Yeah. Dad called me when I got back to the clubhouse. He needs me back at home. Amy's mother Brenda was killed yesterday." Joker slammed back another shot, staring down at the counter in front of them.

"Fuck, man, I'm sorry."

"She wasn't my mom."

"No but she was important to you." Brenda wasn't as important as Amy but she'd been a stepmom to Joker for the few years he'd lived at home. They'd been close.

"Yeah, she was important." Demon looked in time to see Joker's hand trembled just a little. Nothing ever fazed Joker, but the prospect of going home clearly did.

"How long has it been since you've seen Amy?"

"Five years, maybe more, maybe less."

Joker knew the length of time. He was trying not to let it affect him. Demon took the bottle from him, pouring them both out a shot. He didn't know exactly what had gone down between Joker and Amy, but it was something that sent Joker away. From what he knew, Joker tried to make sure he was never alone with Amy.

"Dad's pretty distraught. He needs some help back at home. Amy's trying to deal with the death of her mother." Joker stopped talking. His voice had become thick with emotion.

"The club's here for you when you need us."

"Thanks, man. I appreciate it." Joker clinked his glass with Demon's. They both took another sip, each man lost in their own little worlds. "So what is going on with you and Deanna?"

"Nothing."

"Come on, Demon. You and I both know if a bitch ran from you, you'd leave her alone. She's shown more than once that she doesn't want to be here. Why did you go and get her?"

Demon didn't answer right away. He poured another generous shot of alcohol into his glass. The truth was, he didn't know what the fuck was happening. What started out as a simple transaction had changed dramatically in the course of a day. Deanna wasn't going to take anything lightly. She didn't want this life, yet he wanted her. Demon didn't even know if he was going to be able to let her go. She'd entered his life and now there was no saying when or if he was going to be able to move on.

Running a hand down his face, he tried to clear his head. All he saw was his semen trickling out of her ass. Fuck, the image along was enough to thicken his cock. He wanted her again, badly.

"I can't let her go."

"I hate to say this to you, Demon, but you may not have a choice."

He rubbed at his temple, staring at the dark amber liquid in his glass. There was no way he could handle this right now.

"You can talk to me," Joker said.

Glancing over at his friend, Demon stared around the club. This was his life, where he intended to spend however long he had left on this planet. The club wasn't just a fad to him. It was his life.

"She's different." She was, too. He didn't know why he wanted her the way he did. She was a weakness he couldn't handle in his life right now.

"Most romantic thing I've ever heard," Joker said, snorting.

Demon slammed his fist against Joker's side, shutting him up.

"Okay, so different is good. You can work with different."

"Joker, no offense, we just fucking killed her father 'cause she couldn't stand being in the club."

"We took her against her will. She's got no one. Look at her from her perspective. She goes to see her dad and suddenly ends up being taken by a bunch of bikers. I imagine that shit is hard for anyone to handle, let alone a young woman. She's what, twenty-one?"

Demon tensed up. He didn't have a fucking clue how old she was. Glancing over at Joker, he saw that the other man looked concerned.

"Do you know how old she is?"

"Fuck." He downed the shot of scotch and jumped out of his chair. There was no way in this world he'd just fucked a minor. He wouldn't do it. No fucking way.

"I'm going to head out first thing in the morning."

"Let me know when you get there." He headed back upstairs to the woman who had him in knots. Demon opened his bedroom door and paused. Deanna was still fast asleep in his bed. She looked so sweet, so tempting, too fucking innocent. Her leg was curled around the blanket, showcasing her full, voluptuous ass.

His cock tightened to the point of pain. He ached to be inside her once again.

Take her.

Fuck her.

Is she even legal?

Yeah, he was a hardened criminal, an asshole and murderer, but sleeping with a woman not legal, a fucking child, was a sick fucking thing. He'd never cross *that* line. He was so fucked up he didn't even want to think about it.

Closing the bedroom door behind him, he stepped toward the bed. Demon stared down at her and knew he couldn't wait to find out the answer. Reaching out, he grabbed her arms and gently shook her awake. No way had he just fucked a minor. The very thought had him sick to his gut.

Deanna screamed as she was brought out of her dream with a rough shake. Strong arms gripped her tightly and it took her a few seconds to clear her thoughts.

"Demon, what's going on?" She held onto his arms as he dragged her off the bed.

"How old are you?" He snarled the words close to her face.

She started to recoil. The sheer anger inside him scared her.

"W-what?"

"You heard."

"I-I'm t-t-t-twenty-o-one." She'd never stammered before in her life. Faced with Demon's anger, she couldn't control her voice.

"You better not be fucking lying to me."

"I-I'm not." She held her hands up in front of her, which was hard to do because of the way Demon held her immobile.

"Fuck, compared to my thirty-eight years you're a damn baby." He started pacing.

Seconds passed but they felt like minutes as he kept staring at her. She became aware how naked she was while he wore a pair of a pair of jeans. This was not the man she'd woken beside hours earlier. The kind man who fucked her into oblivion was long gone. In his place stood a man who ran a biker club with an iron fist.

"You're scaring me."

Slowly, he released her. She stepped away from him, needing to be as far away as possible. He terrified her, which she hated more than anything. Licking her suddenly dry lips, she chanced a glance at him.

"Do you really think I would have slept with you if I was younger?" she asked.

"You'd be surprised how much underage pussy we have to kick out of the club."

She flinched as if she'd been struck. He had to go and remind her exactly what the club was about. Biting her lip, she stared at him, wishing she knew what was going on inside that head of his.

"You don't make any sense to me."

"What? You think because I fucked your ass it makes us ... what? Fuck buddies, best friends, lovers?"

"Why are you acting like a dick?" She reached out to grab the blanket. Deanna would gladly take anything to cover her nakedness. She didn't like this other side to him. He was being mean and an ass on purpose. What had she done to deserve this?

"No, I want to look at the goods." He stepped forward, tearing the blanket from her grip.

She stood there nude, waiting for him to make his next move. "What? You thought you fucked a minor? Did you start panicking or did it turn you on?" Why was she egging him on?

Folding her arms across her breasts, she tried to find as much dignity as she could as he faced her.

"You don't get to talk to me like that. You're club property. You belong to the Soldiers of fucking Wrath. You do as you're told, when you're fucking told." He advanced toward her. She held her hands up as if to ward him off.

He took hold of her wrists, pressing her against the wall. She hit the wall with a bang. Releasing a gasp, Deanna stared up at him. For some strange reason she wasn't afraid anymore. No, she was turned on and she hated it.

Demon glared down at her. "There's nowhere for you to go."

"You killed my father. I don't owe you shit."

He burst out laughing, glaring down at her. "You're wrong, Deanna. He's your father and you're pissed at him. It makes you the number one suspect."

"Why are you doing this? What happened to you?" She wanted to ask him some other questions but she was afraid that he would laugh at her. This was not a side to Demon she ever wanted to see.

"Do you really think that just because I put my dick inside you that you're different?" He chuckled. "Baby, you've got to do a hell of a lot more than spread your legs and let me take your ass. There are a hell of a lot more women out there like you, willing to fuck."

She started to struggle against him. In all of her life she'd never been spoken to like that. No man had ever left her feeling so small. Against her own wishes, tears filled her eyes. She tried to force them down. He didn't deserve to see her cry.

Get yourself together, Deanna.

"Get the fuck away from me."

"So, the little wildcat has claws."

She growled at him, wishing he'd just leave her alone.

"I look forward to you using those claws on me." He released her, backing out of the room. "Until next time."

"There will never be a next time."

"We'll see."

He closed the door behind him and she heard the lock click. Glancing around the room, she ran her fingers through her hair several times. Did that really happen? Her tears spilled down her cheeks as she became aware of the ache throughout her body. It had happened and so had Demon's rejection. She hated him, despised him. Grabbing the blanket, she couldn't even bring herself to get back on the bed. Sinking to the floor, she wrapped her arms around her body, trying to hold onto her sanity.

Everything will be okay.

She didn't know how it was going to be okay. Deanna was alone in an MC with no one to know she was still alive.

I'm alone.

Curling around herself, she started to sob. Her mother was dead and gone, as was her father.

"I'm sorry, Mom," she said, hoping that her mother could hear her. "I tried. I tried to get him to clean up his act. You must hate me so much." She wiped a hand down her face, trying to clean away her tears. What had she done to deserve this?

Demon blew hot and cold. Could she last in this club, watching him with other women?

She was just one of many different pussies he had on offer. The very thought of seeing him with someone else left her sick. She shouldn't want him, especially after what he had just done, how he had just acted toward her.

Pulling the blanket over her head, she tried to hide from the world and everything she'd been through. Her mother wouldn't answer, nor would her father.

Alone, so alone. She didn't even have Demon anymore and that thought alone was enough to send her life into a spin.

Joker stared up at the house he'd not been back to in over five years. The last time he'd been here was at a party his folks had. Pulling the shades from his eyes, he looked up at the large house set back from the road. He climbed off his bike, pocketing his sunglasses.

Pulling out his cell, he dialed Demon's number.

"Yeah?"

"I'm here."

"Keep in touch, brother."

Hanging up, Joker didn't know if he wanted to step closer to that house or run. There were so many memories coming to the fore. Memories he'd locked up years ago. Amy... this house reminded him so much of her. She was the one woman who'd torn at his defenses, making him vulnerable for the first time in his life.

The door opened and there stood his father. David Michaels was over six feet, a giant of a man covered in a shit load of muscle. Standing still, Joker looked at his father, who had just lost his wife.

Joker closed the distance, wrapping his arms around him. "Hey, Dad."

"Hey, son."

"I came as soon as I could."

"I called you last night. I should have called you sooner but it has been a little crazy in here." David led the way inside the house.

The moment the door closed, Joker felt the loss of Brenda's presence. He couldn't even count the number of times he'd walked inside to the scent of baking. The moment the door closed, he heard her.

Amy. She was sobbing her heart out.

"I've not been able to get her to eat or shower. It's like she's lost. All she does is cry and sleep. Son, I'm out of my depth. When she had the nightmares in the past, you were there to handle them. I don't know what to do."

For his father to admit that, it took a lot of guts. David was not a man to admit defeat. Staring into his father's blue eyes, Joker nodded. "I've not spoken to her in years."

"She always listened to you. Please, you've got to try."

David didn't know the truth of what happened five years ago to send him running. No, that was between him and Amy. No one knew the truth, not even Demon.

"Where is she?"

"In her room."

Removing his leather cut, he walked toward the steps.

"Reese?"

He turned back to look at his father.

"It's good to have you back."

Nodding, Joker made his way upstairs. Amy's room was across from his old one. He stopped when he saw the door was open. Leaning against the doorframe, he stared at the woman who'd done nothing but plague his thoughts. She was a tormented soul at the best of times. Some bad shit had happened to her when she was younger that had changed her life completely.

That same tortured soul was collapsed on the bed, stricken by grief.

Clearing his throat, he entered the room, and quietly closed the door.

The sobbing stopped and when she turned around, green eyes were focused on him.

"Reese," she said. Her voice was croaky from the hours she spent crying.

"Hello, Amy."

Her head lay on the pillow. She held onto a teddy bear as she looked at him.

"Mom's dead."

"I know, baby." He took a step closer to her. She didn't fight him like last time. He moved behind her, lying down next to her.

She didn't fight him but she did tense by his side. "I'm not going to hurt you, Amy. I'd never hurt you."

Wrapping his arms around her, Joker closed his eyes as she turned toward him, burying her head against his chest.

"She's gone, Joker. She's gone and she's never coming back."

He held her tighter, afraid of letting her go. He didn't want to let her go but remain on the bed, holding her. "I'm here. I'm not going anywhere."

Running his hand down her back, he soothed her, promising her that he'd stay. He didn't know how long he'd be with her. Joker would stay for the funeral—afterward, he didn't know. Slowly, the tears began to dry up and Amy fell asleep. Joker didn't know how much time had passed until his father poked his head in.

"Do you want anything to eat?" David asked.

"Not yet. I don't want to disturb her."

She snuggled a little closer to him.

Joker didn't like how frail she felt in his arms. He remembered her being full, rounded in all the right places. What had happened to his little hummingbird?

Chapter Thirteen

Amy wasn't asleep, but instead lay there, letting Reese hold her close to his body, protected from the world around them. It had been years since she had seen him, so long that right now felt like a dream almost. Her mother was gone, killed by a drunk driver, and she was alone in this world. She might have David, a second father to her after hers had ditched her and her mom when Amy was little, but she knew that David had to deal with his grief himself.

She wasn't a child, and was old enough to have to deal with this sooner or later on her own. But staying in her old room, holding the bear her mother had given her when she was younger, seemed like a pretty good idea to try and deal with all of this.

"I'm so sorry, Amy," Reese said softly, right beside her ear, and continued to smooth his hand up and down her back. "I'm so sorry about everything."

She knew he wasn't just speaking about her losing her mom, but of the shit that had happened five years ago. At twenty-one she had her own home, a life, a job, and shouldn't be trying to find comfort in a man that she had run from. All those years ago she had made a fool out of herself after what they had done, and since then she had stayed away. But all of that seemed so silly and ridiculous now. Reese pulled her closer, and she heard him inhale.

"I know you're up, baby." He smoothed his hand over her hair again, speaking softly.

She pulled back slightly, looking into his face. Reese, or Joker as the motorcycle club he was affiliated with called him, was such a strong man. Even after she had probably made him feel like shit for freaking out all those years ago, he was here comforting her. "How can you even want to see me after..." She couldn't even finish her sentence, too humiliated by everything.

"Amy, I won't lie and say that I still don't think about that night five years ago, because I do. It consumes me sometimes."

She swallowed and closed her eyes. When she opened them again it was to see Reese staring at her with his deep blue gaze. His dark blond hair was a little on the longer side, and he had a days' worth of scruff on his face. He was so big, taking after David in his height and muscle mass, but it was the way he looked at her that had her speechless. It was a vulnerable, sorrow-filled look. Here was this hardcore biker comforting her, holding her like she was the most precious thing in the world. He probably did things that would make her cringe, run screaming because it frightened her, but right then she didn't care.

She couldn't help it. She started crying harder.

"It's okay, Amy," he said softly again.

She shook her head. "No." She squeezed her eyes shut, feeling the tears falling harder. "I lost my mom. Nothing will ever be okay again."

Demon stared at the mirror behind the bar in the clubhouse, feeling drunk as fuck, pissed at himself for the way he felt for Deanna, and at the way he had handled that encounter with her. He had locked her in the room, knowing that it wasn't the right move after the way he'd treated her, but feeling like he was on a razor's edge right now. He had grown agitated at the emotions he had for her, at the fact she made him even crazier, and had him feeling this obsession for her that boarded on insanity. He hadn't gone back in there all night, just laid in the meeting room on the couch. Yeah, he needed to go back there and get her out. But he was still upset with himself that he wanted her like a fiend tweaking for their next hit, like a serial killer needing that rush of blood being spilled.

The sun was starting to rise, and although he had been in the meeting room, he hadn't really fallen asleep. He was too wound up, too on edge for this woman that had come into his life, twisted it around, and made him realize that he wanted only her.

She was his, and he knew that no amount of backlash toward her, trying to push her away because he was angry with himself, would change that fact. Demon lived a hard life, fucked with purpose, and immersed himself in his biker life. Deanna had become ingrained in their world, in *his* world, and it was clear that he wouldn't be able to shake her from the moment he saw that first picture of her.

He pushed away from the bar, turned and faced the stairs that would lead to his room, and grunted out a curse. He was going to just lay it out for Deanna, tell her exactly how he felt, and knew that it would come out harsh and crude. He wasn't a romantic man, wasn't used to telling anyone how the fuck he felt. He did whatever the hell he wanted, when he wanted, and fuck anyone who stood in his way. He didn't become president of this club, run this dammed town, by being some pansy ass motherfucker. He'd die with his cut on, with his men behind his back, and with his patch inked on his skin. That was the way his world worked, how it would always work, and he was content living that way.

Stalking toward his room, he pushed away the club pussy that advanced on him, drunk still from the previous night, and smelling like his brothers. He wasn't a sloppy second kind of male, and sure as fuck wasn't interested in their dirty cunts now that he had his woman. Yes, Deanna was *his* woman, and damn anyone who got in his way of claiming her.

Deanna paced. She was infuriated that she was still locked in this damn room. It was barely morning, but she hadn't been able to go back to sleep after Demon had locked her in here and had shown her the dick side of him. She had showered, gotten dressed in a pair of his sweats and an oversized t-shirt. Fuck him, his pompous, alpha and domineering ass. She was not going to put up with his shit, not going to be talked down by some biker that thought he could fuck her and just walk away. She wanted Demon, yes, and damn her for being so fucking stupid on that account. But she couldn't help it, couldn't help her heart and what it wanted, even if the man she was growing to care for was Demon.

She heard the lock being disengaged and stopped pacing to face the door, ready to give Demon an earful. Maybe the skanks that hung out at the club were okay with being talked to like this but she wasn't some club pussy. She was a strong, independent woman, and she could handle herself.

Keep telling yourself that, Deanna, especially when it comes to a man like Demon.

He pushed the door open and stood there, intimidating, strong, powerful, and with this expression on his face that had her actually taking a step back. But she held onto her strength, her reserve, and straightened her shoulders.

"Demon, you can't keep me here like a prisoner every time you have a fucking hissy fit—"

Demon stormed forward and she snapped her mouth shut, felt her eyes widen, and took a step back, but the wall stopped her retreat. He slammed his hands on the wall beside her head, lowered his face to hers, and curled his lip. "You infuriate me, make me insane with lust, and have my fucking dick harder than it has ever been." He growled, cursed, and stared at her right in the eyes. He was so tall, so muscular, and his dark hair was slightly brushing his forehead. He was a menace, a reckoning of death, pain, and lust, and she felt all of that directed right at her. "I want you, Deanna, and I won't walk around pretending like what I want with you isn't something new." He sounded pissed at himself, and the angry slash of his dark eyebrows told her he was pissed at himself right now.

She swallowed, not knowing if she should push him back or pull him closer. "You can't talk to me like that, treat me like that, Demon," she said, softer this time. Something flickered in the depths of his eyes, and she wanted to believe that he realized how he had acted was wrong on every level, psycho even, but then his hard composure came back.

"The way I want you, want to fuck you, claim you, and make sure that no other man touches you ever again is driving me out of my fucking mind, Deanna." He said her name on a growl. "I've never had this possessive need inside of me to own every part of a woman. I fuck pussy when I want, never twice even, but with you—" He lowered his gaze to her mouth, and lower still until he was staring at her breasts. She wasn't wearing a bra, and her nipples hardened. "With you I want to beat a motherfucker into the ground that looks at you, tear them apart if they even think about you, and fucking kill them if they touch you."

A soft gasp of shock and also arousal slammed into her. What in the hell was wrong with her that she was getting wet hearing him proclaim his psychotic obsession with her? Was she so needy for affection, for a man to notice her, that she was blind to the fact that Demon was an animal, a criminal, and a murderer?

He killed for you, *Deanna.*

Yes, he had, and he had done it without a flicker of emotion on his face, without showing any kind of emotion or remorse over the fact. He had killed her father because of what his junkie ass had done to her; how he had betrayed his own flesh and blood.

Demon placed his hand in the center of her chest, smoothed it down her belly and slipped it between her thighs. He added pressure, just enough that she rose on her toes, opened her mouth, and felt her clit swell.

"This is mine." He leaned in closer. "Your pussy, your tits, all of it is mine." He ran his tongue along her bottom lip, and she knew she should catch him off guard, kick him in the nuts for the way he had treated her, but she knew that right now, what he had admitted to her was something he had never done. Demon was a man of few words and harsh actions. But he had told her he wanted her like no other, and a part of her, every part in fact, knew that hearing him say that was a big deal.

"Demon—"

He shook his head. "No, Deanna. You will admit that you're mine, that everything about you is mine. I own you, and not because your piece of shit old man handed you over to the club." He sucked on her bottom lip, dragged his tongue along the swell, and growled like some kind of animal. "I own you because you want to be owned, but only by me. And I want you to admit that, Deanna."

The he kissed her, claimed her in a way that no other man had ever done before, and she felt her anger mixed with her pleasure. She bit his bottom lip, heard him hiss out, and felt this surge of power go through him. Now she just needed to decide if she really did want to be owned, and by a man like Demon.

Chapter Fourteen

Deanna sizzled in his arms. He couldn't believe she was so responsive, especially after he'd treated her like shit. She didn't deserve his bad attitude. He'd make sure he'd never, ever, treat her like he did. The last thing Demon wanted was for her to leave his ass.

Banding his arm around her waist, he kept her close, inhaling her feminine scent as she ravaged his mouth. She bit his bottom lip and he plunged his tongue into her mouth. Their moans echoed together.

Reaching down, he gripped her ass tightly. The fleshy mound filled his palm, making him want more. He wanted her cunt squeezing his cock, washing him with her cream.

"Fuck, baby," he said, muttering the words against her lips.

"Please, Demon."

"What do you need, baby?" He pulled away from her to stare into her beautiful green eyes.

"I want you to fuck me."

He groaned as she ran her hand down the front of his chest to land on his cock. Instantly hard, he knew exactly what to do with it. Drawing his hand around the front of her body, he rubbed her pussy through her sweat pants. The clothes she wore were too big and swamped her smaller body. Sliding his fingers over her clit, he felt the wetness of her pussy through the fabric.

"You're so fucking wet."

"Please." She rubbed him a little harder as he teased her.

"You want my cock inside you?"

"Yes."

"Are you going to run away from me again?"

"No."

He released her pussy to cup her cheek. "Why?"

"Why what?"

Her pupils were dilated clearly filled with arousal. She looked so fucking sexy and he didn't want to question her sudden submission to him. Deanna wasn't the kind of woman to take the shit that he'd dished out to her last night. What had happened? Why was she giving in? Was it a ploy?

You're completely fucked.

"Why are you giving in so easy?"

"You're scared and I get that." She licked her lips. Her gaze moved to his chest and her hand trembled where she touched his chest. Her other hand still held his cock firmly in her grip. "I've got nowhere else to go, but I want you and I've never wanted a man the way that I desire you. It scares me."

He ran his thumb over her full bottom lip. It was so plump and inviting. Sliding the digit into her mouth, he groaned as she sucked him inside.

Trust her.

"You want to stay here. Be my bitch?"

Her cheeks went flush at his words. "I want to be yours."

"I won't share you."

"Then don't. You're the only man I want."

"Then strip," he said, stepping back. Demon sat on the edge of the bed, looking at her. The sweats were the least attractive thing he'd ever seen and yet on her, they looked fucking hot.

She fingered the edge of her shirt, staring back at him. "You want me naked?"

"Yes. I want you naked and doing what I say."

He leaned one elbow on his knee as he rested his chin on his open palm. His cock was rock hard, begging to be inside her.

Deanna licked her lips and he saw her hand shake as she started to lift the shirt up her body.

She didn't wear any bra and he grew more aroused as she revealed her creamy flesh to his gaze. The hard tips of her nipples called to him to suck. His mouth watered for a taste of her lush skin.

No other woman called to him like this. He'd not liked to lick or kiss any woman. They were used goods, not good for anything other than to fuck. Demon wasn't used to doing anything loving or nice. All he ever knew was the sheer force of fucking. The women he'd been with knew how to take his cock and accept it. He didn't offer exclusive nor did he offer long term. If a woman wanted him then they had to handle the club, being passed from one man to another.

He'd never settle down with an old lady but when he looked at Deanna, stared into her mesmerizing green eyes, he felt something stir within him. There was a sort of peace that settled over him. He wouldn't ever grow bored with this fiery temptress. She'd keep him on his toes, making sure he didn't stray. But he knew he'd never want another female, never desire anyone but Deanna again.

They'd only fucked once and yet it was the best experience of his life.

She dropped the sweat pants to the floor, and he simply stared at the sheer perfection of her body.

"Open your legs," he said, stroking his length through his jeans.

Deanna spread her legs where she stood.

"Thrust your cunt out and spread your lips. I want to see your pussy." She did as he asked without question. The hard nub of her clit peeked out of the hood. She was soaking wet. He saw her cream glistening in the light of the bedroom. The scent of her arousal surrounded him. What little sense he had vanished. "Dip your finger inside and bring it to me."

He opened his mouth as she presented her cream-slicked digit for him to suck. Running his tongue along her finger, he groaned at the explosion of her cream. She tasted so fucking sweet and clean. He liked the fact she was his. Deanna was all his to explore, to pleasure, to fuck, and he intended to make sure she didn't want another man's touch. The only touch she'd ever need or want is his.

"Give me some more."

She dipped her finger back into her cunt, presenting it to him. He made her do this for five minutes. Each taste of her drove him to the edge of insanity.

"Come here," he said, when he couldn't stand to simply taste her. He wanted inside that tight heat, to explore her body. She stepped closer and he opened his thighs to welcome her. Skimming the tips of his fingers over her skin, he caressed up and down her thighs. "You're going to do exactly what I say, when I say it. You're not going to argue with me, do you understand?"

She licked her lips once again. "Yes."

"Good. You're mine, Deanna. You're mine to do with whatever the hell I want to do."

The very thought of doing everything Demon instructed should scare her, yet Deanna was excited. She wanted to give herself up to Demon's instruction. Her whole life she'd taken care of her mother or tried to be there for her father, only to have all of her hard work thrown in her face. Her father had tried to use her to pay off a debt and her mother had passed away. She'd spent the whole of her life worrying about what would happen next in her life. Paying bills, dealing with her mother's health, school, work, everything had always been a worry to her. When she was with Demon, she didn't worry. The moment he looked at her, everything floated away and it was like the only two people to exist was them.

She didn't know if she cared about him but there were feelings. Was it love? Deanna really didn't know what she felt for the man before her.

"Yes," she said.

It would be a welcome relief to live for the pleasure of the moment. Demon wouldn't want anything else from her but pleasure. Her pussy was soaking wet. The hard ridge of his cock pressed against the front of his pants and she wanted to taste him.

"Then get on your knees."

She sank to the floor before him. Staring up into his eyes, she waited for his next instruction.

"Get my dick out."

Reaching out, she tugged on his belt then on the zipper of his jeans. She fumbled around trying to grab his cock from the confines of the pants he wore. Deanna smiled up at him as she stroked the hard length of his cock in her palm. He was warm to the touch.

"Now, take me in your mouth."

She didn't need to be told twice. Leaning forward, she licked the tip, swallowing down the pre-cum glinting on the tip. He tasted so fucking good, masculine, and exactly like a biker. This was what danger meant, danger and excitement felt like. Demon excited her.

His fingers stroked over her hair, sliding through the length until he gripped her hair within his grasp. She groaned as the pain went straight to her pussy, flooding her with more cream. Pressing her thighs together, she tried to work her clit without even touching herself.

"I'll make you come when I'm good and ready. You focus on my dick. I want my dick slick with your mouth." His voice was husky.

Taking the tip of his cock into her mouth, she moaned as he hit the back of her throat. The grip he had on her hair controlled the depth of her thrusts. Demon took over, thrusting into her mouth. She sucked as much of him as she could until he withdrew from her mouth, only to slam back inside.

She gripped his thighs, holding onto him in an attempt to hold onto some sanity. Nothing helped. The control he had over her went far beyond his grip.

"Fuck, I need to be inside your pussy." He tugged her off his length by her hair. Within seconds his hands were on her arms, dragging her over his lap. His superior strength should have scared her but she was aroused. He had her straddled over his hips with his cock at attention between them.

She was naked while he remained fully clothed. The scent of leather filled her senses and she watched as he grabbed his cock, sliding through her wetness.

"Do you see how wet you are? It's going to be so fucking easy to slide inside you." He tapped her clit with his cock, making her cry out from the sudden burst of pleasure. It didn't last. He moved the tip of his cock to her entrance, where he teased her. She tried to slam down on his cock but he wasn't having any of it.

Demon controlled when he entered her. The one grip he had of her hip kept her in place. When only the bulbous head of his cock was inside her, Demon gripped both of her hips.

"Look at me, Deanna."

She stared into his silver grey eyes. They held her captive as easily as he held her body.

"What?" she asked. Her skin was on fire with a burning need that only he could put out.

"I want to look into your eyes when I fuck you." On the last word, he slammed her down onto his cock, forging his way inside. He was long, thick, and she felt him fill her to the hilt. Demon was so deep that it was almost painful. Sinking her nails into the flesh of his shoulder, she screamed out at the dual hit of pleasure and pain.

"Fuck, you're so damn tight." He bit her shoulder, growling the words against her flesh.

Closing her eyes, she tried not to move. The moment she did, she became aware of the depth of his penetration. Demon wasn't small, but so damn huge.

"Does it hurt?" he asked.

She nodded.

"You'll get used to me."

"I don't think I will."

"I'm not going to give you a chance to forget about me, baby. I'm going to fuck you day and night. You're not going to be able to walk straight without thinking about me. Whenever another man looks at you, you're going to be so full of my cum that you're not going to even think about straying."

"I'm not going to stray," she said, taking a deep breath.

"I know. I'm not going to give you a chance to leave me."

Why was he worried about her leaving? He ruled a club full of whores who'd gladly spread their legs for him. If anyone should be worried about straying, it should be her, even if he knew in his heart he'd never do that to her.

"Now, I'm going to fuck you, and you're going to enjoy it, because you're mine and know it."

Chapter Fifteen

"Get on the bed, baby, and lie on your back." Running a hand over his mouth, she watched as Demon tried to control himself. She could see it in his hard expression on him, in the way he was poised tightly, as if he wanted to pounce on her like a wild animal wanting to devour her.

She moved to the bed, lay back fully on it, and felt her cream slip from her pussy even more. She was so wet, so aroused, that staring at him fully dressed with his cock only visible through the fly of jeans was heady and arousing.

"Open for me."

It wasn't a question, and that alone had Deanna moaning even louder, ready for Demon. She never thought she would like dominance in the bedroom, never thought she could be submissive and allow a man to control every part of her. But with Demon she realized that he wanted her to give herself up to him totally. And she was more than ready to be that way with him. Having Demon control the situation made everything more heightened within her. She didn't hesitate to place her heels on the mattress and spread her thighs open for him.

The cool air drifted along her swollen, wet pussy, and she bit her lip as she waited for him to come to her, to order her to do whatever he wanted. She could see him staring at her body, and didn't need to hear words to know what he had to say.

"Fuck, Deanna," he said and grabbed his cock, stroking himself. "Compared to me you're so damn sweet and innocent, just waiting like a ripe fruit to be plucked and sampled." He took another step forward. The flavor of his flesh, of his mouth and pre-cum was still in her mouth and she wanted more. His erection was a hard rod between his thighs, and she knew he would fill her pussy completely. When he was at the edge of the bed and his body heat coated her like a blanket, she shivered, feeling so aroused she was lightheaded. Before she could say anything Demon was moving on the bed and between her legs. His mouth was on her chin, and he slowly moved his lips lower, dragged his tongue along her cleavage, and gripped her shoulders to hold her down for his erotic abuse.

He made the same path over and over again, over her breasts and back up her neck. It was pure, unadulterated torture. He ran his tongue over her chin, down her throat again, and nibbled the hard tips of her breasts. Throwing all sane thoughts aside, she let her head fall back and her eyes close as Demon memorized her body with his tongue. He didn't miss an inch of her, and Deanna felt as though she was being devoured. Her nipples were stiff buds, and when he ran his tongue over them her pussy walls contracted involuntarily. This was enough foreplay, because there was no way she would live through any more.

"Take off your clothes, Demon, and fuck me already. Claim me as your woman." She was stunned with herself for those words coming out of her mouth. She meant each one of them with every part of her body. In a move faster than she thought a large man like him could do, he was off the bed, tearing his clothes away until the hard, tattooed flesh of his huge body was on display. She braced herself on her elbows, breathing heavily as her desire moved so high she felt like she was about to explode from it. He was between her thighs again and the hot, hard length of him pressed against her slit.

"You want me, Deanna?" He thrust against her. "You want my cock? Want to be my woman?"

She nodded her response, not able to speak because she was too lightheaded, too crazed with lust. Reaching between their bodies, he aligned himself at her entrance. His cockhead was thick, bulbous, pressed snuggly to her opening, and she parted her lips. She thought he would ease their suffering and just shove right into her, but instead he pushed the head in slowly, continuing the same momentum until his length was fully inside of her. Her pussy stretched around his girth, and it made the whole situation hotter when he placed his hands by her head, lifted up slightly, and stared at where their bodies were connected.

"Your cunt is stretched so wide around me, baby." The sight of him closing his eyes, of his biceps shaking from the force it was taking him to go slowly, had her lifting up her hips and causing another inch to slip into her. He growled low and snapped his eyes open. "Christ, baby, don't fucking do that or I won't be able to control myself." He growled low. "You're playing with the devil, and it is taking a hell of a lot of control for me not to fuck you like some kind of wild beast."

Panting from the anticipation and trepidation of allowing herself to fall for this hardened biker, she said, "I want you to be an animal with me, Demon."

Right before her eyes he seemed to snap, seemed to just detach from everything around them. He pulled out of her, and when the head was lodged in her entrance he shoved back into her so fast and hard tears of pleasure/pain filled her. She bowed her back and shifted up the bed from his forcefulness. This was what she wanted, though, what she had asked for.

"Are you ready for me?"

"God, yes, Demon," she breathed out. Closing her eyes and baring her throat, she parted her lips, sucked in a breath, and held on as he really fucked her. Demon's hips slammed so hard against her that sparks of intense pleasure rocketed through her clit. She kept moving up the bed, and so he placed a hand on her shoulder to keep her stationary.

"So. Fucking. Good," he seemed to roar out. She forced her eyes open to watch the ecstasy morph her biker's face. His muscles straining and tensing, his hips thrusting back and forth, and the gruff, almost unnatural sounds coming from him were an auditory and visual orgasm for her. Her pleasure came on strong and hard, stealing her voice and her vision as it claimed her.

Demon stared in lust at his woman. Her breasts bounced from the force of his thrusting, and she was screaming out as she came.

"Oh God. It hurts so good." She moaned, but he wasn't nearly finished with her yet, not even close.

"Baby, you haven't seen anything yet. Tomorrow you won't be able to walk straight once I'm done claiming you." He slammed into her again and again, bottoming out in her pussy, then pulling almost out. Over and over he did this, feeling the sweat fall down his temple.

Demon didn't hold off any longer; he was barely leashing in his control as it was. Taking hold of her clit between his fingers, he rolled the nub around until it became so engorged he knew she'd come again. "Just once more, baby. Give it to me one more time because you're mine and I own you." Her cunt was pink and glistening and her clit stood out, begging him for more attention. She thrashed her head back and forth on the mattress, and just like that she came for him again. Yeah, she was also fucking receptive to him, so damn giving. She'd always be his, always submit to him because she liked his coarse, harsh attitude and darker side. He wanted to follow her into oblivion, but he held off for just a moment longer.

When she breathed out and marginally relaxed on the bed he slowed his thrusting, then pulled out. Before she could say anything he flipped her around, shoved a pillow under her hips, and spread her ass cheeks. "Oh yeah. Fuck yes, baby." Her asshole was smooth and pink, and although he wasn't the kind of man that liked rimming, he wanted to taste every part of her. Holding her ass apart, he started licking the tight, clean hole. She smelled good, so fucking good. Her ass was tight, and when he moved back, grabbed some lube to make her good and slick for his cock, and placed the tip at her hole. He had to grip her hips to control himself. He didn't want to hurt her, but he wanted to fuck her raw, too. He groaned out when he started pushing into her.

"It feels so tight, Demon. I feel so stretched," she gasped out. He eased off, not wanting to hurt her, but wanting her fuck her ass good and hard. He wanted to feel the ultra-tight muscles clench around him, and come so hard everything went black, until she told him he owned every part of her, and that nothing would ever be the same because she was all his.

Deanna shook as Demon continued to thrust into her ass. She loved it, even if it was a strange sensation. The sheet beneath her mouth grew moist from her increased breathing. He leaned over her, pressed her mouth to his nape, and licked her like he was an animal and he was memorizing her flavor. He tightened his hands on her hips. Demon palmed her ass, massaged the globes, and had her skin heating within seconds.

"I want you everywhere." How strange things had escalated as fast and powerful as they had. The hard slap to her ass had a pleasurable gasp leaving her.

"That's it, baby, take all of me." He moved his hands back to her ass, squeezed the globes hard, and she knew she'd have bruises. They would be marks of his domination, and that sent a thrill through her. He pulled out slowly until just the tip was lodged in her ass, then he pushed back inside just as agonizingly easy. He did this over and over. Deanna found herself thrusting back, wanting him to really take her like he meant it. A hard slap to her ass again had her movements stilling. A look over her shoulder showed a hard mask on his face and sweat dripping down his hard, toned chest. Their gazes locked and he increased his speed. Soon he was fucking her with abandon, giving it all to her so she was forced to reach up, grip the slates of the headboard, and hold on. Her breasts bounced from his hard thrusts, and the sound of their wet skin slapping together filled the room.

"Fuck, yeah." He slapped first her right cheek then her left. "Do it again, baby. Squeeze my fucking dick."

A wave of pleasure slammed into her, taking her breath and having her moan out. Reaching around her body and finding her clit, he pinched the tiny bundle of nerves between his fingers like he had before. Lights flashed behind her closed lids, and just like that she came again. Her body shook from the pleasure, and she took comfort in the all-consuming ecstasy that stole her very sanity. He placed his big hand on the center of her back and continued to push into her and pull back out. He slid his hand up her sweaty back and stopped at the nape of her neck. For several seconds he held her immobile, but then he moved his hand to the front, gripped her throat in a loose hold, and thrust into her several more times before stilling. He came long and hard, shuddering behind her as he emptied himself.

"That's it. I'm going to fucking fill you with my cum until it comes out of your ass and soaks the bed." His words were sharp like broken glass, and another shiver wracked her already exhausted body. He pulled out of her and she immediately collapsed on the bed. He pulled out of her, and she immediately felt his semen slip from her bottom. He moved on the bed beside her, collapsed on his back and placed his arm over his eyes. His hard chest moved up and down, and the definition of his six pack and muscles became apparent.

He turned and looked to her, this hard, unyielding look covering his face right away. Before she knew what was doing he rolled over, placed his hand on her throat in a loose grip, and said right by her mouth, "You're mine, will always be mine, and I'll kill anyone that tries to say differently."

She could have fought, could have said no, but instead she leaned up, causing his hold on her throat to tighten, and said, "I'm yours."

Chapter Sixteen

Days passed and Deanna fitted into Demon's lifestyle with ease. She hadn't been back to her job, and she had told him that she had probably lost it. But the relief in her face after she said those words told him enough that he figured she had hated the damn thing. It didn't matter because he didn't plan on allowing her to go back to working anyway.

There were no more tantrums or angry outbursts out of her. Demon loved spending time with her, which surprised him. Some of the club whores were not happy, as he'd not even given them the time of day since Deanna had entered his life. He fucked her every chance he got and Deanna would spread her thighs for him whenever he demanded. He fucking loved it. She was so fucking hot and the only woman he got a hard on for was Deanna.

Joker returned after the funeral of his woman's mother. He looked like shit and he was constantly on the phone, but no one talked to him.

"Can you go back for me?" Deanna asked. She was laid out naked on Demon's bed and resting on his chest. He'd just fucked her and seconds before had her screaming out in orgasm. Running the tips of his fingers down her back, he stared into her green eyes.

"What?"

He'd not been paying much attention, basking in the afterglow of fucking her pussy. She'd settled into his way of life a hell of a lot better than he ever imagined.

"I was wondering if you'd go back to my apartment. The rent is due at the end of the week and the landlord can be a real jackass. He'll trash my shit before I get them back."

"What?" He frowned, confused.

"My clothes. The furniture could stay behind. I don't want to spend the rest of my life borrowing other women's clothes. They're not my style."

"You want clothes?"

"I don't want you to buy me any. I want you to take me back to my apartment. I'll grab my clothes and settle things up with my landlord."

He didn't like the thought of her going back to her old life. If she got a taste of freedom would she even want to come back to him? He couldn't lose her. In the short time they'd known each other she'd come to mean so much to him.

Caressing her arm, he thought about it.

"I could buy you new clothes."

"Or you could let me get the clothes that I paid good money for. Come on, Demon, they're decent clothes." She slid her fingers through his chest hair. "I can go on my own. I'll be back before nightfall."

"You've not got a chance, baby. You're not leaving the clubhouse." He tilted her head up as he leaned down to claim a kiss. She melted against him instantly and Demon was lost. His cock thickened, ready for action. Rolling her over, he slid her thighs open, finding the wet heat of her pussy. He didn't bother to get a condom. Demon loved the feel of her tight cunt surrounding his dick. "Fuck, baby, you're always so tight." He'd fucked her every chance he got and yet she was still so tight. Demon couldn't catch a break.

She gripped his shoulders, lifting up to meet each of his thrusts. "Please, Demon."

Was she begging for his cock or for him to go to her apartment?

Claiming her lips, he silenced her begging as he drove his cock inside her. Slamming in, he went to the hilt, hitting deep into her cervix. He wanted his cum swimming inside her.

Get her pregnant.

Once he had her pregnant with his kid, she wouldn't have a chance of getting away from him. He'd possess every part of her. There wouldn't be a chance of her ever leaving.

Thrusting his tongue into her mouth, he groaned as her pussy fluttered around his shaft as he drove in and out. Her cum washed over his length, making it easier for him to slide inside.

"I can feel you getting off, baby. Give it all to me." Holding her hands above her head with one of his, he lifted far enough away from her to work over her clit. She was slick because he'd cum in her twice already that day.

"Demon." She screamed his name and it echoed off the walls, teasing him with her own need. He slammed into her twice more, rubbing her clit. She splintered apart in his arms. Her tight cunt was squeezing the life out of his cock. Demon closed his eyes, enjoying the feel of her warmth wrapped around him. He basked in her contracting pussy, the heat, along with the heady sensation of her nails sinking into the flesh of his back. Everything felt so totally right. He didn't want any other woman warming his bed.

Opening his eyes, he glanced down at Deanna, pulling out of her body at the same time. Staring deep into her eyes, he slammed into her hard again, making her scream. Her head tilted back and he relished the sounds coming from her mouth. He wanted her completely drunk from the pleasure of his cock.

"That's it, baby. Take my dick. Your pussy is so fucking tight. It's not going to know any other cock but mine. I'm going to fill it with my spunk, own every inch of you." Tightening his hold on her hands, he rode her hard, pounding deep inside until all she could do was beg him to not stop. The headboard slammed against the wall. Anyone passing by the room would know exactly what he was doing to her. He brought her to orgasm a second time before he allowed himself to come. Plunging inside her a final time, he filled her with his cum, grunting out his release. He held her close to him as he saw stars from his orgasm.

When it was over, he collapsed on her, panting from the sensation.

"Fuck, Demon. I could get used to this," she said, stroking his back.

He was already used to it. There was a lot more going on between them than simply screwing. He didn't know what it was but he had an idea. Demon believed he was in love with her. The very thought of loving Deanna scared him. Could she even love him? He'd killed her father.

She would be dead if you didn't.

Gritting his teeth, he pulled away, dropping a kiss to her lips so she wouldn't ask any questions about his withdrawal. "I'll get some boys together and we'll go and get your shit."

"Thank you."

Demon sat on the edge of the bed, tensing as she wrapped her arms around his back.

"Don't mention it. Stay here and don't piss anyone off." He got to his feet, escaping to his bathroom. Staring at his reflection, Demon wondered what the fuck was going on inside him. This wasn't like him at all.

No woman got under his skin, apart from Deanna.

"Demon, are you okay?"

He heard the concern in her voice.

"I'm fine."

Get your shit together before you lose everything.

Splashing cold water onto his face, Demon wiped the remains of the water off with a towel, leaving the bathroom. He found Deanna sitting on the edge of the bed, facing the bathroom. She wore his discarded shirt. He liked how the sight of her in his clothes had him feeling.

"You look good," he said.

"Are we okay?"

"Yeah. Of course. You were right. What's the point of me getting you anything new when I can pick up your old shit?" He quickly dragged on his jeans followed by a fresh shirt. Demon sat beside her to tie up his boots. When it was done, he stood, grabbing his leather cut. "The sooner I'm done the quicker I can get back."

"Okay."

Before she said anything else, he left her alone, heading downstairs. Joker was entering the clubhouse as Demon made his way down the stairs. Steel and Shakes were already there, drinking coffee.

"What's up, Demon?" Joker asked. He looked awful, as if he'd not slept in days.

"I'm heading over to Deanna's old apartment to pick up some shit. You want to come with?"

"Sure." Joker opened the door, ready to leave.

"Road trip? Can I come?" Shakes got to his feet, looking way too excited.

"What the fuck has gotten into you?" Demon asked.

"Nothing. We've not rode in a few days. I'm missing it."

Rolling his eyes, Demon looked toward Steel. "You want to come too?"

"Now that you ask so nicely." Steel jumped to his feet following them outside.

Demon didn't say anything as he straddled his bike. He didn't bother with his helmet. The need to feel the open road was too strong for him to be trapped under the confines of a helmet.

Driving out of the clubhouse, he saw Deanna was standing at the door. She was dressed in only his shirt and it looked like she'd followed him down. The sight of her twisted his gut.

Pushing the thoughts aside, he focused on the road and winding around the bends without causing himself a serious injury. He loved the thrill of the ride more than anything.

They stopped at a diner a few miles from Deanna's apartment. He needed to take a leak and eat something. Entering the bathroom, he saw Joker follow him inside.

"What's going on?" Joker asked.

Pulling his dick out, Demon blew out a breath. "I don't fucking know."

"It's with Deanna, isn't it? She means something?"

"Yeah, she means something. What, I don't actually know but it means something." He stared at the wall in front of him.

"None of the club would think less of you if you decided to lay claim to her."

Demon wasn't worried about the club or what they'd think if he decided to take Deanna as his woman.

"She's not for the lifestyle."

"Are you sure about that?" Joker asked. "She seems to have taken to it to me."

"You think?"

"She hasn't run off scared yet. I'd take that as a sign that there's a lot more grit to her."

He'd not thought of it like that.

Finishing his business, he washed his hands and headed out. Steel and Shakes had ordered them each a burger with fries. They ate quickly, all of them wanting to get Deanna's crap and be gone.

Within no time at all they were back on their bikes and heading toward Deanna's apartment.

Demon paused as he took in the rundown area.

"Fuck me, Demon. She was living in a fucking shithole," Steele said.

Her father had been living a better life than Deanna. Demon didn't like it nor did he like the abandoned look to the area.

"Come on. Let's get her stuff and go."

He climbed off his bike and started to walk toward the building. Opening the door, he went up to the first floor. Demon froze when he saw her door was open. She hadn't said anything about a roommate. Warning his three men, he pulled the gun out of the back of his jeans that he always kept there. Pulling the safety off, he slowed his pace until he got to the door.

Kicking the door with force, he charged into the room with Joker, Steel, and Shakes at his back.

Guns went off and Demon yelled for his men to get down.

Chaos ensued until someone called, "Enough."

The firing stopped.

"Fuck, Demon, I'm hit." Glancing toward Joker, Demon saw a bullet had gone into his shoulder.

"Anyone else hit?" Demon asked.

"No," Steel and Shakes called out at the same time.

"The president of the Soldiers of Wrath is in my company. This is a real treat."

Raising his gun to stare at the man who sat at Deanna's dinner table, Demon focused on him. He wore an expensive looking business suit, a smile filled with evil deeds, and several men stood at his back with guns trained on them. This was not your average businessman.

"Who the fuck are you?"

"I'm, well, I'm an investor of sorts. A businessman always looking for an investment." He held his hands out as if it was a natural conversation to be having with guns trained on each other.

Joker got to his feet with his gun still trained on the man in front.

"I'm not interested in any fucking investment," Demon said. He never trusted men in suits. They were fucking dangerous.

"No?"

"No."

"Well, you see, I've got a problem as I paid Deanna's father quite handsomely with the understanding that she'd come and work for me." The man before him crossed his legs, resting his hands on his knees.

Demon didn't like this. "You're a fucking pimp?"

"I like to think more of a contractor who helps women to stay safe."

"A pimp."

"Well, you see, I've got a problem as I gave her father a lot of money." The man tapped his fingers on the table. Someone placed a video player on the table with the screen facing him. On the screen was the inside of Deanna's father's house. More importantly, his murder played out. Demon tightened his hold on the gun as he watched Deanna struggle for breath. "You see, I like to take proper care of everything that belongs to me."

"Deanna isn't for sale."

"No, well, you see I've got a problem. I'm a very good businessman and I've got a reputation to protect. This man, this piece of shit offering me second hand goods after he'd given Deanna to you, is a problem for me. I don't like the way it makes me look." The man slammed the screen down with enough force that Demon was sure he heard a smash.

"What's your name?"

"Zeke."

Demon froze. Zeke was a well-known criminal lord of everything. He controlled everyone and everything. Soldiers of Wrath hadn't done business with him ever but they'd heard of him. From the tensing of his men, he saw Joker, Steel, and Shakes all realize who he was.

"I see you know who I am."

"What do you want?" Demon asked.

"Well, I've got a business proposition for you, Demon." Zeke stared right back. There was no fear in his eyes. Demon had to respect that. There were not many men who'd continue a conversation with a gun trained on them.

"What?"

"I need competent people to use as bodyguards at my exclusive club. It's a VIP club. I will leave Deanna alone if you show your alliance with me."

"Why the fuck should I do that?" Demon asked.

"Well, I could take your club and fucking crush it, take your woman, use her until there's nothing left, passing her from one man to another until she's nothing but a cum bucket."

Demon saw the true colors of Zeke. He was a man known for being brutal.

"Also, as an act of faith on my part I can give you something he wants," Zeke said, pointing at Joker.

"There's nothing I fucking want."

"Really?"

"Yeah, really."

"What if I can give you access to Amy's father?" Zeke asked. Joker tightened his grip on the gun. "Ah, I see I've struck a cord. It's bad business, you know, raping and abusing your underage daughter."

"Shut the fuck up," Joker said, losing his shit right in front of him.

Reaching out, Demon blocked Joker from doing anything stupid. "We need to have a talk."

"Take your time but remember there really isn't an option here, gentlemen. I can fuck you all up or I can make life easy for you."

Grabbing Joker, Demon headed out of the room with Steel and Shakes at his back. "What the fuck was that about?"

Joker paced, completely oblivious to his bleeding arm.

"Amy, she's my step-sister."

"The woman you've just gone to see for your dad?"

"Yeah. Bad shit happened to her. I don't know the complete details, I never asked. I only know that her father was put away for physically abusing her. I don't know his name or anything else. Brenda and Amy kept that information to themselves."

"You want to know where he is?" Demon asked.

"I want to murder the bastard for putting his hands on Amy, yes."

There wasn't anything he could do. If he denied Zeke's request, he put the club at risk. What the fuck was he supposed to do?

Chapter Seventeen

Deanna was dressed and sitting outside of the clubhouse. Demon and a few of his men had left just ten minutes ago, and although she had always wanted this freedom from her father, from the shitty apartment she lived in, and the equally crappy job she worked at, she couldn't deny that the clubhouse made her feel safe. Yes, it was a compound of sorts, with fencing around the perimeter to keep out trespassers, she should have felt like she was in a prison, but she didn't. In fact she felt safer and protected here, more than she had ever felt at any time in her life.

The sound of the remaining club members could be heard from the open doorway. She glanced over her shoulder and saw one of the guys standing in the doorway, smoking a cigarette and staring at her. After a few more seconds he inhaled, flicked the smoke away, and exhaled. He tipped his chin toward her, then headed back inside. The bench she sat on was old, scarred, and was situated under a tree that was probably as old as this town. There had been a prospect guarding the front gate, although she wasn't sure why someone needed to watch what was going on because it was locked. But he had gone into the clubhouse about ten minutes before, and she could imagine that he was getting drunk and sleeping with the sweet butts.

She closed her eyes and breathed in the sweet scent of the fresh air and flowers. Although the clubhouse was mainly atop a thick slab of asphalt, there was a patch of grass out front, with this one tree and a bench. The cigarette butts that were in this metal tin beside the bench ruined the peaceful effect she was going for. She opened her eyes, and instantly the flash of something shiny had her lifting her arm to shield the light.

A dark car parked right in front of the gate, and the tinted windows hid whoever was inside. As the car idled there, no one moving out of it, and the car not driving off, she stood. Should Deanna go inside? Maybe they were lost? Although the latter didn't sit well with her, and she took a small step back. The gate was only a few feet from her, and when she looked over her shoulder she saw that no one stood at the doorway.

She heard the car window roll down, and the sight of a barrel of a gun flashed right before she could move or scream. Whatever they had shot her with went right into her neck. Lifting her hand, she pulled out a small dart. The world spun instantly, and she thought about Demon, and how she wasn't ready to leave his side yet. The last thing she saw was someone climbing out of the backseat of the luxury car, wearing all black, and walking toward the gate.

Demon stood in the hallway of Deanna's building, pissed and ready to fucking kill someone. One of Zeke's men came out of the apartment, his black trench coat and sunglass making the motherfucker look like the grim reaper.

"Zeke wants to speak with you," the asshole said in a bland, "don't even fucking think about saying no" voice.

Demon stared at the prick, about to tell him to screw off, but in the end he knew that when it came to Zeke, the Soldiers of Wrath weren't as damn twisted. Zeke had power and money, and a whole lot of manpower behind him in several cities. He owned businesses across the state, and Demon had heard several stories about the man and his tactics for getting what he wanted. They were sick and deranged, fucked up to the nth degree. When it came to Demon and his club going after what they wanted, yeah, they were brutal in acquiring it, but they didn't mess around. They beat the shit out of people that screwed with them. Zeke, on the other hand, was the type of man that pulled fingernails off with a pair of pliers and blowtorched skin while still wearing his expensive-as-shit designer suit.

Demon went back into the apartment, and his boys followed close behind. If shit got bad up in here, the MC might not be able to come out victorious, but they sure as hell would make these bastards hurt.

Zeke was still sitting at the table, and two of his guys were still behind him, looking like they should be in some fucking Matrix movie with their dark clothes and black sunglasses.

"If that was your idea of giving me some time to think about it that was shitty." Maybe Demon needed to watch his step, but right now he felt rage burn inside of him, and didn't much care.

Zeke smirked, tapped his finger on the table again, and one of his guys set the laptop down once more.

"What is this now? I already saw the murder tap—"

Zeke hit a button on the laptop and right in front of him, flashing on the screen like some kind of sick fucking snuff film, was Deanna. His Deanna. She was sitting on a chair with a blindfold and gag in her mouth. A light shone above her, bright and fluorescent. Demon's blood boiled and he took a step forward. But Joker grabbed his arm, at least being the only levelheaded one here at the moment.

"You do this and they will kill you before you can get your revenge," Joker said in a low voice. "Right now let's do what they say and get your woman safely back at the club."

Demon nodded once, shrugged off Joker's hold, and stared at the motherfucking Zeke that was grinning at him.

"She's unharmed, but I wanted you to have a bit of a sway concerning your decision to work for me."

Demon clenched his hands at his sides, tightened his jaw, and tied to reign in his control. What he wanted to do was fuck this asshole up, but he wouldn't be able to find Deanna very easily, and Zeke could have a gun pointed to her head and have the trigger pulled in a second. "You're messing with the fucking Soldiers of Wrath, Zeke."

Zeke had the balls to laugh, but he sobered quickly, and tapped the table again. One of his men lifted a cell and made a call. Like some kind of damn horror movie, Demon watched the computer screen as a man stepped beside Deanna and placed a gun right by her head. Because she was blindfolded she couldn't see him, but she was struggling.

"I can kill her without even pulling the trigger, Demon," Zeke said seriously, and with malice.

He never let anyone walk over him or his club, but this was his fucking woman in the line of danger, his club on the line, and if it meant that the end result would be Demon and his men taking out Zeke, then he'd roll over this once. "You have the muscle of the club, but only when my woman is safely back with me."

Zeke grinned widely. "I knew you'd come to see reason." He closed the laptop, said something softly to the guy with the phone, and stared at Demon again. "I hate going to drastic measures, but I wanted to get your attention."

Demon clenched his jaw hard enough he felt like his teeth might crack.

"Your woman will be delivered safely back to your club, and I'll be in touch with you later to go over the arrangement." Zeke stood, smoothed his hands over his dark suit, and said, "And as long as the club holds up their end of the deal, I will deliver the girl's father to Joker."

Demon sensed Joker tensing beside him, and glanced at the other biker. Joker looked pissed, about ready to crack skulls, but right now he had to focus on Deanna. "I want her delivered to my club now."

"Already in the process." Zeke nodded once, and he and his men headed out of the apartment.

For several seconds Demon couldn't move. His rage consumed him. "I want to know who fucked up and wasn't watching the gates." He stared at his men. "They are finished for putting Deanna in danger."

Shakes opened his mouth to say something, but Demon held his hand up to cut him off. He stormed out of the apartment, needing to get back to his club, to his woman.

Deanna had gone from being at the clubhouse, to in a car and knocked out, to in some room sitting on a chair like a hostage. But now she felt the bumpiness of a car going over uneven ground. The vehicle stopped suddenly, and with her hands still bound and her eyes shielded with a blindfold, she had no idea where in the fuck she was going. The gag in her mouth made cursing these assholes out impossible, but everything in her stilled when the door beside her opened and she was hauled out. She moaned and struggled, but before she knew what in the hell was happening she was being hauled somewhere else. The guy that had been holding her arm let go of her.

"A gun is trained on you. Don't fucking move."

Her entire body started shaking. The sound of the door slamming, and of the car driving off had her on the edge of this cliff, waiting to see what in the hell would happen. Was someone still pointing a gun at her? Was there even one trained on her? She started crying out of fear and anger, but the sound of motorcycles coming closer had her tears drying and this hope springing up in her. Was Demon coming for her? The deep rumbling of the bikes were right on her now, and the heavy footfall of steps coming toward her had Deanna moving backward. What if it wasn't Demon?

"God, baby."

His voice pierced through her emotions, and she fell to her knees. The blindfold and gag were removed, and then Demon was taking the bond on her wrists off. She blinked, trying to calm her nerves, but started crying harder than before.

"I'm so sorry, Deanna. I didn't know the bastard would have the balls to come to my club and take what was mine." He cupped her cheek. Demon had a mixture of rage and relief written across his face.

She wanted to hit him, curse at him and his club for putting her in this situation, but instead she threw herself in his arms. Relief swamped her, and she knew this man had ruined her for all others. She was gone for Demon, and she knew that this was her life now, as scary and fucked up as that all was.

Chapter Eighteen

Demon had faced the barrel of a gun, death, and hadn't been as afraid as he was in those moments when he saw the gun held to Deanna's head. He was pissed off, furious for what that fucker did to his woman. Zeke would pay, but not yet. It would take time but no matter what happened Demon would make sure Zeke paid for taking what was his.

"I've got you."

"I was so scared." She started to sob and he picked her up, forcing her to wrap her legs around his waist.

"I've got you, baby, and I swear I'm not letting you go."

"I love you, Demon. I love you so much. I didn't want to die without you knowing the truth."

Her admission broke something inside him. "I love you too, Deanna. Fuck, baby, you've got to make sure you're safe. I can't handle anything happening to you. I don't even want to think about that shit." He gripped her ass, pulling back enough so she could see his face.

"Really? You love me?"

"Yes. Heart and soul, babe." He meant every word. If he'd ever been in doubt there was no room for that after what he'd just gone through. "No more women. I promise you. You're the only one I want." He gripped her head, drawing her close to inhale her sweet scent. "Fuck, do I love you."

She wrapped her arms around his neck, squeezing the life out of him. "Don't let me go."

"Never."

Joker cleared his throat. "What do you want to do?"

"I want the asshole waiting for me in the fucking barn. Make sure he's there in twenty minutes, Joker."

"Clean up?"

"Yeah."

"I'll let the others know." Joker nodded at him before leaving him alone. Without waiting, Demon carried her through to the clubhouse. In the main room his men, the prospects, and the sweet butts were waiting. The seriousness of what just went down was clearly felt by all of them.

Deanna held him even tighter. This wasn't the place for her; she was better than this life, but he wouldn't let her go. She was his and he'd protect her.

Staring at all of his men, he made sure they saw his face. "Deanna's mine. She's an old lady, my woman, and will be treated with fucking respect. I see any of you talking shit to her, you'll answer to me. She's to be given the respect that you all give me. I don't want any arguments."

They nodded. When he was sure they all understood where he was coming from, Demon made his way up to his room. He kicked the door shut, going straight through to his own bathroom. Turning on the shower, he helped her inside, putting her on her feet. Removing his jacket, he draped it over her shoulders. The water cascaded around them but he didn't give a shit.

"This, this is yours."

"You've just claimed me in front of your club."

"I'll marry you as soon as it can be arranged. You're not going anywhere." He cupped her cheek, tilting her head back. Her full lips begged to be kissed. Demon gave in, slamming his lips down on hers. Banding an arm around her waist, he pulled her close, moving down to squeeze her full rounded ass. "You're mine."

She ran her hands up his chest.

"They didn't touch you? Rape you?"

"No. They stuffed me into the trunk of a car, tied me to a chair, and stuffed me back into a trunk again. Demon, I hate the trunks of cars. What the hell happened?"

Taking a deep breath, Demon knew this choice would come to him. He wouldn't lie to her. There wouldn't be anything between them ever again. "Your father. He's what fucking happened."

"My father? What do you mean? He's dead."

"Yeah, and before he died he made another fucking deal with you as his bargaining chip."

What little color Deanna had faded instantly. "Bargaining chip?"

"Yeah." He took the jacket off her. "This is yours."

He started to undress her.

"In what way?"

"You really don't want to know, baby."

"No, I need to know."

"There's a guy. He's a criminal lord around here, possibly all over the country. Goes by the name Zeke. You do not ever want to get involved with him."

"But my father did?"

"Yeah. You were supposed to go on Zeke's books. He pimps out girls, among other things."

"Seriously?" She started to shake. Tugging her into his arms, Demon kissed the top of her head.

"I've made a deal with him."

"You've done something you wouldn't have done before?"

"I'll handle it."

"What would have happened if you didn't agree?"

Demon stared into her beautiful eyes. "He would have shot you in the head and we wouldn't be here having this conversation."

She sobbed, pressing a hand to her mouth. "I'm so sorry."

"No, you don't get to be sorry."

"But you're in danger and it's all my fault."

Demon silenced her with his lips. Massaging the cheeks of her ass, he drew her close so she didn't have any choice but to feel his raging erection.

"You will shut the fuck up about blaming yourself. You haven't got anything to worry about. I promise you. The club and I will handle Zeke and whatever shit comes our way."

"I love you, Demon."

Smiling, Demon stroked her cheek. "That's all I need from you."

He stripped away the rest of her clothes before he started washing her body. She was so beautiful, but he wasn't going to fuck her yet. No, he had business to attend to and he wasn't interested in losing himself in her sweet cunt before he did it.

Washing away the muck from her body, Demon tended to her, showing her all the love and affection he could. She moaned, sinking against him. He removed his own clothes and allowed her to wash his body.

When they were finished, he turned the shower off, taking his time to dry her body. He carried her through to his bedroom, putting her underneath the covers.

"What are you doing?"

"I've got something to deal with. I want you to stay here and keep the bed warm for me."

"Demon, don't go."

"I've got to, baby. It's club business. I won't have any secrets from you but the club still has to come first." He stepped away from the bed, grabbing a pair of jeans and a shirt. In quick movements he had on a pair of socks followed by his boots.

"Okay."

He kissed her head before making his way toward the door. The need to hurt, to kill struck him hard. With Zeke in their lives he didn't have room for a half assed prospect.

Walking downstairs, he saw the grim expressions of his club. He didn't give a shit.

Joker was waiting for him outside of the barn.

"What's he saying?" Demon asked.

"He was distracted by the blonde sweet-butt. I don't even know her name. I just hear the brothers say she has one tight cunt."

Demon gritted his teeth, fisting his hands.

"You sure this needs to happen?"

"We're working for Zeke now. You want a fucker who wants to get his dick wet more than take care of shit? He had a job. He failed and look what had happened. Zeke was in control today because of Deanna."

"You love her."

"If that was Amy what would you be doing?" Demon asked.

Joker's jaw tensed.

Demon watched as he pulled his gun out of the back of his pocket. "Here, use this."

He took the gun Joker gave him. Entering the barn, he saw that Steel and Shakes were guarding the prospect.

"Shit, Demon, I'm so fucking sorry."

The prospect, Ben, he believed his name was, walked toward him. Demon kicked out, slamming his boot against the guy's middle. Ben went down, gripping his stomach.

"I'm sorry."

"You had one fucking job and that was to stand at your bastard post." He gripped the back of Ben's head, pulling him close. "Instead you were more interested in having your dick in some whore." He pushed him away.

"I know. I'm sorry."

His three men stood by the door, stopping anyone from entering or leaving. No one fucked up as a prospect. There were rules for a reason. Ben had fucked those rules up.

Ben was sniffling, crying out.

There was no remorse inside Demon. All he saw when he looked at the fucker was Deanna strapped to that chair with a gun pointed at her head.

"They took my woman."

"I'm sorry."

"There was no excuse." Removing the safety from the gun, Demon stepped closer, pressed the tip of the gun to Ben's temple. "There's no room for mistakes in Soldiers of Wrath." He fired the gun and Ben sank to the floor.

Demon put the safety back on, handing the gun to Joker. "Let the others come and see. It's a warning. You do the job you were supposed to or you end up dead."

He passed his men, leaving the barn.

Deanna stared at the door waiting for Demon to return. She wasn't an idiot. The prospect who was on duty wasn't going to have a good time of it. She knew she should feel bad for him but she couldn't. If he'd been there she wouldn't have been taken.

Pushing some damp hair out of the way, she kept her gaze on the door. She didn't care what Demon was doing. She wanted him back so that he could hold her. The cold was seeping into her bones and the only person she wanted was him.

Time passed, she didn't know how much, but when he opened the door, relief swamped her.

"I thought you'd be asleep," he said, closing and locking the door.

She watched him remove his clothes before sliding under the covers. He gathered her up into his arms and she rested her head on his chest. Breathing out a sigh, she wrapped her arms around him. "I couldn't sleep but now I can."

"Why?"

"You're here and I don't want to be anywhere else but in your arms."

She traced a pattern on his stomach. The silence stretched out between them. "You killed him, didn't you?"

"He put you in danger."

"There's no room for mistakes?"

"Not this big. Screwing up a drink order, sure, but one of our women being taken, no. It was too big and with Zeke in our lives now, I'm not going to risk that shit. He had to go." He ran his fingers over her back. "You're not running away scared."

"He wasn't the one who had a gun held to his temple with a blindfold on. Why did he leave his post?" she asked.

"To fuck a sweet butt who's getting a bit of a reputation."

She snorted. "Great, I was taken because someone wanted to get their dick sucked."

Demon took hold of her chin, forcing her to look back. "I took care of it. That shit is not going to happen again. You're protected here."

Guilt hit her hard. A man had just died because of her. Tears filled her eyes. "I'm a horrible person."

"Hey, no you're not."

"Yes, I am. My dad, that prospect, they're all dead because of me."

"No, they're all dead because they fucked up. This has nothing to do with you, baby. They're the ones that screwed up, not you."

He held her tighter, stroking her back.

His soothing touch helped to calm her down.

"What happens now?" she asked after some time had passed. She couldn't think about anything else. Her thoughts were all over the place; nothing made any sense to her anymore.

"We wait for Zeke to call. I handle the club as best I can, and you service my dick."

She laughed. "You're so romantic."

"Wait until you have my ring on your finger. You'll see how romantic I can be then. I've got a right treat for you." He reached down, gripping her ass. "God, I love you."

"You sound surprised."

"I am. I promised myself I'd never love a woman."

She stared up at him. "I'm glad you broke that promise for me. I love you too." She stroked his chest, thinking about how they met. "If it hadn't been for my dad I wouldn't be here now."

"Then I guess the fuckhead did something right."

He lifted her up in his arms, kissing any protest from her lips. This was what was right in her life, and nothing else mattered.

Chapter Nineteen

One month later

Joker sat at the table and stared across the smooth glossy wood at Zeke. They had been working for this lowlife motherfucker for the last month as muscle. They hadn't dealt with a lot of shit, because whenever someone looked at them they seemed to back the hell off. It was good for them, but for Joker he wanted an outlet for his rage.

"You said if we helped you'd also tell me where to find the bastard that hurt Amy." He clenched his hands on his thighs and stared at Zeke. The asshole looked smug sitting behind his expensive desk, surrounded by his extravagant décor and furniture, and having armed bodyguards watching his every move.

"Yeah, I told you I'd deliver the fucker that went after his daughter." Zeke tapped his fingers on the table. "I may kill people, but I find child molesters the lowest of the low. In fact, I've castrated a few that I've caught in the act in my clubs, because I don't play with that shit, and don't allow it around me."

Well, good for you, asshole.

Zeke smiled like this smug fucking bastard. His dark hair was slicked back, his forehead prominent, and his fucking face made Joker want to hit something over and over again. "Well then, you can see why I'd want to handle this my own way, seeing as I am personally involved." Joker's nails dug into his palm, and he felt his skin slice open from the force of his actions.

"I did promise to hand the motherfucker over to you, and you and your boys have been doing a very fine job of keeping shit in line." Zeke opened a drawer on his desk and pulled out a manila envelope. He slid it over the glossy wood tabletop, and Joker grabbed it. Inside were images of Amy's father, locations where he had been the last five years, daily routines, and even where he currently lived. Joker gripped the paper tightly in his hand, stood, and stared at Zeke. When they didn't say anything to each other, Joker turned and left.

He headed down the steps, away from Zeke's office overlooking the downtown nightclub, and pushed his way through the throng of college students all but fucking on the dance floor.

"Hey, watch it, fucker," some bleach blond asshole said, and when he turned around his eyes grew big and his mouth opened in a silent "O" at the sight of Joker. "Yeah, ugh," he held his hands up, but Joker had already snapped. All he could see in his head was Amy and her father, that motherfucker hurting her, making her do things she didn't want to, and the fact he fucking loved that girl with everything inside of him.

Joker slammed his fist into the punk's face, and when he went down Joker kicked him hard enough he slid across the floor. People scattered back, the music still pumped loud in the room, and the scent of beer, sweat and sex filled joker's head. He had to get the fuck out of here, kill something, fuck something up, or just get high enough he couldn't even walk. All he knew was that if he didn't calm down he'd find this bastard, hunt down Amy's father before he was to follow through, and take him out faster than he wanted. Joker wanted this shit done slow, agonizingly slow, because he'd make the fucker pay for everything he ever did to Amy.

Two months later

"Come here, baby," Demon said, pulling Deanna onto his lap. They were having a picnic several miles from the clubhouse and the only thing that surrounded them was fields and woods. She loved this section of land. The whole of the Soldiers of Wrath MC owned the land surrounding the club, acres and acres of it. She heard some of them were planning on building other houses or even a couple of businesses. Deanna loved being part of the club but what she loved more was wearing Demon's cut. This was his brand, a sign of his ownership.

The other sign of his ownership was the ring that decorated her left wedding finger. They'd gotten married a month ago, with Joker giving her away to Demon. The whole club had been present and she'd loved every second of it.

Reaching up, she cupped his cheek to smile into his face.

"I love you, Demon."

"I love you too, baby." He cupped the back of her head, claiming her lips in a searing kiss. This was a side to Demon that she loved to see. Everyone else got to see the boss, the hard-assed biker who didn't let any shit stand. When they were alone she got to see the tender, loving side to him. She put up with all of his shit just to be with him like this.

"I want to stay here forever."

"You know we can't." He ran his fingers down her body to stroke over her breasts. She moaned as his fingers circled the bud of her nipples.

"You're heading out to help Joker?" She'd heard him talking with the other men. They were going hunting for some man that hurt a girl named Amy.

"Yes. This is part of the club business."

"I'll miss you."

"I'll call you every day, baby. There won't be any other woman for me. You know the only pussy I want is yours."

Heat filled her cheeks. This was the kind of man Demon was. She'd accepted it long ago.

"I know." She wasn't worried about him being with another woman. Deanna trusted Demon. "I'm worried about what will happen if things go wrong."

She looked down at their locked hands. The love that had bloomed between them had taken her breath away. There were times she couldn't believe how lucky she'd become. If her father hadn't owed them money then she wouldn't be sitting across Demon's lap right now.

They were stronger than ever before, solid in their relationship. The club life was not always going to be smooth and she accepted that. Demon was a bastard to the core but he was her bastard and there wasn't anything she wanted more than to be owned by him.

"Nothing is going to happen. I'll be back before you know it."

Before she could say anything else, he took her to the floor, opening her legs, and sliding between them. "Now, let me give you something to remember me by when I'm gone."

The End

BENT, NOT BROKEN

The Soldiers of Wrath MC, 2

BENT, NOT BROKEN (The Soldiers of Wrath MC, 2)

Sam Crescent and Jenika Snow

http://www.CrescentSnowPublishing.com

http://www.SamCrescent.wordpress.com

sam_crescent_fanmail@yahoo.co.uk

www.JenikaSnow.com

Jenika_Snow@Yahoo.com

Published by Crescent Snow Publishing

Copyright © February 2015 by Sam Crescent and Jenika Snow

Digital Edition

First E-book Publication: February 2015

Edited by Editing by Rebecca

Pain is a lasting feeling, emotion, and can consume a person without any discrimination. Amy Holland knew all too well what pain did to someone. She has been living with it for far too long, and it is all because of her father.

Reese "Joker" Whitman has put his old life behind him. He is now just Joker, part of The Soldiers of Wrath, an outlaw MC that rules his town. Despite the hard edge he carries around, the violence and destruction he's been known to deliver, Joker wants Amy, the daughter of the woman his father married. Amy might be considered family, but she isn't blood, and he wants her more than he's ever wanted anyone in his life. However, he has to tread lightly, because she's been hurt, and she may never be able to give herself fully to him.

When she finally sees Joker for who he is, it isn't fear or pain that consumes her; it is hope and desire. But can she give herself to the biker when she sees herself as too damaged be loved?

BENT NOT BROKEN

SOLDIERS of WRATH

USA Today Bestselling Authors

Sam Crescent
Jenika Snow

Chapter One

You shouldn't go down there, Amy. It's dangerous and wrong.

Even as Amy gave herself a warning, her sixteen-year-old body just wouldn't stop, turn around, and go back the way she came. No, she kept walking toward the pleasured moans coming from her step-brother's bedroom. This was dangerous, but she couldn't stop. She wanted to see what was going on and at the same time, she didn't want to know. The moans were self-explanatory.

Licking her dry lips, she crossed her arms over her chest, wanting to find some comfort. Finding none, she stepped closer to his bedroom. Her mother and step-father had left to go out to dinner. She hadn't really been paying attention. Her mother, Brenda, asked her not to bug Reese.

She stepped closer to the door. He hadn't locked the door and looking up from the carpet, Amy's heart literally stopped. There was no turning back. Reese was completely naked, and she saw several of his many tattoos. None of them made sense as she stared at him across the room. He was four years older than she was, so much more mature than even that though. He'd not seen her yet. She couldn't look at anything but him. His body was a work of art, rock hard, ripped, muscular; it was everything she'd read about in the romance books she kept hidden in a drawer. The past, and her horrors, reared their head, and she clenched her hands. She wouldn't think about her father, about any of the things he had done to her, not during a time like this. She could never tell anyone. The pain of the past had to stay in the past where there was no escape. It was her and Daddy's little secret. It had been until Amy had finally told her mother, finally shared the shame she lived with.

Just thinking about her real father made her shudder.

Cutting off the memory of him, she gazed at Reese's body. The way he stood before the bed, she got a clear side shot of his body. He stood in direct sight of the door. When he turned to show his back, she saw the tattoos, then when he faced his prey, she got the length of his body. His cock was covered in a condom and stood out, slick. In the light of the room she saw he was covered in a woman's cream. Her gaze moved to the bed. There, she was shocked. A woman was bound to the either side of the headboard and not just her hands and legs. Her tits were bound separately by rope. The binding was a little tight, and it gave them a red tint in contrast to the woman's otherwise pale flesh. The woman's mouth was open slightly and between her lips was a thick piece of rope.

"What's the matter, baby? Do you need to come? Do you need your Master to let you come?"

Reese stroked his fingers up the inside of the woman's thigh, going farther up until he landed on the lips of her pussy. Amy was rooted to the spot as he stroked from the woman's cunt up to her clit. The woman tensed on the bed. Her screaming muffled by the rope in her mouth.

"Bad girl." Reese slapped her pussy and Amy couldn't control the whimper that came from her lips.

Before she could cover the sound, Reese tensed, looking toward the door.

"Fuck, Amy."

She didn't wait around. Turning on her heel, she ran from the room. Charging downstairs, Amy needed to find escape.

There was no way she could face him. She ran out of the back door, rushing past the garden. Reese yelled for her to stop but she couldn't stop. Escape was the only thing on her mind. She had to get away from Reese and what he was doing to that woman.

And yourself. Don't forget that, Amy. Run from yourself.

Watching Reese's control over the nameless woman had done something to her body that she didn't understand or didn't want to think about. From the first moment she'd met Reese there had been something about him that lured her in. When they were alone, she wanted to tell him all of her secrets, the same secrets she'd been forced to keep to herself. He'd never once judged her. Gripping the nearest tree, she dragged in a deep breath. Closing her eyes, she rested her head against the rough bark.

Breathe in, breathe out.

Each inhalation and exhalation was hard for her to do.

You're useless. No one is ever going to want you. You're broken, Amy. Broken and so alone. Who will want anyone who is soiled like you?

She sobbed as her inner fears refused to be pushed aside. Tightening her grip on the tree, Amy broke down. She dug her fingers into the bark for support.

That's a good little girl. Just lie down and Daddy will take care of you.

The echoes of the past were too close.

"Amy," Reese called out to her.

Keeping her eyes closed, it took every ounce of strength she had to push the demons away. No one could help her. She was all alone.

He pried her hands from around the tree. He held her tightly, stroking her hair. "I've got you, Amy. I'm not letting you go."

"You've got to," she said. He didn't know the truth about her. She was broken, ruined, soiled.

Reese didn't let her go. He held her tightly, kissing the top of her head. "You're stronger than this. Push them back, Amy."

He'd always known she fought some demons yet he never asked her what they were. She broke down, sobbing against his chest. He had put on a shirt before he came for her.

There was no rush or demand that she hurry up so that he could get back to the woman he wanted to be with. Slowly, little by little, she opened her eyes. His masculine scent surrounded her. Glancing up his chest, she stared into his eyes.

"Where's the woman?" she asked.

"She's gone."

There was no other explanation.

"You didn't have to get rid of her."

"Yes, I did, Amy." He stroked her cheek. "She was never going to satisfy me. The whole idea was one big fucking illusion. I can't have what I really want."

He ran his thumb across her bottom lip. Her nipples tightened at his words. She was afraid to ask him what he really wanted. There was no way she'd ever handle this man. There was already more to Reese than she'd ever imagine.

Three months later

The party was in full swing with bodies crushed together. Amy didn't like the fact she had to brush against different people just to get to where she needed to go. She'd never liked tight confines, and this was certainly that.

"Excuse me... thank you... yeah, sorry..." The apologies went on and on as she smiled at people. Her face hurt from being nice to people she didn't know. This was a good-bye party for Reese. He was moving out of the family home and would be away from her for good. She hated the thought of him leaving completely but there was no keeping him in one place. Travel was in Reese's blood.

Passing the people on the stairs, she entered her bedroom, closing the door and flicking the lock behind her.

Resting her head against the wood, she closed her eyes, seeing Reese naked like she had a few months ago. The woman that he had been with hadn't stayed around that long, but the image of the two together was forever ingrained in her mind. It was a constant reminder of what she'd never be for Reese.

Not that he'd ever want her.

Damaged, broken, dirty, they were the words she used to describe herself. There was no getting away from what happened to her. Turning around, Amy cried out as she saw the man who was always on her thoughts sitting on the end of her bed.

"Reese," she said.

"Hey, sweetheart. You okay?"

"What are you doing here? This is your party."

She stayed by the door. The last thing she wanted to do was make a fool of herself and start begging him to stay.

"Yeah, this is not really my crowd anymore." He rubbed his palms together. "You've not been the same since that night."

She knew what night he was talking about. It was hard for her to look at him without thinking of him naked. The biggest problem in her mind was that she kept putting herself in the other woman's position, and that terrified her.

"It's nothing."

"You've not been the same since saw me with Candy."

"Candy? Is that her real name?"

Reese smirked. "It's what I call her. Names are not important to me."

"They're important to me." She'd hate it if he forgot her name.

"I'll never forget who is most important to me, Amy."

Her heart raced as he stood up, walking toward her. Her mouth went dry as he pressed both palms on either side of her head, trapping her between the door and his hard body.

"What are you doing?" she asked.

"Nothing. I'd never hurt you, Amy. I need you to look me in the eye and tell me you forgive me."

"I don't need to forgive you, Reese. There's nothing to forgive." She licked her lips. His gaze went from her eyes to her lips.

A groan escaped him.

"Don't do that," he said.

"Do what?"

"That with your tongue and lips. There's only so much control I've got and you're too fucking young and innocent for the likes of me."

Amy snorted. Innocent was not a name she'd use to describe herself.

"I don't want to stop doing it."

"You're playing with fire," he said.

In response, she licked her lips once more.

It was a big mistake.

Reese sank his fingers into her hair, tightening his grip as he tugged her close. In the same instant, his lips were on hers, ravishing her mouth. Gasping, Amy kept her hands by her side, not knowing what to do. The passion he was expressing, took her breath away.

"Open for me," he muttered the words against her lips.

She opened her mouth, and he took full advantage, plundering his tongue within. Moaning, she fisted her hands at her sides, not sure what to do with them. Her body was awakening under his touch.

He groaned. His free hand gripped her ass, drawing her close to him.

"I've tried to be good around you. I've tried to be the big brother, but I can't stop these feelings. You're like a drug, Amy. A dangerous drug. Touch me, angel. Please, I need your hands on me."

Opening her hands out flat, she placed them on his chest.

The pleasured sounds coming from him increased and he spun her around, moving her back toward the bed. Reese had her wrists tightly clasped in his hand, holding them to his chest, and keeping her immobile. She felt safe with Reese, felt that he would be the only one that could bring her back from the brink of madness and self-destruction. He'd never hurt her, she knew that, but she also knew that she wasn't normal and could never give him what he wanted.

Everything faded into the background as the past merged with the present. When Amy opened her eyes, it wasn't Reese she saw but her father. Panic, fear, disgust, and shame rushed over her and she couldn't stop the scream that bubbled up.

Pulling at her arms, she fought him, refusing to do what he wanted. It was too much for her.

"Please, stop. Please, stop. I'll be good. I've always been so good."

She begged and pleaded with the ghost that had stolen her childhood, her innocence. He wasn't a ghost. Her father was out there, living his life.

Fighting, Amy did everything she could to get away.

"Let me go."

"Amy!"

Her name was shouted, but it wasn't her father who said it, it was Reese.

Opening her eyes, she found Reese holding her tightly in his arms. He wasn't forcing her to submit to him. Reese held her tightly in the cocoon of his arms. His heat and warmth surrounded her with love and care.

"I've got you, sweetheart, I'll never hurt you. I'll always protect you. I'm sorry I lost control."

The tears that blurred her vision finally fell, sliding out of her eyes, down her cheeks, and onto his arms.

Nothing was ever going to be the same for her. She loved Reese with all of her heart and soul. His passionate kiss would stay with her forever as would his touch, but her demons would overshadow everything.

There was no way she'd ever be able to live her life to the fullest. She was broken from the inside out. There was no future for her. Amy knew she'd be doomed to live her life in misery.

Holding her demons close in Reese's arms, she fell asleep to troubled dreams. When she woke up the following morning, she discovered from her mother that Reese had gone.

He'd not even said goodbye to her.

Chapter Two

Five years later

Amy was lost in thought, her mind replaying the images of her mother lying in that casket, her lifeless body so cold and ashen. God, she was going to cry right here at work, in front of everyone, because she couldn't control her emotions all these months later. Leaning back in her chair, she stared at the other members of her team that worked in the office with her. At twenty-one she had her own life, a good job she had landed right out of college, a home of her own, and a step-father that she thought of as her dad. And then those thoughts led to ones of her piece of shit father, the one that had done so much damage to her that she couldn't even function sometimes all these years later.

"Hey, are you okay?"

Amy glanced up from her keyboard and stared at Michael, one of her co-workers at *Frances and Son's, a* realty firm. He had a stack of papers in his hand, a concerned look on his face, and she felt like a fool for not being able to control herself and her emotions.

"I'm fine, thanks." She smiled, but it was totally forced. He nodded once and went back to work. She stared at her computer, started working again on entering data, and told herself that she needed to move on from this. The years of therapy she'd undergone had helped somewhat, but the darkness she had inside of her would never really go away. She'd need to find her own path, find a light that would have everything illuminated so she was afraid of it anymore. Taking a deep breath, she tried to focus on something other than the shit that always brought her down.

That, of course, was easier said than done.

"Tell me how you're feeling today, Amy."

She stared at her therapist, a man who had been helping her for the past three years. She started seeing Gregory when the nightmares had become too much for her. The night sweats, crying out in the middle of the night, and the overall stress that from holding her emotions in had burst forth. The therapy sessions helped to a point, but now that her mother was gone, she was slipping back into this darkness that she hated.

"I'm feeling fine today." It wasn't a lie, but it wasn't the complete truth. She stared at Gregory, watched as he jotted down his notes, and looked at her hands. She twisted her fingers together, knew that she'd have to be honest with him if she was going to make any progress.

"Amy, why don't you tell me what's bothering you," Gregory said, crossed a leg over the other, and stared at her. His blond hair was perfectly styled to the side, and his thin glasses balanced on the bridge of his nose. He was sophisticated and professional and had helped her through a lot.

"My mother died."

"I know," he said without sarcasm, only interested in what she had to say and encouraging her to share more. "How have you been dealing with that? I know it's been a few months, but you have to be struggling with your emotions."

She stared at her hands again, looking at the redness of her skin from the constant rubbing of her fingers over her flesh, and nodded. "It's hard, I won't lie, but I am working with that more than I am with the fact I will always be damaged."

"Amy, I thought that we were going to work on the fact you are not damaged, that you need to start seeing yourself as a strong, independent woman."

She nodded, knowing he spoke the truth, but having such a hard time coming to that realization. "I want that, I do, but when I close my eyes, I can still see him, still smell his rancid cologne and cigarette breath as he comes into my room and climbs onto my bed." She wanted to move on, to be a woman that didn't let the past hurt her, cripple her life, and take things away from her.

"There is no time frame to make things better, Amy. That's why we are here, to try to help you get through it one day at a time." He smiled at her. "But you have to start with yourself first. You have to realize that you are better than everything that happened to you."

It was hard though, but she was working toward that, and hoped that one day she could look behind and see that all of this hadn't destroyed her, but had made her even stronger.

Joker sat in his SUV, the piece of shit man he stared at was just asking to be sliced right across the throat. He watched as Amy's father, Bruce, a fucker that needed to die a slow and agonizing death, took another hit off his cigarette and snubbed it out on his boot. He had gotten the information on this motherfucker from Zeke several months ago, had tracked Bruce, and now he knew exactly where the piece of shit was staying.

He also knew his routine, where he hung out, and the fact he was a fucking low life that was an infection on the world. Joker inhaled from his joint, let the smoke slowly billow out of his mouth, and watched as Bruce headed back inside. He could have killed the asshole last week when he had locked down his routine, but the truth was that Joker wanted to prolong this; he wanted to make the fucker suffer before he begged for death. So he wouldn't be killing this piece of shit tonight. No, he was going to torment him first, make him beg and scream for mercy.

Joker started the engine and headed toward a bar out of town that was known for back alley and bloody, raw fighting. Right now, he needed to let his aggression go, needed to fucking hit someone over and over again so that he would have a semblance of control when he finally took down the piece of shit that had hurt his Amy.

He drove for an hour before the small bar that specialized in illegal fighting came into view. Joker had gone there on more than one occasion to try and ease some of the destruction housed inside of him. Getting into a fucking crazy fight helped erase the darkness inside and helped him cope with the fact that he would probably never have the woman he wanted: Amy. If she knew the shit he liked to do in the bedroom, stuff she hadn't seen all those months ago when she'd come into his bedroom, she'd probably run in the other direction and never want to see him again. He wasn't into the conventional way of sex. Domination, submission, and bondage, along with the mixing of pain and pleasure is what he liked to indulge in.

He parked his vehicle, took off his cut and left it in the SUV, and headed toward the front of the bar. Once inside, the place reeked of cigarettes, nasty fucking alcohol, and vomit.

The women walking around were glorified, trashy whores. He walked right past them and moved toward the rear of the building. Joker pushed open the back door, walked into the large building reserved for the fighting, and stopped to watch the fight currently underway that was just about to end. There was blood and sweat everywhere and the scent of the anger and testosterone in the air was suffocating.

The fight was over quickly, and Joker was putting his name in to be next. He needed this fight, needed to feel bone breaking, blood spraying, and pain filling his body. He stepped into the center of the room, took off his shirt, and stared at the man he'd be fighting. He was a big motherfucker, tatted up like Joker, rippling with muscle and rage: the perfect contender. The guy bared his grilled-out teeth at Joker and didn't waste any time in attacking.

The hit that came from his right cracked his head to the side. Ears ringing and head fuzzy, Joker let the pain further fuel his rage. This asshole was about to feel some fucking pain of his own. He knew how to fight dirty, and in fact, loved it, reveled in it. Joker was really fucking looking forward to this. He let them have the first hit, but that was all he was getting.

The guy came after him again, started swinging like he was on fucking speed, and Joker smelled the alcohol coming from his pores. He was drunk, probably fucking high, too, so he moved slower. His punches were sloppy, and his hits were off the mark. Joker slammed his fist into his nose, grew even more excited when he heard the sound of bone crunching from the hit, and immediately went after him again. He tossed him against the side of one of the wall, and the assholes watching cheered for more. The guy went down like a rag doll when his head cracked against the wall.

"You motherfucker. You broke my nose." The bastard slowly stood and spit out a mouthful of blood. Blood poured from his nose, flowed over his lips and chin, and covered his white shirt like a grotesque painting. "I'm going to kick your ass and piss on your body." He charged forward, but Joker was ready. A man that wanted to win never lost control and never took his eyes off his opponent.

The asshole came swinging like a damn freight train, but his anger was a cloud of amateur movements that Joker had seen a hundred times before. He swung out again, but Joker caught his fist midair and used his opponent's momentum against him. Slamming his fist into first his right side, and then his left, he kept his composure when the guy doubled over and grunted in pain. He'd be pissing blood for a week after those punches. Joker stood there and waited for him to come back for more or turn the other way and end the fight.

"You're not going to win. You can either get your fucking ass out of here or you can come back for more and get your ass handed to you again."

He lifted his glossed over eyes and snarled.

"I can make you really hurt." It wasn't a threat, but a promise. And then the guy spit once more, straightened as much as he could, given the fact he was clearly in pain, and turned away. Yeah, that was fucking right. He wasn't about to throw down the white flag and lifted his hands for the next motherfucker to get their ass kicked.

Chapter Three

Amy walked into the home where her step-father, David lived. This was the place they had all shared growing up, she and Reese. No, he wasn't Reese anymore. He belonged to a biker club, Soldiers of Wrath and he was called Joker. Nothing she knew about Reese made her think he was a Joker, anything but someone to be laughed at. He was always serious, never pretending about anything.

Pushing thoughts of Reese to the back of her mind, she walked into the kitchen. Staring at the cupboards, an image of her mother, Brenda appeared before her.

"It's going to be okay, honey; you just forget about him." Her mother would tell her constantly to forget about her real father. She had forced the memory of him out of her mind so long ago that she couldn't even think of what he looked like, refused to remember what he looked like. Before her mother met David, she would sit with Amy, crying and holding her, telling her how sorry she was. Her mother had always been so sorry for not being able to protect her.

Brenda was dead now. Closing her eyes, Amy counted to five and when she opened them again, the image of her mother was gone. Tears filled her eyes, but she forced them back. Nothing good ever came from crying.

Putting the bag of groceries down, she made her way toward the fridge. David *was* her real father. He'd treated her like one of his own. Reese should have been her brother, yet after all the years together, Amy felt anything but sisterly toward him. For the longest time, she'd felt like a freak for not cutting off thoughts of him that were anything other than brotherly.

Then their friendship had changed; *he'd* changed. There was something in his eyes when he looked at her, something akin to yearning. After witnessing him with that woman on his bed, she'd tried to find whatever she could on the Internet to understand what it all meant. She hadn't found anything that had given her any clue as to what it meant to be controlled by someone like that sexually, at least not where she had been looking. Amy couldn't bring herself to look deeper into website or books. Everything about *that* scared her. Until one day, she decided to take the next step to understand exactly what Reese was.

In a bookstore in the city, she finally understood what Reese was: a Dom. There were so many books out now about Doms. She'd been so embarrassed that she hadn't even purchased the book from the store. Instead, she went online, ordering it for a speedy delivery. Ever since then, she'd been trying to find everything about what it meant to be a Dom. When she first started out, she'd not had the courage to look, whereas now, she wanted to know it all. Her intrigue about the subject grew and sent her searching for more details until she'd found everything she needed.

She'd wanted to ask Reese questions about his lifestyle. However, since her mother's unexpected death, she couldn't bring herself to talk to him about something so personal.

"Hey, honey, I didn't know you were coming over tonight," David said, breaking into her thoughts.

Turning around, Amy blushed. She'd been so lost in her thoughts that she had been standing in front of the open fridge for the past couple of minutes.

"I thought I could cook for you. I bet you hadn't gone grocery shopping and looking at this cheese, I was right." She pulled out a block of mold disguised as cheese. Amy chuckled, hoping he wouldn't ask her why she was blushing.

"That would be great. No, your mother, I mean, she always took care of me like that." David stopped talking, looking down at the floor. The emotion in his voice broke a part of Amy. She hated seeing him in any kind of pain.

"I miss her, too."

"I'll never stop waiting for her to appear. I love her so much." He gripped the counter until his fingers were bright white from the strain. "I can't handle it at times, Amy. She was only going to the fucking store."

Amy rarely heard him curse but accepted it now.

"I hate this. She shouldn't be dead. Brenda should be standing at that fridge, smiling at me. She should be by my side." He shook his head. "I'm sorry, Amy."

"If you want me to leave, I understand. I hate to impose."

"No, I want you to stay. With you around, it is almost like it was before."

Leaving her spot near the fridge, she reached out to touch his arm. "I understand."

The love Brenda and David had shared was the stuff generally reserved for books and movies. Seeing him like this broke her heart.

"I'm going to make you a lovely meal. Go and relax, David. I'll deal with the food." She watched him walk away before going back to the fridge. The only love she'd ever felt similar to what David had with her mother was the love she felt for Reese.

Pulling her cell phone out of her bag, she scrolled through her contacts until she saw his name.

Hovering over his number, she threw caution to the wind and sent him a text.

Amy: *Hey, it's me. I miss you. I hope everything is fine with you.*

She sent the message before giving herself time to change her mind. Putting her cell phone down, she started to put the groceries in the fridge, humming softly.

Her mother had been an amazing cook, teaching Amy everything she knew. Amy loved cooking and once wished she'd have a family of her own to cook for. She doubted that would ever happen. Who would want her? Her cell phone vibrated on the counter. Putting the vegetables down, she picked up her phone.

Reese: *How's my best girl?*

Her heart turned over. Was she his best girl? Amy wanted to be more but her stupid reaction to the heated kiss five years ago had stopped that. She doubted Reese would have gone any further. He was rough and hard, but too much of a gentleman to take her at such a young age.

Amy: *I'm good. Missing you.*

Without second guessing her response, she sent the message. She really did miss him.

Joker's fingers were blooded from the weeks of fighting. Tonight he was going after the bastard who called himself a father. The anticipation had built inside him to a fever pitch. He couldn't let it go on any longer. Soldiers of Wrath needed him back to deal with whatever Zeke threw at them. His cell phone went off, and when he looked at the screen, he saw it was Demon's number.

Letting out a breath of disappointment, he put the cell to his ear.

"Hello," Joker said.

"What's happening? You've been gone for a while over this."

"I'm going to end it this weekend." Starting tonight, Bruce wouldn't be getting an easy death. Joker intended to prolong it, making it agonizing for him. The fights he'd entered had only set to fuel his wrath, not ease it. He wanted Bruce's bones breaking; he wanted to tear the flesh from his body. Before Bruce died, Joker was going to sever the bastard's cock and feed it to him. The list of his torture plans was endless and Joker couldn't wait to get started.

He didn't know the whole truth of what happened, but Zeke had filled him in on a few gaps in his knowledge. Amy's sealed hospital records had filled in the rest of the blanks of what that monster did to her. No wonder Brenda had been so damned protective and secretive. She'd done everything in her power to make Amy's life as easy as possible.

Blowing out a breath, he looked across the parking lot. Bruce was drinking in his local bar, loving the attention. He wondered what the residents of the town he lived in would think of the man they drank with if they knew he'd abused and raped his little girl.

"Are you handling this okay? You're not sounding... right?"

Joker laughed. "Nothing about this situation is right, Demon. This fucking bastard hurt my woman. He made her scared of men, of me." He stopped. No one but Demon could get him to spill the truth. Amy was his woman, and he'd always considered her his. The love he had for her was never going to go away. It wasn't just love, it was outright obsession. She was a submissive at heart, a broken submissive. With the right care, he could bring her out of her shell, but she was so damned scared because of what that fucking evil bastard had done to her.

Gritting his teeth, he closed his eyes.

"I've got to go, Demon."

"Do you need support there? This is not something you need to do alone."

"This is what I *need* to do alone. I've spent a great deal of time imagining this moment. I'm prepared, and I'm ready. The evil fucking bastard is going to die."

Demon sighed. "Okay, I'll call you tomorrow."

Joker closed the call to see a text from Amy.

She missed him. *His* woman missed him.

Joker: *How's everything going with Dad?*

Amy: *It's not good. He's sad. Will you come by at some point? I'd really like to talk to you. I miss talking to you.*

He hesitated. Amy's texts always made him smile. She hated the small text talk and when they were growing up he'd sit in his room texting her in short talk. She'd get so angry that she would storm into his room, shouting at him.

Joker: *I'll be there Sunday.*

Once he sent the message, he sent a text to his father letting him know he was going to be stopping by on Sunday for dinner. He missed spending time with Amy. The sluts he slept with now were his way of trying to forget her. Amy couldn't be what he wanted. Not yet.

Doubts filled his mind. Given the right amount of care and love, Amy could be exactly what he wanted and needed. It was almost too good to be true for him. His anger raged inside him as he watched Bruce leave the bar, laughing.

Joker couldn't hear what was being said, and he didn't care about it. Putting his car into drive, he followed the fucker down a quiet road. In a couple of minutes, Bruce would cut down a darkened alley that would give Joker the perfect opportunity to grab him.

He bided his time as Bruce stopped against a wall to take a piss. It wouldn't be long until he didn't have a cock to piss with. Pulling the car against the curb, Joker climbed out. Shoving his hands into his pockets, Joker followed close enough behind the bastard who was going to experience some pain. No, not some pain, a lot of agony. A shit load of pain.

Rounding the alley, Joker grabbed Bruce from behind, slamming against the cement wall.

"What the fuck?" Bruce said, turning around to face him.

"Go on, Bruce, hit me. Let me see how you fare with hitting a real fucking man instead of terrorizing little girls." Joker got right up in his face, almost begging for the bastard to take a shot, any shot that would give Joker a chance to hurt him.

"Who the hell are you? I don't know what you're talking about." Bruce had paled though.

"You don't know me, but I know a lot about you. We've got a mutual acquaintance: Brenda, your ex-wife." What little color Bruce had disappeared at the mention of his ex-wife.

"I've stayed away. I told her I would."

"You see, Bruce, I've got a problem. Amy's my woman, and you hurt her. You took something away from her that she'll never get back, and now it's time for you to pay the price." Wrapping his fingers around Bruce's neck, Joker fought the temptation to end him now. "And I'm going to make sure you beg for death long before I deliver it."

Chapter Four

Joker dragged an unconscious Bruce by the arm, tossed his ass on the floor of the abandoned warehouse owned by The Soldiers, and stared at his body. The fucker was still breathing for now, and the energy inside of Joker to end his life now ran him hard. But he had been planning this for a long fucking time, and would make the fucker beg for mercy before he was finished with him. He spit in Bruce direction then turned and faced the metal table pressed against the wall. There was a chair and rope beside the table and on top of the scarred, rusted-out metal was an array of things that would bring Joker a hell of a lot of pleasure.

After he picked Bruce up off the floor and tied him to the chair, he moved back and pulled a joint out of his cut. He didn't need to be high or drunk for this, but a little weed sounded good before the party got started. For about five minutes he waited for the motherfucker to wake up, and when his impatience got the better of him, he walked over to the sink. After filling up the bucket with cold water, he turned and stared at Bruce. Leaning against the sink, he inhaled his joint, took it out from between his lips, and exhaled. The smoke billowed out in front of him in a hazy white cloud, and when it dissipated he moved the joint to the counter, set it on the edge, and picked up the bucket.

He threw it on the bastard; he loved it when Bruce sputtered awake and started coughing as he inhaled some of the water. When Bruce caught sight of Joker, he started struggling against his bindings, but there was no fucking way was he getting out of the knots Joker had tied. He watched Bruce struggle and scream out, and then amusement filled Joker.

"You sorry piece of shit. We are out in the middle of nowhere." After he had knocked Bruce the fuck out, he'd driven an hour out of town to this secluded spot. "Ain't no one hearing your soon-to-be dead ass."

The rapist sputtered out pleas that he was a changed man, but Joker blocked everything else out. He took a step back, took off his cut and T-shirt, and grinned over at the tools on display. He'd be using many of them on this asshole and enjoying every second of it. He picked up his joint again, inhaled from it, and blew the smoke out softly until a cloud covered his vision. It dispersed, and he grabbed a pair of brass knuckles from the tray, slipped them on, and moved back to Bruce.

"I didn't mean to do anything to Amy. She's my daughter and I love her—"

Joker didn't let him finish; he cracked him in the side of the face with the knuckles. "You don't talk about her, think about her, or fucking say her name. She is no one to you anymore and least of all your fucking daughter." He hit Bruce again until blood sprayed out of his nose and mouth. The rancid shit got on Joker's chest, but he didn't care. He wanted blood running down his chest, wanted it covering the ground, and draining the life right out of this rapist pedophile.

"Please, stop," the man sputtered out. Blood dripped out of his nose and mouth and fell onto his chest and the ground. His shirt was already soaking in the shit, but it didn't matter, because he'd be deader than a damn doornail soon enough.

Joker swung out again without responding and connected the brass knuckles with Bruce's face again. He felt power move through him when Bruce's nose cracked. The rapist howled in pain and tried to get up, but all he accomplished was falling to the side, still tied up like a hog. Something inside of Joker broke, and he reared his leg back and kicked Bruce hard enough that the chair and Bruce's entire body skidded to the other side of the room. He stalked forward, but not before he grabbed a blade from the tray. Yeah, he had wanted to prolong this, but this evil feeling inside of him rose up, demanding that he finish it. Amy deserved peace, and he knew she'd get it once this waste of space was finished.

Bruce howled out in pain, struggled against his bonds, but then started to slowly still as Joker moved forward. He hauled Bruce up, took the knife and cut Bruce free, and then immediately strung him up on the meat hook that he'd rigged up for this special occasion. Blood continuously flowed, and a small pool settled on the floor beneath him.

"Amy kept saying stop, didn't she?" He hit Bruce again, and again, and once more until the prick as now hanging on to the ropes that bound him. "But you are one sick motherfucker, and couldn't, stop could you? You wanted to see how far you could push her." He took the knife and dragged it across the asshole's cheek, watching as the skin opened up.

"But you didn't stop for her, and I bet you didn't know someone would come calling all these years later, ready to extract revenge in her name." Joker stopped talking and shook his head. He inhaled deeply for a moment, trying to get the image of Amy, scared and crying, out of his head. The rage that came over him stole his breath away, stole his very fucking sanity. He had said he didn't need liquor, but seeing a crying Amy in his head almost did him in. He turned and grabbed the bottle of whiskey from the counter, popped the cap, and took a long drink from it.

"No, you're not passing out yet, fucker," Joker said through his teeth. He took one more drink and put the bottle down. "I wanted to make this last, but I better end this now before you pass out again and can't feel how much I make you hurt." He grabbed a serrated knife, ran his finger over the blade, and walked over to the man who had hurt the woman Joker loved. He grabbed Bruce's chin, turned his beaten face up so he was forced to look at Joker, and growled out low. He felt feral, felt like he was going to snap even further until he couldn't control himself enough to enjoy this.

Joker took the blade and ran it along each side of the asshole's face, watched the blood pool and slip down his flesh. He would be dead soon, and then he'd focus on making Amy his.

"You made my woman afraid of being with me." Joker stabbed Bruce in the gut. "Your death will make her rest easier, breathe at night, and not flinch and push me away when I want to comfort her." He felt rage burning brightly inside of him. Joker moved the blade up, opening up Bruce's stomach, and taking the blade out to press it to his neck.

The blood dripped off of the blade and landed on his chest. He stared into Bruce's eyes, saw them widen when Joker pressed the blade into his flesh, and then he bared his teeth at the asshole. Joker continued to move the blade slowly across his throat, heard the gurgle of Bruce choking on his own blood, and looked down to see the bright red blood start to spurt out of his jugular.

He took a step back, the knife he held dripping the red, viscous fluid onto the ground, and this warmth and release filled him. He stared at Bruce, watched the life fade from him, and knew that this was what true vengeance felt like.

Amy sat at the kitchen table, across from David, and thought about how many times she had done this with her mom, her step-father, and Reese back in the day. The silence between them right now wasn't uncomfortable, and in fact, she saw the smile on David's face and knew he was thinking about her mother.

"Your mom used to make the best sweet rice I have ever had." He stared at her and smiled wider. "Do you remember the first time she made it; you and Reese were hesitant to taste it because you said it looked slimy?"

She started chuckling and nodded. "Yeah, but Reese is actually the one who got me to try it. It was the best."

David nodded. "Yeah, your mom could cook like no other."

The room was silent again, and she thought about Reese. "David, how is he doing anyway? I mean I've spoken to him, but how is he really doing?"

David didn't speak right away, but instead picked up the sandwich she had made for him and took a bite. He chewed for a moment, swallowed, and then he took a sip of water. He set his water down as he looked at her again. "Reese has changed a lot since he was a teenager. The few times I've seen him in the last few years he was a harder man, more dangerous even."

She nodded, knowing exactly what he meant. "Yeah, I've seen a change since he became a member of the MC." There were times, at first, when staring at him, just being in his presence, had made her nervous. He was big and strong, easily over six feet in height, with muscles that were stacked on top of each other. He was dangerous, there was no doubt about that, and he was violent. She knew he had killed men, knew that he did illegal things, yet she still wanted him. God, did she want him, but who in the hell would want a woman like her?

Chapter Five

"Did you get it all out of your system?" Demon asked.

Joker climbed off his bike. He'd cleaned up the remains of Bruce in the warehouse. No one would ever find his body and if someone did try to look for him, or even care about where the sack of shit was, there wouldn't be anything left to find.

"Yes."

"So long as it's where it needs to stay."

"I don't have a fucking problem anymore. He's gone."

"You're going after her now, right? The bitch you claim not to care about?" Demon walked beside him as they made their way toward the clubhouse.

The only thought Joker had was of Amy. He couldn't stop thinking about her. Killing Bruce had been designed to set her free. She needed to know he was dead to start living her life.

"Amy's not a bitch. You be careful what you say about her." Joker turned on his friend.

Demon raised a brow. "She's special all right. You're going to have to bring her by the club."

At the mention of the club, Steel walked out with three bitches on his arms. They were running their hands up and down his body, and the women were completely naked.

"I'm going to fuck each of you and then you're all going to lick each other the fuck out."

"Yes, Steel," all three women spoke together.

"That fucker is dirty," Demon said, scrunching up his nose.

"Amy wouldn't last two minutes in this club." The very thought of bringing her to the club broke Joker out in a cold sweat.

"You don't have a choice. There's no out from the club, Joker. You're my VP. The only out is six feet under."

"I could be voted out," Joker said.

"It's not going to happen. You're too well liked for them to get rid of you. You've got more chance of being fucked by one of the boys than voted out."

"I didn't peg you as the kind of club that fucked each other," Deanna said, coming out of the clubhouse. She went straight to Demon, wrapping her arms around his waist. "I missed you."

"I missed you, too. I'm trying to convince Joker that he's got to bring his woman around here."

Deanna asked, "What kind of woman is she?"

"A civilian, like you. She's not had the best life starting out. The club, it's not for her." Joker gritted his teeth. He didn't want to leave the club nor did he want to live without Amy. Could he have both? Was there a way for Amy to move beyond the demons of her past? "I've got to head out. I hope that's okay?"

"You're going to her?"

"I've got to see her. When I know she's ready, I'll bring her around. I'm not leaving the club. I'm by your side all the way until the end. We're brothers, Demon. I wouldn't dream of turning my back on you. We've still got Zeke to take out." Joker reached out to grab Demon's hand.

Demon pulled him in for a hug. "Good thing, bro. You're the best man I've got."

"I'm going to take a shower. I'm not seeing my best girl stinking like a pig."

He passed Demon and Deanna, making his way toward his room. Several women tried to stop him but he shoved them away. He wasn't interested in free skanky pussy. There was only one woman he wanted, and he wasn't going to stop until he got what he wanted.

Inside his room, he locked the door, and stared at his space. Closing his eyes, he imagined Amy's sweet face. Her innocence went bone deep and yet she'd never felt worthy of his love. That's what he hated more than anything... the complete lack of respect and value she had for herself. Her past made her think she wasn't worthy of love. In his opinion, she deserved love more than anything else. He'd give her a life that she'd only ever dreamed about.

Scratching the back of his head, he walked toward the shower, knowing he'd done the right thing. There's no way Amy would be upset by what had happened. Everything he'd done was for her.

Steel stared at the three bitches on the ground. They were club whores, used pussy, and fucking willing snatch. He didn't have to do anything but snap his fingers to get what he wanted. They didn't demand better of him or ask him to take them on a date. Swigging from his bottle of Jack, he watched the fake blonde start to unbutton his jeans. He wanted his dick sucked, and this slut was just the one to do it. The brothers talked about her. She had a mouth like a fucking vacuum. He doubted miss prim and proper, Eloise, would have such a nice fucking mouth. The bitch who worked at the supermarket wouldn't know the first thing about sucking dick. He'd first seen the mousy woman three months ago when he went in for a pack of cigs after a long ride with the Soldiers. Steel didn't know what it was about her that drew him in. She was rounded in all the right places and had nice big tits. Fuck, no she wasn't perfectly rounded... she was chubby. He could have any bitch he wanted and did. Eloise wasn't worth anything, yet she drove him fucking mad. He couldn't stop thinking of her.

She'd done nothing wrong other than turn him down. Who turned him down when he was offering sex? It was ridiculous. He may not have been nice about it, but she didn't need to tell him to fuck off.

"That's it, bitch, suck my dick."

The woman on her knees smiled up at him. "Anything for you, Steel." She tugged down his jeans, revealing the hard ridge of his cock. He was ready to explode just from the sight of her tongue. Her tongue was pierced and the little barbell was a little cold against his flesh. Damn, he loved fucking.

Closing his eyes, he fisted his hand in her hair, and slammed his dick so deep into her mouth that she started to gag on his length. He didn't care. With his eyes closed, he imagined another woman taking his shaft. Steel didn't have the first clue who Eloise was. He'd only ever seen her at the supermarket either serving customers or stacking shelves. She meant nothing. There were far more willing women out there, yet the only one he imagined was her. It didn't make any sense to him at all.

Speeding up his thrusts, he imagined her smile, and that was all it took. He exploded his load into the bitch's mouth. She swallowed his spunk, moaning as she did. When he was finished, he opened his eyes, and looked at the three women. None of them were the one he wanted. This was not what he desired at all.

"What's the matter, Steel?" the one on the left asked.

Shit, he didn't even know any of their names.

"I forgot my shit back at the house." He turned on his heel and made his way back to the clubhouse. By the time he reached the building, he leaned against the side, dragging in lungful's of fresh air. This shouldn't be happening to him. He never thought too long about a particular woman.

Resting his head against the brick, he stared up at the night's sky, wishing something would come and give him a sign. Years ago he'd lost the right to want a woman. This life, the club life was in his blood. He'd killed people in the name of the Soldiers. Eloise was not a club whore. She was like Deanna, Demon's woman. The kind of woman a man kept by his side to treasure and adore. He didn't deserve a good woman. There was nothing good about him, yet what he wanted was the shy woman that consumed his thoughts. What would she say if she knew the kind of pleasure he liked? She'd fucking run in the other direction, and rightly so.

Amy stood on the landing outside of her room listening to David as he answered the door. She'd decided to stay the night at his home because going back to her place seemed lonely. Her mother was dead and she couldn't bear the thought of leaving David alone. She leaned over the staircase railing and looked at David and Joker.

"What's the matter, son?"

"I wanted to see Amy. Do you know where she is?" Reese asked.

No, he wasn't Reese anymore. He was Joker. There was nothing laughable about him, yet that was his name. When he'd lived with them he'd make her laugh. She loved watching him be silly, stupid really. But he was definitely a changed man now, a dangerous, violent man.

"Reese, what's going on?"

"My name is Joker. Now where the fuck is she?"

"No, you're not Joker to me. You're my boy and I'll use the damn name I gave to you. Do you understand me?"

She could practically hear Joker grit his teeth. "Yeah."

"What's going on?"

She tensed up, expecting to hear Joker lash out. He didn't.

"Nothing. I just want to talk to Amy."

Silence descended on the room for several seconds. She wondered what David would decide. Why did he have to decide anything? She was a full-grown woman. It wasn't up to David to keep men away from her.

"She's upstairs in her room." David turned away.

Rushing toward her bedroom, Amy closed her door and quickly jumped on her bed. She picked up the book she'd been reading. Her heart was racing with anticipation, excitement... fear. Shaking her head at her own thoughts, she looked up when Joker opened the door.

Joker. Joker. Joker.

She kept saying his name inside her head so that she'd get used to it.

"Hey," she said.

"Hey. I heard you run across the landing; you were listening again."

Opening her mouth, she went to deny it, but Joker raised his finger and shook his head. "Don't lie, sweetheart. It's not a good look for you."

"I was worried about David. I didn't want anything to happen to him."

"Right and you just happened to be listening in for his good?" he asked, stepping farther into the room.

"Exactly. I care about David. You could have been an axe murderer."

"What did you plan? To beat him to death with a book?" Joker sat on her bed, grabbing the hardback book from her grip. She reached out to take it from him then started hitting him on the arm.

"Do not underestimate the power of a good book bashing." She didn't hit him hard. Joker took the book from her fingers, throwing it into the center of the bed. "That's no way to treat books."

"Dad tells me you're seeing your shrink again."

Amy closed her mouth then opened it before closing it again. What could she say to that? There was no point in lying. "Yes."

"The nightmares? They're back?"

"Mom's dead; I was struggling. But I'm dealing with things." She grabbed her pillow and placed it over her lap. This is what she hated about Joker. He saw everything. He saw every little detail to her very soul of what was wrong with her.

"It's about him again, right? You're dreaming about him."

Her heart started racing. What was he referring to? Did he know about her father? "This isn't any of your business."

"He's dead. You don't need to worry about him anymore."

"Dead?"

"Yes, he's dead. Bruce, your father, he's dead." He said with a stoic, hard expression on his face.

Amy jumped up from the bed, pacing the short distance of her room.

"He's dead?"

She didn't know how to cope with this information. Yes, her family knew about her going to therapy, but they hadn't known about the why behind it all. Why was Joker even telling her this? Wait, how did Joker know? Her mother kept everything a secret for so long. "How do you know anything about this?"

"I have ways of finding out."

"Are those ways through that club?"

Joker tensed up. "I love my club, Amy, they're good men."

"You've just told me that my father is dead. How the hell did you even know about him, find him, and know what happened? These are not questions I should be asking you, Reese."

"No, these are the questions you *should* be asking me." He stood up, advancing toward her. She took a step back, but he came at her again. Her back hit the wall, and Joker just kept coming.

He placed his hands on either side of her head, trapping her against his hard body and the wall.

"You're not going to get rid of me. You know who I am. I'm not Reese anymore, baby. My name is Joker and I take care of the people I love. I love you, and I had to end the fucker who made you afraid of life. That is what I do."

"You're a murderer." It wasn't a question.

He didn't say anything to deny it.

"He's gone, Amy. That bastard is never coming back to lay a finger on you. He's dead, and he died screaming and begging forgiveness."

Tears filled her eyes at the image he created for her. She didn't want to know this or even think about what he'd gone through. The bastard had hurt her more than anything.

Relief swamped her as it suddenly dawned on her that Bruce was never going to knock at the front door. He'd never show up at work. His ghost wasn't lurking around a corner waiting to take the life from her.

He was gone; it was over, but what did it mean for Joker?

What would happen when the cops found out? Would he be taken from her, too?

Chapter Six

Eloise bagged the last of the groceries for her customer and handed her the receipt. "Thank you for shopping at Markam's; please come again." She leaned against the wall behind her, so tired from working a double shift today, but having no option. She didn't make a lot of money, not as a cashier at the small grocery store in town, and although she had never seen herself doing this for a career, not everyone got their dreams in life.

She could see her reflection in the reflective window across from her, the "Boss's Cage" where her pig of an employer, Hanson, sat all day. She assumed he just watched everyone work while he claimed to do paperwork. Eloise could feel his eyes on her all the time, and although she hated feeling like this while working, it was a necessary evil. Unless she wanted to leave Markam's and start over, making even less than she made now, quitting because of her creepy boss wasn't even an option.

The bell on the front doors dinged as another customer entered. It was almost nine in the evening, and although they closed in about ten minutes, there was always that one person that waited until the last minute. She turned, about to greet the customer in the generic, almost robotic way she was trained to, when her voice stalled and her whole body tensed recognizing who it was. The man that stepped through the front doors was huge, muscular and tall, and deadly-looking. He looked like a killer, a gorgeous, hardened killer that had her thinking of very inappropriate and sick things. This wasn't the first time she had seen the man who called himself Steel. And the leather biker vest he wore told her he was part of the outlaw biker gang in town, The Soldiers of Wrath. The memory of his last visit played through her mind, and although she thought wicked things concerning this man, things that were perverted and made her feel dirty, she had turned him down when he had so blatantly and lewdly asked to take her home.

No, not asked. Practically demanded she give up her body to him.

He moved through the store, his gaze locked on hers at every available opportunity. He watched as he went to the fridge section and grabbed a couple of cases of beer. When he went over to the locked case that held the cigarettes, the sound of the manager's door opening had her turning and looking at Hanson. He was only in his thirties, and although he wasn't much older than her twenty-eight, he had the whole "Creepy Pervert" look going on. His dark hair was greasy, combed over to the side, and his face was riddled with old acne scars. It wasn't his appearance that disgusted her; it was his attitude and clear disrespect of her and women in general that did it. She had lost count of the number of times she had heard him speaking on the phone, coarsely talking to what she presumed was a woman, and the disgusting things he said to them.

"Eloise, can you explain to me what this is?" Hanson asked in an annoyed, slightly raised voice.

She glanced at the man named Steel, and had this uncanny feeling that he was aware of everything going on behind him, even though his back was to her while he continued to scan the shelving of cigarettes. The sound of Hanson slamming a piece of paper down on the counter in front of her had Eloise looking down at the form and knitting her brows. It was an order form for paper goods in the store, and although she dealt with ordering things from time to time, this was not on her.

"Can you explain why there were two cases of paper towels, toilet paper, and napkins ordered, yet there is only one case of each accounted for?" Hanson asked, his beady black eyes staring at her with annoyance and interest.

"This isn't my signature, Hanson," she said and placed her finger next to the name who signed the order form. "Robert ordered these, and he isn't coming back from his vacation until next week. You should probably take this up with him." She glanced over at Steel again, took in the way his dark hair was on the longer side, how his biceps were so thickly corded with muscles, and the tattoos that seemed to cover every square inch of his arms.

"I don't care whose signature it is, you were working with Robert on this."

"No, I wasn't, Hanson."

"Listen, Eloise," he leaned in, and she moved an inch back. The scent of fast-food wafted from him and when he smiled, flashing his crooked and yellowed teeth, she felt her stomach roil with disgust. He reached out, picked up a small lock of dark hair that fell over her shoulder, and made this gross sound deep in his throat.

"Back off, Hanson."

He ignored her comment. "I think you're wild, aren't you, Eloise? I bet if we got you naked and took off those glasses you'd be the naughty librarian—"

Hanson's words were cut off when Steel pulled him away from Elise so quickly she hadn't even seen him approach. He didn't throw Hanson on the ground, but he did toss him aside with enough force that Hanson stumbled backward and caught himself before he fell.

"When a woman says back off, you back the fuck off, man." Steel said in a hard, commanding, and take no shit voice.

"Being a motherfucker to women is going to get your ass handed to you and your body six feet under."

Chills raced up her arms and legs at the deadly calm voice that came from this outlaw biker. When Hanson stumbled away and back into the manager's office, Steel turned back around to face her. His leather vest showed a patch of his biker club, and a small patch that said 1%er. She didn't know what that meant, didn't plan on asking either. This man scared her, but there was also a part of her that was aroused that he had stood up for her, pushed Hanson away as if he were nothing more than a nuisance, and now stared at her with this possessive gleam in his eyes.

"He bother you like that often?"

She licked her lips and glanced away. "It's okay. He's harmless for the most part." She looked at him again. "Thank you for that, by the way. You didn't have to step up and help."

He picked up the cases of beer he had set aside to help her and then put them on the conveyer belt. He also grabbed the two bottles of whiskey and set them beside the beer. She was nervous as she checked him out, because she could feel his gaze on her, intent and strong, and it had her hands shaking. Once he paid, and she had the items bagged, she glanced at him again, saw the way his dark eyes were still trained on her, and didn't understand what it was about this man that had her so on edge. It wasn't because he was violent and dangerous, or that he was associated with the biker gang. It was simply *him,* and that scared the shit out of her.

He grabbed a slip of paper off the register, took the pen on the counter, and jotted something down. He handed her the paper, and she stared a down at it. "If that little fucker bothers you again, you call me, okay?"

She stared at him and then looked back at the number he had written down. She didn't know what to say, how to respond. So she just nodded and watched as he gave a deep gruff as if he liked her response and then left.

Amy breathed heavily as she stared up at Joker. He was so close to her, keeping his body right in front of her and blocking any escape, if she had planned to do that. The wall was cold behind her, and she placed her hands flat on wallpaper, feeling her heart race and her nerves go on high alert.

"We aren't going to talk about any of that, Amy," he leaned in closer. "We aren't going to bring up that motherfucker's name ever again, because he is dead, literally and figuratively. You understand?"

She was scared of Joker, of the man he had become, even though she knew he'd never hurt her. He was just menacing, so big and strong, watching her like he wanted to devour her. He also had no problem in killing anyone that stood in his way, or as it turned out, had hurt her. A part of her should have been disgusted and horrified that he had murdered her dad, but the truth was that she wasn't. Amy actually felt this intense relief fill her, felt like he had just done something for her that showed how much he loved her. And Amy loved him, God, did she love him, but she also thought she could never be what he needed or wanted.

His scent was strong, powerful, and faintly hinted at his wild essence and the aroma of motor oil. She loved the combination and actually felt her eyelids flutter as if they wanted to close on their own.

"You are scared of me." He didn't phrase it like a question.

"I am," she said on a breath, not knowing why she had admitted that.

"I'd never hurt you."

"I know." And she did, with everything inside of her.

"I'm a dangerous man, Amy, but with you I feel this lightness inside, a calm and ease that makes me want to just hold you and protect you from this fucked up world."

She didn't respond for a few seconds, just reveling in the feeling the heat of his body, his scent invading her senses, and feeling truly protected by his nearness. "I don't think I can be what you want me to be, Reese." She swallowed hard, hating to say the words, but knowing he needed to hear them.

"And what is it that you think I need you to be, Amy?" Reese asked softly and lifted his hand to run his finger over her cheek.

"You want me to be like those women you are with, the one I saw you with all those years ago." She closed her eyes, imagining that night, the domination that had flowed from him in waves. Maybe he wasn't like that anymore? Maybe he didn't like that kind of hardcore sex anymore? Amy didn't know, but she had a feeling his desires were just as powerful as they were back then, if not more so.

He stared into her eyes, didn't respond, and didn't move for several seconds. And then he surprised her by leaning forward and placing his lips on hers. The kiss wasn't forceful, wasn't demanding. It was soft and gentle, and she actually relaxed against him and opened her mouth. It felt good, really good to have him so close, kissing her and smoothing his finger over her face. He pulled back, kept his hand on her cheek then rested his forehead on hers.

"I don't want anything from you that you're not willing to give, baby." He cupped the either side of her face. "I just want you, and we can work through whatever issues you have with this." He pulled back, the hardness coming back on his face.

"Because I want you, and I won't leave you this time, Amy. I want you as my woman, and despite your fear, I know you want me just as badly."

Chapter Seven

Joker pulled away from the woman he loved and saw her glistening tears. "I'm going to spend some time with dad and leave you alone for a little bit. I'm not going away, Amy. We're in this together." He pressed another kiss to her lips, rejoicing when she kissed him back. "We're going to work through this together."

"He's really dead?"

"Deader than dead, baby."

"And you're not going to be put away for his death?"

He chuckled. "I'm not going to be put away for anything. I promise you. Everything is in the clear. I made a deal with some guys at the club." He stroked her soft cheek, wishing she hadn't been hurt before. Joker would gladly take her to bed and make love to her but she wasn't ready.

"Your club scares me."

"The club keeps me sane, Amy. They've kept me grounded for a hell of a long time."

"But they kill people and I don't know if I can handle that."

He held her head between his hands, staring down into her eyes. Compared to him she was so small, delicate, and soft. Joker knew he'd have to take care of her, love her with every part of him when he finally got her. She was the only woman he'd ever loved and even though he'd fucked plenty of women in his time, none of them ever compared to this sweet, delicate woman in his arms, even though he had never slept with her.

Fuck, he was a goner, and he'd never actually tasted her. He didn't have the first clue about how tight her pussy would be, or the sweetness of her cream as she came on his face. Amy was his woman, had always been his, and yet there was so much for him to learn about her, and learn, he would.

"Without them, Amy, I'd have been dead long ago. I couldn't have you. We didn't do anything that night all those years ago, yet I knew I'd hurt you. I couldn't live with myself. When I met Demon, I was dying inside. You're my life, Amy. The club is part of me, and I love them like the brothers I never had. Trust them the way you trust me."

She placed her hands over his. "I'll try."

"You're stronger than that asshole, baby. Stronger than anyone I've ever known. We can do this and we're going to do it." He pressed another kiss to her lips, but this one far more demanding than the other. "I'm going to speak to my father. Get some sleep and I'll join you soon."

He eased her away, making his way out of the room before closing the door behind him. Resting his body against the door, he stared up at the white ceiling with the single light bulb glowing down at him. His cock was rock hard, begging for him to go back into Amy's room and fuck her.

Not now. Take your time and give her a chance.

If he walked back into that room to her frightened screams, he'd regret it. The only screams he wanted to hear were hers calling his name in utter pleasure.

Joker forced himself to remember that night their kiss got out of hand, the way she'd fought him as he led her back toward the bed. All of it came crashing down around him and cut off all his pleasurable thoughts. His cock deflated and, after taking a deep breath, he left her door and made his way downstairs.

His father was waiting for him at the table.

"I made you a coffee; I figured you'd need it." He pointed to the cup on the table.

"Thank you."

"Are you going to be staying awhile?"

He glanced over at his father, seeing his slight weight loss along with his grief. The loss of his step-mother had hit his father hard.

"Yeah, I'm staying. I'm going to lay my cards out here, Dad. When I go back to the clubhouse, I'm taking Amy with me."

"Reese—"

"No, don't cut me off. I mean it; Amy's mine. She has been mine for a long time. You know this."

"I promised Brenda when I married her that I would always keep Amy safe. I can't let her down. Amy's all I've got of Brenda now."

"I killed him, Dad."

Silence fell between them. Staring at the man he'd loved his whole life, the same man he admired and respected, Joker waited for him to speak. His father, and even Amy, could call him Reese, but he wasn't Reese anymore, he was Joker, VP of the Soldiers of Wrath, and he wouldn't change. So much had happened in his life that he didn't even know if it was possible to change. The only thing that had remained the same was his love for Amy.

"What?" David asked.

"I killed him: Amy's father, the fucker who ruined her childhood and put her into years of nightmares and therapy. He's gone, and he's never coming back. You don't need to protect her anymore. Amy's protection is my job. It's time for you to go out and find someone for yourself."

David cut him off laughing. "What the fuck has happened to you, son?"

"I grew up."

"Killing men doesn't make the problem go away. Bruce hasn't been around for years, and Amy's still fighting what he did to her. It's not just going to go away because you killed him." David slammed his hand down on the table. "Amy's delicate. She needs to be cared for."

"And you don't think I've got it in me to care?"

"I don't think you've cared about anything for a hell of a long time. Soldiers of Wrath, Demon, and the crap related to the club have been your life. I love you, son, always have and always will, but you're not coming into Amy's life with the intention of taking her away. You do that and you're going to send her on a downward spiral. I won't let that happen."

"I love her. She's all I think about, all I care about. You're not going to keep her from me."

"Then you better show me that you've got her best interests at heart. I don't mind you being here. Just don't rush Amy. She needs to have her life and live it, and you need to respect that."

Joker clenched his teeth together, angry at himself and his father. His father was right, but then he was always right and that just pissed Joker off.

"I'll stay." He picked up his coffee, finding it lukewarm. Swallowing down the dark liquid, he nodded at his father before heading back to Amy's bedroom.

Entering the room and finding Amy already fast asleep in her large bed, he removed his jeans and shirt. He'd been so long without her that he wasn't going to spend another night not sleeping with her.

He was down to his boxer briefs and climbed into bed, making sure he didn't make any sudden moves. He didn't want to wake or frighten her. Wrapping an arm around her waist, he moved in closer, molding his body against hers.

"I'm going to love you for the rest of our lives. I'll give you everything, and if anyone tries to hurt you, I'll kill them." He kissed her temple, resting his head near hers, and breathing her in.

For the first time in years, he closed his eyes and slept.

Amy slowly became aware of the warm body behind her. Turning her head, her heart stopped pounding when she saw Reese asleep next to her. Breathing out a sigh, she allowed herself to just look at him. In sleep he appeared much like the boy she'd known growing up. There were no frown marks or hard angles decorating his face. He was completely relaxed. One of his arms was underneath her head while the other lay across her waist.

This was the first night in months that she hadn't woken up frightened. She must have been really tired not to notice when he crawled into bed with her.

"You're awake," he said, opening an eye.

"How did you know?" she asked, smiling.

"You moved, and baby, you're not a light mover. You tug on the bedding and shift a hell of a lot. There's nothing covert about you."

She giggled.

"That's a sound I could get used to."

"Why are you in my bed and not your own?"

"Do you remember what happened last night?" he asked.

Amy thought about last night and her heart started to pound. "You're not going anywhere?"

"No, I'm not. I'm not going anywhere and I'm going to stay here until you're completely comfortable with me. This is the bed I'll sleep in. I'll be there to meet you after work."

"You're not going to back away?"

"No, not even if you beg me to."

Amy licked her lip, pulling away from him a little. Reese stopped her from moving by tightening his hand on her waist. Should she call him Reese or Joker? She didn't know what to think.

"I need to go to the bathroom."

"You're not running from me."

"I'm not going to run, but you've got to admit this is pretty damn confusing." She moved off the bed, making her way toward the bathroom.

"It's not confusing, baby." He moved toward the edge of the mattress, sitting up. She couldn't help but glance down. His penis pressed against the front of his boxer briefs. Amy swallowed past the lump in her throat. He was huge.

"I need to use the bathroom." Opening her bathroom door, she sat on the toilet, and her thoughts returned to Reese. "Stop it," she said, scolding her mind.

She squealed when he knocked on the bathroom door, her nerves running wild.

"Yeah?" she said, clearing her throat after the words left her. Her face felt bright red at the fact Reese could come in and see her on the toilet.

"Can I come in?"

"No." she said right away. "Hold on." She finished going, flushed the toilet, and washed her hands. She opened the door and saw Reese leaning against the frame, his arms crossed over his chest.

He grabbed her hands in his in the next second. "You're going to be mine. I'm not going to leave here until you're by my side on the back of my bike." He gripped her hands even tighter. "I'm not expecting you to be all right with this straight away, but with time, I want us to be more." His thumbs stroked across her skin. "Nothing you can do or say is going to push me away. I know what happened to you. I know what Bruce did to you. Look into my eyes, Amy."

She did as he ordered, unable to look away from him.

"Everything with us is real. I love you, baby." He placed one of her hands over his heart. "You're in here and nothing is going to push you away. Tell me you understand."

"I understand."

He pressed a kiss to her lips. "No pressure, no pushing, we'll take our time together."

She smiled as he pulled away.

"You're gorgeous even when you're embarrassed." He chuckled, leaving her alone.

Turning and staring at her reflection, she blew out a breath. *It's all going to be okay.* She wanted to be with Reese and if that meant learning to accept him and the club then she would.

"You can do this, Amy. He's gone and nothing is ever going to happen to you again."

She found her hand shaking. This is what she hated the most. One part of her wanted to give herself over to Reese, to have what she'd witnessed that night all those years ago with the other woman. She wanted to give in and to know what it was like to be kissed, loved, and desired. However, another part of her was scared. All she'd ever known was fear and pain. Her mother and her therapist promised it would take time, but she'd be able to live normally. How could being frightened of everything in life be living normally? So far, she hadn't been able to allow herself to experience new things, and she knew it was because of fear.

Fisting her hand, she was determined to ignore that inner fear and try. The bastard who was supposed to love and protect her would no longer be allowed to rule her. Her father was dead and she would learn to live life to the fullest.

Chapter Eight

Amy was afraid of what she was about to do, not because she feared Joker, but because she was afraid of taking this first step toward her new future. The reality was that she could hide in the past forever, never being able to live her life fully because she worried she'd always be afraid. She thought about Joker, about him lying beside her in bed all night, holding her, and just being there for her. He had killed her father, the man who hurt and tormented her for far too many years. She hated him, hated that he still had this kind of control over her. Why should he dictate how she loved or was loved? Why should he control who she gave herself to?

She stared at herself in the mirror; her long dark hair was messy around her face, and light blue eyes. She had never thought of herself as pretty, never even thought she could truly be loved by someone. That was all thanks to her father, and what he had taken from her all those years ago. He hadn't just taken her innocence, but her self-confidence, too.

Amy heard the front door close as David left for the day. Could she really do what she was about to do? Could he give herself to Reese? She wanted him, had for so long. He might be considered her step-brother, but she was a grown woman, knew who she loved and what she wanted, and she couldn't let her life be dictated by her past any longer. She might not be able to give him the type of pleasure he sought, at least not at first, but she wanted to be with him, wanted to give him what he desired, and right now she'd just take baby steps.

Leaving the bathroom and standing right inside the room, she stared at Reese, who stood across the room, and looked at the hard planes of his muscular back and his biceps, at of all the ink that covered his golden flesh. His hair was messy from the night before, and she wanted to run her fingers through the shorter strands. She wanted to tug at the dark hair and tell him she wasn't going to be afraid anymore. He was doing something on his phone, and when he set it aside and turned to face her, she took in the glorious expanse of his chest. His hard lines and planes, his rippling six-pack, that V of muscle that disappeared down his boxers... all of it was on full display and showing proudly through his ink.

For a second they just stood there while she checked him out, feeling her body grow warm and wet. She put all other thoughts aside so she could focus solely on the here and now.

"Hey, baby..." his voice cracked at the end, and she knew he could see that she was growing aroused. It was not something she tried to hide because she wanted this desperately.

"I want you, Joker." she said his club name, knowing she needed to get used to saying it, because that's who he was now. "I don't know how well I will do in that department and I'm afraid, but I love you, and I want this." She was standing up for herself, taking her life by the reigns, and saying fuck you to everything else that dragged her down.

He had no clue what the fuck was going on. Well, of course that wasn't true, because he was currently letting Amy lead the way. She wanted this, was coming to him. However, he didn't want to rush her.

"Baby, really, we don't have to do this. We can wait because I have all the time in the world."

She lowered her eyes to the bulge he knew he was sporting then slowly lifted her gaze back to his face. "I trust you."

That was all she said, and he nodded once. "You have the power, Amy. You control me." Joker had always been the one to take control, to dominate, and although that desire was in his blood, it was the very essence of who he was, he knew Amy didn't need that shit. If she ever decided to submit to him, he would take care of her, treat her like his Queen, and never make her feel like she couldn't trust him. He'd never betray her.

"I don't know where to start, Joker." The long T-shirt and sweat pants she wore were maybe not the most flattering apparel, but to him she looked fucking gorgeous. "But I want to see it, Joker," she swallowed. "I want to see your... erection."

God, the way she said that, all soft and hesitant, had his dick jerking. He started removing his underwear nice and slow because he didn't want to frighten her. His erection sprang free, his breath hitched as her eyes widened, and he swore to fuck he could have come just from the sight of her staring at his cock. Her breathing visibly changed, her breasts rose and fell under the thin material of her T-shirt, and his cock jerked. He didn't know how far she'd allow this to go, but she did have control over this moment, and he'd go along for the ride.

"Are you sure about this, baby?"

She licked her lips and took a few seconds to answer. "I don't want to live in the past anymore. I want you, have never wanted anyone else, and I know you'll never abuse my trust. I love you, Reese."

He smiled a real and genuine smile because he loved this woman so fucking much. He swore his dick visibly pulsed with each passing second that she stared at him. Hell, he could feel cum starting to seep out the tip. The slight worry that marred her face pulled at his heart. Joker reached out and stroked her face with his thumb. "You have the control, baby. I am here for whatever you need." He was large man in every aspect, and he could see the thoughts running through her mind. She worried about the pain, about him stretching her, and just about being with *him*. His Amy was scared, and he fucking hated that.

All thoughts fled him when she moved closer and wrapped her hand around his length. She started stroking him with slow strokes. "Am I doing it okay?" she asked softly.

Oh fuck, yeah she was. He nodded once, unable to speak. A harsh sound left his throat when she dragged her hand over the underside of his cock. Joker could have come right then and there, but the first time he got off with Amy would be with her under him and coming as well. It felt so damn good that he was having trouble keeping his eyes open. All he wanted to do was give himself over to her, but he wanted to prolong this moment with her. "Jesus *Christ,* Amy." He groaned loudly, cursing, murmuring how good it felt, how good she made him feel. "You're doing such a good job, baby, but we have to stop, or it'll be over before it really begins." He was far too sensitive and needed a breather. "Shit, baby," he couldn't catch his breath. "Let me make you feel good, Amy."

She licked her lips, let go of his dick, and nodded slowly. She moved onto the bed, and before he could follow her, she lifted up the bottom of her shirt and took it off. Glancing down at her chest, he felt arousal the likes of which he had never experienced move through him. Her breasts were big and round and her tips were a dark pink. Her nipples were hard, and he could see she was embarrassed by her nudity.

"You're beautiful," he said in a husky voice. "And you're mine."

She glanced up at him, and a smile covered her face. She was staring up at him, her eyes so big and blue he felt like he could get lost in them. The thing was that he had no intentions of letting her go, ever. Joker moved onto the bed and very slowly leaned in and kissed her. He slid his tongue along her plump lips before slipping it into her mouth. When she pulled back he thought maybe he was moving too fast, but she surprised him by taking off her sweats and panties.

"I want you, Joker," she said very hesitantly. Joker was scared of pushing her, but oh, fucking hell, he wanted her so badly.

He reached out to touch her gently and kept his gaze trained on her. When he slipped his hand between her thighs and felt her slickness coat his fingers, he groaned.

"Kiss me, Joker. I'm dying here," she smiled, but it was soft, almost weak.

He kissed her with so much passion, so much love. He cradled her body close to his and kissed her for long, gentle seconds. He was hard as steel, but he was taking his time. When she started moving against him, pressing her breasts to his chest, he groaned against her mouth. Adjusting his body so his hips cradled hers, he breathed out roughly at the feel of her wetness coating the length of his shaft. She was hotter than hell and he was going to burn alive. He wanted to go slowly, ease her into all of this, but he was too far gone already. Hips jerking on their own accord, his length spread her labia apart as he moved back and forth against her. She liked what he was doing, and he knew by the little mewls and cries that left her parted lips.

"It feels good, Joker."

"Good, baby. I'm going to make you feel even better." He kissed her harder, with more passion. "You tell me when you want more."

"I want more," she breathed against his mouth. Her breath fanning against his mouth smelled of the mint from her toothpaste. Arching, she pressed her hard nipples against his chest.

"I want you so fucking badly, baby." Thrusting against her with a little more force than necessary, he groaned, "I want to feel your tight, hot little body spreading around my cock. I want to make you feel good, make you only think about me."

She panted, but didn't stop him.

"You want that, too, don't you, sweetheart?"

"God, yes. Yes, I want that." Her pussy cream coated him completely, verifying exactly what she'd said. He could feel it slip along her thighs, making him wet; it was such a turn-on.

He stared at her face, looked right into her eyes, and reached between their bodies to grab his cock. He placed it at her entrance, but didn't push into her. "I want you to be completely ready. I'll ask you over and over again until I know for sure you are on- board. I don't want to rush you about anything, baby." He cupped her cheek and kissed her. Murmuring against her mouth, he said, "I'm clean, and I know you are. I can wear a condom, but I want to feel you, baby, be with you without anything between us." He breathed out. "I'll be careful, pull out even, but I need this, Amy. I need you."

"Just be with me. I trust you more than anyone, Joker."

He could have died right then and would have only felt bliss. As he started pushing into her, inch by slow inch, he watched her face. He wanted to gauge her reaction for the slightest doubt or that she was uncomfortable and wanted him to stop. Her eyes were wide and full of emotion. Ecstasy filled him, and he gritted out, "Damn Amy, baby, it feels so good." She was his, and he was claiming her. He bit his lip and continued sinking into her, feeling every hot part of her pussy ripple along his length.

Dipping down, he dragged his lips across hers, stared down at her, and pulled out of her eager body. When just the head of his cock was at her entrance, he took a deep, calming breath and pushed back. He groaned, never before going so slow, or so gentle. But with Amy he found it more pleasurable taking his time and making sure that she was comfortable. He wanted this to feel good to her and he would go as slow as he needed to. She was slightly stiff beneath him, and her nails were lodged in his biceps, but she made these little mewling noises as he worked his cock in and out of her. Then she closed her eyes and tilted her head back, moaning out long and low.

"That's it, Amy, let me make you feel so fucking good. I'll take care of you." He kissed her face, not stopping until he touched every inch of her. Joker gripped the back of her thigh and lifted it out slightly to deepen his penetration. He made sure his movements were easy and slow, giving her body time to adjust to him, to stretch around his cock. With his mouth pressed to hers, he could hear her whispered pleas that she trusted him, and that she loved him. He whispered, "I'd never hurt you and will always protect you. I love you, baby." They were so close, so fused together that they breathed the same air.

The more he moved within her, the more she cried out for. A blush stole up her chest, her nipples hardened even more, and she tugged at her bottom lip with her tiny, straight white teeth. In and out, he thrust into her, going as far as he could until the heavy weight of his balls rubbed along the crease of her ass every time he pushed into her. The whole experience was made hotter by the fact they were covered in sweat now, their skin slapping together every single fucking time he sank into her. He was mesmerized by the beads of sweat that dotted her flesh, and he followed those droplets as they made their way down her body to pool in the dips and hollows of her curvy body. He wanted to savor every inch of her until there was nothing left for him to taste or memorize.

Not able to help himself, he let his tongue follow a bead of perspiration that started its descent down her chest. He tracked it, dragging his tongue between her breasts before moving back up and sucking the dip and base of her throat. Even her sweat was sweet. All the while he kept pumping his hips into her, bringing them both closer to a mind-altering pleasure.

"Oh, *yes*," she hissed the last word out. He lowered his mouth to hers, letting her taste the flavor of herself on his tongue.

Her pussy milked his cock, and he grated out, "Christ, baby, I'm going to come. Please tell me you're close." Over and over he plunged into her.

"I'm so close," she whispered, her eyes wide with surprise and pleasure. She continued to make small noises in the back of her throat. Yeah, she was so fucking close. He could feel her tightening around his cock, drawing out his cum in fast, hard pulls.

"You clench around me and it feels like a fist, like fucking heaven. I'm going to come so hard, baby. So. Fucking. Hard." He pushed into her on the last word, and she cried out in climax. *Yes.* Harder and faster he sunk into her, needing her to come like he needed to breathe. It was there. Right. Fucking. There.

The roar that left him was loud and harsh, and it was a good thing his dad had left already. He could feel the heavy jets of his cum fill her pussy. He loved knowing it was his semen that coated her insides before sliding out of her and making a wet spot on the bed. Joker knew he would never let her go. He couldn't.

When both of their bodies stopped shaking, he collapsed on top of her. "Everything is going to be okay, sweetheart." He pulled back and ran the pad of his finger between her eyes. "I'm going to make sure of that. No one will ever hurt you again." He kissed her forehead, knowing that he'd never been this gentle with a woman before. Amy brought out this side in him, and the fact she'd given him this moment, this gift, despite the trauma she'd endured, made him feel like the luckiest fucker on the planet.

"I know you'll take care of me," she murmured sleepily, even though they had slept all night. He wanted to hold her, inhale her scent, and keep her protected against him. Joker rolled off her, pulled her close to his chest, and kissed the top of her head. He felt her acceptance in every word and every move. She rested her head against his chest, her hand draped on his stomach.

Joker felt the tendrils of his love for her encompass him, but he only felt like his with Amy. *His* Amy.

Chapter Nine

Amy opened her eyes and found Joker smiling down at her. "Hello, sleepyhead."

"Hello," she said.

Everything they had done together came rushing back. They hadn't fucked, it hadn't been seedy. It had been beautiful. They'd made love, come together as one.

"How are you doing in there?" he asked, stroking his fingers over her temple. "Are we still okay?"

"I'm more than okay." She snuggled closer, running the tips of her fingers over his chest. "I never knew it could be like that."

"Of course you wouldn't know how it could be with someone that loved and treasured you."

"Joker?" She gave him a look.

"No, Amy. You don't remember him. You were a virgin in every way that was important. I'm not thinking about *him* and neither are you. That's an order and I expect you to remember that. I was asking how you were feeling, not about anything else."

"You're so bossy. I don't know if I like bossy." She scrunched her nose.

"There's a difference with me, baby."

"Yeah? What is it?" she asked.

"You like me, so you like me being bossy."

"That's weird logic."

"It's my logic."

His cell phone started to ring, interrupting their little moment together. He reached over her looking at the screen. "I've got to take this, honey."

"Okay. I'm going to take a shower and then I'll make us some breakfast."

"Good." Before she moved away, he cupped her cheek, claiming her lips. She gasped as his tongue thrust into her mouth. Opening up to him, she cupped his neck, holding onto him. The cell phone stopped ringing halfway through the kiss.

When it was over, she pressed her head against his. She didn't want the kiss to end.

"Your phone stopped," she said.

"I'll call them back. We're going to explore this a little more." He laid a gentle kiss on her lips before getting up.

Releasing a sigh, she watched his naked ass disappear out of the room. "Great, he's gone."

Pushing the blankets off her body, she stood up, stretching out. She became aware of the small aches all over. The kind of aches that came from being thoroughly loved.

The mirror across the room caught her attention, and she stood naked staring at herself.

"You did it."

It wasn't exactly a hardship. She'd not done anything great or challenging. There had always been a connection between the two of them. From the moment they'd first met as kids, she'd been caught up in his world, loving him. For so long she'd loved him from afar, taking her time to get to know him. Touching the pulse at her neck, she released a groan remembering the way his lips touched her sweet spots. He knew what buttons to press to turn her on. Sliding her hand down her body, she caressed over her breasts. Her nipples were a little redder and swollen from his kisses.

"I belong to Joker."

Smiling to herself, she held her head up high. There was nothing to be ashamed of. She'd loved Joker for so long, and now she was learning what it was like to be his woman. The thought of him finding anyone else scared her. He'd never pressured her and this morning, it was all on him.

She entered the bathroom, running the water for a shower. She held her hand up to the spray waiting for it to warm up. Once it was ready, she moved under the water, basking in the warmth. She picked up the soap and her sponge and began to lather her body. Her mind kept returning to Joker's patience that morning. She'd been in charge, not Joker. Setting the pace of their lovemaking had made it a lot easier for her.

Washing the soap down her body, she gasped as she grazed over her nipples. They were hard, and she moved her hand down, hovering over her mound. She couldn't touch herself.

Amy had never touched her body in that way, never wanting to go that far even with herself.

New you, new life, new chances.

Dropping the sponge she was using, she slowly lowered her palm over her mound, cupping her pussy. Slipping her fingers through her slit, she gasped at the instant pleasure that overcame her. This was hers. Joker had touched her, bringing her to orgasm. This time, she'd bring herself to orgasm.

Running her fingers across her clit, she gritted her teeth, struggling with her own inner battle of what was right and what was wrong. This wasn't wrong.

Closing her eyes, she imagined Joker's smiling, approving face. She wanted to be perfect for him, whole. Sliding her fingers down, she plunged them inside her pussy, groaning as she clenched around her digits. With her other hand, she pressed it against the tile wall. All the while, the water of the shower washed over her.

The sensation startled her in its intensity. Brushing her thumb across her clit, Amy couldn't contain her cry. Freeing her desire, she fought the war within her and won.

No one could stop her. She no longer needed to be afraid of the unknown. This was who she was. She was going to become a new woman who intended to grab hold of life and never let go.

Her nipples ached with need. She didn't dare let go of the tile wall. Leaving her pussy, she stroked her fingers over her clit. Each time she stroked her nub, she felt the beginnings of her orgasm getting closer. Biting her lip, she imagined Joker on his knees in front of her, lifting her leg up over his shoulder.

She became fierce in the strokes over her clit. For the first time in her life, she fantasized about what Joker would do to her. The way he'd touch her, hold her, love her. She wanted to know what it was like to have his lips on her pussy, his touch hard and demanding within her.

It was more than she could stand. Gasping out, Amy threw herself into orgasm thinking about straddling Joker's cock as he slammed deep inside her. Nothing felt more perfect in that moment than the thought of being with Joker, his cock sliding in her body.

When it was over, Amy couldn't stop smiling. It was perfect. All of it was perfect. Raising her face to the shower, she finally felt like she was living life, loving life. No one was going to take this moment away from her. Once she finished in the shower, she blew out a breath as her body grew heavy.

Turning off the water, she walked into the empty bedroom. She heard Joker talking somewhere in the house. Dressing in a summer dress, she left the bra and panties in her room. For once in her life she was going to start living dangerously, well, as dangerously as she had ever lived.

"What's going on, man?" Joker asked. Demon wasn't the kind of man you ignored and Joker knew he'd pushed his luck with the club recently.

"You're needed for church. Zeke has another favor and I need you here."

"A favor? What the fuck are you talking about?"

"It seems our good friend wants to use us to escort his daughter from college back home. He doesn't trust anyone else and we're an MC that is known for getting the job done. No one fucks with us."

"We're not a fucking escort service."

"I don't think he wants us to fuck his daughter."

"No, but she gets attached to one of the men, we're all in fucking trouble." Joker cursed. He didn't want Amy to hear him and so he made his way downstairs, moving toward the back porch off the kitchen. "I bet she's some pampered princess who's used to getting what she wants. Fuck, when do you need me up there?"

"Tonight. He wants his daughter back pretty soon," Demon said. "Look, he's given you Amy's dad and we're all clear on everything. We pick his daughter up and we're pretty fucking even. It's all business from here on in."

"I don't know. We keep doing this kind of shit and it's going to go wrong."

"Look, it's a simple thing. We pick the girl up, drop her at her dad's and we're all fine," Demon said. "I don't want to leave Deanna for long. She's still getting the hang of club life."

An idea sprung up in Joker's mind. "Do you think I could bring Amy over while we do this? It'll be good for her and Deanna to get to know one another."

"Do you think she's ready for that?"

"I don't have much of a choice really. If I don't get her used to it then she'll never be. I won't stay for long after we make this run. In fact, why don't I come up with Amy and then Deanna can go with Amy back to my dad's place? I'll clear it with Dad for them both to be here. It'll get both of them out of the clubhouse for a while." Joker liked the idea of Amy having someone to talk to that wasn't in with the club. Deanna was Demon's old lady but hadn't grown up in the club life.

"Sure. I'll talk with Deanna. It'll be interesting to see if the two women get along."

"Great. I'll be there shortly. I just have to a call my dad."

He hung up after Demon said his goodbyes. Putting a call through to his dad, he gave him the heads up about what was going to happen.

"Do you really think Amy's ready for that kind of involvement?"

"I'm only going to take her to get used to it. Afterward, she and Deanna will be coming back here. I don't want her on her own right now. I promise you, Pop, Deanna is safe all the way. She won't cause any stress to Amy."

"If you think this is what Amy needs then sure, go ahead. I trust you, Son."

"Thanks, Dad. I appreciate it."

"Son?"

"Yeah, Dad?"

"I've missed you and I can't think of anyone better to take care of Amy."

Joker felt a lump from in his throat. Out of all the men in his life, the only one he wanted to impress was his father. Demon was his friend, and all the MC men were important to him, but nothing meant more to him than family. "Love you, Dad."

"Love you too, Son. Brenda, she'd have been proud of what you've done for Amy."

"Even with Bruce?" He fisted his hand, almost unable to complete the bastard's name.

"Yes. It doesn't really matter because I'm proud of you."

Glancing behind him, he saw Amy in the kitchen.

"I've got to go."

Hanging up the phone, he sent a quick text to Demon to let him know his father was okay with Deanna stopping by. Entering the kitchen, he saw Amy looking through the cupboards. She wore a summer dress that showed off the fact she wasn't wearing any underwear. The material was sheer and his cock was hard instantly. He wasn't wearing a shirt and had grabbed a pair of sweats while Amy was in shower before returning Demon's call.

"Did your call go okay?"

"Yeah, there's something I want to talk to you about."

"Can you talk while I make pancakes? I'm starving. I've also got bacon, are you good with that?"

"Yeah, load me up woman." Joker took a seat at the counter, watching her work. "Demon called. He's president of the Soldiers of Wrath."

"I know. You've told me before; you must think I ignore you." She smiled at him.

"You're right," he chuckled. "Anyway, he needs me to take care of some business and I can't ignore it. I've got to head over there in a little while."

"Oh, um, okay, sure."

"I want you to come with me." He held his hands up stopping her from saying anything. "I'm not going to leave you there while I take care of business. I want you to come with me and meet Deanna. She's kind of like you. She's Demon's old lady. They're together and I think you'd like her. I've spoken to Dad. He's happy for both of you to come back to his place for the night. I'll be back tomorrow morning."

He watched her mix flour, eggs, and sugar together.

"You're going to be away until tomorrow?"

"Out of everything I said that's the only thing you noticed."

She stopped what she was doing and rounded the counter. He swiveled around in his chair and she stood between his thighs.

"I was hoping we could have some fun." She placed her hands around his neck, moving even closer to him. Although she fought it, he could feel her hesitancy. Joker was so proud of her right now. She was his little fighter.

He cupped her hips, feeling no break in the line. "You're not wearing any panties. I like it."

Her cheeks heated to a delightful red: the red of a ripe strawberry ready to be bitten.

"I'm not wearing a bra either." She leaned forward, showing off her naked state underneath the dress.

"I did say later on, not immediately." Running his hands up to her breasts, he stroked over her nipples, watching her mouth open a little. She was getting aroused. Her cheeks were flushed, and he thought about her shower. He decided to take a big leap. "Did you touch yourself in the shower?" There couldn't be any other explanation for her flushed cheeks.

"Yes."

This is what he liked about Amy. She never lied to him and gave it to him properly.

"What did you think about?"

"I thought about you."

Sliding his hand down her dress to the hem of her skirt, Joker watched her eyes. Her eyes were the key to what she was thinking and feeling. She was with him the whole way.

Her stomach growled, interrupting the moment.

"We're going to eat and one day soon, Amy, you're going to play with yourself while I watch. Would you like that?"

"Yes, I would like that."

"Good." He leaned down, kissing her lips. Even sitting on a chair he was much taller than she was. "Now, go and make me some pancakes."

She walked back to the stove and heated up a skillet.

He couldn't tear his eyes away from her.

His cell phone went off and when he looked down, he saw an unknown caller.

"I'm just going to take this outside, baby."

"All right."

Answering the call, he stepped outside, closing the door behind him.

"Hello," Joker said.

"I take it you got my message," Zeke said, taking him completely by surprise.

"What the fuck are you calling me for?"

"I wanted to let you know we disposed of the body. You did good there. I was actually impressed. For a man of your age and upbringing, you can make quite a mess." Joker's stomach turned over. What he'd done to Amy's father wasn't something to be lauded.

"What does my age and upbringing have to do with shit?"

"Your father is a tough man, yet he's pretty much father of the year. You've not had a particularly hard life. You've got a talent for creating pain and I've got a talent for men who like to give pain."

"What the fuck do you want?"

"I want you to consider a job in the future. I could use a man of your skills."

"This is not going to happen."

"Do you really think the Soldiers of Wrath is going to stop this partnership? When they get a taste for the money and the risk, it's going to be a long profitable relationship, one I intend to keep. All it takes is a call to Demon and your ass is mine, Joker. You need to start thinking about the future with that little step-sister of yours. You want her to be happy then you've got to make some sacrifices. We'll talk soon."

All good humor and arousal left him as he closed his burner cell phone. He was pissed off; what he'd done to Amy's father was sick, yet he hadn't cared. Not a second had gone by when he actually cared about the pain he was creating. Was this the kind of man he was? He wouldn't dream of inflicting pain on anyone else unless they hurt the ones he cared about.

Bruce had been a scumbag, and he didn't doubt there were plenty more to fill the gap. Entering the kitchen, he smiled at Amy so she wouldn't know anything was wrong. There were kids, women, men who were all suffering because of assholes like Bruce. He'd set Amy free by killing that bastard. Would he do it again? He killed for the club but never for sport. Could he look in the mirror and call himself a decent man?

"Are you okay, Joker?" Amy asked.

She cupped his cheek at the same time she put a plate full of breakfast in front of him. He went to protest when he saw her plate wasn't full as his.

"Tell me you're happy, Amy."

"I'm happy. I'm with you and everything is great in the world. How can I not be happy?"

She smiled at him and any fight in Joker disappeared. He didn't want to work for Zeke or be part of that bastard's life, any more than he had to be. He was a member of the Soldiers of Wrath, but if he could help others by doing what came naturally to him, then he'd do it. He'd do it for the club, for Zeke, for the people he'd help, but he'd also do it for Amy. One less scumbag on the street made it easier for him to let her walk out there alone.

"Joker," Amy said, grabbing his attention.

"What is it, baby?"

He took a large pancake, pushing it into his mouth. Amy scrunched up her nose. "What? It tastes delicious."

"I love you."

Joker stared at the love of his life. Reaching over the counter, he touched her cheek, caressing her soft skin. Leaving her had been the hardest thing he'd ever done, staying away, even harder. This, being with her, was his reward for keeping the distance.

"You own my heart, Amy, you always have. I love you, and I promise I'm not going to let anything happen to you ever again." It was a promise he intended to keep.

Chapter Ten

They rode toward the large college town of Portsmouth to pick up Zeke's daughter Daniella. It was three hours from Auberdanne, the city where The Soldiers of Wrath held camp. Three of the members were riding on their bikes in front of the SUV Joker was driving. Demon and Shakes were in the vehicle with him. They were silent, nearly at their destination, and had to deal with the trip back with the pampered daughter of the man that Joker still considered their enemy because of how it went down with Deanna. The fact that they were helping Zeke, the man that had crossed them, pissed Joker off, too. But Zeke could still do damage, he was deadly, had an army behind him, and part of their agreement was helping him when he asked.

"I bet she is one uptight bitch," Shakes said from the backset. They had all been thinking that. Her father was a coldhearted sonofabitch, and because of that, they could only imagine what she was like.

"And why couldn't he do this himself, or get one of his fucking henchmen to pick her up like a damn taxi service?" Shakes asked again, his annoyance clear.

"Man, I don't know, but bitching about it isn't going to make this trip any better," Demon said. All of them were annoyed that they had to drop what they were doing just to go pick up the underground Princess.

Joker didn't want to leave Amy, not after they had finally found a good place in their relationship, but she was safe at home, and that thought was getting him through this. He hated having to be at the beck and call of some psycho that had the club by the balls.

"So, Amy is yours now, yeah?" Demon asked. Joker glanced at the President of club and saw the other man staring straight ahead. Joker had known this was where the conversation would go once they were trapped inside this metal box on wheels.

"I want her as my old lady, have claimed her, and ain't nothing stopping me from making Amy fully mine."

"I hear that and understand," Demon said.

"I don't understand any of that woman and old lady shit. Man, I'll stay single and fuck all the sweet-ass pussy I can get my dick into." Shakes said from the backseat, his voice growing a little more animated. Shakes had never made it a secret that he didn't want an old lady. Hell, the man got more cunt in the clubhouse than most of the members put together. He was a man-whore to the nth degree.

"A lot of shit has happened in her past, shit that I won't even go into, but I am not about to turn my back on her or let her go. She's mine."

"Whatever gets you off, man. I don't have anything to bitch about that because it's your life. But for me," Shakes said, "I don't want any woman to tie my ass down. I'll be doing the tying down." Shakes started laughing, and they all knew that the brother liked to get down and dirty with the women he screwed.

Demon switched on the radio, and rock blasted through the SUV. That was their cue to end their conversation and focus on the task at hand. They drove the rest of the way in silence. When they pulled up to the university that Zeke's daughter attended, all Joker wanted to do was turn the shit around and get home to his old lady. They pulled to a stop in front of the main building of the university, but he couldn't see who in the hell they were looking for. Zeke was supposed to have sent a picture to their cells, but of course, the motherfucker hadn't done that. Zeke had assured them that Daniella knew to be on the lookout for them and would contact him when she was safely with them.

"She's probably one of those made-up bitches that has all the luxuries her piece of shit underground father gives her." Shakes said, but no one responded.

Joker stared out the passenger side window, watched as the kids came and went out of the main building, before he saw a young woman that was probably the daughter of that piece of shit. She had long blonde hair, tight as fuck clothes that left little to the imagination with several guys hanging around her. She had one of those little designer purses hanging from her arm, a cell pressed to her ear, and even from this distance, he could see how much make-up she had plastered on her face.

"I bet that's the bitch right there," Demon said, and Joker nodded even though neither of the members were looking at him. She pushed her way through the crowd, looked like she had a stick up her ass. Joker knew that whoever was tied to Zeke was probably just as fucked up as he was. The blonde looked at them and started making her way toward the SUV. Before she got to them, a red convertible pulled up, stopped between the SUV and the Harleys, and the blonde climbed in.

"Okay, so not Zeke's uppity bitch daughter," Shakes said, and they all watched as more people filed out of the building. Another five minutes and Joker was getting pissed because all he wanted was to get back home. But then, there amongst the crowd of pierced, tattooed, and preppy punks, was this mousy young woman with nerdy as fuck looks. She was on the shorter side, definitely plump, and not like the other females walking around in skintight clothing. Her looks screamed she either didn't care, or she didn't know what the hell she was doing.

Joker took notice of her because she was pulling out her phone, staring at the Harleys and SUV like she was confused as hell, then started dialing a number on her phone.

"I think that's her," Demon said, and pointed to the brunette. After a moment, she closed her phone, looking slightly annoyed, and moved closer to the SUV. The closer she got the clearer her looks became. She had pin straight brown hair, her bangs touched her glasses, and her cardigan looked a size too large. Her long plaid skirt touched her ankles and the black Mary Jane style shoes she wore screamed school-girl-geek.

"That's her?" Shakes asked, his confusion clear in his voice.

Joker glanced at him in the rear view mirror. "She's coming closer, so I'm gonna say yeah."

"Damn, she isn't anything like I imagined." Shakes stared out the window. "She's kind of a hot mess in a fuckable way."

Demon and Joker both turned fully in their seats to stare at him. "Man, remember whose kid this is. No fucking her just because you want to stick your dick in any warm pussy."

"Unless you want your cock cut off and fed to you by Zeke and his men, I'd say back the fuck away from that idea," Joker said.

The sound of someone tapping on the passenger side window had all of them facing Zeke's daughter.

"You're here to pick me up, right?" she asked, her words muffled through the glass.

Demon rolled down the window, and she pushed her glasses up the bridge of her nose. She was a cute girl in a very non-made up way. She was plain Jane for sure, endearing maybe, but she was Zeke's daughter. Because of that he had this bitter taste in his mouth.

"You're Daniella?"

She nodded.

"Zeke's kid?" Shakes asked, and Joker saw him in the rear view mirror move closer to the passenger side window. She scrunched her nose, as if disgusted to hear Shakes say that, and Joker found that confusing.

"Yeah, I'm related to him," her voice was distant, slightly soft, but most definitely disgusted.

Demon turned and glanced at Joker, his dark eyebrow lifted as if he, too, was surprised at hearing her say that. Joker's phone vibrated, and he grabbed it out to see Zeke had messaged him.

Zeke: *Daniella said you're there.*

Joker: *Yeah. We're heading out now.*

"That was Zeke; we better head out." He looked over at the two club members ahead of him, gave them the motion to go, and he gestured for Daniella to climb in the backseat. Shakes opened the door for her from the inside, grabbed her bag when she set it on the seat, and Joker watched her climb in. Once the door was shut, Joker continued to stare at her in the rear view mirror. The way she had reacted when they mentioned Zeke led him to believe she might just hate him as much as they did. Shakes was watching her, too, and Joker wanted to smack him upside the head, because the look on the other man's face screamed that he didn't care about anything but getting his dick wet with this young woman.

"Let's roll, man," Demon said, and Joker snapped out of his thought and started the engine. He pulled out of the parking lot and followed the bikes back onto the highway. It would be a long three hours in the car, especially with Daniella looking stiff as fuck, uncomfortable, and trapped in the metal box with three badass bikers.

Amy stared at Deanna and three women that were known as sweet-ass in the club. She knew, at least she had heard, what being a sweet-butt meant, and it slightly nauseated her. To know that a woman would willingly share her body with men she didn't really know, and would have no relationship connection with, baffled her. She had never been with anyone sexually—willingly that is—aside from Joker. Her bastard father didn't count.

"You have a lot on your mind," Deanna said, and glanced up from the pot of spaghetti sauce she was stirring. "I can see the thoughts moving across your face as if you're worked up about something."

She stared at the other woman, knew from Joker that she had been given to the club as payment by her father. Her own father. But she also knew that Deanna was a strong woman. Amy and Joker had talked about the shit that had gone down with Deanna, and although Amy knew club business was not her business, she knew Joker had been honest with her. As she stared at Deanna, knowing that her deadbeat father had traded his daughter because of a debt, Amy knew that her life now wasn't as bad as it could be. Yes, she'd had a shitty past, had lost her mother far too soon, but she was alive and trying to live a healthy life.

"I know you're thinking what I thought when I first got here."

Amy didn't answer, but smiled.

"I was thinking how in the hell could these women essentially whore themselves out? I mean they fuck any and all of them at the snap of a finger, and for what, in hopes of being an old lady or something?"

Amy nodded. "Yeah, that's what I thought, but I know that I shouldn't think and worry about what others do. My life certainly hasn't been perfect, and I have no right to judge others."

"Sweetheart," Deanna set the spoon down. "We can judge, because we've lived a shitty life, know what it means to have to struggle, and because of that, we see things on a different level."

Amy knew what Deana was speaking about and understood where she came from. She'd been an introvert her whole life, and she knew it was because of what had happened to her. To give her body willingly to a man in hopes that he'd love her, just seemed... wrong and sad.

"You're doing okay here though?"

Amy thought about Deanna's question. She had only been here for a few hours, and so far everyone had been nice and accepting. The women that walked around made her a little uncomfortable, because she thought about Joker being here, seeing them, wanting them, and being with them.

"Hun, he doesn't want anyone but you," Deanna said and smiled, and Amy realized she hadn't thought those words, but rather, said them aloud. "There are all these girls walking around, their bodies on parade, and the raunchy shit they do out on display." Deanna shook her head. "When one of these men claims a woman as their old lady, there isn't anyone or anything that will deter them from having them fully." A smile filtered across Deanna's face, and Amy knew that the woman, even if she had been here against her will at first, was totally, madly in love with Demon.

"You're really happy here?" Amy asked her and Deanna didn't even hesitate.

"I am, and I know that if you allow yourself to realize you deserve to be happy, then you'll be happy here, too."

Amy knew that and knew that Joker was the one for her. She just needed to realize and accept that she was worthy of being loved and being happy.

Chapter Eleven

After Amy finished eating Deanna's spaghetti, they made the trip back to David's. Before Joker had headed out on this trip, they'd promised they wouldn't stay too long at the clubhouse alone. She was glad they were heading out. The thought of spending any more time with the women who used their bodies to attract the club members made her uncomfortable. She'd never be like those women.

"So, you and Joker?" Deanna asked. "Who knew he could be like that?"

Amy chuckled. "You sound surprised. Joker's not someone you should underestimate. He'll surprise you." Amy smiled thinking about the Reese she had grown up with.

"He cares about you. Anyone with eyes can see that," Deanna said, reaching over to touch her hand.

"How do you handle this? When the men go on jobs?"

"I don't handle it. To be honest, I've not had a lot of experience with this. Demon and I, we're very new, really new, actually."

"Do you love him? I mean, after everything you've been through, do you love him?"

"Of course; Demon is the only man I've ever loved. I know our situation is not normal for most couples but who needs normal? I love being with him. The club isn't all that bad. You just have to take what you love and leave what you don't." Deanna ran fingers through her hair as she weaved her way through traffic.

"Is that what you did? Take what you liked?"

"Being Demon's old lady, I don't really have a lot of room to choose what I like. He needs me to be strong at his side." Deanna bit her lip. Amy couldn't look away. She really wanted to make this work with Joker. "You know Demon's the President of the Soldiers, right?"

"Yes, Joker told me."

"Then you know it's going to be different for every woman. Before Demon, I was all alone. My mom had passed away shortly before all this happened, and I didn't have anyone. Then out of the blue, the shit happened and my father gave me to the Soldiers to pay a debt. I met Demon and even though it was tough, something eventually just clicked between us. Do you ever have that with Joker? Where it doesn't matter what you've been through, you've got that connections?"

Tilting her head to the side, Amy thought about Joker. Her man, the one she could talk to about anything and not be afraid. "Yes, I've got that with Joker."

"That's how I can handle the club."

"Aren't you worried he's going to use those other women when you're not around?"

"Honey, I don't let him get the chance to be with anyone else."

"What do you mean?"

"I don't know why men stray, but I'm not going to let my Demon get away from me. I'll be whatever he wants me to be. He gives me the freedom to be myself, never judging me. I love him with my whole heart and I love sex just as much as he does."

Amy thought about Joker and his touch. The way his hands caressed and stroked her.

"I see you know what I'm talking about."

"It's down at the end of the street, last house on the left," she said, pointing out the window. Deanna followed her directions.

"You know you can talk to me, right?" Deanna asked. "I'm not going to run back to Demon and talk about this. It would be totally gross."

Amy laughed. "I'm not a very, um, open person."

"Neither am I. I like you, Amy. There's something about you. It could just be the fact I know you're not going to try to steal my man." Deanna parked the car. "This is a nice place. My old place was a shit hole."

"This is my parents' house. My mom, she passed away recently. David, my step-dad, Joker's dad, he lives here. I crash here every now and then." She climbed out of the car. There was no sign of David's vehicle. "It's a nice area though, quiet. Not a lot of kids."

"I love kids. I want a ton of them. I just hope Demon can keep up with the supply I want," Deanna said.

"You want kids?"

"Yeah. I've always wanted a big family. It was only me and my mom, you see. My father was a deadbeat crack head; I hated him. So, I've always wanted a big family."

Amy had thought about kids but completely dismissed the idea. Could she be a Mom? Be responsible for kids? Thinking about Joker, she imagined a little boy who looked exactly like him. The very thought touched something deep within her. Would Joker even want kids? And with her?

No, she was going too fast. They were only just starting out in this relationship. There was no pressure to have kids or get married.

Entering the house, Amy went straight for the kitchen. "You can make yourself at home," she said, calling over her shoulder to the woman.

"Really?"

Amy chuckled. "Is this completely different from the club?"

"Yes. I didn't realize how much time I'd spent at the club until now." She looked toward the sofa. Amy laughed even harder as she sat down, closing her eyes in rapture.

"Don't you have furniture at the club? I didn't see much of the club."

"We have a lot. When you watch what happens to that furniture, you don't trust it. This is like heaven." Deanna relaxed back, looking completely happy. "Peace."

"Why don't you talk to Demon? He'll probably get you some furniture."

"He probably would, but you see, not at the clubhouse. They're animals. Let's not talk about the clubhouse."

"I'll get us some drinks." Amy went back into the kitchen, happy to have finally found a friend. Deanna was a friend. She liked the other woman and for once, Amy was going to try and make sure everything worked out. Joker was her man, and she'd put in the effort to give him what he needed.

Joker glanced in the rear view mirror to see Shakes hadn't turned away from Daniella. The nineteen year old was reading a book. Every now and then she'd push the bridge of her glasses up on her nose. She didn't try to drag them into a conversation nor did she beg for them to stop for a piss break or food.

"So, you're Zeke's kid?" Shakes asked.

Daniella turned to look at Shakes. "Yeah, I guess. Last time I checked I was."

"Checked?" Joker asked, chuckling, thinking Zeke forced a paternity test.

"I didn't want it to be true, so I went to one of those clinics to see if it was real. It's real." Daniella closed her book, letting out a sigh. "What do you want to know?" she asked.

"You paid for a paternity test on Zeke?"

"Yeah, it cost me over three hundred bucks. God, it was the worst day of my life."

"Why would you even want to know if he was your father?"

"Hello, have you met Zeke?" She slapped her hands on her thighs. "He's not exactly the nicest man you're ever going to meet. You're working for him, right? You've seen what an ass he can be, well, why don't you try being his biological daughter. Believe me, it's not exactly fun."

Demon's cell phone ringing interrupted her.

Joker saw her face was bright red and her hands shook a little as they ran through her hair. He thought about Amy. She kind of reminded him a little of her: the vulnerability and the pain, along with the anger. Amy didn't realize it, but she had a lot of locked up anger, and he was worried about that.

"Yeah," Demon said. "Are you sure... No, she shouldn't be there... Her age... Fuck, fine, whatever." Demon hung up the phone. "We need to take her to the clubhouse. Zeke's not finished with business and he'll come to the club to collect her."

"I want to get home to Amy."

"I've still got to pick Deanna up."

Daniella pulled out her cell phone and before anyone could stop her, she was already on the phone.

"Zeke, what the fuck? You told me I had to be home tonight. If you weren't ready for me to come home, I'd have stayed at school. I'd prefer to stay at school."

Joker kept driving even as the young girl's voice grew louder.

He heard Zeke's raised voice over the line.

"Whatever," Daniella said, terminating the conversation. "Sorry, I've got to go to your clubhouse. I wish this wasn't happening."

"You'll be safe there."

"I'm not worried about my safety. You see the three cars behind you? That's my special entourage that goes wherever I go. Dad's that much of a psycho that I've got to have people with me at all times. He also needs you guys to transport me because he knows I try to get out of going to him." She leaned her head against the window.

Joker had already clocked the trailing cars but not thought much about it. "If you've got those men why use us to pick you up?"

"I don't know. Like I said, I hate my father and everything he stands for. I'm sorry to put you guys out like this."

"Don't worry about it. You're just a kid," Demon said.

"Yeah, a pretty big kid for my age." She picked her book back up and no one else spoke for the remainder of the journey. Joker was itching to get his hands on Amy, which he couldn't do until he dropped Daniella back at the clubhouse.

Demon turned the radio on for the last hour of the journey. Joker hadn't heard from either his father or his woman.

Once he was outside of the clubhouse, he watched Demon, Shakes, and Daniella get out of the car.

"I'll be back in a minute. Don't go anywhere," Demon said.

Sitting outside of the clubhouse, Joker let out a breath. He needed to see Amy to make sure she was okay. After their night together, he didn't want to leave her alone for long periods of time. He'd been away for over eight hours and their relationship was new, but more importantly, this had been a huge step for Amy and liable to bring up a lot of painful memories.

Demon climbed back into the car.

"She settled?"

"Do you really think a young girl like that will ever be settled in a clubhouse?"

He thought about Amy and hoped to God she was.

"Let's get this over with."

Joker put the car into gear, heading toward his father's house.

"So, you and Amy are step-siblings?"

"Cut that shit out. We're not related so don't even try to gross me out with it. I'd never touch any real sister and you know it." Joker shuddered at the thought. Amy had always been different.

"Sorry." Demon held his hands up. "When you're like this I forget you're young and you've still got your whole life ahead of you."

He was in his mid-twenties, not exactly young.

"Do you really think Amy has a place in the club?"

"When you took Deanna in, did you see her as the woman you were going to love?" Joker asked, answering Demon's question with a question of his own.

"Look man, I'm sorry; Amy and Deanna are two different people."

"I know which is why you need to back off. I love Amy. She's my woman and with time she'll fit into the club just like Deanna has. It's not going to be easy, but I promise you, I'm going to make it work."

He gripped the steering wheel tighter. Joker refused to have doubts when it came to Amy.

Demon didn't say anything else on the drive. The silence was tense. All he wanted to do was take Amy in his arms, make love to her, and make all of her fears go away. He couldn't give up the club nor could he give up the love of his life. It was a decision he didn't want to have to make.

Blowing out a breath, he parked behind Demon's car—the one that Deanna had obviously driven.

"Well, my woman is still here. That's got to be a good thing."

Demon climbed out of the SUV while Joker locked it up. The moment he opened the door to his father's home, he heard the laughter: Amy's, his father's, and Deanna's. All three were giggling over something.

"Come on, you ladies are totally cheating."

"Am not, it's the rules of the game."

Entering the room, he saw his father shuffling cards as Deanna and Amy were laughing.

"Hey, son, good trip?"

"The best," Joker said, his voice void of emotion.

Amy looked toward him, her eyes twinkling with excitement. "I'm up a hundred bucks."

"What the hell are you playing?" Joker asked, taking a seat behind his woman. He reached out to stroke her neck, touching her rapidly beating pulse.

"We're gambling on snap."

"Seriously?"

"It's fun." She leaned forward, gathering up her cards to show him how much fun. All three of them were pressing cards into the pile, laughing as they caught the same card. His father didn't stand a chance.

"Snap?" Demon asked.

"It's not poker of any kind but it's fun. How long has it been since you played?" Deanna asked.

"I'm a grownup."

Joker snorted.

"Whatever, party pooper."

"How was your ride?" Amy asked, leaning back against his legs.

"Great." He leaned forward and pressed a brief kiss to her lips. He wanted so much more and yet that simple kiss was enough for him for now.

"I'm going to head on up to bed." His father got to his feet. "Deanna, it has been a pleasure to meet you. You must come around again soon."

"I will. It was nice meeting you."

"Come on, baby, time to go."

They both said good night to Deanna and Demon. When they were alone, Amy spun in his arms, wrapping hers around his neck.

"I've missed you," she said.

"Yeah?"

"Yeah," she raised a brow at him. "And, uhm, I was hoping we could have more of what we did this morning."

His cock was on alert and ready.

Chapter Twelve

"I want you so fucking much, Amy," Joker said against her mouth, and she molded into him even more. She felt comfortable with this man, trusted him, and although she knew she had a lot to learn and heal when it came to being with a man, Joker was the person she wanted to experience it all with.

He started kissing her again, wrapped his hand behind her head and tangled his fingers in her hair. God, she wanted to feel him touch her intimately... possessively. She wanted those strong, long fingers stroking her flesh, those lips caressing the most sensitive parts of her. To have all that raw power wrapped up in a six-foot-five frame and over-two-hundred-pound package was almost too much for a woman to handle, but she wanted it. Desperately.

The way he kissed started off almost gentle, but with each passing second he became more demanding. She felt his hand slide along the back of her neck, gripping her nape tight and pulling her forward another inch. She let him fuck her mouth, because, in all honesty, that was exactly what he was doing. But Amy loved it and wanted more of it. He was fucking her lips and tongue with his own, fast and hard, and she could almost picture him above her, his cock thrusting into her with all that aggression. God, she had never met a man that had so much raw sexuality pouring off him like it did from Joker. And right now, she didn't feel fear or her past creeping up on her, threatening to ruin the moment with the man she loved.

He tilted her head to the side, deepening the kiss. Amy's heart pounded hard; she heard it in her ears, felt it in her throat. Her pussy was wet, so incredibly wet that she felt her panties getting saturated. He used his teeth to bite her lip, causing a flash of pain before he smoothed the sting away with his tongue. But strangely, she enjoyed it, craved more of that passion from him. She knew that being with Joker meant she didn't have to be afraid.

"I want inside of you, baby. So. Fucking. Bad." He broke the kiss, and she was left feeling bereft. A chill coasted over her and cooled her overheated flesh. The feel of her nipples poking obscenely against her shirt wasn't lost on her, and the way Joker zeroed in on them made her painfully aware that it wasn't lost on him either. He wrapped his hands around her waist and pulled her against his body until she felt the hard length of his shaft right on her jean covered pussy. All his hard, defined lines were flush with her softer ones. A gush of moisture left her at the contact.

"I want you, Joker. God, I want you so badly." She felt like she was burning alive, and only Joker could ease the fire raging inside of her.

He ran his hand along her sides and cupped her breasts. Acting totally out of character, she arched her back, thrusting her chest further into his grasp. The slow glide of his lips along her jaw had her closing her eyes and letting her head fall back, giving him better access. His other hand pressed against her lower back and slowly made its way lower until he cupped her ass.

"Oh, God. It feels so good, Joker."

"Yeah, it does, baby."

She hadn't meant to say anything, but the feel of one of his hands covering her ass and the other cupping her breast was driving all common sense out of her. When he started moving his thumb over her hard nipple, back and forth, using slight pressure, she would have given him anything he wanted at that moment.

"Amy, you feel so good against me, so right." He breathed against her throat, and as if to emphasize his point, he thrust up, grinding his dick against her material-covered pussy. His voice was so deep and rough it was like a wild animal growling and she turned her head to the side, needing to feel his mouth on hers. He dragged his mouth back up her neck, over her jaw, and ran his tongue along the corner of his mouth. "You know what I want from you, baby?" He continued to kiss and lick the side of her mouth, not giving her what she really wanted.

"What?" Right now Amy wanted pure, unadulterated sex with him, and it was a scary feeling for her because she'd never been so bold with her thoughts, feelings, or desires. He pulled back and looked into her eyes. Her breath caught at the look he gave her. He searched her face while his thumb teased the puckered flesh of her nipple and his hand caressed her ass.

"I want you to strip, get on your knees, and suck my cock." He whispered softly.

Had he just said what she thought he said? From the look on his face, she had to assume she had heard correctly. Swallowing the lump that had suddenly formed in her throat, Amy thought about his request, about if she could really do that... follow his command and pleasure him.

Yes, yes you can, because you love this man, he'd never hurt you, and don't you want to make him feel as good as he makes you feel?

Yes, she did.

"No pressure, baby," he said in his harsh, gravelly voice.

"I want this, want you, Joker."

He groaned and his hands went to the cut he wore. After that was off, he removed his shirt, showing off his hard, muscular and defined chest, and the ink that covered it all. The rolls of muscles that made up his six-pack, his defined pecs, and his bulging biceps were jaw dropping, but that isn't what had her heart pounding in awe.

God, but was she turned on.

Joker stood, gently helped her to stand as well, and cupped her cheek. "Baby, strip for me."

Hearing him say those words had her pulse throbbing between her thighs. It was as if his words alone elicited something deep inside of her, drawing out her needs and wants and combining them all in one hard package that represented Joker. Her hands shook as she gripped her clothing and slowly peeled it up and over her head. She took off everything until she stood before him bared, totally unobstructed. When the air hit her chest, she shivered.

"Now the rest, baby girl."

The way he spoke had her lifting her gaze to his. His voice hitched and she could see his chest rising and falling a bit faster as he looked at her breasts. As if his gaze alone could draw the tissue taut, she felt her nipples pull tighter, felt the blood rush just below the surface of her skin. Amy didn't wait, didn't try and say things should go slower. Even though the chilled air hit every part of her, the very knowledge that he was staring at her had her body hot.

Maybe she should worry that David was just upstairs, that if he wanted to come downstairs, he might see something he'd regret. But knowing that someone could very well walk in on her with Joker was an aphrodisiac all on its own.

When she kicked the garments free, she stood there, her gaze locked on his. She tried to decipher what was going through his head. She let her gaze travel down the length of his body again, stayed a little longer admiring the tight *V* of muscles that disappeared beneath his jeans, then swallowed hard when she saw his erection pressing against his zipper.

"Come here, baby." Voice low and deep, Joker looked fierce at that moment. She found herself right before him again, the heat of his body spearing into hers. Amy's breath came in short, hard pants. His eyes seemed riveted to her chest, but she saw him lower them until she knew exactly what he was looking at. Just knowing that he was looking at her pussy had her shuddering. She felt soaked and squeezed her legs together, praying that her inner thighs weren't wet and he couldn't see it if they were.

"Goddammit, baby girl. You're so fucking hot." He sounded out of breath.

She hadn't realized she dropped her head until she felt Joker lift her chin with his finger. She was caught up in his liquid-blue stare and found herself drowning in the depths of it. Their combined breathing was harsh, and she knew that there had never been a point in her life when she had wanted someone as much as she wanted him; she loved him so much.

"On your knees," his voice was soft, gentle, yet still held a command. His hand landed on her shoulder and he gently pushed her down. The soft carpet beneath her knees sent a flash of heat and a chill up her body, but the sight before her had everything vanishing. His erection was right in front of her, straining against the material, insistent on being freed. Lifting her head, she looked into his face and held her breath at the expression he wore. It was haunting, and she didn't think she had ever seen anything so beautiful.

"Amy." Her name from his lips sounded pained, strained. He cleared his throat and dropped his hands so they hung at his sides. "I need you to touch me, suck me." He breathed out hard. "I *need* you to put my dick in your mouth, but only if you're ready, comfortable. I want you to be able to explore sexually with me, trust me, and not worry about ever being afraid with me."

She took a shuddering breath and pushed all her uncertainty aside. Feeling strength rise inside of her, she lifted her hands and undid his belt buckle, before going after the button. When everything that obstructed her access to his dick was out of the way, Amy licked her lips. Joker groaned above her and she lifted her gaze up to his. Gaze heavy lidded and face a little flushed, he looked fierce with need.

"Go on, Amy, take my dick and suck it into that pretty little mouth of yours."

She didn't waste another minute. Reaching into his pants and boxer briefs, she wrapped her hand around the hard, impossibly thick length of his shaft. He grunted at the contact but she didn't stop. Joker was a large man, and that included everything on his body. She squeezed her thighs together as if that would solve *her* current problem.

His cock was just as strong and powerful as the rest of him, and the bulbous head was flushed red with a drop of pre-cum dotting the slit at the tip. Her mouth watered and she found the thought of her hungering for the taste of him absurd, but then she found herself leaning forward and engulfing the crown into her mouth. He groaned above her and his hands speared into her hair, his nails digging into her scalp. The sting of pain had her sucking in more of his length and running her tongue along the underside of his penis. His taste was slightly salty with a hint of something more masculine, more potent. Amy moaned around him, trying to get even more of him into her mouth, until she felt the tip of him hit the back of her throat. Amy couldn't get enough of him.

"Christ, baby girl." Joker groaned and his cock jerked in her mouth, and a spurt of pre-cum bathed her tongue. She braced her hands on his muscular thighs at the same time he started to pull out of her mouth and then push back in. He fucked her mouth slow and easy and she found herself moving her tongue along his flesh, tasting a burst of saltiness as his semen coated her taste buds.

"That's it. You're doing so good, Amy."

A carnal need to taste all of him, to have his cum slide down her throat, spurred her on. She started bobbing her head along his length at the same time he thrust in and out.

"Yes. Oh fuck, yes." His hold on her hair tightened and his thrusting hips became more frantic in his need for release. "Take it all, baby. Take all of my fucking cock."

"Mmm." Closing her eyes, she focused on getting him off. She'd never really thought about giving a man head, but giving it to Joker had so much pleasure moving through her. Her pussy was soaked and her pulse was pounding in her clit. Hands gripping his strong thighs, she moved them around behind him until she felt the firm, taut cheeks of his ass. They flexed while he pumped his hips. Once, twice, and stilling on the third time as he buried his dick all the way in her mouth, she felt his balls bump her chin and his cum coat the back of her throat. His orgasm was powerful, and she felt her own pleasure mounting.

She wanted to reach between her thighs and rub herself, knew that it would only take a few hard strokes and she would be going right over with him. But he pulled out of her, breathing hard and fast, and lifted her up so she was standing once again. He lifted his thumb and brushed a drop of his cum from her bottom lip and forced the digit into her mouth. He made her lick it clean, made her drink all of him. Her breasts swayed from the force of his movements and then she was pressed against his chest. His mouth crashed against hers and his hands slid down her body to cup her ass.

His cock was starting to harden again between their bodies and she pressed closer, needing the feel of his body. Joker ran his tongue along her bottom lip, and she wondered if she'd be able to deny him anything, especially when it seemed her body was now running the show.

Joker had a firm grip on her hand as he led them upstairs and to her room. Once they crossed the threshold, he let go of her hand and shut the door. "Get on the bed, Amy, let me see you sprawled out for me."

She was still nude, and if he hadn't assured her David wouldn't walk out and see them, she probably wouldn't have allowed herself to walk around naked. But he fucking loved it, loved every inch of her body. She moved onto the bed and scooted to the center. Knees bent and hands flat on the bed, she braced herself up, and watched him with hooded eyelids.

"Lay flat on your back and spread those thick, gorgeous thighs so I can see the pussy that I own."

She did as he asked without hesitation. He moved closer, loving that she was all his. The sight of her lying on that bed, offering herself to him, had his cock fully hard again. He shucked off the rest of his clothing, grabbed his dick, and started stroking himself. Every inch of her body on display for his visual pleasure was slowly draining his self-control. The idea of teasing her to the brink of orgasm was a delight he was not about to pass up. Here she was, ready for his taking, and he wasn't going to say no. He didn't want her thinking about anything and anyone else, seeing or hearing anything that didn't directly result from what he was doing to her.

He moved onto the bed and took up residence between her legs. Placing his hand on an inner thigh, he pushed them open even farther. She stiffened for only a second before she opened fully for him. Her cunt was a thing of beauty, all smooth and pink, glistening with the wetness *he* caused. She was primed for him, but he wanted her soaking, dripping with nectar, until she drenched the sheets beneath her.

"Your pussy is a pretty shade of pink, sweet Amy."

Her chest rose and fell and his gaze was torn from her mouth to the smooth lips of her pussy. He lifted his hand and ran his finger down the center of her wet pussy. Her body visibly shook, and he smiled, loving that just the slightest touch from him affected her so quickly. Placing his thumb on her clit, he pressed into it while he slid his index finger over her slickness and circled it around the opening of her body. Her legs seemed to fall open even wider and a soft mewl left her. Slipping his finger into the wet, hot depth of her body, he grunted when her pussy sucked the digit inside.

He finger fucked her in long strokes while he rubbed hard, slow circles around the swollen little bud of her clit. The breathy cries that came from her had his cock throbbing and leaking cum. He used his other hand to grip his shaft. Tightening his fingers around his aching member, he started tugging at it as he thrust with his finger into her. He could have come just from watching his finger dip into her body, but he wanted to hold off until he could blow his load inside of her, feeling her snug little pussy gripping him.

He wanted her on the verge of coming. He wanted her to beg him for it, to give him anything he wanted just so she could get off. She would get there. There was no doubt that, by the end of the night, he would fuck her good and hard, and giving in to what they both desperately wanted.

"Joker, oh God." The way his name fell from her lips, all breathy and full of need, had him gripping his shaft harder. Fuck, he wanted inside of her so bad. "Please. I'm so close." She squirmed on the bed, her breasts thrust out and her hips rising to meet his plunging finger.

Leaning forward, he pressed a kiss to the side of her mouth, and slid his tongue out to run it along her bottom lip. He ran his fingers over the swollen bundle of tissue again and she cried out, her pussy gripping his fingers. She was close. He could feel it as her inner muscles tightened around the digits. He knew it would only take a little pressure on her clit and a little twist along the bundle of tissue and she would go off.

Joker removed his fingers, and she moaned. He ran his palm over one of her breasts, needing to touch her mounds. Joker sucked her cream from his digits, not able to help himself. Her nipples were hard and tight, the air making them poke up as if begging for his mouth. Leaning over, he suctioned his lips over the turgid peak.

"It's so good."

He grinned around her flesh and ran his tongue over her nipple. She tasted so fucking good. Her flesh was as smooth and he knew he'd never get enough. While he sucked and licked, he moved his hand back down her stomach and to the hard little knot of nerves at the top of her pussy again. A cry left her, and she begged him for more.

He let her nipple go and closed his eyes as pleasure moved through him. "I love you so much, baby girl."

"I love you, too, Joker," she whispered, and strained forward.

He circled her clit, harder, faster, drawing out her pleasure. Latching his mouth onto hers, he stroked her body until she shook and cried out against his lips. He swallowed her cry of pleasure, feeling his own need to be buried inside of her mounting to an uncomfortable level. He found himself pressing his hips into the mattress, trying to let off some of the lust he had for her. It was no use. There was no denying that there wasn't a substitute for what he really wanted.

He placed a hand on each of her thighs, feeling the delicate flesh of her skin, dampened from her need for him. He was harder than he'd ever been. Placing the very tip of his cock at the entrance of her pussy, he lifted his eyes to her. Amy's cheeks were flushed and her hairline was wet. He pushed into her, filling every succulent inch of her pussy with his cock. Her mouth opened and her back arched. It was the most erotic thing he had ever seen.

Oh. Yes. More. *So much more.* Amy couldn't help the long moan that spilled from her when Joker thrust his massively huge dick into her. She could feel the coarse hairs dotting his thighs as he moved inside of her, scrapping her delicate flesh. She could feel his sweat-slicked skin glide effortlessly against hers. Joker thrust his shaft into her, her wetness and arousal making his movements fluid, easy, and fast. The very tip of his cock hit the very end of her and she gasped, loving that she burned at being stretched. It was an intense sensation and one that she wanted to experience over and over again.

"Jesus *Christ,* baby."

Her vision wavered and the tendrils of another orgasm swirled around her, leaving her gasping out his name, begging him for it harder and faster. As her climax burst inside of her, spiraling outward, with flashes of stars in front of her eyes, there was a part of her mind that spoke up, telling her that this is what it meant to be owned and claimed by a man that loved her.

He thrust three more times into her willing body, but he wasn't done with her yet. He rubbed his thumb on her clit and pumped his hips forward, sliding his dick in and out of her still-clenching pussy. "Come for me again, baby. Now."

Another orgasm ripped through her and she felt the world drifting away, but not before she heard Joker grunt from his own climax. His big body stilled and everything around her darkened as she felt him fill her with his cum. He collapsed on top of her, panting for breath, the same as she was, and finally he rolled off her. She stared at the ceiling, hoping David hadn't heard what they had done. But she was too exhausted, too sexually satiated, that she honestly didn't care at the moment. All she wanted was to be wrapped up in the arms of the man she loved, not worrying about anything.

"I love you, Amy," Joker said in a deep, sleep thickened voice. He wrapped a thickly muscled, tattooed arm around her waist, pulled her close, her back to his chest. He ran the tip of his nose up her neck, and inhaled deeply, murmured something she didn't understand, but she knew it was positive and filled with love.

"I love you, too." She closed her eyes, feeling so good, and not because she had been sexually conquered. She felt whole, wanted, and invincible, but it wasn't just because of Joker. She felt like something had started to shift inside of her, move through her, and make her stronger. Amy let herself slip into a contented sleep with the man she loved behind her, protecting her, and her future looking brighter.

Chapter Thirteen

Joker rolled over the following morning to the blaring of his cell phone. He didn't want to wake Amy up but the stupid device seemed to be getting louder.

"You better get that," Amy said, pulling away from him.

Falling out of the bed, Joker scrambled for his cell. He found it in his jeans pocket and Demon's name lit up the screen.

"What?" Joker asked. He didn't expect to be called about club business for a couple of days let alone the next morning after picking up Daniella.

"We need you at the clubhouse."

"I just left you a few hours ago."

"Fuck, Joker. Zeke's coming down, and he wants to see you."

"He's not collected his daughter yet?" Joker asked, sitting up and paying attention. He saw Amy leave the room and head toward the bathroom.

"Nope. She's been at the club all night. Do you want to hear some interesting piece of news?"

"Yeah, sure." He rubbed the sleep out of his eyes and figured he might as well hear it all.

"Shakes gave up his room. He slept on the couch in the main fucking bar, Joker."

"For Daniella?" Joker asked. "He gave his room up for her?" Out of all the men, Shakes was a selfish prick who only ever did anything for himself. This was entirely out of character, but on the drive back, it had been out of character for him to ask her questions. Shakes didn't give a shit about anyone or anything except getting laid.

"Yeah, he gave up his room. Told any man that if they went in, he'd slit their goddamned throat."

"What did you do?"

Joker sat on the edge of the bed, running a hand down his face.

"What do you think? I added to the warning. I don't give a fuck who Daniella is related to. She's a fucking teenager in college. There's no way I'm letting any of these guys think they can play with her. Fuck, this club is not for girls like her."

"I can't believe that bastard didn't come and collect her. Did she put up a fight? Any trouble?"

"Nope, she stayed out of everyone's way. She took the Chinese food Shakes ordered for her and closed the door. It was like she wasn't even here." He heard Demon blow out a breath across the line. "Zeke's a business partner for the foreseeable future. I can't have his kids jeopardizing that relationship we're building up."

"I get it." As VP, it was Joker's job to keep up to date with everything happening in the club. "I'll get Amy and I'll be down there as soon as I can."

"I'd prefer it if you were here when Zeke arrives. Deanna loved Amy. She wants to know when Amy can visit again."

"We're working on it. Amy's still... delicate. I don't want to push her too hard. I don't expect her to just get over shit in one day."

"I get it, Joker."

"I'm patient; I can wait, and I'm going to help her get through this."

"You really do love this woman, don't you?"

"Yeah, I do."

"Okay, see you when you get here."

Demon hung up the phone and Joker dropped his head.

"Problems at the club?" Amy asked.

Glancing toward the bathroom doorway, Joker hadn't even heard her come back. She wore his shirt, and he held his hands out. "Come here, beautiful."

She smiled, walking toward him. Amy was a natural, sensual woman. She didn't need any tricks or teases to make him want her.

Gripping her ass, he drew her close to nuzzle her stomach. "There are always problems in the club. Everywhere I turn there are problems."

"Isn't that the fun part of being in the club?" she asked, sarcastically.

"No, baby." Resting his head on her stomach, Joker closed his eyes. Peace was hard to come by in his world. "There are other things that are a lot more fun being involved in the club."

She started to stroke his hair. Her delicate touch making other parts of him rock hard.

"How did someone so young get to be a VP? What does a VP do?"

"I am Vice President of the club. I took a bullet, almost died, and I've got a pretty face. All the guys listen to me. I think they want to fuck me," he said, raising a brow, trying for coy.

Amy laughed. "There's nothing pretty about you but I can see why they want you. You're incredibly handsome." She leaned forward, dropping a kiss to his lips.

Joker groaned as she deepened the kiss. "Fuck, baby, I've got to stop this."

"Why?"

"The club needs me for club business. It's entirely shit 'cause I thought I had the rest of the weekend with you."

"The girl you picked up?"

"You do listen when I talk?"

"I don't really have a choice." Amy covered her ears. "You make sure I hear you."

She headed to her closet. He slapped her ass, watching it wiggle underneath his shirt.

"You're a little vixen, baby."

Amy chuckled and Joker made his way into the bathroom. She really was the love of his life. His very reason for breathing, and he couldn't imagine anything happening to her. He wouldn't survive it.

After taking a piss, he washed his hands, and then brushed his teeth, which he'd grabbed from his old bedroom, before splashing water on his face. This was not how he imagined the day panning out. Getting dressed, he walked downstairs to find Amy cooking in the kitchen. His father was sipping some juice while reading the newspaper.

"Morning, son. I didn't expect you to be up this early."

"I've got to be heading out. Club business. I'm taking Amy with me."

David nodded. "Good. It'll do her good to get out of here every once in a while. She's spending too much time here again."

"You know, I do own my own place," Amy said, looking back at them.

"I know, and you're more than welcome to come back here anytime. You know that, honey."

"Love you," she said, smiling at his father.

David nodded back. "You better treat that girl with care, Reese."

"I will."

Twenty minutes later, Amy placed a plate full of bacon, eggs, and toast in front of him with a cup of coffee. She took a seat beside him with the same food she'd given David as well.

"You spoil me."

Their breakfast went by in silence as they ate. Joker kept reaching out to touch or stroke Amy, cupping the back of her neck, pulling her close to him.

"Will you two lovebirds be back tonight?" David asked.

"I'm thinking of sticking around at the clubhouse. We're having a bit of a barbeque. Family thing, it'll be good for Amy to meet a few people."

"Sure."

"Do you want to come?" Amy asked, looking pointedly at David.

"Nah, honey. Football's on and I've got a six-pack in the fridge. I'm all set."

He knew his father was still hurting from Brenda's loss. He wondered when he'd start dating again and if he'd even considered it. When Amy left to do the dishes, Joker sat back and asked him.

"I'm old, son. I'm not going to get back in the saddle or whatever you kids call it these days."

"Dad, you can't live the rest of your days alone. You're only fifty."

"To some, I've come and gone." David sat back in his chair, looking sad. "I can't do it just yet. This is the house I shared with Brenda. I just can't think of looking for another woman. Brenda, she was my soul mate... the other half of me. I loved your mother, Joker, I really did, but not like I loved Brenda."

He understood. His parents had a volatile relationship, which meant they could be kissing one moment and fighting the next.

He left his father an hour later, and with Amy on the back of his bike, he headed toward the clubhouse. She had on the helmet he was insistent that she wear even though he broke the law by not wearing one. He was a good, strong, competent driver, but he wouldn't have her putting her life at risk.

Once inside the clubhouse compound, he saw Zeke's vehicle was already waiting. Two of his guards stood outside smoking.

Parking his bike in his spot, he waited for Amy to climb off first before getting off his bike.

"Who are they?" she asked.

"You're about to meet a partner of the club." He took her hand, leading her toward the doors. From the outside they heard shouting.

"I can't believe you left me here." The voice sounded like Daniella.

Entering the club, Joker kept a firm hold of Amy's hand. There, right in the center of the club, Zeke and Daniella faced each other. Behind Zeke were his two bodyguards and behind Daniella, he saw Shakes. His club brother kept his distance and only people who knew Shakes, knew how protective he was being.

"I had business to attend to."

"You could have let me stay at college. You must think you're some kind of god. You call me to tell me we're spending the weekend together. What happened to inviting me?" she asked.

"You wouldn't have come."

"So, you order. It's all the same with you. You're always ordering everyone around to get them to do what you want."

"You're my daughter."

"I'm sure you've got a stash of those around as well. I bet every freaking city has a daughter of yours. My mother wasn't the only one you screwed." Daniella spat each word, glaring at her father.

Zeke didn't lose his cool for a moment.

"I don't have any other children."

"That you acknowledge." Daniella folded her arms underneath her breasts. "Where is my mom?"

"Last time I checked she was vacationing in France."

Daniella shook her head. "I hate you."

"Unfortunately, Daniella, I'm the only one you've got. Your mother doesn't want anything to do with you. I married her so that I could gain custody of you. Providing she stays out of the picture, she gets paid handsomely for it."

From the stricken look on Daniella's face, Joker could tell she'd been aware of the fact her mother didn't want her. It wasn't a shock, no; it was pain, pure and simple. Daniella hurt because no one else wanted her and she didn't want anything to do with the one who did.

"Thank you, Demon, for coming to get me," Daniella said, smiling at him. She moved past Zeke, who reached out to touch her. "Don't you dare! I may be your daughter, but I've not been paid to kiss your ass."

She barged out of the door, leaving the club speechless.

"I'll have to save our business meeting for another time," Zeke said. "I'm sorry for my daughter. She can be emotional."

"It doesn't bother me. Daniella behaved well," Demon said, clearly rubbing it in.

"Yes, well, I've not exactly been the best father to her. I'm sure she blames me for everything that has gone wrong in her life, including her whore of a mother."

"You're married?" Joker asked.

Amy tightened her hold on his hand when Zeke turned to look at him.

"Yes, I was married for a very, very short time. Make no mistake, I love my daughter, and I don't want anything to happen to her. Children, they can be your greatest joy and your greatest pain... I have to go." Seconds later, Zeke left the clubhouse with his bodyguards trailing behind him.

"Well, I have to say, he kind of goes up in my estimation," Steel said, standing away from the bar.

"Why is that?" Demon asked.

"Some fathers would have slapped her silly for the way she talked to him. He may be a bastard to us, but he does love his daughter."

Joker couldn't argue with that.

Several days later, Amy sat inside her office thinking about Joker. She'd spent the entire weekend with him at the clubhouse. He'd wanted to show off his room, and the place he called home more often than not. She'd loved every second of being in the clubhouse. What she didn't like was being surrounded by all the sex that went on. She'd gone to the kitchen while Joker was in the shower and there, she found a couple fucking on the kitchen table. She didn't know what the hell to do, turn away or get the soda she'd been after. Deanna had come down, rolled her eyes, and told her to get what she wanted. "No one stops for anything or anyone here."

After that, Amy was very nervous about who she approached.

Tapping her lip with a finger, she scrolled through the website to make sure everything was up to date on the company's property. *Frances and Son's* was booming at the moment, but with the recent pitfalls with the recession, everyone was on tenterhooks to see where everything would land.

In her two years with the company, they had seen the ups and downs of the market.

"Hey, stranger, it's good to see you back with us," Michael said.

After her last appointment with Gregory, her therapist, she'd taken some leave. Among all the things she had worked through with him, she still needed to deal with the issues surrounding the loss of her mother.

"Thanks, it's good to be back."

"I'm really sorry about your mom."

"Me, too." She offered him a smile even as tears welled up in her eyes. No matter how much time had passed, the loss of her mother was still hard for her to bear. There were times she'd wake up, sure she heard her.

Joker's arms around her kept her safe and grounded.

"So, I was wondering, do you think I could buy you a drink after work?" he asked.

Opening her mouth, Amy was shocked. Michael had always been a nice guy, attentive, but friendly.

"Um, I don't think that's a good idea. My boyfriend is picking me up after work." Calling Joker her boyfriend still gave her a thrill.

Michael held his hands up. "No need to say more. You're taken. I should have known." He stepped away.

Amy smiled, watching him retreat. When he turned his back, she went back to the screen again. The house she was currently looking at was one that had been booked to show that afternoon. Scribbling the address down, she finished up her early duties before heading out.

Driving to the location, she saw the house was luxurious from the designed garden to the private gate. She used her realtor's key code to enter.

Waiting in the car, she saw the vehicle enter the property ten minutes later. Amy tensed up, recognizing the car, and the guy who stepped out of the vehicle: Zeke. From the other side of the car, she saw Daniella climb out. Her palms sweaty, Amy forced herself to leave her vehicle.

"Hello," she said.

"You're Joker's old lady."

"Yes, I saw you at the clubhouse Saturday." Amy held her hand out to Zeke then to Daniella. The younger girl looked shocked to be acknowledged. "Shall we?"

For the next hour, Amy showed Zeke around the house. She noticed Daniella walked a few steps behind her father, never getting too close to him. There was a lot of damage between the two and it broke her heart to see it. Zeke was a bad guy, and Joker had warned her about how dangerous Zeke was, but he loved his daughter. When the tour was finished, Amy turned to them. "What do you think?"

Zeke looked at Daniella. "What do you think, sweetheart?"

"Why are you asking me?"

"I'm buying this for you and me."

"What?"

"You heard me. I'm tired of this fight between us. This house, it's going to be ours but if you don't like it, tell me what you do like, and I'll have Amy look into it."

He was a good father. Amy knew the difference between a good one and a bad one.

"I could find something more to your taste," Amy said, smiling between the two.

"I like it. This is the one," Daniella said.

"Amy, you've just sold yourself a house."

Smiling, Amy went through the necessary paperwork to start the process of buying a house. By the time she made it back to her office, it was past lunch. For the next couple of hours, she took down appointments, and showed another couple a property. At five, she was exhausted and ready to call it a day.

Joker met her at work.

"I came here in my car," she said, wrapping her arms around him.

He held onto her ass, rubbing his cock against her.

"Go and get your car. I'll follow you back. We're going to your place. I think we should give Dad some space."

She nodded, leaving him to grab her car.

The drive back to her small apartment made her feel lonely. It reminded her that her mother was gone and it didn't matter how much she tried, she was never coming back. She hated being lonely more than anything.

Joker was right behind her when she parked her car in the parking lot. He gripped the back of her neck, pressing a kiss to her lips.

"You won't believe what happened to me today," she said, opening her apartment door.

"What?"

"I showed Zeke a new house today. It's a good one, expensive, and nice."

"Zeke bought a house?" She saw the tension in her man. Running her hands up his chest, she tried her best to ease his worry.

"Don't fret. He was nice. I think he's just trying to make a go of it with his daughter. He's trying to break down some of her walls that keep him locked out."

"I don't like it."

"It's work, and I made one hell of a commission off him today by selling it."

"Well, if you're getting money out of it, I say take it."

He kissed her, biting on her bottom lip.

"I missed you today," she said, resting her head against his chest.

"Missed you too, baby."

That moment, her stomach started to protest that she hadn't eaten.

"Go and cook us something to eat."

"Okay." She kissed him again on the lips before walking into the kitchen.

"You've got a couple of messages on your machine. Do you want me to press play?" he asked.

"Sure."

The first message was from over a week ago. She hadn't been back to her apartment in over a week, preferring to spend time with David.

After three messages, Amy paused at Gregory's voice.

"Hello, Amy, this is Gregory. You've missed your last two sessions. Please, give me a call so we can arrange for your next appointment. You're aware how important these are. Thank you."

"Gregory's your therapist," Joker asked, leaning against the fridge.

"Yes."

"Why have you missed your last appointments with him?"

"I didn't think I needed them. I've been doing better. Much better."

"Amy, you can't stop going now."

"But I'm doing so well. We're together, and I feel happy."

Joker closed the distance between them, cupping her face. "Look at me, baby."

She looked up at him.

"I love you. I love you with all my heart and soul. When I decideded to take the next step with you, I did it, knowing you were not completely fixed here." He pressed fingers to her head. "And here," he pressed his hand to her chest, right over her heart.

"What?"

"What that man did to you, it's a miracle you're able to be with me." Joker pressed a kiss to her lips. "Those appointments are important to you. I love you and that's never, ever going to change."

"But I feel fine."

"Now, you feel fine now. That could change in a couple of weeks. Don't stop going, Amy. I'm not going to let anything happen to you."

"You still want me to go?"

"Yes."

Nodding, Amy shrugged. "Then I guess I should go."

"Good, now feed me woman."

"I'm pleased you decided to come back and see me, Amy," Gregory said.

She took a seat in the chair across from him. Her hands were sweaty and a big part of her didn't want to be there. It reminded her of why she'd had to see Gregory in the first place. Joker had taken care of her father. She was never going to see him again, and that made her fixed.

"I see you don't want to be here."

"I just don't feel I need this anymore."

Gregory removed his reading glasses to look at her. He only ever used them to look at the chart he was writing on.

"And why do you think that?" he asked.

"I don't have nightmares anymore. I'm sleeping through the night, too. I'm in a committed relationship. I'm growing up."

"Amy, being here isn't about being a grownup. You've had to grow up faster than a lot of women your age. This is about talking and dealing with the problems that you've faced." Gregory tilted his head to the side. "You're in a relationship?"

"Yes, Jo-Reese, my... friend." Her cheeks heated thinking how gross it would sound if she said step-brother.

"I know who Reese is. I'm not here to judge you, Amy. I'm here to help you so that you can overcome some of your anxieties and fears."

"I'm doing much better."

"And I want you to continue with that progress, Amy. This room, I don't judge you here. You talk freely about everything going on in your life. It hasn't been long since you lost your mother, and a new relationship can add to the stress."

Amy rubbed at her temple, wishing she could express more clearly how much she didn't want to be here.

"I can see you're still not happy being here."

"I just—I want to be with Reese. His name's Joker. He's part of a club. I love him, Gregory. I love him with my whole heart and I want to be everything he needs and loves."

"I imagine Reese loves you very much. Is he aware of your past?"

"Yes."

"How would you feel if I invited Reese in to talk with me?" Gregory asked.

"Wait, what?"

"I'd like to get to know him a little better. I want to help you, Amy. Your mother, she cared about you very much."

"I don't think that's—"

"You're nervous about this aspect of your life. In order to build a successful relationship, you must be willing to open yourself up. Reese needs to know how important it is."

"He does."

"Would *you* object to me talking with Reese?"

The more she thought about it the more she decided her protests were silly. "No, I don't think he'd have a problem."

"Excellent. I was thinking on your Thursday appointment. I'd like the opportunity to talk with him separately and then with you."

"I don't like this," she said. Over the years she'd come to trust Gregory so that she could just say exactly what she was thinking and feeling.

Gregory put his glasses back on. "You've got nothing to be afraid of. I'm more concerned about your absence the past couple of sessions. From the look of you, I can see you're doing great. This is one of the reasons I want to see Joker. I've never seen you looking this happy before, Amy. In all the years I've known you, you've never once entered this room with a smile on your face or your eyes twinkling. The change within you... it's beyond my comprehension. I'm a doctor and I like to see my patients are well taken care of. Brenda, she was a friend of mine as well as a client. I'm here for you," he said.

"Thank you, Gregory."

She was happy. Joker was finally in her life and for the first time ever, she felt safe.

Chapter Fourteen

"Would you like me to call you Joker or Reese?" Gregory asked, and Amy glanced at Joker, feeling all kinds of nervous at this appointment. When she'd asked Joker to come with her to a therapy session, she didn't know if he'd actually agree, although she'd hoped he would. But he had been so willing, especially when she told him she thought it would be good for them to get everything out. Although she was comfortable with where their lives were, and with where hers was going, she wanted to make sure she truly was healing. Amy wanted to know that Joker understood she might be okay on the outside, but there were times that she would struggle with her demons on the inside.

"I go by Joker."

"Okay, then that's how I'll address you," Gregory stated, and wrote something down in his notepad.

She stared at Joker, knowing he had to be semi-uncomfortable in this situation. She knew she had been her first appointment.

"Did Amy tell you why I asked you to attend a session?"

Joker nodded. "She thinks that I should come because of what she went through, and that you want me to understand how fragile she is." She was surprised by his answer because she hadn't been in-depth with him like that. But Joker was so smart and insightful, and nothing got by him.

"I wanted you here because I know you are aware of the past abuse she suffered at her father's hands." She noticed the way Joker curled his hands into fists.

"Yeah, I know all about that asshole, but he won't be hurting Amy ever again."

Gregory didn't speak for a moment, just stared at Joker, and she worried that he'd pick up on the unsaid statement. Yeah, her man had done something horrible, so violent that it should have frightened her. She would never tell anyone that Joker had killed her father. He'd done it to protect her, to save her from her nightmares, and she loved him even more for that.

"I'd ask what you mean by that, or how you could guarantee that, but I don't think you'd tell me, would you?"

Joker didn't respond, just leaned forward and braced his elbows on his thighs. "You know the answer to that, Doc. But I want you to know that I would never hurt Amy. She's my life, the woman I love, and I'd do anything to make sure she's healed and whole. She knows what she means to me; that's why I agreed to come here today. I want her to know that I support her all the way."

Gregory nodded, made a low noise, as if agreeing with what Joker said, and jotted something down.

For the next forty-five minutes they talked about everything Amy had gone through, her progress, and Gregory let Amy and Joker speak together. It was a little awkward and embarrassing to have such a personal conversation with Joker in front of someone else even though she knew she had nothing to be embarrassed about. Maybe it was admitting all of this to Joker and Gregory, or maybe it was admitting it to *herself*?

The first step to healing was healing within; she knew that from her therapy and living her life. If she could accept that life sometimes wasn't picturesque, even if it seemed like it, then she knew she'd be able to accept anything that was thrown her way.

They left Gregory's office after their hour session was up. They stood by the bank of elevators, neither speaking, with this weird vibe surrounding them. She looked at him, knew he was tense and uncomfortable, but he looked relaxed. Maybe she was the only one feeling that way? The elevators opened before she could say anything, Joker had his hand in hers and he pulled her into the elevator.

He wrapped his hand around the back of her neck, and with his other hand, pulled her closer, holding onto her as if his life depended on it. He used his body to press her even more firmly against the wall of the elevator. Amy was suffocating, but in the good way, in the kind of way that stole her breath and made her realize that life was precious.

Taking hold of the short hair at the base of his skull, she tugged lightly on the locks, trying to get him closer. She wanted to be ingrained in this man, let him take everything away so all she ever thought about was being with him. She pulled away, kept her eyes closed, and rested her forehead on his chest. "I love you so much, Joker."

He stroked her back with his hand, and she heard him inhale deeply right by her ear. "And I fucking love you, baby."

Leave it to her man to say it like it was.

"This is all real?" she murmured.

"I sure as hell hope so, Amy." He pulled back, cupped her face, and leaned down to kiss her. "I know this seems so damn crazy, but this is so right." He smiled at her, and she felt her heart rate pick up. "I am not going anywhere, and I won't let you run. You're stuck with me, baby girl, and that's a damn fact." He placed a hand on her chest, right over her heart. "Nothing else matters aside from what we feel in here, and baby, you own my heart."

Two weeks later

The wind was chilly as the sun lowered behind the horizon, and Joker had never felt happier than he did right now. He was on his bike, riding free, with his woman behind him and holding on tight. He was doing something that he'd wanted to do for a long fucking time, but had never had the balls to follow through with. But because Amy was on the road to becoming healed, he knew this was the right step. She was doing so damn well, and he couldn't be happier. The deeper they went into the woods, and the higher they ascended the mountain, the more the temperature dropped and the trees became thicker all around them. He wasn't much of a nature person, didn't give a fuck if he was surrounded by pavement or covered by trees. But for what he wanted to do he sought privacy, seclusion, and needed nothing artificial surrounding them.

He had his old lady on the back of his bike, her arms wrapped tightly around his waist, and her head resting on his back. He was in fucking heaven right now, and couldn't have asked for a more perfect outcome to some shitty situations in his life. There was nothing better than this feeling of freedom with the woman that he loved and knowing that she was the one he wanted to spend the rest of his life with. But his nerves were already getting the best of him and twisting his gut uncomfortably; it was not something he was comfortable or used to.

Another twenty minutes driving up the mountain and Joker finally pulled to a stop in front of a clearing. The trees surrounded them, a creek ran parallel to the small dirt road, and there wasn't a soul in sight. It was perfect, absolutely-fucking-perfect. He cut the engine and climbed off then helped Amy off the bike, too. For a second he kept his hands on her waist and stared down at her, loving that this woman was his. He'd sampled her, couldn't get enough of her, and he knew he'd have the rest of his life to spend with her. It took a strong woman to be with a man like him, a member of an outlaw biker club that killed when the time called for it, dealt out violence, and did shady shit. But his Amy was strong as hell, and he loved her even more for it.

Did she knew what he was about to do, that he had this ring sitting in the inner pocket of his cut and was nervous as fuck? Shit, he hadn't felt this unsure about anything in his life, but he supposed even the toughest motherfuckers felt skittish when they were about to pop the big question. He grabbed a blanket from one of his saddlebags and led her to the center of the clearing. There was a break in the trees and they could see the city below, the lights starting to brighten as dusk fell over the sky. He laid out a blanket and gestured for her to sit down.

"You look nervous, Joker, and that makes me nervous." She smiled, but he could see that it was a little forced.

Fuck, his hands were even shaking, and he hated the fact that this one thing could make him feel so off kilter. "Dammit." He sat down beside her.

"Joker, is everything okay?" she asked, twisting her hands together. She touched his shoulder, and he could see that this was worrying her. He felt like an asshole for not keeping his shit together.

"Everything's okay, baby." He turned and faced her, and before he lost his nerve, he reached inside his cut and pulled out the small velvet box. She looked down at it, and her eyes widened. "I meant to say all this sweet and endearing shit, tell you how important you are to me, that I love you more than anything else, because Amy, all of that is true." He ran his free hand over his hair and exhaled roughly, needing to say this because he wanted her to know she was his world. "I feel out of my element here and have never felt so nervous in my fucking life." He chuckled, hoping to ease some of the tension. He hadn't been good with all the sweet, sappy shit, never had. Hell, he'd never made a woman his like this. It seemed that he was at a loss for those sweet as fuck words that would tell his woman he loved her more than anything else.

"You're my old lady, and that means a lot, but I want you as my wife, too, Amy."

"Oh God, Joker," she breathed out. Her eyes were wide as she stared at the box he had yet to open.

He popped the lid.

"Oh God," she said again. "It's gorgeous."

He took the ring out, snagged her left hand, and slid the platinum band with the big circular diamond in the center on her ring finger. "Look at me, baby girl."

She lifted her gaze so she was looking at him, and he heard her swallow. Now he swallowed and tried to calm the nerves inside him. He had beaten the shit out of grown men, killed anyone that hurt those he loved, and did illegal shit, but asking his woman to marry him made him feel like a vulnerable bitch. "I love you; I have loved you for a long time. I don't care that we are considered step-siblings. I don't care that my past and yours hasn't been a fairytale. I want you, and I know you want me. I want all of you, Amy, and I am offering my life for you, because that's what you mean to me... life."

She started to become teary eyed, and he hoped he wasn't screwing this up. She was going to cry, and he didn't know if that was a good thing or a bad thing.

"I want you by my side as my wife, not just as my old lady, baby." He took her hand in his and lifted it to his mouth to kiss her knuckles. "You've always been mine, Amy, always. Even when we were younger, I knew you'd be mine. I just didn't know how to process those emotions." He stared at her. "Will you marry me Amy?"

When she didn't answer right away, Joker felt his heart start to pound fast and hard. Would she say no? The tears were the next thing that came from her, big, fat tears that slid down her cheeks. He moved an inch back, giving her some space, as those beads of wetness slid down her cheeks. She continued to stare at the ring, and with every passing moment he worried that she was ultimately going to say no.

"Joker..."

"Baby, you're making a man feel pretty fucking worried here, especially when you won't say anything and are looking like you might say no." She looked up at him, and he reached out and brushed her tears away. "Baby, will you marry me?" he asked again. He was a man and didn't know jack shit about women and what it meant when they cried during these situations. Was she happy about this?

"They're good tears, Joker," she chuckled and wiped her tears away. "God, they are really good tears." She fell into his arms, wrapping her arm around his neck.

"So, that's a yes then, baby girl?" He cupped her face and looked into her eyes.

She grinned wildly. "Yes. Yes, of course, I'll marry you."

He kissed her senseless, loving that he was about to make the woman he loved his legally, officially, and forever.

Chapter Fifteen

Six months later

Running her hand over her swollen stomach, Amy stared in the full-length mirror. She wore a white dress that did its best to hide her very pregnant state. Joker had wanted to get married before the baby started to show but she wanted to wait until everything was perfect. It was close to Christmas and throughout the clubhouse everyone was preparing for her to walk downstairs to her man.

"You look so beautiful," Deanna said, running her hand down the full skirt.

"Thank you."

The last six months had been beautiful. She'd loved every second of getting close to Joker. He visited with Gregory regularly now, and they were developing as a couple. For the first time in her life, she was stronger than she'd ever been before. Joker helped her to heal. There were times she was still plagued by the demons of her past but they were so few that she didn't even think about it. He was her rock, and she loved him with all of her heart.

"Can I come in?" David asked, knocking on the door.

"Yes."

"I'm going to leave you two alone," Deanna said, making her way out of the room.

David closed the door behind him. "You know, I always knew there was some connection between you and Reese."

"You know he prefers to be called Joker, right?"

David chuckled. "I don't care. He's my son. My little boy and right now, I've never been so proud in all my life. You both deserve happiness and when I look at you two, I know you're both going to be so happy."

"He completes me, David."

He wrapped his arms around her, holding her close. "Amy, I loved your mother. I always have and I always will. We're not related, but after this day, you will be my daughter for real. I'll always be indebted to you for bringing my son some peace."

Someone else knocked on the door.

"It's time," Demon said.

Everyone was knocking on her door today.

Blowing out a breath, she took David's arm and together they made their way downstairs. They passed brothers who wore the leather cut of the Soldiers of Wrath. She hadn't cared what kind of wedding she had so long as she was getting married to the love of her life. Joker, the man who was the answer to her dreams, had pulled her out of the pit of fear and despair. Rounding the corner, Amy smiled when she saw Joker standing before the priest. She fell even more in love with him in a tuxedo and not the leather jacket she had been expecting.

David handed her to Joker. "Take care of her."

"With my life." He took hold of her hand, leading her to the priest.

"You didn't have to wear this," she said, finding him even sexier than ever before.

"I know. I wanted to wear this. It's our day and when you look back, I want you to always remember that my heart, my body, and my soul belong to you and only you."

Facing the priest, she held Joker's hand more firmly. He was hers and she was his. At the end of the ceremony, when the priest asked if anyone objected, there was silence all around the clubhouse. No one would dare question their union. Joker slid his ring onto her finger and she did the same with hers. She was his old lady, and he was her old man, and it would be that way until they breathed no longer.

"It hurts," Amy said, panting after she tried to push. It had been several months since their marriage and Joker was regretting getting her pregnant. Every part of their life was bliss, filled with happiness and love.

"I know, baby. One more push. You heard the doctor."

"He's not even crying yet," Amy said. "Ouch, it hurts."

Stroking her head, he whispered words of love and encouragement. Amy was his heart and soul. There wasn't anything he wouldn't do for her. If she asked him to jump, he'd ask her how high. He was devoted to her.

In the last few months he'd proven to her that she was not broken. For so long she'd truly believed she was a broken woman incapable of love and being loved. He'd showed her something different. His woman wasn't broken. She might be a little bit bent, but they all were, and he loved her even more because of it.

She gave another push and then the sound of a squealing baby filled the room.

The nurses started to clean up the baby and then Joker looked up. Held before them in a blue blanket was a beautiful baby boy: their boy, his and Amy's first child.

"I love you, Joker."

Staring at the precious gift she'd given him, Joker held her tight, both of them embracing the little life they'd created.

"What should we name him?" she asked.

"It's your choice, baby girl."

She smiled and looked down at the baby. "I guess we don't have to decide right now." She looked at him then, her eyes full of love, her face covered in sweat and exhaustion. "I want more, Joker. I want a big family so no one will ever feel alone again."

They'd both been only children, and he would have given her, would give her, anything she wanted. Pressing a kiss to her head, Joker agreed. "We're going to have more children. You can count on it."

The End

HARD AS STEEL

The Soldiers of Wrath MC, 3

HARD AS STEEL (The Soldiers of Wrath, 3)

Sam Crescent and Jenika Snow

http://www.CrescentSnowPublishing.com

http://www.SamCrescent.wordpress.com

sam_crescent_fanmail@yahoo.co.uk

www.JenikaSnow.com

Jenika_Snow@Yahoo.com

Published by Crescent Snow Publishing

Copyright © April 2015 by Sam Crescent and Jenika Snow

Digital Edition

First E-book Publication: April 2015

Edited by Editing by Rebecca

Eloise has kept her desires in the dark her entire life. Not sure if she should feel ashamed over her need to have a sexual relationship that consists of pain, she focuses on keeping to herself, knowing that she can never have what she really wants.

Steel is a member of The Soldiers of Wrath MC. He is a man that takes what he wants when he wants it; he is never denied. But he wants Eloise, and her refusal to give herself to him makes Steel want her even more. He's determined to break the composed and collected exterior that she carries.

When Hanson, Eloise's boss, attacks her, it's Steel that comes and rescues her. Steel feels something for the woman that's seemed to turn his world upside down in such a short time.

But Hanson isn't about to be put in his place, or lay down without a fight. He'll show Eloise and Steel that he'll take what he wants regardless of any threat.

Can Eloise give herself to Steel fully, or will her fear for what she really wants hold her back? Can Steel finally allow himself to commit to a woman and show her that what she wants is exactly what he desires to give her?

Chapter One

Steel leaned against his bike, watching Markam's store for a sign of Eloise. He was going fucking insane with this bitch, and he needed to get her out of his system. Something needed to fucking give before he went insane. Tipping back the bottle of beer, he glanced around the dark parking lot. It was summer and hot as shit. He wasn't wearing his leather jacket and had removed his white vest hours ago.

Night wasn't any reprieve from the heat either. It was too damned hot and sticky. The boys back at the clubhouse were partying it up, fucking all the pussy they could ever want. What was he doing? Oh, yeah, standing outside a damned supermarket waiting for a bitch who wouldn't even give him the time of day.

He was tired of this shit.

Running fingers through his hair, he growled as the long length fell over his eyes. He hadn't taken the time to slick it back with gel to keep it out of the way. What he really needed was to get his hair cut. He didn't trust strangers with his hair. No, that wasn't true; he didn't trust anyone close to him with scissors or any kind of weapon.

Throwing the beer into the trash bin, he watched the final customer walk out of the store. In the next moment, Hanson, the piece of shit boss, started to close up the store. Steel could just make out Eloise at one of the registers. She wore the uniform shirt and a skirt this time. Her long hair was tied on top of her head. She looked tired even from where he stood.

The way Hanson made his way toward Eloise didn't sit well with Steel. He recognized the look, the intent, and he knew instantly something was going wrong.

What if she's fucking him?
What if she doesn't want you?
What if she wants him?

He'd tried to get Eloise in bed, ordering her to fuck him, but that hadn't worked. Women fell for him hook, line, and sinker, yet Eloise wouldn't give him the time of day. She plagued him every moment of every day with her beauty. When he closed his eyes at night she was the person he saw, and it was the same when he woke up. It didn't matter if he was balls deep inside a cunt. Her face appeared before him like a vision.

It was messing with his head, messing with his ability to disconnect with the world. He didn't like it. She had this power that no other woman had before. What was it about her? She never wore revealing clothes. The only thing he'd seen of her body was her arms and her plain but gorgeous face. She wore clothes that were way too big and not attractive at all.

She was pissing him off, and he didn't like it, not one bit.

What had she actually done to him? Nothing. She served him when he went to her register, nothing else. She didn't lead him on or make him think something that wasn't there.

It's all in your head.

He stared at the doors, waiting for them to open or for one of them to come out. Steel frowned as he took in the front of the shop. Eloise and Hanson were not there anymore. He didn't like it. His gut clenched as if something was wrong. Moving closer to the supermarket, he stared through the glass but couldn't see anything. Trying the doors, he found they were locked, not that he expected them to be open.

Annoyed, he was tempted to leave it at that.

"Fucking women." Eloise didn't want anything to do with him. It was the heat and the fact he'd not had a nice warm pussy in so long that put him in this annoyed state.

What if something's wrong?

Glancing over at her car, he growled in frustration. He couldn't just walk away. A few months ago he'd found Hanson treating her like shit. What could the bastard possibly want with her now?

Before he could talk himself out of anything, he started making his way around the back. What would it hurt to check on her?

"Will you come to my office, Eloise? There's something I want to discuss with you," Hanson said.

Glancing toward the parking lot, Eloise couldn't make out her car or anyone outside. It was late, she was tired, and just wanted to leave. "Can we take care of this tomorrow?"

"No, I want to talk with you now!" He shouted the last word, causing her to jump. She hated being yelled at. Taking a deep breath, she nodded.

"I'll finish up my register and be back to see you."

"Make it quick. I don't like to be kept waiting."

Ben had called in sick so there was only the two of them to run the whole store. Rubbing her temple, she tried her best to ignore the twisting in the pit of her stomach. Being alone with Hanson wasn't something she liked. The guy gave her the creeps. Using a cloth, she wiped the sweat from the back of her neck. The heat wave they were getting was making life even more uncomfortable.

Once she finished, she grabbed the bag of money to be taken to the bank, and made her way into Hanson's office. He was sitting behind his desk, looking smug about something.

"Here are the deposits. Everything is there, no problem."

He took the bag from her.

"Sit down, Eloise."

She took a seat, staring across the desk at him. "Is anything the matter?"

Ever since Steel had threatened Hanson, he'd kept his distance. She'd noticed his gaze on her, but he'd never been alone with her until now.

"I have to say I'm a little disappointed in you, Eloise."

"What? Why? I work hard for the store." If she even tried to think of working any harder for him, it would make her sick to her damned stomach. Hanson was a slave driver. He'd do anything to get out of paying overtime, or crediting the staff with good work. They put up with it because at least a shit job was better than no job at all.

"Oh dear, we're not going to see eye to eye." He stood up, moving around the desk to lean on it. She didn't like how close he suddenly was. "What will you do to keep your job?"

"Are you firing people?"

He leaned forward, putting his hand on her thigh. "Come on, Eloise. You must know what you do to me."

She panicked as he moved his fingers down her thigh, past her knee, and grabbed the hem of her skirt. He teased her flesh, making her sick. Slapping her hand over his to stop him from moving farther up, she glared back at him. "What the hell are you doing?"

"If you want a job, you're going to have to spread those pretty fucking thighs. I'm sick of seeing you in those skirts, of teasing and tormenting me."

Eloise pushed the chair back. Hanson didn't stop as he reached out and grabbed her. There was nowhere for her to go. He grabbed her arm, hauling her up against him. "You're going to give me what I want."

"Let go of me." She screamed the word, kicking him in the shin. He released her long enough for her to step back. It wasn't far enough for her to get away, though. Before she got to the door, he'd reached out, tugging her hair back. She cried out at the sudden burst of pain. He threw her away from the door with enough force that she fell. Out of the corner of her eye, she watched him shut then lock the door, closing off her way toward freedom.

"You've not got a choice. If you want your job, you'll fuck me."

Getting to her feet, Eloise didn't have much time as he shoved her back down. She fell to the floor, and he was on top of her. He pushed her skirt up and started to claw at her panties. Fear, unlike anything she'd ever felt, consumed her.

"Stop! Stop it! Let me go!" She screamed, yelled, and fought him as he tried to take from her what she wasn't offering.

"You little bitch. You've done nothing but tease me."

She'd done nothing, had not teased him, or lured him in. Eloise had done everything to stay out of his way.

Fighting with all of her might, she was no match for him. He was bigger and outweighed her.

There was a loud bang and, suddenly, the door to the office slammed open. Eloise barely had time to think before Hanson was pulled off her.

"You filthy, fucking, piece of shit." Steel slammed Hanson against the wall. He glanced down at her. She quickly pushed her skirt down, trying to calm herself down mere seconds from being attacked.

Steel didn't stop. He started to attack Hanson, slamming his fist in the other man's stomach, face, and body. She was amazed as he threw the other man around as if he weighed nothing.

"When a woman says no, she means fucking no," Steel said, yelling each word.

Getting to her feet, she stumbled after Steel. Hanson tried to land a few blows but nothing hit flesh.

"Stop, Steel. He's not worth it."

Steel slammed his fist into Hanson's face one last time. She heard the distinctive sound of something breaking, and Hanson fell to the floor, out cold now.

Eloise couldn't believe what had happened only moments before.

"Shit, baby, are you okay?" Steel reached out to cup her face.

"I don't know what I'm feeling right now." She glanced over at Hanson. "He's alive?"

"Yeah, the fucker should be dead for what he was about to do."

"Should we call the cops?" she asked.

"No, no cops." Steel said.

He was right. "No, I can't talk to the cops." She couldn't talk to anyone. The thought of telling anyone what happened freaked her out. There was no way she'd survive it.

"Do you want to talk about it?"

"No, I don't." Tears filled her eyes, spilling down her cheeks as she looked at him. "I don't want to do anything like that right now." She shook her head. "This is insane and crazy. I can't believe this has happened." Staring down at her hands, she saw they were shaking badly.

"Come on, I'll take you home."

"What about him? We can't just leave him like that." Fuck, what about her job? What was she going to do? This was a shit job but at least she had one, one that paid the bills.

"I'm going to get you home, and then I'll come and have a talk with him."

"I need this job, Steel." She stared into his eyes.

"You can't work here after what just happened."

"I don't have a choice. I've got bills to pay." She couldn't believe she was even thinking about this.

Steel caught her face in his hands, cupping her cheeks, and stopping her from pulling away. "I'll think of something. Come with me." He eased an arm around her and before she knew what was happening, he was helping her into her car.

"I can drive."

"You can't even think straight right now. I'll handle it. I'll handle everything." He moved toward the driver's side, climbing in. She was so confused right now. What was he doing?

Eloise couldn't find her voice. She was all over the place emotionally.

Steel surprised her even more by driving her straight to her apartment building. *How does he know where I live?* Before she could ask, he climbed out of the car, helping her toward her place.

"Steel?"

"Don't worry about it. I'm going to sort everything out and you don't have to be concerned about a thing."

She reached into her skirt pocket, pulling out her apartment keys. Eloise had such a small set of keys that they fit into her pocket and she hated carrying around a purse. He took the keys from her, escorting her up to her apartment.

"I want you to take a shower, drink some hot chocolate or coffee, or whatever the fuck women drink, and I'll be back as soon as I can."

"Why are you helping me?" she asked.

"Someone has to. Tell me you can do this. I've got to go and settle things with Hanson."

She nodded, biting her lip. "Go, go and take care of what you need to."

He stared at her for several seconds before he nodded. "I'll lock the door on my way out."

Steel was gone, leaving her watching after him. What the hell had just happened?

Chapter Two

Steel drove back to the grocery store, parked her vehicle in the back of the parking lot, and felt adrenaline and rage move through him. He'd called a couple of his brothers from the MC to come to the store and follow him back to Eloise's so he'd have his bike and her car at one place.

He should have killed the bastard, made him suffer and pay for putting his hands on Eloise. It didn't matter that she wasn't Steel's old lady. It also didn't matter that she'd turned him down. He wanted her, and this dark desire to possess her, to own her completely in any way that he saw fit, consumed him. Hell, he knew where she lived because he'd followed her home one night. How fucked up was that? He could have been called a damn stalker for coming to her employment and just watching her through the window, but the truth was he didn't care what label someone put on him. He'd seen Eloise and something had sparked inside of him; he knew he had to have her no matter what.

He moved through the store and placed his hand on the office door as it barely hung on its hinges. Steel leaned against the doorframe and crossed his arms over his chest. Hanson was awake, holding a bloody rag to his face, and looking like he'd just gotten the shit beat out of him.

He's lucky that's all that happened. He's lucky he's still breathing.

When Hanson saw Steel standing there, he scurried back against the wall and tried to stand. His eyes were wide, and the stench of fear filled the small office. Good, the motherfucker needed to be afraid, needed to worry about his life.

"No more," Hanson said and raised a hand in front of him, as if that would really keep Steel away if he'd wanted to approach.

Steel pushed away from the doorframe and stalked closer to Hanson. No matter how much that man squirmed and tried to move away, Steel came closer. The wall stopped his retreat, caging him in so he had nowhere to go. When Steel grinned, not one of amusement, but one of predatory delight, Hanson started stuttering.

"No more," the other man said.

"Listen up, motherfucker," Steel took a step closer. "You fucked with Eloise, the woman that I've claimed as mine. I don't want anyone touching her, even coming up to her and speaking to her if it causes her harm." Steel felt anger boiling inside of him as he pictured this little weasel touching what was his. He pointed his finger at Hanson's chest, jabbed the digit into the other man's boney fucking flesh, and bared his teeth. "You understand me, asshole?"

Hanson nodded frantically.

"Because if I ever find out you put your hands on Eloise again, touched her in any damn way, I'll hunt you down like a dog and slit your fucking throat."

Hanson stuttered out something, looked away, and Steel reached out and slapped him across the face.

"You fucking look at me when I'm talking to you, asshole."

Hanson promptly looked up.

"Eloise will no longer work here, but what I said still holds true." He leaned in an inch. "I know how to make a person look like they died on accident, or fuck, not found at all, got it?"

Hanson nodded.

Steel turned and left, not about to deal with this piece of shit a second longer. He wanted to go back to Eloise and make sure she was okay, make sure she wasn't alone after that fucking prick attacked her. He wanted to tell her that he wouldn't give up on what he wanted with her, wouldn't just walk away. There was something about her that Steel wanted, something innocent and pure, totally different from what he was used to. Steel fucked hard and liked dark temptations. He saw a glimmer of something in Eloise that called out to the man that was not only a biker, but a Dom as well. The images of Eloise tied to his bed, her body stretched out for him, and the thought that he could do anything he fucking wanted, had his cock so hard on so many occasions that not even beating off had relieved his ache.

Shakes and Striker showed up shortly after he stepped outside. Shakes climbed out of the SUV, and once Steel handed over his keys to his bike, the three of them headed toward Eloise's place. Striker could take Shakes bike to the clubhouse once they got to Eloise's, and then Steel was going to have her all to himself.

He was going to lay it out there for her, tell her that he wasn't just going to walk away, not until they sated each other into sexual exhaustion. If she was done with him after that then Steel could try to step back. However, if he fucked her and needed more, well then, he might not be able to walk away.

Eloise twisted her fingers together and stared out her window. She knew Steel would return, felt that knowledge in the pit of her stomach. He might not know she was aware that he'd been outside the store on several other occasions, watching her, maybe trying to convince her that she was for him, or at least for one night. Maybe she should have called the cops, because hell, wouldn't that constitute stalking? He knew where she'd lived. Despite the creepy factor, there was another part, an almost forbidden part, which liked that he had taken such an interest in her. What man had ever done that? She'd never been attractive in school, not with her chubby, short body, or the fact she was the geek. She'd never been so desired that a man felt the need to watch her, or insist that she be with him. Well, to be fair, he'd only asked her to go home with him once, but even though she'd said no, he still came to the store, still looked at her as though she were his prey.

The sight and sound of a vehicle pulling into her apartment complex parking lot had her heart beating faster, and a tightening in her gut. She was nervous, so nervous, because the truth was she did want Steel. Eloise wasn't a virgin, but she had never spoken of what she really wanted in the sexual department, too afraid of what the two men she'd slept with would say to her, think about her.

Although Steel scared her on a primal level, and one of the reasons she'd turned him down, she knew he wasn't like the men she'd been with in the past. He was harder, stronger, and darker in every aspect. Would he want to tie her up, want to spank her until her flesh burned and turned red? Would he like denying her pleasure, only to see that it heightened hers even more? She'd been ashamed of her desires, of the pain that she wanted to experience with sex. She was humiliated because she wondered who would want to do those things with a Plain Jane like herself.

Moving away from the window, she smoothed her hands down her thighs and felt her heart skip a beat. What would he say right now? What would he want from her? Was he the type of man that would demand she offer him some kind of payment because he'd helped her out? He certainly had that hardcore, take no shit look and attitude to him. Eloise might be many things, but she wasn't a weakling that would take shit from anyone, least of all a biker that would want her to sleep with him because he'd saved her from a prick like Hanson.

The knocks on the door had her jumping slightly. They were hard, forceful, dominating. Eloise moved close to the scarred wood, wrapped her hand around the tarnished brass knob, and pulled it open. She'd be strong in the face of Steel, but her desire for him also made her weaker in that sense. But being with him, giving herself to him wouldn't be the worst thing in the world...right?

Chapter Three

Steel leaned against the front door of Eloise's apartment door, waiting for her to open it. He didn't want her alone after the shit that had happened. He'd already spoken to Demon, and it was fine with him to have her working at the club. She'd serve beer and do the general cleaning around the main part of the clubhouse. All Steel cared about was the fact she'd be closer to him. He didn't like the thought of her being out there all alone.

"It's me, Eloise," he said, calling through the door.

She opened the door, staring at him. "I didn't know who it was, but I'd hoped..."

"That it was me?"

"Yes."

"It's a good thing it is." He noticed she hadn't taken a shower like he'd told her to. "Do you want to go to the police?"

"No."

"Why didn't you want to take a shower?"

"Because nothing happened. You stopped it."

"Let me tell you something, Eloise. I stopped him from raping you. That fucker was going to try and shove his dick where you didn't want it to be. If I'd not come along when I did, you'd be telling a whole different story."

"Who's going to believe me anyway?" she asked.

He frowned. "What?"

"Who in their right mind is going to believe that someone wants to rape me? Look at me? I'm nothing pretty to look at. Why would anyone go through the effort of getting into trouble over me?"

Steel was shocked, too stunned to even say a word.

"I'm ugly and plain. There's nothing amazing about me. They'll all just laugh." Tears were streaming down her face and he wanted to kill Hanson for being responsible for them.

Reaching out, he grabbed her arms, hauling her up against him. "Don't ever fucking put yourself down like that again. Do you hear me? I don't want to fucking hear that kind of shit coming out of those pretty plump lips."

"It's the truth."

"No, it's not. It's not the truth." Sliding his hands up her arms, he cupped her face, forcing her to stare right back at him. "You've got no idea how beautiful you are." He couldn't look away from her even if he'd wanted to.

"You're lying."

"Baby, even though I shouldn't be admitting this, I've spent a great deal of time camped outside that place you work just to see you. I'm not fucking lying and I'm not blind." He took her hand and pressed it against his stiff cock. "You feel that? That's how fucking hard I am for you right now. You're not plain or ugly. You're fucking beautiful and you don't even see how gorgeous you really are." He stroked her cheek, releasing her hand from his cock at the same time. "Don't ever put yourself down in my company or I swear to God, I'll make sure you can't sit down for a damn week."

"You swear a lot."

"Get used to it. Now, you're going to get washed. I don't care what you say. I'm going to take care of you and for me to do that, you're going to learn to listen."

He watched as she bit her lip, clearly wanting to fight him. Steel wasn't prepared to listen to a word of what she had to say.

"I'm not used to this. You don't have to stay."

"I'm staying. I'm going to order Chinese. You do like Chinese, right?"

"Yes, I do." She stared down at his chest, licking her lips. "What about Hanson? You hurt him pretty bad, and he's not a nice person."

"I've talked with Hanson. He's not pressing any charges and if he does, I'll tell the cops exactly what I was breaking up. You wouldn't let me be put away for helping you, would you?" he asked.

"No. Of course not."

"Good. Go and get washed. I'll be right here." She nodded her head, taking a few seconds before she finally turned on her heel and walked away. He waited until she was gone before removing his jacket.

Her place was nice, a little small, but then he didn't know much about her. She didn't seem to have any family close by or many friends. The only real thing he knew about her was the job at the grocery store. Glancing around her living space, he didn't see any personal photos of friends or family. Was she a loner? Was she trying to run from a life she didn't like?

So many questions and yet so few answers from looking around her space. She liked to read, he saw that with all the used books. They were all well read, but he didn't recognize a single author or title.

He put the order in for the Chinese, asking for half of the menu since he didn't really know what she liked. When that was finished, he walked into her very small kitchen, which consisted of a sink, stove, fridge, and a small counter. Rubbing the back of his neck, he groaned. He didn't like the small space that she lived in. She deserved something bigger, grander than this. What the fuck was he talking about? Grander? He didn't even know her, not well anyway. Yet here he was, unable to even go a day without her on his mind. Something about her called to him, and he couldn't deny that having her in his head caused this pleasure to fill him. Shaking his head, he opened the fridge, sighing even louder as he saw she only owned soda. Was Eloise that repressed?

Taking out a plain soda, he took a seat on her couch, and started to drink. He didn't know what he planned to do for the remainder of the evening. The sweet-butts back at the clubhouse didn't hold any appeal. There was no challenge to them nor were they enticing. He heard Eloise moving around in the tub and his cock became alert to the smallest of sounds she made. She'd be naked and wet. Fuck, he couldn't get the image of her out of his mind. He hadn't seen her naked yet and already he was hard as a rock for her.

He didn't have the first clue what to do with her or what he was going to tell the rest of the brothers at the club. The only thing he knew for certain was he didn't want any of them fucking with her, or hell, fucking her in general. Eloise was his to play with, his to own, and his to fucking claim.

There was a man, a rough and hardened biker in her apartment, possibly on her couch. Eloise leaned back in her small tub, trying to make sense of whatever was going on. Here she was, naked in her bathroom, soaking in the tub because that man out there deemed it so. Why was she even listening to him, deciding that it was safe to be with him? Yes, he'd saved her from a situation gone horribly wrong, but he was still a stranger. Thinking about him, about how she'd seen him lurking in the parking lot of Markham's should have told her he was dangerous, unstable, bad for her. But the truth was she'd never had this kind of attention, and in a strange, screwed up way, it made her feel good. The last person she'd ever expected to come to her aid was Steel. She'd been such a bitch to him. She'd noticed him lurking in the parking lot. There was no way he was waiting around for her. He could and probably did have many women begging to be fucked. She wasn't interested in sex, not at all. *You lie.*

Closing her eyes, she counted to ten in an effort to push down the awakening need that Steel inspired in her. Her pussy grew slick, and it wasn't because of the water. No, it was because of one man she couldn't get out of her mind. Steel was breaking past all of her barriers. She couldn't let him know what she wanted or craved. He'd take and take from her until there was nothing left. Letting out a breath, she opened her eyes, happier that she'd not been overcome or swamped by desire or lust. She'd seen how disastrous giving into a person's need was.

She'd seen it in her parents. Her mother and father had been destructive to each other and to everyone around them. But Steel had come to her rescue and now he was waiting for her. Lifting her arm out of the water, she started to sponge down her body. Eloise should have hurried, but for some reason she felt slower, less concerned about having to rush. She felt safe having Steel around. She couldn't get him out of her mind or the way he'd hurt Hanson to get the beast away from her.

Everything about Steel screamed mess and chaos. After getting out of the tub, she quickly dressed in her ducky pajamas, and walked out of the bedroom to find Steel sitting on her couch.

"You didn't take long."

"I didn't need to take long." She didn't admit that she'd felt like she was in there forever.

"Dinner should be here soon."

"You ordered already?" she asked, fisting her hands at her sides. She didn't know what to do with him in her apartment. The space was so small and yet he was still here, making the place feel smaller.

"Yeah, Chinese."

She tried her hardest to smile, but the truth was, she didn't feel in the least like smiling.

"Come here."

She should have argued. Any ordinary, sane woman would have. Instead, she went to him without putting up a single fight, because the truth was she liked that he had this dominating aura to him. It called to the darker side of her, the part she'd never shared with anyone.

"Sit down."

Taking a seat beside him, she folded her arms across her breasts, trying her hardest to ignore the uncomfortable, misplaced need rushing through her. It wasn't her fault what happened.

"How are you holding up?" he asked.

"I'm fine."

"Seriously, Eloise, you don't need to lie to me."

"I'm not lying. I mean, I know it happened, and it scares me, but you stopped him."

"He'll think twice about trying that with another woman."

She gasped. "What if he does try to, erm, try to force another woman?"

"I'll handle it, baby. You don't need to worry about a thing."

Eloise glanced at his hand on her knee. She liked his touch way too much. Looking back into his eyes, her heart started to pound. She really wanted to say or do something to change what was happening. He leaned in closer. She didn't pull away or put a stop to it, even though she should have. She shouldn't be in this situation, allowing him to touch her, be in her apartment, because she knew nothing about him. He was a biker, hardened who probably did illegal things.

The knock at the door interrupted them.

"Fucking door."

For the first time in her life, Eloise really wished they'd not been interrupted, and that scared the hell out of her.

Chapter Four

They'd just finished eating, and Eloise stared at Steel, wondering why she felt so comfortable around a man like him. All her life she'd had to rely on herself. Her parents had been a disappointment and keeping control in her life was key. She was shy and quiet, reserved even, but she was comfortable at this point, and that suited her just fine. But she'd never admit to anyone the darker things she liked, the deeper, masochistic desires that she housed inside, too afraid to reveal them to anyone else.

"You're staring at me," Steel said with amusement in his voice.

She turned away, feeling her face heat with embarrassment. "I'm sorry," and she was, because she'd just made an ass out of herself. She'd been watching him, thinking about what he'd do if she just blurted out the things she wanted to do, the things she wanted someone—him—to do to her. He moved closer to her, and when she felt his hand on her chin, turning her head so she was forced to look at him again, her breath stalled. He was such a big man, intimidating and frightening in many aspects. Eloise felt so small compared to him, so thin and fragile, despite the fact she'd always seen herself as a bigger girl, plumper than she liked at times, but generally accepting of herself. But sitting beside Steel, having his nearly six and a half foot height towering over her, his big, muscular body seeming to dwarf hers, had this tingling sensation moving through her. Her breath stalled in her lungs, her heart started to beat faster.

His gaze was on her lips. "I can tell you're wet right now, can see the arousal on your face," he said in a low, deep voice. "I can see the blush on your face, the way your pupils are dilated, and the fact your nipples are hard as fuck."

She wanted to cover her chest, block out her embarrassment, as she knew everything he spoke was the truth, but she was frozen.

"I also know I make you nervous, unsteady, and a part of you is afraid of me." He slowly lifted his gaze, so he was looking into her eyes. "Isn't that right?"

She felt herself nodding. Of course, he was right. This man might be in an outlaw biker gang, but he was intelligent. She could see that in his eyes, in the way he looked at everything, calculated what his next move would be. She inhaled deeply, took in the scent of motor oil, clean sweat, and something stronger, something more untamed. He smelled of leather as well, and she lowered her gaze and stared at the leather vest he wore. There were patches stating the club he was affiliated with, a 1%er patch, and she knew on the back of that vest was the Soldiers of Wrath logo. It was frightening in appearance, dangerous and violent almost, but she also liked it. It made her feel this realization that she was awake and didn't have to hide.

"If I kissed you right now what would you do, Eloise? Would you slap me, tell me to stop?"

His question had her looking at his face instantly. She licked her lips, moved an inch back on the couch, and thought about his question. Before she could really contemplate what she should have said, the words tumbled out of her mouth. "Would you even ask me? Would you just do it and not care what I thought?" Eloise didn't know why she'd blurted that out, but before she could even think about what had happened or what she'd said to Steel, he had his mouth on hers and his tongue thrust between her lips. For a second, she didn't know what to do, how to react. He pulled back, his breathing harsh, and his pupils dilated in clear arousal.

"I know what you want, baby." He kissed a path along her jaw at the same time he moved his hand behind her head. "You want me to take control, to make it so you don't have to think, right?" He phrased it like a question, but it didn't sound like he really expected her to answer. "I can see it in the reserve you wrap around yourself, the fact you try to be the one in control. You've got that written like a damn flashing sign around you." He had his mouth at her throat, licking, sucking at her pulse point. "Fuck, maybe I'm the one that wants all of that, wants to have you tied to my bed, your body on display, there for the taking."

Wetness coated her pussy, saturated her panties, and she heard this mewling little noise escape her.

"That's it, baby, give it to me, just let go and let me take control," he murmured against her mouth, and she opened wider, let him lead, because he really knew what she liked, the things he'd described. She wanted to be tied up, wanted to be able to relinquish her control to someone she could trust. He kissed her harder, more determined in the way he stroked his tongue along hers, and just as she wanted to tell him everything, she pushed Steel away, her breathing coming in short pants.

"I just can't. This is too fast, it's too much." She touched her lips, felt them tingling from their kiss, but couldn't do this. It was too fast, and she felt too unstable right now. She didn't know why he was coming on so strong, why she was even allowing him to be in her apartment, taking control like this. Turning in her seat, and facing the wall, she still had her fingers on her lips.

Before either could say anything else, Steel's cell went off. He stood, and she glanced over at him.

"Yeah?" he said into the receiver. His back was to her, the skull logo of his club on the back of his black leather vest, watching her, taunting her.

She scrubbed a hand over her damp hair, looked down at her pajamas, and felt utterly ridiculous that she'd decided to wear these when he was here. Maybe she should have worn two pairs of sweats and a sweater, trying to hide her desires, her body. But she wanted Steel, wanted him with a desperation that startled and confused her. She may have been sexual with other men in her life, but they'd been vanilla, hadn't been anything in terms of what she'd *really* wanted.

"Yeah, I can be there in ten," he said, and looked over his shoulder at her. "I'm just finishing up with something, but I'm leaving now." He shut his cell and shoved it in his jeans pocket. When he turned around fully, they stared at each other, the silence stretching, awkwardly. He moved closer to her, got down on his knees, and grabbed her hands. She was stunned, not able to say anything at the sincere expression on his face.

"Steel..." Eloise didn't know what to say after that.

"Listen to me. I am not going to walk away. I'm not going to fucking turn my back on you. I felt the desire in your kiss, felt the fucking heat coming from your body." He smoothed his fingers over her hand. "I fucking want you, Eloise. I want every part of you, want to devour you, and I know you want that, too."

"I don't think you know what I want."

"That's where you're wrong, baby, but it doesn't matter, because whatever you need, I'll be the one to give it to you." He cupped her chin, and she found herself nodding, even if it was ludicrous. "Now, I have to leave, which fucking sucks because more than anything, I want to strip you bare and devour you, but that's for another time." He leaned in and claimed her mouth, sucked at her lips, and before she knew what was happening he was moving away from her and striding forward to her front door. He stopped right before he left, looked at her, and cocked the corner of his mouth. "We'll finish this later." He held her gaze. "And I entered my number into your cell, so if you need me, call me, no matter what, okay?"

She nodded, her mouth probably hanging open, and her shock filling her. He left, and she sat there, trying to grasp what in the hell had just happened. Standing after a few minutes, she locked her door, went into her room, and sat at her computer desk. She stared at the black screen, but then booted up her laptop and went to the place on the web where she'd always felt comfortable expressing her desires. It was a site that catered to people who liked things like she did, pain and pleasure, being held immobile as she was controlled and brought to heights she only fantasized about. Would Steel want to do those things with her, spank her, leave marks on her body, and really tie her up because that's what she craved?

It seemed like she might have found someone who understood her, because he led a hardened, no rules life. It frightened her, but it also aroused her, and she knew she needed to decide how she was going to go forward, but she didn't need to decide tonight. Steel was the first man that didn't seem to be giving her a choice if he was walking away. He'd told her he was staying, and she wanted that. She was just afraid. She was frightened of herself and what she desired, but if anyone could accept her and what she wanted, wouldn't it be a man like Steel?

Chapter Five

"We're not a fucking hotel for his daughter. He's got something going on," Shakes said, growling out the words. Steel found it hard to listen to the conversation as his thoughts were on Eloise. Daniella, Zeke's daughter had been ordered to stay at the Soldiers of Wrath club and he saw it didn't bode well with Demon, the Club president. The truth was, Shakes clearly liked Daniella staying at the clubhouse and was simply putting on a front to pretend he didn't like it.

"We're putting her up. He's entertaining certain men that he doesn't want his daughter ever to know. It's not her fault and Zeke may piss me off but I'm not going to blame his daughter," Demon said.

"Aw, isn't that sweet. What he means is he's dealing with men who probably use and abuse women as if they're personal toys." Daniella caught their attention walking down the staircase. She was dressed in a pair of blue jeans that were torn at the knees along with a ratty shirt with a skull on it. She pushed her glasses up her face as she stared at the room. "Believe me, I don't want to be home and I don't want to be here. He seems determined to order me around."

None of them knew what to do with her. She folded her arms across her breasts.

"You're more than welcome to stay here. Shakes also doesn't have a problem either." Demon spoke as graciously as he could. Deanna stood beside her man, holding onto his arm. None of the men were fooled by Shakes. They saw the interest he had in Daniella.

"It must bug you though." Daniella leaned against the bar looking around the room.

"What must?" Shakes took a step closer and Steel grabbed his arm. When it came to Daniella, Shakes wasn't thinking clearly.

"He thinks a tough biker group is tamer than a group of tubby businessmen. I think it sucks for you," she shrugged. "Can't say I don't mind but I'm getting tired of being ordered around."

"Would you like something to eat?" Deanna asked. "I know I'm starved."

Deanna took over, leading the young woman out of the room toward the kitchen.

"Well, Zeke is treating us like a fucking babysitter for his kid," Shakes said.

"It's not what you think. Joker's with Zeke right now taking care of one of the men while also sending out a message. Zeke didn't want Daniella near that shit. We've already talked about this," Demon said.

Steel stared at his President. "Why did you need me here?"

"We need to talk about this woman you want working at the bar. I figured you'd rather I ask you all the questions than go find her myself."

Following his President to his office, he took a seat on one of the leather sofas. He was tired and couldn't get Eloise out of his mind. The way she'd given herself to him in that kiss alone was playing over and over inside his head.

"What do you want to know?"

"We don't need someone to serve drinks, Steel. We're not an average fucking club that caters to the general population."

Running a hand down his jeans, Steel stared at his boss, the man he'd willingly die for. Demon was one of the Presidents who wasn't afraid to step in front of a bullet for each of his members. "Eloise is the woman who works in the local supermarket."

"The one you've been getting a hard on for?"

"I was there tonight and found her being attacked, nearly raped by her boss. The bastard is still breathing, but Eloise can't work there anymore. I won't allow it."

"You won't allow it?"

"She needs someone to take care of her otherwise she's a walking, talking disaster, and not a good one. I can keep an eye on her here. It's not just serving at the bar. She can clean the club or do something."

"Are you serious about this woman, Steel?"

"I don't know what I'm serious about. I only know that she can't go back there."

"I'll talk to the boys and get it settled."

"If you have to, take her salary out of my cut. I don't care."

"Steel, you're willing to give money up for this woman. You need to face facts that she could mean more than just another pussy you want to take control of."

"Can I go?" Steel asked.

"Yeah, go." Demon walked toward his desk and Steel left the room. He didn't wait around for the pussy to bombard him. Going straight to his room at the clubhouse, he locked himself inside, sitting on the edge of the bed.

Leaning forward, he rested his elbows on his knees and placed his chin on his hand. The kiss had been the first sign that he was sure of Eloise's need to submit. She held herself back, and she was a submissive craving control if ever he saw one. He knew what he was looking for since he needed to be the one in control.

Sitting beside her, he'd noticed a great deal about her. The childish pajamas were the first warning, trying not to show any sign of maturity. He would bet all of his money that underneath her control there was a woman begging to be set free. Her nipples had been rock hard, pressing against the front of her shirt. She'd spent a great deal of time clenching her thighs together. Every part of her world was neat and orderly, yet when he looked into her eyes, he saw the need shining back.

Given the right person in control, he didn't have a doubt in his mind that Eloise would open up like a flower in bloom.

He couldn't do it. Steel couldn't sit on his ass waiting to find an answer to his question.

Standing up, he left his room, making his way downstairs, ignoring the women who were trying to get his attention. He wasn't interested in any other pussy but the one he was going to see. Climbing on his bike, he rode toward her apartment. He'd either get turned away or embraced.

Either way, he'd get his answer.

Eloise thumped her pillow, tossing and turning on the bed. The air was too hot and even though she had the window open, it wasn't doing anything to stem the heat. When Steel had left she'd put on a shirt and some boy shorts. More of her body was on display, but in the privacy of her bedroom, she didn't care.

Staring up at the ceiling, she gritted her teeth. "It didn't mean anything. It was just a kiss."

A demanding, firm kiss that let her know who would be in control. Her pussy was soaking wet, but she refused to touch herself. Nothing would ever come of it. She was one of the few women who couldn't find release with her own hand. If she could have brought herself to orgasm, she didn't think she'd have these problems.

Thumping her pillow again, she scrunched it up under her head, letting out a sigh.

"Nothing could ever come of it anyway."

Closing her eyes, she started to count sheep in the hope of getting to sleep.

The sudden banging on the door had her sitting up abruptly. Frowning, she started to climb out of bed as the banging kept on going. Rushing toward her door, she opened it up without checking who it was.

"Did you check to see if it was me before you opened that fucking door?" Steel asked.

He pushed his way into her apartment, closing and locking the door behind him.

"You could have woken the neighbors." She pressed a hand to her neck as her pulse started to beat rapidly.

"From now on you check who is knocking before you answer the fucking door." He took a step toward her and Eloise took one back.

There was something different in the way he spoke and moved toward her. Licking her lips, she stared up the length of his body.

"Why are you here, Steel?"

He didn't answer her.

She let out a little squeal as her back hit the wall, halting her backward movement.

"Why didn't you wear this when I was here?" he asked, pressing a hand to her head as his other hand caressed over her thigh. His touch was electric on her skin.

"What are you doing?"

Eloise gasped as he placed his fingers over her mound.

"Ah, my little baby is soaking wet."

Her cheeks heated as he moved the boy shorts out of the way and started to touch her pussy.

He tutted as he found her pubic hair. "I'm going to have to shave this all off. I like my pussy bare when I eat it."

"Steel?"

"Open your thighs."

She did as he asked without argument, getting more aroused as he teased her pussy. God, she didn't even know him that well; he'd come in here, touched her, stroked her, talked dirty to her, like he had the right to. Yet she wasn't stopping him, wasn't even thinking about doing that. He made her feel good, unbelievably so.

"You're very wet, Eloise. Were you thinking about me?"

Eloise didn't answer. She closed her eyes, basking in the pleasure coursing through her.

He pinched her clit, drawing her back to his world. "Answer my question."

"Yes, I was thinking about you."

Steel eased up the pressure on her clit, stroking down to her entrance, circling her before going back to her clit. "I've come to notice some things about you, Eloise."

Staring into his eyes, she couldn't look away, afraid that he'd see more than she wanted him to. "If this pussy was bone dry, I was going to walk away and leave you. You're soaking wet and from now on I'm going to tell you exactly how this is going to go."

"Steel?"

"Shut up and listen, because I know you want this, too."

His words had her gasping. She'd never been so aroused in all of her life. Biting her lip, she tried with all of her might to fight the arousal, but it was no use. She'd never come across anyone like Steel.

"Take your shirt off." He knelt in front of her pushing her shorts down and then off. With shaking fingers she removed her shirt, standing naked before him.

There was something deeply erotic about being nude in front of Steel; he was still fully dressed.

He held the fingers that had been playing with her pussy to her lips. "Lick them clean, Eloise."

She felt her heart beat wildly. He was breaking through her composure, her control. He made her feel alive, like she couldn't even breathe unless he had his hands on her. Catching his hand, she drew his fingers into her mouth, tasting herself.

"Do you taste good?"

She nodded.

"Good, because I'm going to be tasting a whole lot of you."

He removed his jacket, throwing it onto her sofa. "Go and get on the bed. Spread your legs open and hold your pussy lips apart for me."

Eloise knew she should argue or at least question him. This was insane to be taking orders from this rough biker, but she couldn't stop. Walking into her lonely bedroom, she lay on the bed, opening her thighs wide. Reaching between her thighs, she held the lips of her sex open.

Staring at the door, she gasped as Steel walked through the door without a shirt on. He was ripped and inked. Two combinations she never anticipated walking through her door.

"You bite your lip a lot."

Releasing her lip, she couldn't look away as he knelt on the floor. He caught her hips and dragged her toward the end of the bed.

"From now on this pussy belongs to me. When I want it, where I want it, and how I want it, Eloise. You'll give it to me and you'll do it with a smile on your face."

"Steel?"

He squeezed the flesh on her thighs, the small bite of pain making her cry out.

Steel knew!

How did he know what she wanted?

Staring down at him, Eloise saw his brow rise.

"It takes one to know one, Eloise." He ran his hands up and down her thighs. "You're mine now. I've found you, and there's no more fighting."

She didn't want to fight anymore. All of her life she'd been fighting these desires, ashamed of what she actually wanted.

Eloise cried out as he leaned down, licking from her hole up to her clit then back down again. He sucked her clit into his mouth, making her scream.

Steel teased her, showing her without mercy what it was like to have a real man between her thighs. Several times she was almost at the peak of arousal only for him to stop, leaving her shaken.

All of a sudden he stood, gripping her hips, and had her on her knees on the bed.

Eloise cried out as he slapped her ass, hard. He did this to both of her ass cheeks before cupping her pussy. Steel slipped a finger inside her, then another, stretching her.

"It looks like we're going to have a lot of fun together you and I, Eloise."

She didn't doubt it for a second.

Chapter Six

He turned her around so she was still on her knees, but looking up at him now. How did he know what she wanted, what she craved? His finger under her chin forced her attention on him.

"I would never hurt you, intentionally or unintentionally. The pain that I think you need, want, is always in a controlled environment and only meant to heighten your pleasure."

Her breathing came in short bursts; her body feeling like it was on fire as her arousal and need for this man took control. He leaned forward another inch until she could feel and smell the warm, sweet scent of his breath along her face.

"Anything I do to you will bring you just as much pleasure as it will bring me."

If she just rose up a little higher on her knees, stretched a little, and titled her head an inch, their lips would be touching. The desire to do so was so strong she made a small noise at the back of her throat.

"Why me?" She whispered and glanced down, not sure why he'd want a woman like her when he could have anyone he wanted. He was big, strong, and a biker, and although she'd turned him down before, she didn't want to now. When he didn't respond right away she looked up again.

He was silent for a moment, his focus on her, intense, dominating, controlling. "There is something about you, something that I can't ignore. I can't walk away. I want you too fucking badly." He held her cheek in his big hand, and the pressure as uncomfortable as much as it turned her on. She wanted to be this man's, wanted to have him controlling her in the way she yearned for. "It isn't just about sex, Eloise. I can see, deep down inside, you want to be controlled just as much as I want to control you. I'm not offering you extreme BDSM, whipping, beating, or degradation. I'm not asking to let me tie you up and beat you." He smoothed his hand over her cheek. "Although all of those sound pretty fucking hot when you're involved and willingly submitting to me."

Her heart beat fast and hard.

"You want to give up control, to allow someone to take care of you in all things. Isn't that right?"

She found herself nodding, not able to deny what he said even though this whole situation was crazy and intense.

"I don't want a woman that will bend to my will because she thinks that is what I want. I *need* a woman that desires to please me, to pleasure me because it will give her satisfaction. I want you, because I know you'll be the perfect submissive to the sadistic, dominant inside of me." He leaned forward, giving her his full, intense stare. "I know that you are the woman that desires to give me that control, because it will get you off too, baby. But giving yourself to me means you're mine, in every way. I don't share, don't even want another man looking or talking to you because it'll make the beast inside of me fucking crazy."

His words, his demands, had moisture pooling between her thighs.

"Tell me you want all of that, and I'm yours, baby."

She nodded, licked her lips, and knew this man could give her the awakening she desperately desired.

"Good, Eloise." He grinned, a slash of male satisfaction on his face. "I want you sucking my cock. Now."

Steel's tone was so demanding that she found herself wanting to obey without hesitation.

She wanted this. Even though it seemed wrong on so many levels, because she'd told herself that it was bad, she knew she wanted to be controlled by a man like Steel.

No, she wanted to be controlled *by* Steel.

Kneeling before him, she reached out with shaky fingers and started undoing the button on his jeans. A glance up at him showed an expressionless face, yet his eyes held so much more.

Even though she didn't have his pants undone yet, she could see and feel his rock-hard erection straining against his jeans. The steely length pushed against her hands as she tried quickly to free it. The need to see what was hidden behind the material, to fuel her lust-ridden imagination, had her working faster.

When she finally freed his massive erection, it blew every fantasy she'd ever concocted right out of the water. His dick was long and thick and tipped with a bulbous head that was flushed red from his arousal. Veins lined the heavy length, almost throbbing with the force of how turned on he was. She had never seen a man so hard, so needy. The very idea of putting him in her mouth, sucking him until he came in her throat had all her insecurities rushing forward. She had given oral before, but she wasn't an expert, certainly not like the other women he had surely been with.

"Stop thinking and just act." He slid his hand along her cheek and lifted her face to his. "I want that pretty mouth of yours sucking my cock. Now." He slid his hand in her hair and pulled her forward until the tip of him brushed her mouth. Eyes locked with his, she opened and sucked in the head. Instantly, his flavor exploded in her mouth. The saltiness of his cum, coupled with the addictive flavor of his flesh on her tongue, had a fresh gush of moisture pooling between her thighs. God, she wanted his mouth on her, his fingers, his cock. She wanted every piece of him touching her.

Hollowing out her cheeks, Eloise closed her eyes and tried to push her insecurities aside. She tried to suck as much of his cock into her mouth as she could, wanting to pleasure him. When the tip of him hit the back of her throat and there was still half his length untouched, she wrapped her hand around the base.

"Good girl, suck me nice and deep, baby, make me feel good." He cupped the back of her head. "You want to make me feel good, don't you?"

She nodded around his length and moaned.

Fingers not able to touch, she reveled in the knowledge that soon he would be pushing all of massive inches into her. She wanted to hear him groan, hear him curse because he couldn't contain himself, because she was the one making him feel good. The only noise he made, to her disappointment, was the sound of his heavy breathing. His hand was still in her hair, pulling at the strands, causing a delicious sting to travel through her scalp and down her spine. But she wanted more pain, wanted it mixing with her pleasure. She'd seen enough S&M things on the Internet to know that was what she wanted.

Increasing her speed, she made it her mission to hear his pleasure. Sucking harder, she used her tongue to run along the length on the down stroke and tease the underside of his cock head on the upstroke. His breathing became quicker, more labored, and she knew he was close. With her hand she ran it up and down his length, applying pressure at the base and feeling his silky smooth skin move over steel. His legs tightened beneath her and she tasted several heavy spurts of semen hit the back of her throat.

"That's it, baby. Suck harder, Eloise." His breathy yet deep command had her obeying instantly. He swelled in her mouth and even if she had thought about pulling away, Steel wasn't having any of that. His hand tightened in her hair and he applied pressure, keeping her head in his crotch, refusing to let his cock leave her mouth. She accepted his steely dominance because she'd not intended to pull away. She wanted to taste him, to feel the thick warmth of his cum hit the back of her throat.

"Swallow it. Drink it all down," Steel growled right before she tasted and felt the heavy load that shot out of the tip of his shaft. He thrust his cock into her, hitting the back of her throat.

Working her throat around him, she swallowed every last drop he had to give. Tasting him had her nipples beading and her clit throbbing. Her wetness had her pussy uncomfortably wet, but it also turned her on even more.

When there was nothing left to swallow and Steel's cock started to soften, she pulled away. His dick fell free of her mouth and she sat back on her haunches, breathing heavily and feeling a drop of his cum slide down her bottom lip. Bringing her gaze up and looking into his face, her breath caught at the look on his face. He didn't say anything for the longest time and she couldn't find any words that seemed appropriate. Finally, he lifted his hand and ran it over her bottom lip, collecting his cum and holding it up for her to see.

"Open," the dark pools of his eyes were the color of the deepest part of the sky. She wanted to dive in, to get lost in everything he offered. She opened her mouth, and when he slipped his cum-coated finger into her mouth, she wrapped her lips around the digit and sucked it clean.

"Suck it all off."

Doing what he said, she hummed around his finger and savored the taste of him. The digit wasn't nearly as satisfying as having his dick in her mouth, but she was so starved for him that she would take any body part that he offered.

When she had cleaned every drop, he leaned back and stared down at her. "Go stand against the wall, back to me, legs spread."

The way he demanded her obedience had her aroused even more. She obeyed right away. She went over to the wall, her legs shaky. Totally nude, nothing hidden from this man, for the first time in her life, she didn't worry about her curves, the lumps or dips in her body, and thought only about Steel.

The wall beneath her sweaty palms was smooth and cold. Despite the way her body flushed and heat rose to the surface of her skin, Eloise shook uncontrollably. She could sense Steel behind her, could feel his body heat. Her thighs were embarrassingly moist, and she feared he would notice, see her desire coating her skin, as evident as the color of her hair.

He ran his finger up the back of her thigh and she closed her eyes, savoring the feel. She snapped her eyes open when his mouth replaced his fingers, his teeth biting into her flesh. A gasp left her as he smoothed his tongue over the sting his teeth caused. He ran his tongue along the back of her leg and across the crease where her leg met her ass. The feel of his hands creeping up her inner legs, closer and closer to the spot on her body that ached for his touch, had everything around her becoming dizzy with pleasure.

She could practically feel his warm, humid breath. The sharp sting of his palm landing on her bare ass cheek had her gasping and biting her lip. The spot where he struck her was warm from the blood rushing to the surface. Endorphins spread throughout her body and she found herself swaying from the force of it.

"Oh," the one word came out on a sigh and she curled her fingers against the wall. Her fingernails scraped against the wallpaper. And then Steel's hot, wet mouth was latched onto her pussy. His tongue, slightly rough, tormented her in great sweeping waves and his hands were smooth as he caressed her hips. Curling his fingers around her hipbones, he pulled her back, forcing her more firmly onto his assaulting mouth.

"So sweet...so mine." The rough growl of his words sent a spear of carnal pleasure straight to her clit. "This pussy hair will have to go for next time, baby. I want smooth cunt when I'm eating you out."

He pulled away and ran his finger along her slick folds, and then thrust one of his long, thick fingers into her pussy. Immediately her body sucked him in, drawing the digit deeper. Fucking her pussy in slow and steady thrusts, he used his other hand to smooth over the mound of her ass and give one cheek a squeeze.

Smack!
Smack!
Smack!

"Ahh."

He smacked her ass again and his tongue lapped at her clit. He took one hand and placed it on her quivering belly and slid his other hand over her ass and rested it at the base of her spine. Pushing her forward with the hand on her back and pulling her back with the hand on her belly, she was forced to take a step away from the wall and bend forward. His hand on her belly splayed across the entire area, causing heat to seep into her and warm every part of her body.

For the life of her she couldn't find the words to say anything in response. His chest covered her back, and she felt his bare skin on hers. He'd removed his jeans already, and she closed her eyes and breathed out at the feel of him. The heavy length of his now erect cock slid against her slick cleft, teasing her with the promise of what the night entailed. The tip of his shaft rubbed her clit every time he shifted.

His breath blew the tendrils of hair by her face and a gasp left her, almost afraid of what he was going to say. His words, whispered low and husky, slid across the side of her face. "If you knew what was good for you, baby, you'd make sure to obey everything I say."

The hand that spanned her belly slid up her ribcage and covered a breast. His forefinger and thumb found her sensitive nipple and started tweaking it. Pulling the tissue away from her body at the same time, he rolled it between his fingers, and Eloise found herself biting her lip to hold in her moan. The taste of blood hit her tongue, and it was then she realized she had bitten her bottom lip. It was pleasure mixed with pain, agony mixed with ecstasy.

"If you want my cock inside of you, you'll tell me this pussy is mine, only mine, and I can do whatever the fuck I want to you because you'll need me to." He applied more pressure to her aching nipple and then curled his hips forward, bumping her clit once again with the root of his erection. With the dual sensation, her legs started to shake, and she feared she would collapse.

Smack! Smack!

The double spanking coupled with his teasing fingers and thrusting hips had an unexpected orgasm creeping up, but before it could wash through her, he suddenly pulled away and she was left feeling bereft. Resting her head on the wall in front of her, she didn't even bother asking why he stopped, or seeing where he went. His hand was back on her ass, smoothing the pain away.

"Answer me," his voice seemed to be everywhere, or maybe she was just losing her mind from the pleasure he was slowly killing her with?

She licked her lips and blinked her eyes open. "Yes, everything I have is yours. I'm yours." She was vaguely aware of the sound of something crinkling behind her and then she screamed out in ecstasy as Steel shoved his cock in her pussy without any warning. It was so unexpected, so intense that her knees buckled and she started to go down.

Steel pulled out of her after only thrusting twice and gripped her waist, spinning her around so she could face him.

She let her eyes travel down his chiseled chest, all rippling with hard lines of muscles and ink, and that delicious V that pointed down to a dick covered in latex and glistening from her wetness.

When she looked back into his eyes, the intensity, the determination to have her, made everything else disappear into nothingness.

"I'm going to devour you, and you're going to see what it feels like to be owned by a man."

Chapter Seven

Daniella finished off her burger, watching as Demon tugged Deanna out of the kitchen . They were a cute couple, strange yet cute. Licking the mustard off her fingers, she glanced around the kitchen. Considering the club was owned by a bunch of old men, the kitchen had a feminine touch to it.

She imagined Deanna and the club whores used the kitchen more than the men ever did. Picking up her second burger, which she didn't care about as her mother wasn't around to nag her. She hated her mother, more than she hated her father. At the young age of fourteen she'd learned the horrid truth about who her father actually was along with the hatred her mother had for her. Daniella didn't miss her mom. Years spent on a diet, being forced to do nothing but exercise or try on clothes had scarred her for life. Her father was the lesser of two evils. Zeke, her murdering, crime lord of a father, was by far easier to deal with than her mother. He didn't give a shit about her weight or what she did with her time or if she liked to eat two cheese burgers rather than a celery stick.

The years of weight charts, diets, and being compared to every slender girl in the neighborhood was far behind her.

Biting into her burger, she relished the grease, the cheese, the meaty fat flavor as it ran down her throat.

"Are you okay?" Shakes asked, walking into the kitchen.

"Yeah, I'm fine. So, men do come in here after all."

"What do you mean?"

"I figured this was a woman's domain."

"Not really. Boys need to eat, but the whores wouldn't be seen in here. They're good for one thing."

"I figured you had to have a reason for calling them whores." She shrugged. "Not all girls are lucky like Deanna."

She liked Deanna. The other woman was nice, a little too nice for a biker club, but Daniella wasn't one to talk. Her own father wasn't a nice man and compared to him she was sweet.

Thinking about Zeke filled her with regret. Her father loved her. She knew he did but she couldn't bring herself to be his little girl anymore. What he did with his life and the way he killed, it was just too much. She'd seen first hand what he was capable of. There was a time when she'd be sitting at the stairs waiting for the front door to open. She'd run into his arms and he'd stop her mother saying nasty shit to her.

That all changed when her mother left and she learned the truth. There was no more running toward him, in fact she spent more time running away from him.

"What are you thinking about?" Shakes asked, pulling her out of her thoughts.

"Stupid shit." She never bonded with anyone, least of all men. After everything she'd seen her father do, she had a hard time trusting them. "Do you want some?" she asked, pointing to her burger.

"Nah, you eat it."

He moved toward the fridge, pulling out a carton of Chinese food. She hadn't known how old the food was and didn't want to risk food poisoning.

Taking a bite of her burger, she didn't like how he sat close to her. He pulled a chair right next to her so that his thigh grazed hers.

"What are you doing?" he asked.

"I'm eating." It wasn't a hard question.

"No, I mean what are you doing tonight?"

She stared at her food, losing her appetite at how close he was. "Erm, what do you mean?"

"When you've finished your food what are you doing?" He spoke slowly, taking his time to pronounce every single word.

"I'm not thick." She snapped the words out, hating the way he'd spoken.

"I had to ask you the same question twice."

"It's not my fault. I'm going to eat my burger, do the dishes, and go and study."

"You've just come from college. Don't you ever have time off?"

"Time off is for people who don't want to do well in life." She didn't believe that. Some people were just handed really bad deals out of life.

"This is coming from the pampered princess of a crime boss."

"What? You think I've had it all handed to me on a plate? I can do and say whatever the hell I want?"

"Yeah, princess, I do. I think you've got life really fucking easy actually. You've not got to fight for a single thing. All you've got to do is click your fingers and you get exactly what you want."

Daniella snorted. "You have no idea what you're talking about." Putting the burger back onto the plate, she started to push away from the table. Shakes surprised her by putting his hands on the chair, stopping her from moving.

The strength he showed should have sent her running as far away from him as she could get. Instead, she simply stared into his beautiful cerulean blue eyes. She liked his eyes. They made her feel safe and warm when everything around her was cold, as totally cold as the arctic.

"What are you doing?" she asked, licking her suddenly dry lips.

"Tell me how I don't know what I'm talking about, princess." His voice was deep and rough.

"You don't know me, Shakes. Don't try to pretend that you do."

"Then tell me about yourself, princess. Tell me about Daniella and why she gets pissy when people think she's had life easy."

Tears filled her eyes, but like so many times before, she forced them down. Nothing good could come from tears. They made a person weak. Tears didn't solve problems, they didn't make anyone feel good. It was a useless action for a useless emotion.

"I don't need to talk to you."

He let out a sigh, but he didn't back away like she'd hoped he would. Shakes leaned closer, invading her space. "You're right. You don't need to talk to me but you're not a bitch, are you, Daniella?"

She gritted her teeth, refusing to talk to him.

"It's okay, baby, I see it in your eyes. You're not this bitch you portray. I imagine it's very fucking lonely being Zeke's daughter. No boys will ever want to get close to you. They'd be afraid of getting their asses blown off."

It was hard for her to swallow and her tears were still welling up.

"You have no one to talk to. What do you have, Daniella? Your books?"

"Why are you doing this?" She didn't sound strong anymore. No, she sounded weak, pathetic, everything her mother hated.

He reached out, pushing some of her hair off her shoulder. "Why am I talking to you?"

"If my father knew—"

"Your father will never know because you're not the type of girl to go running to daddy, are you?"

She licked her lips, staring into his blue eyes. "It's hard," she said. "It's hard to always be tough."

"You don't have to be tough around me."

"You're the enemy."

"I'm not your enemy, Daniella."

"I don't like being called princess. I'm not a princess. It's not easy knowing I'm going to school, and he's killing people or doing something."

"If your father knew I was talking to you right now like this, he would kill me," Shakes said.

"Why are you risking it? No one else ever has."

"They've never risked it for you." He stroked his fingers over her cheek.

"No, no one ever has." She didn't want anyone to risk their lives for her. Daniella knew she wasn't worth it.

"Come out for a ride with me on my bike tonight."

"Why?" she asked. She'd never been on a bike before. Zeke would go mental to hear her even thinking about it.

"It's time to start living outside of that box he's got you trapped in."

Her heart was pounding inside her chest.

"Shakes, I need a word."

Demon was in the doorway to the kitchen. She wondered why he was in the kitchen after taking Deanna out a couple of minutes ago.

"I'll be back," Shakes said.

She nodded, watching him leave. The two men started talking in hushed voices so she couldn't hear anything.

Go on a bike with him?

I can't do it. Zeke would go insane.

It had been years since she called him dad.

Biting her lip, she tossed the burger into the trash before washing her plate.

Her cell phone buzzed inside her pocket making her jump.

Pulling her phone out, she saw Zeke had texted her.

Zeke: *How are you?*

Daniella: *Fine.*

She went to pocket her phone, but it buzzed again.

Zeke: *Are they treating you well?*

Frowning, she stared at the message wondering why he even cared. He'd made them pick her up.

Daniella: *How are the fat business men?*

It took several minutes for him to respond. She was already making her way out of the kitchen toward the front door. No one was around to stop her.

Zeke: *It's business. I wish you were here. I miss you.*

Daniella: *They're treating me fine. I could have stayed at school.*

Zeke: *You need to learn how to take a break. What are you doing?*

She was tempted to tell him exactly what she was doing but decided against it. Getting Shakes into trouble wasn't ever going to be her intention.

Daniella: *Studying.*

Zeke: *What?*

Daniella: *The reproductive process. Tutor says practice makes perfect. Do you agree?*

Zeke: *What's your teachers name?*

Daniella: *I'm not telling.*

This was the first time they'd had any conversation.

"No, please, I swear I didn't do anything."

Staring at the phone, Daniella felt sick as she recalled the man begging for his life.

Zeke: *You're my little girl. I care. Tell me your teacher's name.*

Daniella: *I've got to go. Busy.*

She would have added something derogatory about him killing people but decided against it.

"I went looking for you in the kitchen," Shakes said.

Putting the phone into her pocket, she offered him a smile. "Sorry, I didn't want to wait around in the kitchen. You're taking me for a ride?"

"Yes, I'm taking you for a ride but first you need this." He grabbed a helmet, and she groaned. "You're wearing this. If it's your first time on a bike. I'm not going to risk your safety."

"This is cruel. I thought this was supposed to be fun."

"It is fun." He slid the helmet over her head, hitting the top. "There, it looks cute on you."

She stuck her tongue out, watching as he straddled the large machine. The bike was huge and she wouldn't trust it if it was under her.

"Climb on, princess."

"I don't want to climb on."

"Get on."

Rolling her eyes at his bossy words, she climbed on. Wrapping her arms around his waist, she squealed as he revved the engine.

"Are you ready for this, baby?"

"No."

She didn't get time to finish what she was saying before Shakes took off out of the compound. When they first started riding, she kept her eyes closed, not daring to open them. The minutes passed, and she finally opened her eyes. She wished she didn't have the helmet on.

The helmet restricted the freedom of the air on her face.

All too soon their ride was coming to a close as Shakes pulled up outside of a garage. They were close to the grocery store.

Daniella climbed off the bike. Her legs now jelly so she leaned up against the wall.

Tugging the helmet off, she giggled. "That was totally amazing."

Shakes stepped closer to her. "Glad you liked it."

He stood right in front of her. His hands landed on either side of her head.

"Why did you take me out for a ride?" she asked, licking her lips. She wasn't going to complain. The bike ride was the best experience of her life, not that she'd had all that many experiences.

"So I can do this." He cupped her face, tilting her head back.

She gasped as he slammed his lips down on hers. His tongue plundered her mouth, stroking over her tongue. Shakes deepened the kiss, rubbing his cock against her mound.

There was nowhere for her to turn to or run to. He surrounded her, consuming her mouth.

Shakes bit her lip, pulling away. "I couldn't do that with everyone looking. We're under strict rules to keep our hands off."

"Then why did you do it."

He took her hand, pressing it against his cock. "From the first moment I saw you, you've made me fucking hard."

"I can't do this. I'm not ready." She was scared, excited, nervous.

"I'm not going to pressure you for sex, Daniella. You're in college and I know there are boys there that don't have control over their dick."

"Why are you doing this?"

"I'm doing this so that when you go back to college, you know who you belong to."

"And who do I belong to?" she asked, intrigued. No man had ever staked a claim before.

"Me."

She shouldn't get a thrill from his word but she did.
Fucked, she was well and truly fucked.

Zeke stared at his cell phone for the longest time. He didn't
like his relationship with Daniella. There was a time when
she'd jump at any chance to spend time together or talk. Her
bitch of a mother had ruined it all.

"What are you doing?" Francesca asked, leaning against his
arm. The devil speaks.

Staring at the woman he'd fucked to get Daniella, Zeke
couldn't think of a reason why he'd been with her. She was
plastic; she couldn't smile because of the Botox in her face. Her
tits were too big, they didn't move. Every part of her was fake
and vile, including her personality.

"Aw, is Daniella giving you the brush off. How is little
tubby doing?"

He grabbed Francesca around her throat, slamming her to
the table. She cried out, clawing at his wrist.

"If I hear another nasty word out of your mouth about our
daughter, I'm going to spend the rest of the night making you
wish you hadn't come back here." He squeezed her throat a
little tighter, relishing the sight of her fighting for breath.

Kill the bitch.

Zeke had a lot to make up for with Daniella. He'd left his
little baby girl with this monster thinking she was going to be
safe. Daniella had become withdrawn as she'd grown up and he
was spending more time away. When he came home, she wasn't
cuddly, just withdrawn. He'd give anything now just to have
her cuddly again. Anyway, when he'd seen the diet shakes in

the fridge and the weight machines, he'd gotten suspicious. Installing cameras around the house, he'd discovered Francesca's true self, how vile and mean she was.

It had given him the out of a marriage he hated, but it wasn't the same with Daniella, not after she caught him hurting someone in their home.

Releasing her throat, he moved away from the table. This was the reason he needed the Soldiers of Wrath to take care of Daniella. He wouldn't allow his daughter to go near the spiteful woman.

"I see you still love her," Francesca croaked out.

"She's my daughter. Of course, I love her." He ran fingers through his hair, hating how her very presence riled him. All he wanted to do was kill Francesca, but her death would bring too many questions. She was his wife, and he had no doubt that Francesca had her way out of everything.

"Are you still going to love her when she's spreading her legs for all the dick that will have her?" She lit a cigarette, staring back at him.

He really couldn't guess what she was thinking. "You don't have a caring bone in your body, do you?"

"Caring gets you killed. I'm resourceful. I want my allowance doubled."

"That's what you've come over here to ask? For more money?"

"What can I say? You're going to give it to me, Zeke. You can't risk me going to the right cop or spilling the beans, can you?" She tilted her head to the side. "A police investigation now would destroy any relationship with Daniella. She can't stand you now. Not to mention how it would hurt your business."

He stepped up to her, lifting his hand as if to strike her when an idea entered his mind. "You want double, fine. You've got double."

"Do you want to fuck for old times sake?" she asked.

"Get the fuck out of my house. If you talk to Daniella, our deal is off." He couldn't believe he'd stopped his time with his daughter for this piece of scum. She might be the mother of his kid, but she was scum.

"Tell me, Zeke. Why did you give in so easily?"

"I don't see the point in arguing. You've got all the cards, Francesca." He stared at her, waiting for her to leave.

"It's a good job you know when you've been beat, Zeke." She grabbed her purse, turning away. "You were so easy back in the day. All I had to do was moan in the right places and you thought you were God's gift to women."

"Get out." She wasn't baiting him.

He had another plan.

"Fine. You don't want to play; that's fine with me." He watched her leave. Only when he saw her climbing into the back of her car did he pull his cell phone out.

Dialing the number he used for this kind of business, he waited for the man to answer.

"Hello, Joker, I've got a job for you. I need someone to disappear and never return."

He gave Joker the details before hanging up. Francesca's biggest mistake was greed and stupidity. No one got the better of him and if anyone thought they had, it was their mistake. He was always one step ahead.

Chapter Eight

Steel had Eloise's legs wrapped around his waist and the head of his cock poised at her entrance before she could even take her next breath. The tip of him was scorching hot, and she feared he would burn her alive once he pushed inside of her. If she was going to die, she couldn't think of a better way to go.

His biceps strained and bunched as he lifted her, his hands on her ass squeezing. Her heels pressed against the base of his spine and all she wanted to do was pull him forward so he was forced to impale her.

"Touch your breasts." His gaze dipped down to said body part, and she didn't wait to obey him.

Letting go of his neck she felt off balance, felt like she would fall at any moment, but Steel's hands tightened around her, stabilizing her.

He whispered, "I've got you, baby. Now, do as I say, and pinch those pretty pink nipples. Obey me because you want to, because it'll pleasure me." Her back pressed more firmly against the wall, the lightly textured wallpaper causing a slow burn to start below the surface of her skin. Taking her nipple between her index finger and thumb, she mimicked what Steel had done to them just moments before. It was so good, but his touch was infinitely better.

His hands gripped the cheeks of her ass a little tighter and then he was sliding into her, all the while his stare riveted to what she was doing to her breasts. Mouth opening on a silent cry, Eloise closed her eyes and let the feel of him filling her up wash through her. When he was fully inside of her, his balls touching the bottom crease of her ass, he stilled.

"You'll shave this pretty pussy for me the next time I see you."

She didn't have time to register what he said because her inner muscles clenched around his girth and he grunted. He pulled out of her so that just the hot tip of him was embedded in her opening and then shoved it back in. He was so large she swore she could feel his pulse beat in his shaft, matching the frantic rhythm of her own heart.

His thrusts, fierce and powerful, rocked her against the wall. Her sweat-soaked skin started to chafe, but the discomfort only seemed to add to the pleasure-filled eroticism of the act.

"So fucking tight, Eloise, so hot and mine." His face was buried in the crook of her neck. "I'm going to fuck you so hard that your pussy will ache for me when I'm not there. I'm going to make you mine, dominate you, make you submit because I know that's what you want. That's what I want, what I need from you."

She pinched her nipples harder as she listened to him talk dirty.

"And when I'm done with you, baby, when you're sweaty and weak, begging me to stop, pleading with me that you can't handle anymore, I'm going to fuck your ass, give you so much more until you're crying from the intensity." At the last word, he shoved into her forcefully and she cried out in climax.

It was an almost out-of-body experience. Having him inside of her, moving, coaxing, stroking her to orgasm was nothing like touching herself, nothing like watching the dirty BDSM acts she'd watched on line. It was hard and rough, gritty and dirty. It was everything she'd been missing, she realized.

She expected Steel to come right after her, but when she felt his teeth graze the skin of her throat, adding a bit of pressure, a bit of pain, she knew he wasn't done with her yet.

"Hold on," his arms tightened around her and she was suddenly moving through the air, the only solid thing keeping her grounded was Steel. Then her back met the cool sheets of the bed, and her breath hissed out of her. Steel was still buried deep within her, and he started pounding her body.

In and out. Harder and faster.

"Hands above your head, and baby," he slammed into her once, stilled, and held her gaze.

She did as he said, anxious and aroused.

"If you move your hands for any reason, I'm going to spank that pretty ass of yours until you can't sit for a week."

Oh God. She wanted that.

He resumed stroking her from the inside, bringing her closer to an orgasm she didn't think she would be able to tolerate. Despite the fact she didn't think she had it in her for another orgasm, Steel was proving that wrong. It was like his mission. The determination on his face said as much.

Hands above her head like he ordered, she held on to the slates of the headboard for leverage as he worked his cock in her pussy. A swivel of his hips on the down stroke, a bump to her cervix with the tip of his cock when he pushed inside, and he had her climbing closer and closer to agony and ecstasy. Steel was the composer, and he was playing her body like she was his masterpiece. Had she ever been with a man that knew exactly how to touch her, that could get off numerous times?

No. God, the answer was hell no.

"You're going to stop thinking and just feel, baby. You're going to enjoy my big cock pounding away in your tight, slippery cunt." He emphasized his point by gripping her waist and pulling her down so her ass hung off the edge of the mattress, and he could get more leverage fucking her.

Was she that transparent that he noticed her mind was elsewhere? She didn't have time to ponder it because his finger was on her clit and he was thrusting into her again. Back arched to try and shift her body so she could slide farther down on him, a hoarse moan of satisfaction left her when he pushed fully into her. The pleasure went on and on, and this time she thought for sure he would get off. But he pulled out as soon as her orgasm subsided and when she opened her eyes she could see his cock was still stiff.

There had never been a man that was so intent on pleasing her, or maybe by him pleasing her he was also pleasing himself?

She was unceremoniously flipped onto her belly and positioned so her toes touched the floor and she had to balance on them. Her ass was in the air and he pushed her thighs apart. There was no question that he could see every intimate part of her, and as if to prove her point she felt him run his finger over her folds.

He gathered her moisture and brought it to her anus, the hole that had never been breached. "I want your hands above you. The same rules apply as before, Eloise." He leaned forward so his chest covered her back and gripped a chunk of her hair, pulling her head up so her neck was bared. He whispered in her ear in a rough growl, "I hope you do disobey me, because the punishment will be oh so sweet." He let go of her hair and smoothed his hand down the length of her spine, stopping at the top of her ass and giving it a forceful slap. The sound of flesh meeting flesh was highly erotic, and she wanted to hear more of it. Lifting her ass, she presented more of it to him, hoping he would take the hint. All she got was a richly dark laugh.

He brought more moisture to her anus, and just as she closed her eyes and savored the taboo nature of his act, he pushed his finger into her ass. On instinct she reached back, not realizing her mistake until Steel pulled away from her. She immediately put her hands back where they were and mumbled an apology.

"Too late, sweetheart."

She heard him move across the floor but didn't dare look back. Would he actually spank her until she couldn't walk? Did he like hearing a woman cry out as he brought his palm down on their flesh? Just when fear started to take control of her he was back, his chest on her back. His heat seeped into her, easing away the fear that tried to control her. She had never had a man do half the things Steel had just done, and although some may have seemed tame, she did want more, wanted it darker.

"What I want to do to you is meant to pleasure you. Fear does not belong here, and does not belong in what we are experiencing together, Eloise." He kissed the side of her head and she was surprised at the comforting gesture. Steel didn't seem like the type of man that would take the time to reassure a woman he was fucking, but he did with her and that went a long way in helping her trust for him grow.

"I just want to make you feel good. Trust me, baby. Trust me to take care of you." He didn't move and just let his words sink in. He seemed to be waiting for her reply.

"Okay." The single word came out on her exhale. Steel gripped her chin and turned her so their lips met. The kiss was soft, sweet. His demeanor right now was so unlike the persona he displayed that she was taken aback by it. When the kiss ended their eyes locked. His silent question hung between them and she swallowed, knowing what he wanted to hear and knowing she had to go with her instinct.

"I trust you."

He didn't smile, just leaned in, and gave his response with a press of his mouth to hers. When his chest left her back, she buried her face in the mattress, breathing in the scent that was all Steel, her hardened biker. There was no time for her to think about what-ifs as the feel of something hard and painful slammed against her ass cheek. She gasped out, looked over her shoulder, and saw he held her brush. He spanked her with the smooth, flat side of it, and the fact that she liked it, like the pain, should have disgusted her. As it was, she grew more aroused.

Over and over he spanked her until, the agony and ecstasy became one. The more he spanked her the more excited she became. Her pussy felt wetter, more swollen, and against all odds, she wanted to come again. She might be sexually exhausted, so sated that she could hardly move, but she wanted more. A lot more.

Steel brought the brush down on her ass for the fourth time and she strained forward. Every part of her back and bottom felt hot, sensitive. Endorphins exploded inside of her and the rush of pleasure had warm tears sliding down her cheeks and coating the sheets beneath her. There was no sound coming from Steel, just the steady noise of the brush hitting her flesh. Every time she heard it, that *thump* on her body, her pussy would clamp down and her nipples would tingle.

"Such a good girl, Eloise." Another strike to her ass. "You're my good girl, my gorgeous fucking girl." He smoothed his hand over her ass. "So responsive." One more, this time on her inner thighs. She had since eased her legs open, loving that every once in a while a strip would graze her labia, causing a sharp lash that had her growing slicker. She wanted his cock in her, wanted him filling her. Most of all, she wanted his dick in her ass. It was such a foreign desire, one that she never thought she would entertain.

He must have spanked her a dozen times before she was crying into the sheets for him to stop, for him to give her more.

"Beg me to fuck your ass. Beg me to spread these red cheeks, covered with my marks, and shove into your tight little asshole." When she didn't answer right away, he slapped her ass with his open palm.

"Yes, please. Do it. Fuck my ass. Fuck it hard." Cool air shifted over her anus when he spread her cheeks. He moved her moisture from her pussy to the puckered hole and slowly started working the digit inside. There was a slight bit of discomfort, but then he added a second finger and started scissoring them inside of her, stretching her for what he was about to push into her.

For several tortured minutes, he fucked her ass with his fingers while his other hand ran circles around her clit. It was a slow burn of desire that made her desperate for him, but it wouldn't get her off. She knew what he was doing, knew he was waiting for her to come until he was buried deep in her ass.

The sheets were bunched in her fists and she couldn't contain the moans that continually spilled from her as he moved his fingers in her ass and teased her clit with his other hand. Her pussy clenched, trying to grab onto something, but disappointment slammed into her when there was nothing for her to grip on to. He removed his probing fingers and replaced them with the very broad, very hot tip of his shaft. He was big and her hole was very small. Pain lanced through her when he tried to push past the tight ring of muscle.

"Bear down, baby. It'll go in nice and smooth if you relax." She did as he asked and felt her eyes widen when he finally slid into her. The discomfort took her breath away, and when he was fully embedded inside of her, the gentle slap of his balls becoming wet from her moisture, she let the breath she hadn't realized she held in, out.

With her eyes closed and her mind trying to wrap itself around what she was experiencing, she didn't realize Steel had leaned forward until she felt one of his hands encompass both of her wrists. He raised them above her so far that she felt the strain in her shoulders. His other hand braced on the spot right between her shoulder blades. He used his weight above her, pushing her into the mattress as he started to slowly slide in and out of her ass. It was a strange feeling, being filled back there, but with each thrust and retreat, she started to feel the fullness and discomfort start to morph into something even more wicked, and even more delicious.

The sound of slippery skin moving together, of his balls slapping against her swollen, wet pussy, was a driving fuel to the ecstasy that was climbing in her body and just lying in wait to explode. She forced her head up and saw the mirror on the dresser right across from her. She could see Steel's powerful body above hers. His skin was golden and sweat slicked, and his muscles bunched and taut as his hips pushed in and pulled out of her. His gaze was riveted to the spot where his cock disappeared and a look of unadulterated lust covered his expression.

"*Jesus.*" Steel's voice was deep and distorted and, as if he couldn't help himself, his speed increased and his thrusts intensified. She felt droplets of his sweat drip onto her back, and she found herself lifting her ass onto his dick, needing to be impaled by him more.

"Damn, baby. Fucking hell, that's so damn good." The pressure on her back intensified, and she stilled, letting Steel control her, do whatever the hell he wanted to because that is what she wanted. *God...yes.* That is so what she wanted. "You are so damn good. So good, that I'm never going to get enough. Never."

His words had warmth spreading through her, but she didn't let the idea that he may want something more from her than one night alter what she knew in her heart. When the night was over, that would be the end of them; she just knew it.

Faster. Harder. He started fucking her so fiercely that her body was shifting up the bed, and he had to stop twice to pull her back down on his dick. The material beneath her became wet from her juices and she spread her legs wider, trying to rub herself on the material, trying to settle the desperation inside of her.

"Please, Steel." Her words were muffled against the sheets.

"Please what?" Gruff, deep and hard, Steel's words gave her the strength to tell him what she wanted.

"I need it. Please, let me come."

"Ah, fuck, baby. All you have to do is ask, and I'll give it to you. I'll give you anything you want." His fingers slipped between her body and the mattress, and he started flicking her clit back and forth. It only took him three hard presses on her clit and she was coming hard. Her ass tightened around his shaft and he fucked her harder.

"Yes, Eloise. Squeeze that sweet little fucking ass on my cock. Suck the cum from me." His hand on her wrists tightened to the point she knew there would be bruises, but she welcomed them. The pain made it better, made the pleasure more carnal. He grunted once and pumped into her hard, so hard that she cried out as an unexpected tremor worked its way through her.

Even though he wore a condom she could feel the throbbing of his orgasm. It was a heady feeling, and she wished there was nothing between them so that she could feel the force of his desire wash inside of her. Steel collapsed on top of her, their breathing ragged, their skin sweat-slicked. She couldn't hold her eyes open, couldn't process the exhaustion that he caused within her.

Her night with Steel had been a surprise, but there hadn't been the kinky BDSM acts she thought their one night would entail, the darker pleasures she desperately craved. But he'd appeased her desire for right now, given her more than she could even understand; yet she wanted more. She wanted so much more. He certainly showed her he liked to be in control, but he had also been gentle and caring. She felt the heavy weight of him roll off her, but before she let the comforting blanket of sleep take her away, she felt Steel pull her into a tight embrace. He whispered something into her hair, but she was already drifting away, letting the pleasurable soreness in her body be the last thing she registered.

Chapter Nine

Steel sat in the confines of church the following day aware of his woman working next door. Eloise didn't know shit about working at the club, but it had been cute for the last hour to watch her try. Deanna was doing everything she could to help her get settled in. There was no way he was letting her go back to that scumbag of a boss. He wanted to keep an eye on her and had already told the other brothers of the club that she was off limits. Steel didn't like to share his pussy, and Eloise was certainly his.

One night with Eloise was never going to be enough for him.

"So, we've got to take Daniella to her father today," Demon said, bringing him back to the business at hand. Church at the Soldiers of Wrath was a chance for everyone to catch up, but to get business taken care of, too. The club didn't run itself. Demon was one hell of a Prez and kept them all in line, and for the most part, out of the line of fire.

"Why are we fucking babysitters again," Striker asked. The other brother sat in the corner, sporting a black eye from Weasel. "We've got better things to do."

"You've got better things to do?" Demon asked. "Maybe you should think about that fucking patch you're supporting on your jacket, Striker."

"Demon—"

"No, you don't get to fucking 'Demon' me. I'm the one who runs this fucking club. I decide what you get to do and not do."

Steel stared at his club president, who was looking at everyone.

"If you've got a fucking problem, stand up, and I'll be happy to deal with whatever shit you've got to say," Demon said.

None of the brothers could take Demon in a fight. They'd all get pummeled into the floor and be lucky to get out alive. Demon wasn't known for taking shit, it was why he'd lasted this long as president. He proved his weight in gold to the club. There were fewer deaths, more respect, and a hell of a lot to look forward to in life.

Before Demon took over the Soldiers, Steel wouldn't have dared bring a sweet thing like Eloise around the club. Demon got in as president and took all the scum out of the club. There were a lot of men around the table today who owed Demon far more than their lives; they owed him their years of loyalty and servitude. A life doesn't even begin to cut it in the scheme of things.

"Zeke's running us around for his daughter," Striker said.

Demon slammed is fist on the table. Something snapped underneath and the men quickly grabbed the table to stop it from falling onto their legs.

"Zeke is a necessary fucking evil in our lives right now. The Soldiers can take care of one little girl. What's the problem?"

"Daniella isn't a problem," Shakes said. "You got a problem with her, you take it up with me."

The whole table grew silent.

"No, Shakes. You can fuck any cunt you want, but you leave that one alone. Zeke's a necessary evil for us. I'm not having that crazy motherfucker coming after us because one of my boys couldn't keep his dick in his pants."

"Prez, Daniella is a grown woman—"

"I don't give a fuck if it's my grandmother, Shakes. Keep your dick in your pants. There are plenty of bitches here who'll be happy to rub that little itch you've got going," Demon said.

The stare off between Shakes and Demon didn't go well. "I haven't fucked her."

"Keep it that way. I'm not going to give Zeke any excuses to come after my men. My priority is this club, keeping you lot alive. We're just an MC club to this guy. He doesn't give a shit."

"Well, I've got some news that's interesting," Joker said, speaking up.

"What?" Steel asked, amused with the way the meeting was going. Every now and then he saw Eloise moving around the bar through the windows. She kept tripping over her own feet; it was so cute. He couldn't wait to get her alone once again.

She wasn't ready to give the guys in the club a show, but when she was, he'd be more than happy to fuck whenever he got the chance. Her pussy was so fucking tight and hot. There was so much he could teach her to enjoy. She was like a blank canvas waiting for an artist, and he was a great artist.

"Zeke's put a hit out on his wife."

"What?" Shakes asked.

This was getting interesting or fucking crazy.

"I got the order last night. He wants her dead by the end of the weekend. It's why Daniella was here. He didn't want her near mommy dearest."

"For fuck sake." Demon got to his feet. They all took a step back from the broken table. "Just once I want to do this shit easy."

"What are you going to do?" Shakes asked.

"Kill her. What else can I do? Daniella can't know."

"So, we escort her back home and Joker leaves the group before we're at Zeke's," Demon said. "I'm not interested in pissing Zeke off. I've got a woman to worry about and he helps us. His name provides protection as well. Zeke's far reaching."

"I agree with Demon," Joker said. "We're not suffering for our association with Zeke. Yeah, we transport the drugs but we've got no fuckers fighting for our turf anymore. Zeke's name helps us and I don't know about you fuckers, but I'm sick of dying for shit like land. We're not living in the past. This is our MC, our town, and I prefer worrying about other shit than war."

"I'm with them," Steel said. They'd all been in many fights over the years over turf. The Soldiers of Wrath had lost a lot of men for the ground they were living on. He didn't want to watch another brother being buried because some little upstart thought they could have the club.

Then men all nodded in agreement at Demon's assessment.

Striker held his hands up. "Fine. I'm sorry I spoke out of turn. I don't want to end up dead for anyone else but this club."

"I made a deal with Zeke. You die; it's because of me. I'm not interested in adding bodies to our scores."

Death was part of the MC life, but it didn't have to be.

Steel glanced toward the window in time to see Eloise laughing. He wondered what made her smile. She was fast becoming an obsession of his.

"None of us want to add bodies," Steel said. "We're all here trying to make a life for ourselves. I, for one, don't want to watch another one of us die." He had blood on his hands from the time he'd spent in this club.

"Then it's done. Joker, we'll ride out now and take Daniella back home. You'll handle the kill."

"Zeke wants her to suffer."

"Take Nerd with you. He likes to make people suffer."

"It's a woman," Joker said. "I'm like Nerd on this one, making a bitch suffer is going to be hard."

"Then do what you need to do. If you don't make her suffer, I don't give a fuck. The whore hasn't hurt my woman," Demon said. "The rest of you, we ride out. We'll leave the prospects to take care of our women." Demon looked down at the table that was on the floor. "And I'll get another table for our next meeting." He leaned down, slamming the gavel onto the table. "Dismissed."

Leaving the room, he saw Eloise talking with Deanna. Several prospects were hanging around the club, talking. He didn't pay them any attention. Walking up to Eloise, he grabbed her hand, and started walking toward his room.

"Hey, Steel?"

He didn't stop to talk and walked up the stairs. When she stumbled, he made an effort to be slower.

Opening his bedroom door, he tugged her inside, slamming her against the nearest wall once the door was shut behind them.

"What the hell?" she asked.

"Shut up. I need to be with you" He tore at the jeans she wore, knowing next time she was at the clubhouse, he'd make her wear skirts with no panties.

Once they were out of the way, he tore her offending panties off her pussy. Sliding his fingers through her cunt, he groaned.

"You're always so wet for me."

"Steel?" She groaned, thrusting herself onto his fingers.

Pushing two digits inside her, he pushed his thumb against her clit.

"Ride my fingers, baby. Let me watch you come."

She bit her lip, sucking that little plump flesh between her teeth. He groaned, wanting to bite that lip for himself.

Cupping her face, he tilted her head back.

"Give me those lips." He didn't let up on playing with her pussy. She gave him her lips, moaning as he plundered her mouth with his tongue. Biting down on her bottom lip, he sucked the tender flesh into his mouth.

"Are you going to come on my fingers or am I going to have to tease you some more?" he asked.

"Please, Steel."

"You're soaking wet, baby. You need my cock, don't you?"

"You know I do."

He smiled, running his nose from her cheek down to her neck. Inhaling her sweet scent, he added a third finger into her cunt, relishing the wet sounds coming from her pussy. "You'll give me this pussy whenever I want it, won't you." He didn't phrase it like a question

"Yes."

"Submit to me every chance you get, Eloise, and I promise you, you'll never regret it."

She whimpered as he flicked her clit, watching the pleasure wash over her face.

"Come for me."

Eloise shook her head from side to side, crying out as he fucked her harder with his fingers. He didn't let up, forcing her to take everything he gave her.

"Come on, Eloise, let go and give me those sweet sounds."

She screamed, coming all over his hand. When he couldn't stand it any longer, he went to his knees before her, licking and sucking her clit into his mouth.

Her taste exploded on his tongue. Slamming his tongue into her cunt, he drank down her cream, loving her submission.

Standing up, he opened his jeans, pulling out his cock. He didn't wait as he lifted Eloise up in his arms and slid her pussy down onto his dick. When the tip was inside, he slammed her down the remaining inches, going so deep within her.

"I'm going to be leaving town for a couple of days," he said.

She was panting in his arms. He watched her open and close her mouth. "Wait, what?"

"I'm going to arrange for you to be brought here and then taken back to your apartment."

"A couple of days?"

"You're not to go back to Markam's. One of the prospects will bring you here and take you home every night. The only person you're allowed to be with is Deanna. She might take you to see Amy. She's Joker's old lady but doesn't spend all that much time at the clubhouse."

"Why?"

"You're mine now, Eloise. I take care of what is mine, and it means you'll have to do as you're told."

"Are you even listening to yourself?" she asked.

He slammed inside her, reminding her who was boss. "Are you fucking listening to me? You'll do as I tell you or you'll face punishment. I'm taking care of you." Pumping inside her, he watched her come apart on his dick. "Do I make myself clear?"

"Perfectly."

"Good." He knew she needed this dominance, this control. He knew she also felt whole when he was in control. She didn't need to tell him that for him to know. Steel could read her as if he'd known her his whole life. He slammed to the hilt inside her, crying out at the pleasure. It was too much. The tightness of her pussy, having Eloise in his arms, once again sent him over the edge into bliss.

Steel looked forward to coming home if this is what he was coming home to.

Steel and Shakes had to canvas the area that Daniella's mother was living in, had to do this right and fast. Although Steel wasn't all about hurting women and children, he'd been given the low down on why Zeke wanted Daniella's mother gone.

To have a woman that had tormented young Daniella, abused her mentally, forced her to feel like she was less than she really was, pissed Steel off. He also knew it pissed off Shakes and the other men in the club. But for some reason, Shakes was taking this more personally.

He looked at the other member who sat in the passenger seat of Steel's SUV. He looked pissed, and the energy and anger came from Shakes like a fucking wrecking ball.

"What's going on with you?" Steel asked.

Shakes didn't look at him. Instead, he grabbed a cigarette from his cut pocket, put it between his lips, and lit the end with his lighter. He inhaled, held the smoke in for some time, and exhaled slowly.

"And don't fucking tell me nothing is going on."

Shakes looked at him then. "Nothing is wrong," he said without emotion in his voice this time.

Steel wasn't about to try to weasel information out of Shakes. If the man wanted to be tight lipped then fine. "You're a fucking liar, but what the hell ever." Steel leaned back in his seat and watched the house that Daniella's mother lived in. It was late, the lights were on, but there were a lot of people walking outside. They were just canvasing right now, seeing what her routine was before they had to do this.

"I can't believe a mother would put their kid through the shit that bitch did to Daniella." Shakes said and took another hit off his cigarette. He rolled down the window just an inch. Flicked the ash out of the open space and finished smoking. "She's a fucking cunt, and the shit that we'll do to her will be the vengeance Daniella needs."

Steel listened, but didn't respond, because frankly he didn't know what to say. This kind of emotion from Shakes was not what he was used to seeing. Shakes liked pussy, fucked a lot of it, and never made anything lasting. He'd been like Shakes, until he met Eloise, felt this all-consuming need whenever he was around her. Was Shakes feeling the same thing for Zeke's daughter?

"You want her," Steel said without question.

Shakes turned and looked at him, his eyebrow cocked.

"Not that I give two fucks about who you want to fuck, but Demon's right."

"He's right? About what exactly?" There was a touch of hostility in Shakes's voice.

"Don't get pissy with me because you want to fuck with Zeke's girl. I mean she's beautiful, and I can see why you'd want her, but she Zeke's daughter, man."

"You have a woman, so don't even fucking try to go after Daniella." Shakes had turned in his seat now, facing Steel, and looking rightly pissed off.

"Man, I don't want Daniella. I have Eloise, and believe me, she's the one for me. She's the only one for me." He rested his head back on the seat, thinking about what he'd just told Shakes. The silence stretched on for a moment, and finally he breathed out.

"So, she's the one? You want her as an old lady?"

Steel looked over at Shakes. He was staring at Daniella's mother's house, his jaw tight, his muscles flexing under the stubble covered skin.

"You want her bad, Shakes, and you're eating yourself up by staying back."

"You all told me to stay back."

This was true, but even so he knew how Shakes felt. He felt something fierce for Eloise, didn't know what he'd do if he didn't have her in his life. She was his obsession, his addiction, and he knew he wouldn't let her go. He couldn't, not now that he'd had a taste of her.

"Yeah, because that's what's fucking smart. Zeke will kill you if you go after her. That's the only saving grace, the only fucking thing that redeems his sadistic ass."

"Yeah," Shakes said and inhaled the cigarette before flicking it out the window. "Let's just fucking report on this bitch and get the fuck out of here. The sooner we get rid of that cunt the better off Daniella will be."

He saw the lights flick off in the house, glanced at Shakes once more, then started the SUV and drove off. Shakes was in for one fucking rollercoaster ride, especially if he went after Daniella. The look on Shakes face, the intensity, possessiveness, told Steel that Shakes wouldn't listen to reason, and would most definitely go after Daniella.

The poor bastard was sure as fuck in for one hell of a ride, and he'd better hold on tight.

Chapter Ten

"So, this is where I live," Eloise said, waiting for Deanna and Amy to enter. After Steel left yesterday, Deanna drove her to where Amy lived. She loved both women even though she didn't know them very well. They were both sweet, lovely, and oh so nice. She couldn't ever recall getting along with anyone so easily. Their men banded all three of them together.

"This is a nice place," Amy said, stepping inside.

Both women removed their jackets as Eloise closed the door. "Erm, should we let the prospect up?"

"Nah, he's happy downstairs. He can keep an eye out and tell our men what's happening," Deanna said.

"He's going to tell our men what we're doing?"

"Of course. Didn't you know they know everything?"

Amy chuckled while Eloise headed toward her fridge. "Do you guys want a drink?"

"I do," Amy said. "I'm so thirsty."

"How's Joker anyway? I've not seen much of him around the club," Deanna said.

Looking toward the two women, Eloise smiled as they sat on her sofa. She'd never had girlfriends before.

"We're doing good. He's taken half of my clothes as it is."

"Finally, you've been hinting at him long enough."

"He doesn't want me to feel pressured by him. Joker wouldn't pressure me," Amy said.

Taking three sodas out of the fridge, she walked into the living room. She handed both women their drinks, taking a seat in her chair.

"So come on, spill," Deanna said, turning to her. "You and Steel?"

"Um, I really don't know what to say about Steel and me."

"Nothing?" Amy asked.

"I don't know what we've got going on. I mean, I owe him a lot."

Deanna and Amy shared a look.

"What?" she asked. "What is it?"

"What exactly do you owe Steel?" Deanna asked.

"Well," she ran fingers through her hair in an effort to stall the conversation. "I used to work at Markam's. Well, a couple of nights ago the manager, erm, he kind of attacked me. Nothing really happened though. Steel was there to stop it."

"Attacked you?" Amy asked, whispering the words.

"Nothing happened." She wished she hadn't said anything.

"Eloise, you should have reported it." Deanna leaned forward.

"Can we talk about something else? I've already argued with Steel about it. Besides, he took care of it." She didn't even want to think of what Steel had done to take care of it.

"I don't like this," Amy said. "If there's a guy out there—"

"Seriously, it's nothing. I trust Steel and he took care of it." She smiled. "Then he took care of me."

Both women looked like they wanted to say more. After several tense minutes, they relaxed, smiling. "He took care of you?" Amy asked.

"Well, he's very intense and...dominating."

"Oh," Deanna said. "Please, do tell."

Eloise giggled. "He likes to take charge in the bedroom. We've only been together a couple of times, but he's made an impression."

For the next hour, Eloise relaxed as she listened to Amy and Deanna talk about their men, Joker and Demon. She found she had a lot in common with the two women. They were nice, strong, but vulnerable. A strange combination to have for biker women.

A cell phone going off stopped their giggling.

"It's me," Amy said. She grabbed her cell phone out of her bag and looked down at it. "Joker, Demon, and Steel are on their way over here."

"We're not doing anything wrong," Deanna said, sitting more comfortably on the sofa. "Let them come up and order us around. Demon looks so cute when he gets all red in the face."

"I doubt he'll like being described as cute," Amy said.

"Cute is not a word I'd describe Steel." Eloise had a lot of words to describe her man, cute wasn't one of them.

"Well, we're here now and they can be mad at us all they want. I'm not going anywhere until I finish my drink," Deanna said.

"We sound like a couple of women drinking wine. We're only hanging out having a soda." Amy started laughing.

During their laughter, someone banged on the door.

Amy and Deanna let out a childish giggle. "Don't let them in, Eloise."

Shaking her head, she made her way toward the door and opened it. Leaning against it, she smiled at the three intimidating men.

"Our women are here," Demon said. She recognized both men from the photos that Deanna showed her yesterday at work.

Stepping out of the way, she watched the three men enter.

"You've been behaving?" Steel said, stepping forward. She noticed there were some bruises on his knuckles when he reached out to touch her cheek.

"I have, but you don't look like you've been good," she said, pointing at his hands.

"I've been busy."

"I see that."

He sank his fingers into her hair, cupping the back of her head, and drawing her closer. "I want those lips."

She couldn't believe how easy she gave herself up to him. It wasn't so long ago that she'd turned him away.

His lips melded to hers and she was too weak to deny him. Opening her lips, she moaned as the instant bolt of pleasure attacked her. He slid his tongue into her mouth. Releasing the door, she wrapped her arms around his neck, relishing the taste of him in her mouth.

"I've missed you," he said.

"I missed you, too." Opening her eyes, she smiled at him.

"I can see that." He brought his hand down from her cheek, to slide across her nipple. She gasped, staring into his eyes. He was fast becoming her drug of choice.

"Has there been anyone else?" Eloise asked. She didn't know what to expect with him on the road.

"Have I fucked anyone else?"

She nodded.

"No, baby. The only pussy I can think about is yours. You're the only one I want." He silenced her with his lips. She didn't like how easy she was giving herself over to him. Steel knew how to work her body.

Eloise didn't fight her need for him. In that moment, all she cared about was the pleasure to be had at his touch.

Someone clearing his throat made her pull away from him.

Turning around, she saw Joker sitting with Amy on his lap and the same with Demon and Deanna.

"Well, we're here and I don't see a reason for us to go back to the clubhouse yet. Let's order food here," Demon said.

"I'm game," this came from Joker.

Amy and Deanna nodded in agreement. "Do you mind us crashing here for food?" Deanna asked.

"Not at all."

Closing the door, she was surprised when Steel waited for her. He held on to her hand as they walked toward the only available chair. Steel lowered himself into the chair before tugging her down onto his lap.

"Well, what should we order?" Demon asked.

"Pizza with cheese, lots of cheese," Joker said.

"You always ask for too much cheese," Amy said.

She watched the couple smile and whisper to each other. The red tint on Amy's face was not hard to miss when Joker leaned in and started to whisper to her. They were a lovely couple and Eloise couldn't help but wonder exactly what she and Steel were doing.

Eloise stared at the Harley's that drove down the street. Steel and the rest of the guys and their old ladies had just gone, and here she was, feeling content, but also itchy with need. Steel hadn't been able to stay, saying they had club business to attend to. She didn't know what it was about, didn't want to know either, but she saw the look of violence on his face, in the way he held himself.

She knew that whatever he had to talk about concerning club business it had to do with his scuffed up knuckles and the blood on his shirt. It was a little frightening to think about what he did, where his club was going, and how they were associated with illegal activity. She'd asked herself if this is what she really wanted, if being with Steel was the right move. But the truth was he made her feel alive, made her desires not feel wrong. He took control, showed her that with pain came pleasure. She couldn't think of herself without Steel in her life, and that was probably the scariest part of it all.

Going into her room, she shut the door, stared at the computer, and knew that one day soon she'd actually have to tell Steel what she liked. He knew, or at least he was good at giving her what she wanted, but what would he say if she actually told him she wanted pain with her pleasure, wanted to be spanked so hard welts showed up on her ass, on her back and thighs? What would he say if she told him she wanted to be restrained, her hands above her head, his hand prints, bruises on her body?

God, she was sick, or maybe she wasn't really sick at all, she just hadn't found the right man to show her that what she felt was okay? Maybe she'd finally found that one person to show her that pleasure and pain could be one? Yes, Steel had certainly opened her eyes, and she didn't want it to end, didn't want it to stop. She wanted more, so much more, and being with Steel made her feel okay to want all of that and more.

And that made her smile, and had her cheeks hurting because she was deliriously happy, and she hoped nothing took that away from her.

Chapter Eleven

One month later

Steel sipped at his whiskey while watching Eloise work around the clubhouse. Deanna had taken her under her wing and the men adored her. She was a great little barmaid and since they'd been together, she'd blossomed. He noticed she smiled a hell of a lot more now than ever before. There was something that she was holding back from him. He sensed it and deep in his heart, he knew she was still afraid.

In the last month, he hadn't held back from her, giving her most of what he could but he was holding back a little. Part of him was worried that if he was to let go and show her the true man he was, she'd run away screaming.

He'd spanked her ass to the point that she'd bruised, crying out for him to go harder. After she'd taken his hand and begged for more, he moved up to the flat edge of a brush. She'd been dripping wet. What really had her going was being held down, controlled as he fucked her, spilling filthy words into her ear. She didn't fight him, at least not to get him to stop. No, Eloise kept trying to get him to go harder, deeper, to take her more forcefully.

"What's going on in that head of yours?" Shakes asked, taking a seat.

"Nothing." He didn't look away from Eloise. She bent down showing off her ass that underneath the jeans she wore, was bruised from his play.

"Something's going on in that head of yours; I know you."

"Are you ready to tell me where you've spent the last month?" Steel asked.

Every other night Shakes would leave the clubhouse and not return for a day or two. Glancing at his friend, he saw Shakes's lips pressed together.

"Until you're ready to talk about that shit, stay out of my business." Steel tipped his glass to his lips. He was buzzing, and there wasn't a chance of getting Eloise home. His room wasn't going anywhere at the clubhouse. He'd take her there.

"You know where I've been, Steel," Shakes said, whispering the words.

He turned to look at his friend. "You're going to get yourself killed."

"One of us just killed her mother. Everyone around her has abandoned her. I'm not going to do that."

"Out of all the women you could play with, why her? She's going to cause you trouble. Her father will castrate you and laugh while he's doing it."

Shakes shrugged. "There's something about her. She's strong even after everything she's been through. I'm not going to abandon her."

"She's not your responsibility." Steel tapped his glass, waiting for Eloise to fill it up again. She smiled at him, her sweet smile that he adored. Grabbing her hand, he kissed the inside of her wrist. "Hey, beautiful."

"Are you drunk?" she asked.

"No, I'm not drunk. I'm fine." He winked at her, loving the way she rolled her eyes. Counting up all of her punishments, Steel had an idea for when he got her into bed that night. He was going to push her just a little further. Two things would happen, he'd either break her or find out what she was hiding. He had a feeling they were two of a kind, only she wanted pain while he wanted to give it out. She was his perfect match.

"I've got to go."

He tugged her down, drawing her lips to his. "Miss me?"

"I do."

Steel watched her walk into the back.

"What's going on there?" Shakes asked.

"If Demon or Zeke finds out what you're doing, you could be killed or lose your place in the club. I hope you're prepared for that."

"I'm not doing anything. Believe it or not, Steel, I've not touched her." Shakes got up and stormed off.

"What's his deal?" Demon asked, taking a seat.

"Nothing as far as I can tell," Steel said, sipping at his drink once again.

"Eloise is a good woman. Deanna speaks highly of her."

"She also allows us to crash at her place to order a shit load of pizza." Steel laughed, hitting Demon's arm. "You don't need to go listing Eloise's good points; I know them."

"Have you made sure Hanson's not getting any ideas?" Demon asked.

Steel paused with the glass against his lips. "What?"

"It has been over a month. He had the guts to attack his own employee. I'd go and just give him a little reminder of what happens when he messes with us."

"You think he's stupid enough to try something like that?"

"I don't know what he's stupid enough to do." Demon shrugged. "Why you kept him alive is beyond me."

"I couldn't just kill him. He owns that fucking store. His death would come back to the club. I did what I had to do." It didn't mean he hadn't thought about paying a special visit to the fucker, to give him a reminder of what it was like to have his ass kicked. "I've drunk too much. I can be an idiot, but I don't have a fucking death wish."

"Good for you, I don't have anything on right now. Come on, I'll drive you."

He followed Demon out of the clubhouse, climbing into the car. There was no way he'd ride bitch for his Prez. The only one to ride at Demon's back was going to be Deanna.

"What's going on with Shakes?" Demon asked as they pulled out of the compound.

"I don't know."

"Zeke was clear in his instructions. Daniella is off limits. I'd hate to punish a brother because he's not listening."

"It's not my business, Demon. You've got a problem with Shakes, take it up with him. My dick is sticking with Eloise. My woman knows exactly how I like my sex." At least, he was going to step it up when he got back home. He only hoped she didn't run screaming from him when he did.

They pulled up outside of Markam's. Climbing out of the car, he made his way inside. A slender blonde was serving a customer at one of the counters. "You seen Hanson?" he asked.

"He's in his office."

"Between us, sweet thing, he behaving himself?"

"Yes."

"Good. That's what I like to hear." He moved down the aisle toward the back office. Steel's anger returned recalling Eloise's terrified scream. She'd not wanted the bastard near her, yet he'd tried to touch her.

He couldn't kill Hanson, but he could hurt him, hurt him a hell of a lot.

Opening the office door without knocking, he watched as Hanson jumped up from his seat the moment he clocked his gaze on him.

"Hey, fucker, long time no see."

"What do you want?" Hanson asked.

"I've come to make sure we're still clear on what we'd talked about?"

"I've not said anything to anyone."

Steel advanced into the room, reminded of the pain this bastard tried to inflict on Eloise. Reaching out, he twisted his arm at an odd angle. The pressure was enough to make him uncomfortable but not enough to snap the bone. "I'm just giving you another friendly warning. You come near Eloise and you're going to be dealing with something far worse than a beating, do you understand?"

"Yes."

Satisfied he'd gotten his message across, he gave a friendly wink to the woman on the counter, walked out of the store, and went back toward his car. "Time for us to go home." He hoped Eloise was waiting for him. His cock thickened at the thought.

Eloise sat on the edge of Steel's bed waiting for him to come back to the clubhouse. He was too far over the limit to take her home. She didn't like driving late at night. He'd spoiled her the past month, driving her everywhere, getting her anything she needed or wanted. She'd never liked driving before and only did it because she had to.

I'm going to do it. I'm going to be open and honest with him.

Steel had given her more in the past month than anyone had ever tried throughout the whole of her life. He didn't leave her feeling like a freak. She'd noticed he was getting harder in his hits to her ass and thighs. The way he held her down was getting tighter, more firm with the right kind of pain.

She could be honest with him about what she liked, the pain, the need to be consumed by him. They'd gotten close to each other, and he'd opened up about the club. Tucking some hair behind her ear, she finally came to a decision. She wasn't going to bottle it in like she had done the last couple of times.

Open up.

He'd either send her packing or embrace this side of her. She'd tried to bury the need for pain for so long that she'd held everything in, afraid of feeling. That wasn't going to happen again. She wouldn't let it.

The door to his room opened and Steel walked in. "Hey, baby, I'm pleased you waited up for me."

Her heart raced. Steel was wearing a belt looped through his jeans. Now was the time to tell him.

"Steel, there's something I need to tell you."

Chapter Twelve

She breathed in and out, stared at Steel, and just told herself to tell him what she wanted. "I want pain when we have sex." She held her breath, waiting for him to say something.

"You want me to hurt you, baby?" he said in a low, menacingly aroused voice. He took a step closer.

She nodded, licked her lips, and stared at him as he stared at her. "I want you to hurt me, because that's what gets me off, what makes me feel good inside."

He didn't move, but after a second he lifted his hand, gesturing for her to stand. "If we do this we do it my way. You do what I say, when I say it, and I promise you I'll make you feel so good you'll be high from it."

Her heart thundered from it. She wanted that; God, did she want that.

"Yes, Steel, that's what I want." He hadn't laughed at her, hadn't looked disgusted. In fact, Steel looked aroused, his cock was hard, pressing against his pants, and she knew he wanted this.

"Move to the center of the room," he said, his voice a deep, guttural sound that had goose bumps popping out along her flesh.

She moved over to the section of light that was an ever-present square in the center of the room. There she stood, waiting for him to give her the commands. Yes, she'd been dreaming of this her whole life, able to trust someone with this deep, dark secret of hers.

"Take off your clothes," he said, and sat on the edge of the bed.

Eloise got undressed, her hands shaking, her need rising. Then she stood there in nothing at all, seeing this man, this dominant man, about to give her the pleasure she desperately desired.

"Turn around for me, baby."

She did as he said.

"Spread your legs, bend at the waist, and grab your ankles. I want to see the cunt that belongs to me."

Her heart was starting to pound fast now, not because she was scared or embarrassed, but because she was aroused, and this was what she'd always wanted. She closed her eyes, picturing him doing what she wanted. He'd be touching her, spanking her, and giving her his mark. When she was in the position that he'd ordered, she waited for him to respond, or command her to do more.

"Grab your ass cheeks and pull them apart. I want to see what I'll be fucking tonight, what I own, Eloise."

Her throat constricted, but she didn't hesitate in complying. God, she'd never disobey him. With her ass and pussy now on display, and the chill in the air moving along her exposed cleft, she forced herself not to shiver.

"Very pretty and all mine. Stand and face me again," he said with that bass voice that did something to her insides.

When she was facing him again, she clenched her hands into tight fists. She took a step forward, but he *tsked* and she instantly stopped.

"I take what I want when I want. That's what you've come to me for, right? That's what you want from me." His voice was hard and unyielding.

"Yes, I'm yours."

"I don't practice BDSM, Eloise. I fuck women that like pain with their pleasure because I like to give it to them. It gets me off, makes me hard, and with you I've never been harder in my life." He stood and moved closer to her. "Before you, I've never had this bone-deep need to control and dominate a woman." He reached out and brushed a stray strand of hair from her cheek. "With you, I only want...you." He moved away from her and sat back down on the bed. "On your hands and knees, and crawl to me."

She was so aroused right now, wet and needy, and she was getting more lust-filled knowing she'd crawl to him. On her hands and knees now, her ass was in the air and her tits hung freely. Eloise took a steadying breath and started to move toward him.

The hard floor was cold and unforgiving, but she blocked out the discomfort and focused on the man in front of her. Steel was this dark, devilishly handsome man, but not in this classic sense.

"I like pain with my pleasure, too, Eloise. I like spanking and restraining, and a lot of screaming," he said. "Does that frighten you, baby?"

When she was right in front of him, she looked at his face, but saw nothing but icy composure. Her mouth instantly went dry when he went for the belt of his jeans. Once he had his belt undone he pulled his zipper down. It was erotically sick, the way he pulled his erection out through only the flap, not even bothering to undo the button. He started stroking himself up and down slowly, and her mouth watered.

"Do you feel like a slut right now baby? Do you feel like my slut, Eloise?" he asked, then grinned when she nodded.

She looked down at his dick, swallowed at the big size, and felt her pussy clench.

"Stop staring at it and suck my cock." He was hard and unyielding in his command. "I'll give the pain you and I both need, but first you'll give me what I want."

He was brutally coarse with his language, but even him calling her a slut for wanting his dick couldn't turn her off. She glanced down at his large size, at the way he continually stroked himself lazily, as if waiting for her to obey him. Leaning forward, she felt her throat constrict and her mouth water. Yes, she did want him in every way imaginable. He grabbed a chunk of her hair and yanked her forward with enough force that she cried out in pain. Pleasure slammed into her immediately.

She moaned.

"That's it, make noise. Let me know that this hurts." He leaned forward, and she heard his breath right by her ear. "But even though it hurts, I know your cunt is all nice and juicy right now."

A gush of wetness left her pussy and slipped down her thigh.

"Now. Now suck my fucking cock." He leaned back and pulled her head forward until the slick tip of his shaft moved along her lips.

She opened her mouth, sucked on his shaft like she was dying for his cum, and if he didn't shoot his load down her throat she'd starve to death.

"Move your tongue around and stroke the underside of my dick."

She did as he said, and the salty flavor of his pre-cum covered her taste buds. Flattening her tongue and doing what he said required her to take in more of his length into her mouth. She actually grew even more aroused at the flavor of him. His cum exploded on her tongue, covered the entire interior of her mouth, and she wanted more.

Eloise wanted the tip of his cock to hit the back of her throat, wanted to swallow his cum until it slipped out of the corner of her mouth and dripped down her chin. God, she really was a slut for Steel, a little whore because she couldn't get enough.

Lifting her hands and placing them on his thighs, she felt the rough material of his jeans. But before she could curl her nails into his muscular, hard legs, he had both of her wrists in one of his hands and had them lifted above her head. The whole action had only taken a few seconds.

Now she stared up at him, his cock no longer in her mouth, and her lips parted in shock. She gasped out when he tightened his hand on her wrists. The pain was immediate, intense, dominating. She loved it all.

"I didn't say you could touch me," he growled. He pulled her forward again, and her face went right into his lap. "Now suck my fucking cock until I come."

God, his coarse and hard language did something wickedly naughty to her. Opening her mouth and taking his cock again, she moaned at the salty flavor of his pre-cum. It certainly wasn't a taste that she thought would ever be appetizing, but coming from Steel made it hot as hell. He had moved her hands behind her back now and growled out for her to keep them there. With her on her knees, her thighs slightly open, she had no friction on her throbbing clit. Letting her mouth do the work, she started sucking him with fervor.

"That's it. Suck me until I come, Eloise." He had his hand in her hair now, pulling at the strands hard enough that she had tears in her eyes.

Looking up at him while giving him head, she saw his attention was on her mouth.

"You should see your lips right now, stretched wide around my dick. You're a good little girl that is hungry for my cock." He started lifting his hips, thrusting his dick deeper into her mouth, and causing her to gag.

She panted, breathing out through her nose, and moved past the need to gag every time his dick hit the back of her throat. But she wanted more, so much more.

"I'm going to have you drinking my cum, forcing you to swallow it until it's coming out between your lips." He was so hard and unrelenting as he lifted his hips in time with bringing her head down into his lap.

She couldn't breathe, couldn't do anything but allow him to use her as a vessel for his orgasm. He started breathing heavier, tightened his hold on her hair, and cursed continuously. A deep groan left him, and then she felt the hard jets of his cum move down the back of her throat. He kept his hold on her head, forced her mouth to stay on his dick and for her to swallow him. His cum slipped out of her mouth, and he yanked her head back, breathed out roughly, and tried to catch her breath. His semen slipped down her chin and land on her breast.

He pushed her back so she sat on her heels and stared up at him. Steel stared at her breasts and she knew he was looking at his seed that lined her chest. He reached out and ran his thumb over her nipple, collecting the semen and lifting it to her mouth. There was more of his cum on her chest, but what he collected he made her suck clean from his digit.

"Go on, eat it, swallow it, and moan because it tastes good."

"I do want to suck it clean, Steel. I want it all."

"And I'll give it all to you."

She opened her mouth when he pressed his thumb to the seam of her lips. Holding her gaze with his, and suctioning her lips around his finger, she sucked slow and hard. He made a low sound in his throat and then pushed her back with enough force that she fell on her ass. Her legs fell open, and she saw him look between them.

"I'm going to color your flesh with my belt, my hand, and my teeth."

Genuine fear slammed into her when he stood. He was semi-hard still, and she gasped out when he took a step closer.

"I'm a sadistic bastard, and I'm going to make you my good little masochistic slut." He stopped an inch from her and used his foot, which was encased in a worn, leathered, shit-kicking boot, and nudged her legs farther apart.

"Touch your cunt." He grabbed the base of his shaft, stroking himself lazily while he waited for her to comply.

Placing her hand between her legs, she felt her slippery flesh and started moving her fingers up and down her slit.

"Rub that hard little clit, make yourself nearly come, and then I want you to stop."

She panted and started rubbing herself harder, faster, and feeling her desire start to move higher. Eloise was already so aroused that as soon as she touched herself she felt on the verge of coming. She watched him remove his belt, feeling her heart rate start to increase.

"Don't stop touching yourself no matter what I do."

She squeezed her other hand into a fist beside her, rubbed her clit fast and hard as she felt her climax start to rise, and stared at his cock. He was hard again, long and thick, and so tempting that all she could think about was feeling him moving back and forth inside of her.

Then she saw the flash of his silver belt buckle, felt the sting of it as it touched her flesh, and she cried out. The immense and powerful pain gave way to something warm and pleasurable. He slapped the belt across her other thigh. He did this over and over again, not especially hard, but with enough force that she felt it down to her very bones. He was breathing heavily, as if he couldn't control himself. Sweat lined his forehead, and then all of a sudden he stopped hitting her with the belt, as if he knew she was about to come.

"Stop touching yourself."

She rested against the floor, panting and staring at the ceiling, knowing that she wouldn't survive tonight if he kept this up.

Chapter Thirteen

Eloise's thighs had a lovely red tint. The way she sat on the floor restricted his view of her. Steel didn't want a restricted view.

"Stand up."

He loved the way she did as he commanded without a second thought. This is what he'd been expecting from Eloise. Slowly, over the past couple of weeks he'd been increasing the pain for her, waiting for her to complain. She hadn't complained and, in fact, did the exact opposite, begging him to make it just a little harder. If she wanted to hurt, then she'd just met her match because he loved giving it.

"Give me your fingers."

She held her fingers up to his face. He inhaled the scent of her cunt before licking her cream off each digit. "That taste is what I want every fucking day." Reaching out, he slipped his fingers inside her core, pumping two digits inside, stroking her dripping heat. She was so wet that her cream coated the inside of her thighs.

"This is what you want, isn't it, baby? You want to be ordered, controlled, fucked, taken over." With his other hand, he gripped her hair while still holding onto his belt. He tugged on a fistful of hair, watching her eyes grow wide. Her mouth opened as she released a gasp. Leaning down, he ran his tongue around her lips before sliding inside. He sucked her tongue into his mouth and finger fucked her at the same time.

"Answer me," he said.

"Yes, it's what I want. I want you, Steel."

Spreading his fingers wide, he added a second then third digit inside her pussy. He stroked over her clit. Her pussy tightened around his fingers. She was close to orgasm. Steel just wasn't going to let her orgasm. She was going to need to earn it.

"Get on the bed," he said, removing his hands from her pussy and hair.

She did so shakily this time. If she wanted pain then he was going to test her to see how much she could take. Within seconds, she was kneeling on the bed. He saw her gripping the sheet beneath her as if it could ground her in some way. Nothing was going to ground her. He intended to fuck her into oblivion. By the time the end of the night came, she wasn't going to even think about ever leaving him.

Eloise was his old lady. She just didn't know it yet. He was going to have her all to himself, to spoil and play with for the rest of their days.

He caressed the back of her legs, her ass, between her thighs, and the lips of her pussy.

"You're so wet, Eloise. Is it all for me?"

"Yes."

"Do you want me to hurt you?"

"Yes."

"Make it burn?"

"Yes."

"Then don't say a word, Eloise. I want to hear you scream, that's all."

He raised the belt in his hand and brought it down on the rounded flesh of her ass. She jumped a little from the contact, her little whimper the only sound to be heard. He brought his belt up again, bringing it down. Five times he slapped her with the belt across the center of her fleshy ass.

Steel liked to cause pain, but he also had rules. He'd never use the metal buckle on her, at least not until she was ready for that kind of pain. The last thing he wanted to do was make it unbearable for her right now, or it feel like abuse. This was not abuse. They both wanted it, craved it.

Against all impossible odds, they'd found each other. He teased his fingers through her flesh, finding her wetter than before. Licking more cream off his fingers, he started working on the base of her back, and down her thighs. He gave her a good working over drawing the leather over her body. Her screams were the most amazing sounds he'd ever heard. She didn't beg him to stop, only to keep going.

Her ass soon turned a delightful shade of red. In some spots there would be bruising come the morning.

Steel wasn't done.

"Turn over, lie down on your back."

She rolled over, settling down on the bed.

Throwing the belt into the corner, he wrapped his fingers around his swollen dick as he glided his hand up her body. He started at her leg, going up her hip to circle her stomach, before circling her nipple. The tight puckered bud was just begging for some attention. Caressing her other nipple, he stared at the tight buds, wondering what would be best. He pinched her left nipple, hard until she was arching up into his touch. Leaning down, he sucked her tight bud, moving his fingers out of the way to replace them with his teeth. He cupped her pussy, sliding a finger in and out of her tight heat. Her body writhed under him at each little touch he gave her.

Whack.

He slapped her pussy while moving to her other nipple. After each slap to her pussy, he slid a finger deep inside her cunt, bringing her closer to the edge. She was so close to an orgasm that she was panting for it.

When he was satisfied she was near the point of no return, he pulled away, and started to tug his clothes off. "Your body is fucking beautiful, Eloise. You're a naked canvas waiting for me to put my mark on you." Kicking off his boots and jeans, he climbed onto the bed naked. Moving between her thighs, he reached for the back of her neck, drawing her up.

Slamming his lips down on hers, he fucked her mouth with his tongue. Her hands held onto his hips, digging her nails into his flesh.

"That's it, baby, mark me just as I'm marking you." Wrapping his hand in her hair, he held her tightly against him. "In this room when we're alone, you're going to be my little pain slut. I don't want you thinking you're anything else; you're not. You're mine and I'm not going to let you go. When we're in here, I'm going to remind you exactly who you belong to and you're going to love every second of what I do to you."

He kissed her one final time before letting her go so she flopped onto the bed. Gripping his cock, he stared at her beautiful body.

"Open your legs wide," he said.

She opened them.

"Lift that cunt to me."

Eloise lifted herself up so that her pussy was close to his cock.

"Yeah, that's what I want. I'm going to fuck your pussy and when I've filled you up with my spunk, I'm going to fuck your ass."

Tonight, he wasn't going to leave any part of her empty. He needed her to know who she belonged to.

"Yes, Steel, I want that. Please, give it to me."

He was going to give it to her all right. Steel was going to have her addicted to his hard cock.

Aligning the tip of his dick against her opening, he slid inside, groaning as her tight pussy walls squeezed him.

He pounded inside her. The odd angle had Eloise falling back. Gripping her hips, he slammed every inch of his dick inside her, making her take it all and beg for more. The tips of his fingers were white where he touched her. There would be bruises on her body in the morning. He didn't give a fuck.

"Please, Steel," she said, begging so beautifully.

He fucked her hard. Eloise had to reach out; grabbing the headboard, otherwise her head would be banging against the wall.

Throughout it all, she screamed for more.

Steel didn't let up his strokes even as he leaned down, sucking on a tight nipple, then the other. Rearing back, he slapped her breasts, watching them darken a little from the taps.

Eloise lapped it up like a bitch in a heat. It was such a beautiful sight to see. He couldn't stop it nor did he want to.

Pulling out of her, he flipped her onto her stomach, dragging her onto her knees until her ass was in the air. He slid back inside her gaping cunt. Steel watched her pussy taking him in, swallowing him up. Licking his fingers, he smeared his saliva over her puckered asshole and started to work into her ass.

He'd meant every word he said. Once he was done in her pussy, he was going to fuck her ass, and spill his load inside her. She was going to be drenched and beg him for more.

"Please, don't stop," she said.

"I'm not going to stop." He slapped her ass, using his palm for her right cheek and the back of his hand for her left. Over and over he marked up her ass then her thighs. She kept pushing back against him so that he could go deeper. He couldn't take his eyes off his cock. The length was covered in her cream, glistening in the light with each thrust he made. Wet sounds of flesh hitting flesh echoed around the room.

She begged, moaned, screamed, and gave as good as she got. The woman in his bed wasn't trying to satisfy him or the club. No, she was here because she wanted to be here. She needed his dick, wanted it.

Pounding inside her tight pussy, he stopped slapping her ass to tease her clit. She was so close that a few strokes over her clit had her hurtling into a screaming orgasm. Her pussy latched onto his cock, and he pounded inside her, finding his own release. His balls grew tight and seconds later he filled her snatch with his cum. By the time it was over, he struggled to even see clearly it was that fucking heady.

Seconds, minutes, hours, time was irrelevant yet it passed. Eloise lay beneath him. He pressed a kiss to her shoulder, pulling his fingers out of her ass in the process. Steel slowly left her body, making sure he didn't hurt her in the process.

Her body was decorated in red stripes from the belt. She looked utterly beautiful with his cum spilling from the lips of her pussy. Coating his fingers in his cum, he pushed more of it inside her.

"Wow," she said.

Steel looked up to see her glancing at him. He helped her roll over.

"I was so scared."

"Why?" he asked.

"I've never been open with anyone about what I want. I figured I was a freak."

"Hey, baby, you're a freak, it just so happens you've found another freak to share it with." He smiled at her to show he was teasing. After such a heady, intense sexual encounter, emotions were raw. "You're not a freak. We just like things a little differently."

Tears filled her eyes. Lying down beside her, he frowned. Seeing her on the brink of tears made him want to find the source of her pain and take them out.

"What is it?" he asked. "Tell me."

"It's so silly and stupid."

"It's not. You tell me now; I want to know." He'd kill anyone who made his woman cry.

"I loved every second of what we just did and now I don't know how I'm going to handle you finding someone else."

Her words registered and Steel chuckled.

"It's not funny," she said, pressing her face into her hands.

"Baby, there isn't going to be anyone else. You're mine. I'm not going to give you up nor am I going to share. You're fucking mine. If you want, I'll have my name inked over these tits, this ass, and this cunt, and over your heart. I expect you to have feelings for me, Eloise."

She wrapped her arms around his neck, holding him close. "I do. I really do."

"Good. I don't want any more talk of you leaving or going somewhere to do some shit. You're all mine, you got that."

"Yes, I got that."

He'd only just found the one woman he was looking for. There wasn't a chance in hell he was going to give that up. Cupping her face, he claimed her lips, determined to complete what he'd started. Next on the menu was her ass.

Hanson rubbed his hands together while also staring over at the Soldiers of Wrath MC compound. A party was in full swing and it made him sick to his stomach to see them all partying and having fun. The men were scum and the women just whores. He was sick and tired of them getting everything in town while he got fucking nothing.

He'd been priming Eloise for months, putting up with her around the store. The moment he first saw her, he knew he wanted to fuck her. Then that bastard Steel had to storm in and ruin fucking everything. He was so pissed off. Now, his face was a fucking mess and the bitch that had replaced her wouldn't take any of his shit.

In one night he'd lost his little toy, and he hated it, seethed because of it. Eloise was supposed to be his, all his.

Gritting his teeth, Hanson smiled. Well, Steel could have Eloise but he wondered if the rough biker would like her once he got a hold of her. He'd cut up that pretty face; scar her for life until she was unrecognizable. She'd come begging for his attention then.

When she was begging him to take her, then he'd really get what he wanted.

He started to plan. All he needed was a moment when Steel and the guys weren't looking. A small moment where they were looking at everything else and they lost Eloise then he'd get what he wanted.

Chapter Fourteen

Eloise finished drying off the counters, went behind the bar, and grabbed the filled trash bag.

"I'm going to take this out," she told the sweet-butt, or club whore, or whatever the hell the guys decided to call the girls that were easy at the club. The girl, Berry, nodded, her focus on one of the prospects as he pushed hair off her shoulder and looked down at her breasts.

She pushed the backdoor open and made her way to the trashcans off to the side of the club, hidden in the shadows. There were a few lights on the outside of the club, illuminating the perimeter, but not reaching this part of the property. Steel was with some of the other club members, working on club business, and she'd decided to stay back here while they did their business. She didn't want to think about what they'd talked about, what they did, or whom they had to hurt to make sure they got the job done.

She glanced to her left and saw a Harley of the prospect that was inside probably getting head by Berry. The music from inside came through loud, and she tossed the trash in the cans and shut the lid. For a moment, she stared up at the moon feeling like her life had finally come round full circle, and she was right where she was supposed to be. Steel had opened her eyes, made her feel the euphoria that came with the pleasure and pain, and she felt like she was falling so hard and fast for him. She felt like she loved him, like she really, really loved that hardened biker.

She wiped her hands on the apron she wore, turned around, but the sound of shoes on the pavement had her stopping. Looking around, she thought she'd see a prospect, or one of the club members that had stayed back coming outside. She didn't see anyone though. Eloise was a few steps away from rounding the corner of the side of the club when someone grabbed her from behind, slammed a hand over her mouth, and hauled her backward. Whoever had her was strong, but she could feel him behind her, and knew he wasn't very large, not compared to Steel.

She struggled, but he dragged her deeper into the darkness. The sound of the front door opening and closing, of men laughing and cursing, came through, but the hand that covered her mouth was unyielding and she couldn't make a sound for help. The stench of garbage and alcohol filled her nose. Eloise was pressed up against the side of the garage, the trashcans surrounding her making her gag.

It took a moment for her eyes to adjust, but when she saw who held her against her will she fought harder. Hanson, that piece of shit was right in front of her, his body pressed to hers, and his smile wide even in the shadowy recesses of this space.

"You know, this was a lot easier than I thought it would be." His breath smelled so heavily of liquor and stale cigarette smoke.

She gagged, and the fear that she would choke on her own vomit slammed into her.

"I've been waiting, bitch, waiting for the right time. Your little boyfriend and his asshole friend came to the store, trying to scare me into staying away."

Eloise felt her eyes widen at his words.

He chuckled almost sinisterly. "Yeah, I want you, and our little party was stopped by that asshole." He looked at her right in the eye. "It's a shame he got in the middle of it, but it doesn't matter, because I have you now, and he isn't here."

Eloise shook her head and struggled against his hold, but it was no use. He was bigger and stronger than she was. She needed to play this safe, and maybe she could get out of this intact.

"Before it was me wanting you, and although it still is, it is also about making my fucking point. No one messes with me, no matter what club they are in."

There was laughter in the front of the clubhouse, and Eloise struggled harder. She tried to bring her knee up and get him in the crotch, but he had his leg wedged between her thighs, making that impossible.

"Next time those MC fuckers want to hurt and threaten me, there will be repercussions involved." His words were slurred, but his drunkenness wasn't what frightened her. He pressed his crotch into her and ground his erection into her belly.

Bile rose in her throat. He took a step back from her, and the surprise that she had enough room to breathe, and to even kick and fight back had her reacting instantly. But he had planned this, and when she went to make that first move he brought his fist to the side of her head. He used so much force her entire body spun around and crashed back into the brick wall. The force went through her whole body, but before she could regain herself, he had his hand wrapped around her throat and lifted her off her feet.

"I just wanted to play," he ground out. He brought his fist to the side of her head again, and again. Blood filled her mouth, and she couldn't hold it, especially not when he hit her again. A mouthful of spit and blood sprayed from her mouth and covered his face and chest.

"Please," she wheezed out.

"You stupid fucking cunt. I'm going to make you pay for that." He spat out, and spittle came from his mouth with as much force as his anger. He tossed her against the brick wall once more.

The pain was like nothing she had ever felt before, so mind numbing and crippling that even breathing hurt. But he wasn't done yet, that was clear from his words and his anger as he kicked her when she was down. Eloise knew one thing: she wasn't going to go down without a fight. He derived his strength and pleasure from hurting others.

He came after her again, and when he wrapped his hand around her throat once more, hauled her up, and pressed her to the wall, she used that moment to bring her knee up. Her entire body protested as pain washed through her.

He wasn't prepared for her act of rebellion, and that worked in her favor as she made contact with his dick. He grunted and the hold on her throat loosened. He tossed her aside like she was nothing but a rag doll, like she was nothing but the trash that surrounded them.

Hanson stumbled back a few paces after she kneed him, but she saw his rage start to escalate and numb out his pain. He charged at her once he seemed to get his bearing again, and she tried to move forward, out from the side of the garage so she could be seen. This low sound left him, one that sounded like he housed the very devil himself inside of him. She wanted to scream, but her throat was so raw from him choking her, and her jaw hurt from his blows that her breath came out like wheezes. She tried to stand and run, but he kicked her in the belly, and she fell back to the ground.

"Eloise, you out here? Berry said you took out the trash a while ago."

She struggled to stand when she heard Greys voice, a prospect in the club.

"Eloise? Where the fuck are you?" Greys called out again. "Come on. Steel will have my balls for lunch if I lose track of you."

Reaching her hand out, she prayed to whoever would listen to her that Greys saw her, or came looking for her over here.

"Shh." Hanson said and pulled her up off the ground. He pulled her to his body, breathed his rank breath in her ear, and cupped her breast.

A small whimper left her, but even that tiny noise hurt her throat. Eloise closed her eyes when he breathed against the side of her face harder this time. "Help..." That lone word sounded pathetic coming from her.

"Come on, girl. I don't want my ass kicked by Steel or the other patched in members." A beat of silence passed. "Fuck, where the hell are you?"

Hot tears were a steady stream down her cheeks when she heard the gun cock behind her, and felt the cold, hard butt of the barrel press against her temple. All she could do was close her eyes and wish things had been different.

"If you're quiet, you'll be okay."

No she wouldn't. Death might be welcome compared to what Hanson had planned for her. He started dragging her backward, but she saw an opportunity and went for it. Kicking her leg out, she knocked over one of the aluminum trashcans, sending it crashing to the ground. Trash fell from the inside, but the sound was what she'd been aiming for.

"You fucking cunt," Hanson said low.

He pushed her forward, and she landed on her hands, the gravel scraping up her palms. Then the sound of a gun firing was so close that her ears rang. Then another shot was fired; Hanson grunted, and she felt something warm and wet land on her bare calf.

Eloise looked behind her, saw Hanson holding his stomach, and then he ran off in the other direction. She looked in front of her, saw Greys running toward her, this horrified look on his face, and all she wanted to do was go to sleep. Her heart thundered, but she couldn't move, couldn't even think straight.

"Oh shit," Greys said.

Everything was becoming more distant, her eyes heavier, and she just rested her head on the gravel, wanting to sleep and forget about all of this. Every part of her body hurt.

"Shit, Eloise. Stay with me," Greys said, pushed her hair out of her face, and then shouted out to someone else that they needed to call Steel immediately. "Stay with me; everything will be okay."

She sure as hell hoped so because right now it seemed far from it.

Chapter Fifteen

Steel paced in the hospital waiting room while he and most of his brothers waited for the doctor to come back. Eloise had been unconscious when Greys had brought her here. There hadn't been any time to call an ambulance or the cops. It was easier to bring her here themselves. It had taken Steel over an hour to get back to the club after handling business with Zeke. He didn't like being away from Eloise any length of time, but when it came to business with the club, he didn't have a choice. Demon didn't mind who he fucked as long as the club came first and would always come first.

"She went out to take the trash?"

"Yes. We didn't suspect anything threatening, Steel. I swear it to you on my very life," Greys said.

"Where the fuck is Hanson now?" Steel wanted to kill the bastard when he first attacked Eloise, now he was going to take his time in killing him.

"Locked up in the shed I keep at the back of the clubhouse," Demon said. Deanna wasn't with him as all the other women had been told to remain at home or the clubhouse.

"I'm going to kill him, Demon. He's done, finished."

"I agree. The moment we know Eloise is safe, we'll finish him, brother."

He turned to look at Greys. Steel respected the kid and would one day make a great brother. He was close to being patched in after showing the whole club his loyalty.

"Do you want me to go and wait," Greys asked.

The last time one of the club women was supposed to be watched and ended up taken and hurt, Demon had killed the prospect when he'd failed. This wasn't a fail. He didn't expect the prospects to be walking side by side with the women. Even he couldn't handle that kind of care.

"No, this isn't your fault."

Steel knew the blame was entirely on Hanson. No one could have predicted when that fucker was going to strike back. After the warning he'd given him, he really didn't think the bastard would have the balls to try it again. He'd underestimated him, but that wasn't ever going to happen again. Hanson was living out his final hours.

"She was smashed up pretty bad. I should have fucking known when she didn't come straight in. Fuck," Greys said, standing up and pacing. "I should have known."

Greys kept repeating the same words over and over again.

"Sit down," Steel said. "You couldn't have prepared for this."

He'd not been there in time to see the mess that Hanson had created, but from the look on Greys face, it was bad.

Sitting down on the nearest seat, he stared at the clock, willing the doctor to put him out of his misery. He couldn't handle this, not knowing what was happening to her. Eloise had gotten under his fucking skin and he loved her. He'd never loved anyone in his whole life and the first woman he did, there was a risk she was going to be taken away from him. No, he couldn't allow it nor would he accept it. If the doctors came out and told him anything but good news, he'd kill every single one of them. No one was telling him bad news, not today.

The minutes passed; and the clock seemed to take its time.

Tick tock.

Tick tock.

He was going to smash the fucking clock in a minute if they didn't hurry up.

Suddenly the door opened, and the doctor called his name.

"I gave them your information as her next of kin," Greys said.

Yep, the prospect was going to get a patch all right.

With his brothers at his back, he listened to everything the doctor said. Eloise's jaw and nose were broken, but they'd repaired them. She'd be in a lot of pain, but with time the bruising and swelling would go down. She had several cracked ribs and a dislocated shoulder, which had been re-set.

The list seemed to go on and on.

"We're going to keep her at least overnight, and probably several days, in case of a concussion and because she needs sedated for her pain."

Steel grew angrier by the second. When he got his hands on that piece of shit he was going to tear him limb from fucking limb. Before he was finished, he was going to make sure Hanson begged for death long before he ever allowed him the pleasure of experiencing it.

"I want to see her." He couldn't settle the score until he saw Eloise.

"She's asleep right now, heavily sedated."

"I don't give a fuck. I want to see her."

The doctor nodded. "She's only allowed two visitors at a time."

Steel looked toward Demon, his Prez.

"I'm right behind you."

They followed the doctor past the double doors then down a long, busy corridor. Steel didn't like the twisted feeling he was getting deep in his gut. He knew it was going to be bad. The long list of problems wasn't going to make for his perfect Eloise now. He didn't care about the risk of scars; he loved her no matter what. Steel was more concerned with how it was going to affect the woman he loved. She'd been attacked and he'd not been there to protect her. He'd pay to help her heal inside and out.

"Be prepared," the doctor said. "She's badly bruised, and the swelling has started—"

"Just fucking show me," he said.

The doctor pulled back the curtain, and the sight before him twisted Steel's stomach. He wasn't repulsed. Eloise was his woman. He'd fallen in love with her and would love her to the day he died. No, he was disgusted with himself. He'd not been at the clubhouse; otherwise he'd have been the one to follow her out into the dark. His obsession for her wouldn't have allowed him not to go out. He'd have used the opportunity for privacy, and to fuck her against the wall, otherwise he'd have taken the trash out for her.

"I'll give you a couple of minutes."

He didn't look at the doctor. Instead, he walked toward his woman. All he wanted to do was take her hand, but her hand was badly bruised as well.

"What the fuck happened?" Steel asked.

Steel knew, but he didn't want to believe it was Eloise lying in that bed with tubes hooked up to her, monitoring her breathing and her vitals.

"Fuck, brother, we're here for you. All of us are."

"I don't care about the fucking repercussions. Hanson is a fucking dead man, and he's dead at my hands, tonight." He glanced toward Demon, and his Prez nodded.

"I'm not going to argue with you. We'll handle any blowback."

Turning back to Eloise, he reached out to touch her hair, wanting, no, needing to touch her even though he didn't want to hurt her. Hovering his hand over her head, he gritted his teeth.

"I'm going to make it better for you. I promise you no other harm will come to you. I'll make fucking sure of it. I promise you." He wanted to kiss her but he couldn't.

Each little thing he couldn't do: touch, taste, kiss built the rage inside him. He was going to fuck Hanson up and laugh while he did it.

Withdrawing his hand, he fisted it by his side.

"I'm going to be back, Eloise. You've got nothing to worry about. The club and I are behind you. You're in safe hands with us." Damn, how could he even promise he that when she'd been at the clubhouse when she was hurt? He leaned forward as if to kiss her but stopped. She was too fucked up to be kissed. "I've got to go and take him out, Demon."

"Greys can stick by her door for protection and if she wakes up."

Steel nodded, getting up to leave. He didn't want to. He wanted to stay by his woman's side, protect, and love her. There was nothing he could do here.

Back home, he could handle business.

On the way out of the hospital he sensed the rest of the brothers leaving with him, preparing to go home. Straddling his bike, he turned the engine over, relishing the vibration between his legs.

In his mind he saw Hanson, gutted and dripping blood from the shed. It was going to be a long night.

With every second that passed, he thought about each mark and bruise on Eloise. Thinking about her lying there on the hospital bed, broken, kept him on the road gunning toward the club. Parking up his bike, he saw Deanna waiting.

He didn't acknowledge her as he passed, going straight for the bar.

"What's going on?"

He heard Deanna asking Demon.

"I can't talk about it, baby. Stay in the club. Don't come out."

Steel entered the large barn. Hanson was tied to a chair and awake. Joker nodded toward him.

"How is she?"

Hanson laughed. "Is the fucking whore dead?"

Walking toward Hanson, Steel smiled down at him. "No, my woman's not dead. She's alive, but I saw what you did to her." Slamming his fist against Hanson's face, he loved the sound of Hanson's nose breaking.

The scream coming from the man's mouth filled him with joy. The bastard hadn't cared if Eloise was screaming or begging. He knew she would have. That kind of pain being inflicted on anyone would have people begging to make it stop.

"You made your first mistake in touching her. I let you live. Your biggest fucking mistake was not leaving her alone like I said and putting your hands on her." He removed his jacket, aware of his brothers around him, watching and waiting. "You're not leaving this place alive, Hanson. I swear, I'm going to fuck you up and you're going to be the one begging. I'm going to have you begging for fucking hours before I allow you to even have the pleasure of dying."

He gripped Hanson's hair at the back of his neck. Pushing his finger against the broken nose, Steel didn't stop as Hanson screamed, begging Steel to stop. Hanson was already bleeding out from being shot in his side but the damage wasn't enough to kill him. Steel was going to have enough time to make him suffer before he finally ended this piece of shit.

"Did you stop for her?" He pressed a little harder, pulling away when he was satisfied with the pain he'd inflicted. He wasn't done. Not by a long shot.

Moving toward the wall, he picked up one of knives that Joker liked to keep stashed in the shed for these kinds of occasions.

Slicing the blade across Hanson's chest, he tore the clothes from the bastard's body until he was sitting on the chair naked.

He started to piss himself and Steel laughed. "You're not a fucking man." Pointing the tip of the blade at the man's flaccid dick, Steel flicked it. "This is fucking useless."

"Dude, that's my knife. You better clean it," Joker said. "I don't want another man's dick on it."

"I'm going to clean it all right, but first I'm going to wash it in blood."

Gripping Hanson's cock, he pulled and slid the blade over his dick, severing that part of his body. Throwing it to the floor, he stood back listening to Hanson's screams.

Closing his eyes, Steel saw Eloise's bruised body. He couldn't touch her or kiss her.

Opening his eyes, he stared at Hanson who had drool coming out of his mouth. "Now we get to the real fun part."

Chapter Sixteen

Steel stared at Hanson, saw the blood drip from his mouth and nose, loved and felt pride that he'd been the one to make this man hurt, and planned on ending it now. He'd been working on the motherfucker for the last hour, his knuckles were bruised and battered from the punches he'd thrown at this prick, and now was the time to end it, while Hanson was still conscious.

He moved forward, and the closer he got to Hanson, the angrier he became. "You touched my woman." Steel stopped in front of him and tightened his hold on the butt of the gun he'd taken from the clubhouse. "You spoke to her after I told you to stay away." He gritted his teeth. "You *touched* her, fucking hit her." Steel didn't hold back his anger from flashing to the surface.

Hanson started gurgling something.

Steel lifted his hand and shot him in the arm. Hanson wailed and thrashed on the chair. Blood oozed out of the bullet wound and started making a small puddle on the floor.

Steel narrowed his eyes and tossed the gun to the side. He grabbed the knife at his waist and held up the gleaming metal.

"It felt damn good to beat the shit out of that bitch. I would have had a fun time sticking my dick in every hole she owned." Hanson gurgled out, blood and spit spraying.

Steel's anger exploded inside of him. He was going to kill Hanson, and he was going to take pleasure in doing it. He brought his fist to Hanson's jaw and sent the man slamming back against the floor. Steel stalked forward. Wrapping his hand around Hanson's throat, he hauled Hanson up, tore the rope from his body, and pushed him up against the wall.

Steel thrust the knife into Hanson's gut and slowly pulled it up. The blade was sharp and went through his abdomen like a hot knife through butter. But he wasn't done just yet. Using his forearm to keep Hanson pressed up against the wall, he held the bloody knife in front of Hanson's face. Blood trailed out of the fucker's mouth, and he started coughing, drowning in his own body fluids.

In a move just as slow as when he cut him the first time, Steel brought the blade across Hanson's throat. He took a step back and stared at the prick gurgling and choking, and clawing at the ground right before he stilled and took one last, labored breath. He should have made the fucker suffer even more.

He grabbed a rag that was on the ground, spilled from the trashcan, and cleaned off his blade. This certainly wasn't the most violent thing he had ever done, but it was the most brutal.

Steel stayed in the corner, his hands tightly fisted at his sides; the anger he felt for a dead man still ringing through his body. It had been days since Eloise had been taken to the hospital, days since he'd taken Hanson out, yet he wanted to kill the man again and again. She'd woken up, but he hadn't been here the last time, and all he wanted to do was hold her. Her face was so bruised and swollen still, and he hated that she hurt like this. But, the doctor said she was healing nicely, would even be able to go home soon.

"Steel?" Eloise's voice was so soft and distant and it sounded slightly confused.

He pushed away from the wall and moved toward her. He took the seat by her bed, held his breath, and felt his heart jump to his throat. With her hand in his, he waited to see if she'd woken up, or if she was just talking in her sleep. "I'm here, baby." He brought their intertwined hands to his mouth and kissed her knuckles.

Her brow furrowed, and she groaned as she shifted on the bed.

"Does it still hurt?" *Of course it does, you asshole.* He closed his eyes and exhaled. God, he hated seeing her like this.

She opened the eye that wasn't swollen shut, and although he knew she was badly hurt and probably scared as fuck, she smiled at him. "It feels like I was run over," she said in a soft voice. Even like this she tried to be strong. "What time is it?"

"It's late, baby. It's really late."

She sighed and nodded. "I feel a little loopy, but the pain isn't so bad so I can't complain," she smiled again.

Steel lightly brushed hair away from her forehead. "The doctor gave you some pain meds, which is why you feel out of it, but he said you're healing nicely and that you'll be able to leave soon."

She nodded, closed her eyes as she shifted, and a wince crossed her face. "I hurt all over, but my face and side hurt the worst." She shifted again on the bed. "He was going to kill me, Steel, or hell, worse I think, because killing me wouldn't have been the worst thing that asshole could have done to me."

He pressed his hand to the top of her head, smoothed her hair away then brought her knuckles to his mouth to kiss them once more. "He won't hurt you ever again, baby. No one will ever hurt you again."

She closed her eye, and he watched as a tear slide out of the corner of it.

Steel brushed it away and kept his hand on her cheek.

"I tried to get away, and managed to knee him in the crotch, so at least I did that much."

"Good, baby. I'm glad you got a good hit in." He ran his hand over her forehead. "You're so damn strong and make me so proud. I'm just sorry, and regret it so damn much that I wasn't there to save you, to protect you."

She swallowed again. "I know, Steel. But God, I hate being a victim, hate that he had that kind of control over me." She lifted her hand and brushed her tears away in an angry manner. "What if he comes back?"

Steel shook his head. "I told you, he won't hurt you ever again."

She stared at him, and then realization of what he was talking about covered her battered face.

"You..." she didn't finish.

He nodded once. "And I wish I could do it all over again." Steel leaned forward and buried his face in the crook of her neck, inhaling her sweet scent and silently promising her that he'd always look after her. He held her for several minutes, and just having her close felt so fucking good. He couldn't get lost in this experience of being with his woman, because the sight of her mangled, the idea that some other fucker had dared to put their fucking hands on her, had him feeling more homicidal than he had ever felt before.

"I just want to go home Steel," she looked up at him. "I just want to go home with you."

He leaned back, but only kept an inch between them. "Let me make sure with the doctor that it's okay for you to leave tonight, because I want you in my bed tonight, with me holding you close." He kissed her softly again. "But I don't't want you at that apartment anymore, Eloise. I want you with me, at my place, and at my side."

She didn't respond right away. "Steel, your place is barely big enough for you, let alone another person," she looked up at him, but he could see her happiness amidst her hesitation. "Besides, we haven't been together that long. Don't you think it's rushing it?"

He shook his head. "Eloise, I have never felt more sure of anything else in my life than I am of having you by my side. I want to be able to hold you every night, to make sure you're safe." He tightened his hold on her hand. "I won't let you leave my side. I can't because I'm fucking in love with you." He brushed his lips along hers. "You're my old lady. And if my place is too small then I'll get a bigger place, one where you can be happy, have your space, and where I know you'll be safe."

She smiled and lifted her hand to cup his cheek.

"I need you by my side, and I need to have you safe, baby."

"I know, Steel, and I want to be with you, too." She was still smiling, and even with the bruising and swelling in her face, he could still see the submissive woman that had opened up something inside of him and changed him for the better.

"I'd like to stay with you, but let's take it one day at a time, okay?"

Steel kissed her once more and stood. "Okay, baby. I'm going to check to see if you can leave." He left the room and strode down the hallway to speak with whoever was in charge of getting her out of here. He was taking his woman home, and he'd make sure she was safe, even if it took his last breath to do so.

Chapter Seventeen

One month later

Eloise didn't know how she got so lucky. Apart from being beaten, almost raped and killed, she'd had a pretty decent month. The bruising was fading fast and her ribs were no longer causing her pain. Her biggest problem was her nose. It still needed to be bandaged up. She hated it, but Steel wouldn't allow her to remove it, which she didn't mind.

"I look hideous," she said, coming out of his bathroom after washing. She couldn't get her nose wet and so she'd been forced to take hand washes because of all the bangages on her body. She didn't want to risk using he bath tub.

"Baby, you do not look hideous. You're beautiful."

"I've got a mask over my nose, Steel."

"When did you get so vain?" He was laid on the bed with one arm behind his back. She crawled beside him, lying with her arm over his waist, being gentle as she placed her face next to his.

"Since there is a club full of hot, sexy, young women with perfect bodies and flawless skin without the broken nose to keep you company." She stroked the tips of her fingers across the expanse of his chest.

"Baby, they could be fucking porn stars, princesses, or the sexiest women in the world down there and they wouldn't hold a candle to you."

"Why?" she asked, getting a thrill at his words.

"Because I know you want me as much as I want you. You're the other half of me, Eloise. I love you and when I love someone, I don't step out on them. I'm yours."

He rolled over so they were facing each other. She tensed as he reached out to run a finger down her nose. "This was broken, but it shows me that you're a fighter, Eloise. To be my woman, my old lady, you've got to be a fighter. This world isn't for everyone, but Demon and Joker have both found women to complete them." He took her hand, pressing it over his heart. "You're in here. I've never met a woman like you."

"Damn, Steel, I didn't know you could be so romantic."

"And you've got the best, tightest pussy and ass I've ever been inside. There really isn't another like it."

She slapped his chest. "Now there's the Steel I know and love." She smiled at him as her pussy pulsed recalling how amazing it could be between them. "You've not bruised me in a long time," she said, remembering their play before she went into the hospital. He'd been brilliant at using his belt on her. She wanted it again, begged for it, needed it, like it was her way of breathing.

"Eloise, baby, you're bruised enough already at the moment. I'm not going to be putting any new marks on you until I know every mark was made by me and not that fucker."

His fist tensed where it lay on the bed between them. Licking her dry lips, she placed her hand over his. "Okay, I'm sorry."

"I wish he was alive so I could kill him again."

She chuckled. "I know I shouldn't be laughing, but you can't think like that, Steel."

"He hurt you and I want to kill the fucker all over again."

"I don't want you to kill him all over again. Once was enough." She knew deep down in her heart she should be terrified of Steel. He'd killed Hanson without blinking an eye. Since her release from the hospital, she'd heard several of the men at the club talking about it. Steel hadn't been nice in his torture methods. Hanson had been a mess, so bad that no one would even recognize him if they tried to get a positive ID, which they'd never do. The Soldiers of Wrath MC never left anything open to chance. They all cleaned up loose ends. Markam's now belonged to the club, and they organized the staff along with the business side of things. That was where she worked, no longer at the club. She didn't want to know how they got Hanson to sign over the deeds, she was only grateful that they had.

As far as everyone knew, Hanson had gone on an extended vacation, skipping town without taking care of anything else.

"You're not running away screaming."

"I'm not as weak as you think I am," she said.

"I killed a man."

"I doubt he's the first man you killed." She raised a brow at him. "Steel, I've spent my whole life being afraid of what I needed, what I wanted. Since I've found you, you've given me more than you'll ever know. I love you. I knew from the start an MC wasn't about fairytales or princesses. You're my dark prince and you're hard as steel. I get where your name has come from. I'm not afraid of you. You'd never hurt me unless I wanted you to."

He cupped her face, caressing over her bottom lip with his thumb. "And you wonder why I'd happily be with you than some of those whores downstairs. There could never be enough of them to satisfy me, Eloise."

"There you go with the charm," she smiled at him.

"I don't give a shit about your broken nose or you bruises. They only serve to remind me how close I came to nearly losing you." He leaned in close, brushing his lips against hers. "I'm not going to make that same mistake again."

"It wasn't your mistake. This is what I'm talking about, Steel. You can't keep blaming yourself when something bad happens. This wasn't your fault and you've got to stop this."

He left the bed, and she frowned as she watched him go to a drawer at the far end of the room.

"What are you doing?" she asked, sitting up.

"My brothers think it's too soon but I know a good thing when I've got it. I'm never going to give you up."

She continued to frown as he came toward her, putting his hands behind his back.

"I'm a little nervous here."

"I've beat your ass with my belt, bruised, and played with you, and yet you're nervous about this." He brought his hand between them. There in his palm lay a deep blue velvet box.

"Steel, what is that?"

"Eloise, will you be my wife," he said.

Her heart pounded inside her chest as she stared back at him. "You're proposing to me?"

"Yes. There's no other woman in the world I want more than you. I promise to be faithful to you, loyal, and to love you forever. What do you say?" he asked.

This man never failed to surprise her. He knew what to say and do to make her feel like the most special woman in the world.

"Yes, yes, yes." She wrapped her arms around him, slamming her body against his. "I love you, Steel. I want to be yours. All yours."

He held her tightly, stroking her hair.

"Good, because even if you said no, I had plans to make you agree to be my wife." He pulled back, dropping his lips against hers.

Eloise melted against him, loving the feel of his arms around him.

"Come on, let's go tell the guys the good news." He took her hand ,leading her downstairs.

"Another brother bites the dust," Shakes said as Steel leaned against the bar. He watched Eloise show off her ring to Deanna, Amy, and a couple of the club whores who were actually nice. The smile on her face was worth every second of pain he'd been through to get to her. She was his soul mate, the love of his life.

"Do you have any regrets?" Joker asked.

"Regrets about what?"

"Asking her to marry you?"

"No. I love her and I'm man enough to admit it."

"The whores are going to be mourning your loss, but I'm sure the prospects will more than make up for it," Demon said, taking a long pull on his beer.

"I can't believe we're standing here now with three of us already settled down."

Steel glanced over at Shakes. Something twisted in his gut as he stared at the other brother. He was going to bring some problems to the club. Steel wasn't a fool. Something was going on between him and Daniella. He didn't know what, but he hoped the brother knew what he was doing.

Eloise walked toward him, swaying her hips. Even with the white plaster over her nose, she was the sexiest woman in the world to him.

"Do you want to back out?" she asked, showing him the ring.

"No, I don't want to back out. I know what I want." He wrapped his arms around her waist, pulling her close. She was his, and he looked forward to the moment he owned her in the eyes of the law.

She pressed her lips against to his.

"When do you want to get married?" he asked.

"As soon as possible."

"Why?"

"I don't want you to change your mind." She smiled, cupping his cheeks. "I want to own you like you own me."

And that was why he wanted her to himself. Eloise was the one woman who completed him. He didn't give a shit about the club whores waiting around. She was the only woman for him. The only woman he wanted to sink his cock into and put his baby inside of.

Banding his arm around her, he held her close, knowing he'd never let her go.

Chapter Eighteen

Their happily ever after

They'd left the BBQ that had been thrown at the Soldiers compound just twenty minutes ago. He wanted his woman to himself, wanted to be able to show her that although she was healed, maybe even still healing inside, she was all he wanted.

She'd moved into his place, and he liked having her around, loved it, in fact. She was everything he'd ever hoped of finding in an old lady, everything he thought he'd never find. Steel had never seen himself settling down and honestly hadn't wanted to. He'd liked fucking, liked the fact there were no strings attached, he could come and go from bitches' beds as he pleased. But all that had changed when he'd met Eloise and fully claimed her. She was sweet and gentle, but also so damn strong it made him proud to have her by his side.

He stared at her as she took off her cardigan and tossed it over the edge of the chair in the living room. She wore this short as fuck dress, but had on these black stretch pants that stopped at her calves. Damn, she was fine piece of ass, and all his.

The dominant side in him rose as he saw the light bruises that marred her upper arms. He remembered when he gave her those, remembered when he'd held her down, fucked her until she'd drifted off, a smile on her face, and the sweet scent of her release coming from her. He loved giving her the pain as much as watching her come around him.

"Look at me." He said in a deep, stoic voice.

She turned around, her eyes widening slightly, and then she started breathing heavily.

"Get undressed for me." He wanted her now.

For a second she didn't move, just stared at him, her desire clear.

"You are here for my pleasure, solely to make me happy," that was true to an extent, but he also was here for her pleasure. When she was totally nude, standing before him in all her nude, curvy glory, he reached down and adjusted his hard cock. "Go to the room and get into position." He knew she was aware of what he spoke of. He watched her walk away, loved how her ass slightly bounced as she moved away.

Once she was in their room, he unzipped his pants and pulled his cock out. He stroked himself, imagining her waiting for him, standing in position, and needing him just as badly as he needed her.

When he made his way into the room, he had to stop in the doorway and stare at her. She stood before him naked and looking so fucking beautiful that he was starving for her. He pulled his belt free from the loops of his jeans and kept tightening his hold on it. The images of bringing the smooth leather down across her ass and the back of her thighs had his cock throbbing.

"Turn around and press your chest to the wall." Their room was set up for the things they liked to do sexually, and he was about to experience Nirvana with his woman, about to give Eloise the pleasure and pain she craved. Even from a distance, he saw the way her pulse beat wildly at the base of her throat, and he wanted to kiss and lick at her flesh, to feel the beat of that fear and anticipation under his tongue.

Steel watched her turn and make her way toward the wall. Her ass was lush and round, and the globes moved seductively as she walked. When he saw the side of her breast press against the wall, flatten slightly and her skin pucker up because no doubt it was chilled, he moved closer to her. Above her was a pulley system, a device he'd installed after she'd moved in. It was something for them to play with, something that he could restrain her fully and give her the pain she desired.

A cord adjusted the height that he wanted her to be presented to him. Moving it so that the leather straps that would hold her in place for him were lowered, he heard her quick gasp as she glanced up and saw what he was doing.

"God, yes," she moaned.

"You won't be saying that when I'm done," he grinned, and although he said that, he knew she'd enjoy it exponentially. She was a slut for the pain only he could give her, a fiend for his hand, belt, or mouth on her flesh, bruising her up nice and good.

He took her hands and lifted them up so he could attach the leather around them. He took a step to the side, adjusted the height, so she was forced to rise up on her toes to keep her balance, and then he secured it so that she stayed in that position. Steel moved back so he could look at her.

Because she was on her toes, her entire body was stretched long, and all he could think about was running his tongue along every inch of her, slapping that ass of hers, and letting her see the marks he gave her when it was all said and done.

He let the belt unravel from his hand and took a step toward her. Steel pulled his arm back and brought the strip of leather forward, right across her ass. The sound of it hitting her flesh, and then her gasp of pain, had him closing his eyes and groaning in pleasure. He was a sadist for her pain, loved giving her what she wanted. The red line instantly popped out along her creamy flesh, and his cock jerked forward at the sight. He used his other hand and grabbed himself, stroked his dick, and tightened his hold on his erection.

Steel brought the leather down across her ass once more, and she cried out, her head tilting back. He moved to the side so he could see her face and saw her eyes close and a tear slide down her cheek. He knew her crying was because she liked it, wanted more of the pain that brought her pleasure.

He gave her a moment to breathe through the pain, but he also knew she was aroused, saw the way she clenched her thighs together, and he was anxious to give her more. "I love the way your skin becomes red when the leather hits your ass, baby." He moved closer to her and smoothed his hand across the two lines along her ass. Her flesh was hot and slightly raised where the belt had struck. As much as he knew that it had probably hurt like a bitch, he could practically smell the arousal coming from her.

Steel tossed the belt aside, got on his haunches, grabbed her cheeks, and pulled them apart. "Open your legs wide, Eloise baby. I want to see the pussy that belongs to me."

She complied instantly, and he curled his fingers into the flesh of her ass.

"That's it, baby." The scent of her arousal slammed into him. He stared at the sight of her slit, glistening with her cream that he'd brought out of her. Steel leaned down and ran his tongue down her cleft, pressing the muscle to the tiny opening of her pussy. Over and over, he swirled it around her hole, licking and swallowing her juices, and needing more. He forced himself to back off or he wouldn't be able to stop.

Moving back once again, he liked how she kept her legs open, loved the fact that her back was arched as she popped her ass out. He would give her more, so much more until she was blind from the lust for her need for pain. Her eyes were still closed, her lips parted, and she seemed almost drugged. Good, because he wanted her to enjoy this as much as he was.

"God, I love you so much, Steel."

And he loved her so fucking much he was blind with it. He brought the belt across the back of her legs this time. He brought the belt across her thighs again, and then her ass. Then Steel found himself staring at her flesh as it turned a vibrant red. "Does this make you feel good, Eloise?" Sweat beaded his brow as he continued to whip her repeatedly until she was crying harder, begging for more.

"It's so good, Steel. You know it's so good."

He tossed the belt aside and stared at the work he had done. Her entire ass and the back of her thighs were red, and he even saw some bruises starting to form. He was on his knees behind her a second later, smoothing his hands up and down her hot flesh, kissing the marks, *his* marks, and loving that she was his. Steel had his hands on either side of her legs as he licked, nipped, and kissed her raised skin.

He was drunk for her, so aroused his dick was about to burst from his desire. All he could think about was the way the belt had sounded as it hit her flesh.

"You're mine, baby, all mine, and that will never change."

"Yes, Steel," she moaned.

He ran his tongue along her pussy, sucked her clit into his mouth until she was grinding her cunt on his face, and then flattened his tongue and slid it up to the tight hole between the firm mounds of her bottom. He stood and lowered the pulley so he could unhook her from her bounds. Eloise sagged against his arms once he had her unrestrained. Steel held her for a few seconds, smoothed his hand over her hair, then lifted her easily and carried her to the bed.

"I love you, Eloise," he set her on the mattress and let her lay back. Her face was red, slightly sweaty, and he loved the glow that came from her.

"I love you," she said softly, almost inaudibly.

This was what he wanted, what he only ever wanted. She was his old lady, his woman, and the only female he'd ever want until he took his last breath. How in the hell had he become such a lucky motherfucker?

She smiled, reached up, and smoothed her hands along his chest. He still had his shirt on, but he knew she could feel his heart beating.

"Say you're mine." She'd said it before, but Steel wanted to hear it, needed to.

"I'm yours, Steel, and I don't ever want to be anyone else's."

And then he leaned down and kissed her, about to claim his woman in the way that she needed.

The End

Where To Find The Authors

www.CrescentSnowPublishing.com

Want to join the Crescent Snow Facebook Street Team?

CPSIA information can be obtained
at www.ICGtesting.com
Printed in the USA
LVHW032306180419
614782LV00010B/208

9 781537 324692